SEEING STARS

A Mashad Family Novel

CANDICE JALILI

HYPERION
Los Angeles New York

First Edition, October 2025

10 9 8 7 6 5 4 3 2 1

FAC-004510-25212

Printed in the United States of America

This book is set in Stempel Garamond LT Pro/Linotype

Designed by Zareen H. Johnson

Library of Congress Control Number: 2025930588

ISBN 978-1-368-09478-8

Reinforced binding

The authorized representative in the EU for product safety and compliance is Disney Trading B.V., Asterweg 15S, 1031 HL, Amsterdam, The Netherlands
email: DCP.DL-EU.bookscontact@disney.com

Visit www.HyperionTeens.com

Logo Applies to Text Stock Only

For the love of my life, my husband,
and my unpaid editor, Brian.

Mona and I both thank you so much.

LUSTRE MAGAZINE

ALI MASHAD & THE TANGLED WEB HE LEFT IN HIS WAKE

The deceased real-estate mogul and reality TV patriarch, fondly referred to as "America's Dad," left behind him a tangled and star-studded legacy.

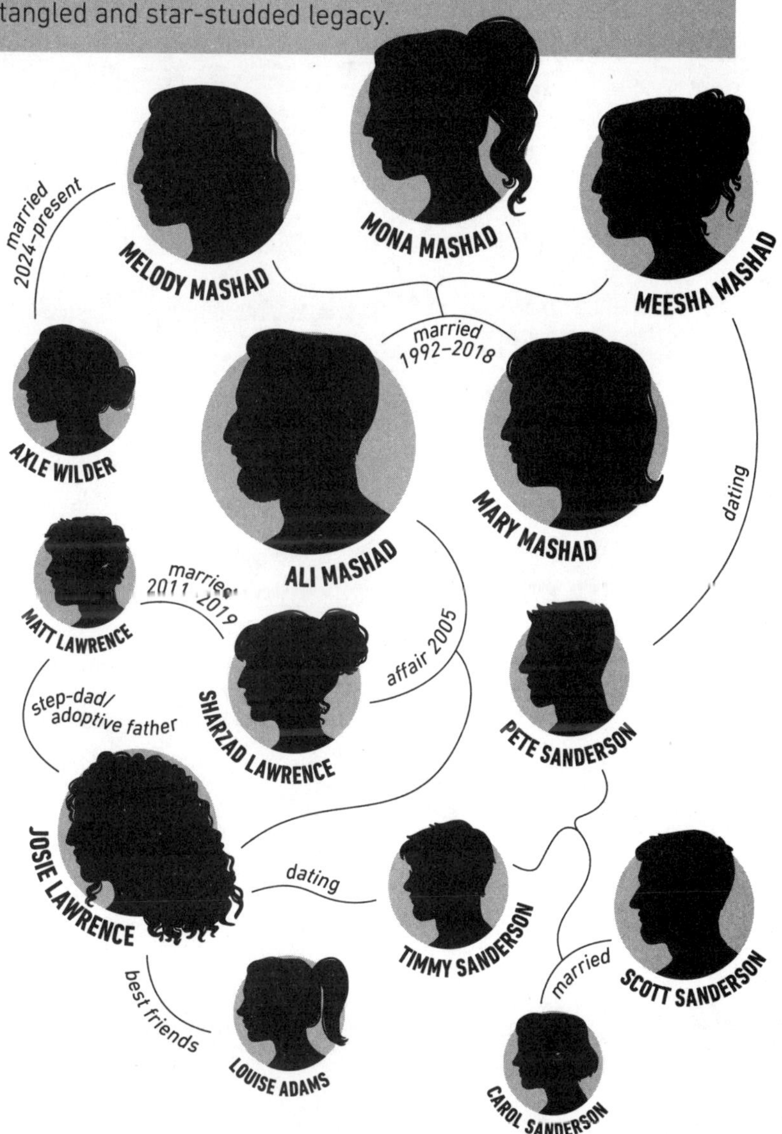

PRESIDENT JORDANA STERLING ANNOUNCES BID FOR RE-ELECTION

President Jordana Sterling stood on the Capitol steps today to formally announce her bid for re-election. Her only son, Harvard sophomore Lucas Sterling, stood by her side as she delivered a moving speech, vowing to continue her already promising legacy.

HE REALITY REPORT

MAKING MASHAD SPINOFF STARRING MONA MASHAD GREENLIT AT YAY! NETWORK

Mary Mashad is set to produce a new *Making Mashad* spinoff series starring her youngest daughter, nepo-baby party girl Mona Mashad, and her new boyfriend. Details remain unclear, but the young starlet assures us it will be "totally unfiltered and an absolutely wild ride." She adds, "The tabloids *wish* they could give you gossip this jaw-droppingly juicy."

COOP360

MONA MASHAD, LUCAS STERLING ROMANCE . . . FAKE?!!!

Our spies at *Scoop360* have gotten hands on a VERY incriminating document that implies President Sterling and Mary Mashad coerced their children into entering a fake relationship to bolster their respective numbers . . . YIKES.

Prologue

Confessional

INT. MARY MASHAD'S LIVING ROOM—AFTERNOON

MONA MASHAD, 18, sits on the massive white cloud couch in her mom's living room.

PRODUCER

So, what's going on? Are you *actually* with Lucas Sterling or are you with that other guy?

MONA

The problem with the tabloids is they always get the story half-right.

[*shows the camera a document that's been sitting next to her*]

This was my NDA.

[*rips it*]

Guess it's no use now. Right?

[*pauses, takes a deep breath*]

Okay, here's what really went down.

Chapter 1

"Let me just practice one more time," Mona demands, bursting into her sister's room at their mom's Belvedere vacation home without knocking.

Meesha is standing stoically still, giant bay windows exposing an unobstructed view of the Golden Gate Bridge behind her as a team of stylists and tailors makes sure her simple black The Row gown hugs her waiflike body perfectly.

"You've practiced two hundred times already," Meesha says, her voice as cool and unbothered as ever. "*I* could give the stupid speech at this point."

Mona looks down at her phone, a vintage photo of their late father carrying three-year-old Mona on his shoulders at the first red carpet premiere of their reality show, *Making Mashad*, staring back at her. "I know. But it's for Dad. I just don't want to mess it up."

"Fine," Meesha, replies, softening. "Shoot."

Mona takes a deep breath, giving her body a little shimmy to shake the nerves out as she snaps into Mona Mashad Mode. "Hi, everyone," she says, her voice booming confidently as she slaps a wide smile on her face. "Thanks for being here tonight. As you all know, the Iranian American Mentorship Alliance meant a lot to my dad— "

Her train of thought is interrupted by the sight of Meesha texting.

"Can you not right now?" Mona groans. "You're distracting me."

Meesha doesn't respond, and Mona notices her olive skin growing increasingly pale.

"What is it?" Mona asks, rushing over to her sister. "You look like you're gonna puke."

"Uh . . ." Meesha says to the small army poking and prodding at her dress. "Can you please give us a minute?"

The stylists and tailors obediently file out, leaving Mona and Meesha alone in the massive bedroom.

"Dramatic much?" Mona asks, snatching the iPhone out of her sister's shaking hand. "What could this possibly be?"

"Just read it," Meesha says, slowly sinking down onto the hardwood floor.

Mona looks at her sister's phone, a new text from Meesha's ex, pop star Bunny Lee, populating the screen. Surprise new album dropping Monday. Thought you deserved a heads-up. You're mentioned. Not in a good way. XO.

"This is absurd," Mona scoffs. "She can't just text you that with no explanation." Without consulting her sister, Mona quickly types back, Send me the songs. The message only says delivered for half a second before Bunny replies, You can listen with the rest of the world Monday.

Mona sinks down next to her sister. "We should call Mom."

Say what you want about their mom, America's most controversial matriarch and momager Mary Mashad, but the woman knows how to handle a scandal.

"No," Meesha says. "I just need to . . . sit with this for a minute."

"Okay," Mona says. "Then I'll sit with you."

Confessional

INT. MARY MASHAD'S LIVING ROOM—AFTERNOON (CONT'D)

MONA

> Meesha and I are only a year apart. We couldn't be more different, which is probably why we fight so much, but we grew up attached at the hip. We know each other better than anyone. When she gets all quiet and emo like this, all you can do is wait. It's the calm before the storm.

The sisters sit quietly side by side for a few seconds before Meesha bursts into tears. "Mona, she knows everything about me. About *us*. Our whole family. Who knows what she'll put in there? And Monday is supposed to be Pete and my red carpet debut at the Met Gala. The *day* she's releasing the album."

Meesha dumped Bunny after cheating on her with their close family friend and Meesha's now-boyfriend, NBA star Pete Sanderson. Let's just say the breakup has not quite gone over smoothly with Bunny's wildly devoted fan base.

"I can't believe she's doing this to me," she continues, yellow-green snot now dripping down her perfectly symmetrical nostrils. "You know what her fan base is like. They're going to destroy me. As if they haven't destroyed me enough already."

To the world, Meesha is known as impenetrably, almost terrifyingly, cool. One *Vogue* profile literally called her "ice personified." But to Mona, Meesha is this. Human. A shockingly ugly crier. Wildly sensitive. Terrified of the very world that seems to be so terrified of her.

Mona scoffs. "Meesha, think about how many people have tried to cancel us before. It just can't be done. Relax. It will be fine."

"Easy for you to say," Meesha sniffles. "You're Mona Mashad. People *expect* scandal from you. . . . No offense."

Mona doesn't bother to take offense. It's not like her sister's wrong. In a way, Mona has it the easiest. Their oldest sister, Melody, is America's sweetheart, which leaves her having a panic attack if she so much as gets a parking ticket. Meesha is a former supermodel who was one half of America's favorite lesbian relationship, so she can't gain a pound or break up with her girlfriend without the world coming after her, pitchforks in hand. Their newfound half sister, Josie, is new to all of this, and America loves that about her—but that sense of "normalcy" comes with an onslaught of hate and skepticism as she gets closer and closer with the Mashads. The public expects so much from them. All they want from Mona is some fun drama. A little mess here and there. And she's great at delivering on that.

"Come on," Mona says to her sister, softening a crinkle on the back of her gold Erdem gown as she stands up. "Enough moping. We're going to be late."

"I can't do it," Meesha says. "I'm fully spiraling. I can't do it."

"Are you kidding?!" Mona exclaims, suddenly fuming. "You're going to miss this all over some stupid text from Bunny? Meesha, it's for Dad."

Meesha shakes her head resolutely, her now-red face puffy and crusty with dried snot remnants. "Mona, I can't. This is the *one* event I can actually get out of without getting the third degree from Mom before the album comes out. Let me have this."

Mona stares down at her sister, her heart cracking a bit as she holds back tears of her own. "Fine."

Confessional

INT. MARY MASHAD'S LIVING ROOM—AFTERNOON (CONT'D)

MONA

My mom couldn't come because she got an invite to some *Forbes*-most-powerful-women-in-the-world-dinner thing. Melody couldn't come because she's on her honeymoon with her husband Axle. Josie had school and I mean, well, she never even knew our dad. I get that they're all busy and this isn't the Grammys or whatever. But this was my dad's favorite charity. We *all* went every year when he was alive. Now it's "the *one* event" Meesha—and apparently all of them—feel fine bailing on.

✦ ✦ ✦

Mona sits quietly in the back seat of the black car, her bodyguard, Majid, seated to her left as her driver, Alice, makes her way up Lombard toward the Fairmont. She stares out the window, counting all the billboards adorned by the faces of her and her family members. A force of habit.

She spots one of an ethereal-looking Melody holding a Vibe Tea can in a field full of daisies. Mona knows for a fact Melody had a horrible migraine that day and spent the entire morning locked in her room with her blackout shades rolled down, but in the photo, she looks absolutely, positively *serene*. Like she's never felt an ounce of pain in her life.

There are a few featuring Meesha teasing out her new couture collection, which is set to launch with a massive show in New York next month. Meesha had to shoot these the day after her split from Bunny got leaked to the press. The hate was so bad that she almost missed the shoot entirely, worrying her puffy snot-encrusted face wasn't exactly camera ready. But Mary dragged her out of bed, dunked her face in some ice water and they got the shot. In the pictures she looks bone-chillingly unfazed, like a psychotically gorgeous robot devoid of human emotion.

On the corner of Lombard and Filmore she spots an old

picture of her own face giving the camera a mischievous wink in an ad promoting a then-new makeup remover. The tagline *Like last night never happened* is scrawled under her face. The irony isn't lost on Mona. A few hours before the photographer got that shot, she had a huge fight with her mom for having stayed out clubbing one night way past her curfew. Had her mom bothered to ask *why* she was out so late, she would have known that Mona was minding her business when she saw her ex, Oscar-winning actor and grade-A jerkwad Max Davenport, strut in with his girlfriend, supermodel Chya. Back then there were rumors they were engaged. Those rumors have since been confirmed.

Confessional

INT. MARY MASHAD'S LIVING ROOM—AFTERNOON (CONT'D)

MONA

[*rolls her eyes*]

It's absurd. They're twenty. Who gets *engaged* at twenty?

That night at the club was Mona's first time seeing them in person. She couldn't just *leave*. She had to stay. Had to look like she was having the best time anyone on planet earth has ever had, like only Mona Mashad knows how to do. She could cry in peace when she got home in the morning. She stares up at the billboard, almost unable to recognize the wildly confident teen staring back at her, dark circles and tearstains seamlessly photoshopped away.

When the car reaches a halt at a red light on Lombard and Octavia, they face a giant billboard of her whole family, Josie included, teasing the new season of *Making Mashad.* Josie, the half sister Mona's late father had with Mona's mother's late cousin (yes, this is some soap opera–level gossip) entered their family last season. Mona carefully considers the poster, which shows Josie tentatively standing off to the side as Mona grips a defensive hand over her shoulder. The words AMERICA'S BIGGEST REALITY TV FAMILY JUST GOT BIGGER are displayed almost ominously below the show's logo. Josie was terrified that day but, unlike Mona and her sisters, she's not trained in the art of hiding it. Her fear is palpable. You can sniff it from here. Mona feels a pang of protection over her newfound sister as she stares up at the image, hoping fans read the body language in the billboard correctly. If they mess with Josie, they mess with her.

Thinking about Josie makes her think of her dad, which brings her back to the speech. "Majid?" Mona turns to her security guard, seated to her left. "Can I practice my speech to you?"

A wave of loneliness hits Mona just after uttering the question. *How sad*. The girl from America's Biggest Reality TV Family has not a single member of her own family to practice this speech to. If her dad was here, this would have never happened. Not just because she wouldn't have to be giving a speech in his memory. But because he was always there. Not just for the big red carpet viral moments. But for moments like this. Quiet, nervous car rides when she felt less like a global phenomenon and more like a normal nervous eighteen-year-old girl having to give a speech in front of a bunch of fancy adults. Mona didn't have to be Mona Mashad for her dad. She could just be Mona. If she was nervous and had to practice a speech a million times, he would be there to listen and tell her she was great a million and one times.

"Of course, sweetie," Majid says, offering her a warm smile. "Go for it."

Mona makes it through the speech twice by the time they finally pull up to the Fairmont. She can hear the fans and paparazzi screaming her name outside for two blocks before she even opens her car door. When she and her sisters used to complain about their dad dragging them to this event every year, asking him why it even mattered if they came, he would always say *this* is why it mattered. "Because when we come, *they* come," he would say. "And suddenly every tabloid in America is talking about our favorite charity. If just *one* of those fans decides to get involved, or even just donate, then we've done our parts."

"You ready?" Majid asks as the car screeches to a halt, mobs of fans in hysterics outside the hotel.

Mona takes a deep breath. "Yeah," she says, taking one last look at the picture of her dad on her phone lockscreen. "Let's do it."

Mona sets one Moschino-stiletto-clad foot down onto the pavement, leaving the hundreds of fans and reporters screaming for her attention. She stands up straight, spreads a wide smile across her face, and blows a kiss to the adoring crowd. "WHAT'S UP, SAN FRANCISCO?" she asks, her voice booming with a confidence usually reserved for rock stars headlining a show at Madison Square Garden.

Confessional

INT. MARY MASHAD'S LIVING ROOM—AFTERNOON (CONT'D)

PRODUCER

We've heard you say there's Mona Mashad and then there's Mona. What's the difference?

MONA

Mona Mashad is Mona on steroids. People expect a show, so I deliver.

PRODUCER

Who are we talking to now?

[*Mona opens her mouth to answer but, before she does, the camera cuts to black.*]

Chapter 2

Mona is cracking a joke to an *E! News* reporter when she spots him. Well, she doesn't quite spot him—she more hears the roar of the crowd and is subsequently *forced* to turn her head and notice him. Lucas Sterling. She watches as President Jordana Sterling's only son steps out of a Cadillac limo, American and presidential flags waving on either side of the black car's hood. Online it usually says guys are taller than they are but not him. Online he seems, like, maybe 5' 11". In person, Mona is surprised to find he's a solid 6' 3". Just the sheer sight of him standing there—signature chestnut hair, hazel eyes, and megawatt smile all predictably on point—is enough to leave the crowd in hysterics. Mona scans the crowd as people cry, scream marriage proposals, and throw roses at his feet. Literal *roses*.

✦ ✦ ✦

Confessional

INT. MARY MASHAD'S LIVING ROOM—AFTERNOON (CONT'D)

MONA

Have you ever seen those old clips of Elvis performing when girls would, like, faint and stuff? It was like that. I've never seen anything like it.

✦ ✦ ✦

Lucas waves to the crowd and, for a brief second, Mona can feel his famous hazel eyes zero in on her. In that moment, it's as though the megawatt smile spread across his sun-kissed face—presumably colored by long days of practice on the Harvard lacrosse field and leisurely weekends spent at his mom's house in the Hamptons—is just for her. Mona can feel her body temperature rising despite the San Francisco chill.

"You know him?" the *E! News* reporter says, snapping Mona out of it. "It felt like he was looking right at you."

"Never met him," Mona responds without missing a beat. "But anyway, like I was saying, Melody and Axle's wedding was *lit*. I'm not allowed to share any content from it yet, but we all know I've never been much for the rules."

The reporter laughs as Mona gives her one of her patent winks. "We'll be refreshing your feed with bated breath, girl."

Mona dutifully makes her way through the line of reporters, stopping to chat with every single one of them. Making sure to give each a unique story they can use for their sound bites, to treat each with the same level of enthusiasm, to mention the charity at the right moment without making it feel too pushy.

At one point a blister on the bottom of her heel pops and starts bleeding, but she doesn't let it show. Just cracks a witty joke about her mom, spills some tea about Meesha's upcoming hard launch with Pete, makes a thinly veiled dig at her ex. Gives the crowd exactly what they want from her. She may only be eighteen, but she's been in this business since she was three years old. She's a seasoned pro.

When she finally makes it into the cocktail hour, she's almost instantly cornered by Silicon Valley billionaire couple and giant Iranian American Mentorship Alliance donors Sherene and Reza Asemani.

"You're not going to college?!" Sherene exclaims, literally clutching the string of Chanel pearls draped over the high neck of her structured tweed butter-yellow gown.

Reza shakes his head in a dramatic display of disappointment, as though Mona just revealed she's taking a gap year to sell crystal meth. "This is just not right. It's not right. Why not UCLA? Both your parents went there! I'm sure your mother could pull some strings for you even if your grades aren't there."

Mona does her best to keep her eyes from rolling at the implication, that she's not going to college because she couldn't get into college.

"I know UCLA's dean of admissions," Sherene says, relief washing over her botoxed face. "I'll call them."

Mona remembers her dad groaning every time Mary would drag him to dinner with the Asemanis. "They're such squares," he'd complain. "I don't think either of them has a singular fun bone in their body." Mona suppresses a smile, imagining her dad chuckling from heaven as he mouths to her, "I told you! Squares!"

"That's really not necessary," Mona tells Sherene as the older woman digs her phone out of her nude Chanel clutch. "Really. I'm good with my decision."

"Nonsense," Sherene says, dialing the head of admissions and putting her phone on speaker. "We'll settle this now."

Mona hears her mom's voice in her head as Sherene's phone rings loudly in the middle of this black-tie affair: "All the money in the world can't buy you class." She's scanning the crowd, desperate for an excuse to get out of this godforsaken conversation before the poor sap on the other end of the line picks up, when a large hand gently grazes the small of her back.

"I'm so sorry to interrupt," Lucas Sterling says, giving Mona a barely perceptible wink as he takes a step to stand beside her. "Mr. and Mrs. Asemani, I'm not sure if you remember me. We met at a fundraiser you hosted for my mother in Atherton four years ago."

Mona looks up at him, perplexed. Was he trying to save her from this brutal conversation? Why? She looks at where his hand is now comfortably resting in the pocket of his crisp black tux. A small part of her wishes it was still on her back.

"Yes!" Sherene says, a nudge from Reza prompting her to hang up the phone and shove it back into her clutch. "Of course! Lucas Sterling! Hello, sweetheart. Is your mother here tonight?"

"She unfortunately had a prior engagement," Lucas says in what Mona instantly recognizes as a line fed to him by PR and practiced a hundred times over. He pauses and adds with a smile, "I hope I'm a worthy substitute."

"Oh, definitely," Reza says. "Absolutely! We are so happy to have you here."

"Thank you," Lucas says. "Actually, if you two don't mind, I was wondering if I could borrow Mona here for a minute. There's someone I wanted to introduce her to."

Mona looks up at Lucas again, a crooked smile making its way across her face as their eyes meet for a split second. So he *was* saving her.

"Absolutely," Sherene says, giving Mona a not-at-all-subtle wink. "Please. She's all yours!"

"Mona Joon, I hope you're going easy on your mother," Reza says, a kind smile making its way across his lightly wrinkled face before they part ways. "She's been through so much."

"I am," Mona lies with a smile. Has she made life *easy* for her mom since her dad's death? Not particularly. But it's not like her mom's done much to make her life any easier, either.

"Shall we?" Lucas asks, his hand once again on the small of her back.

Mona looks up at him, her lips curving into a crooked smile. "I guess we shall."

Lucas guides Mona through the sea of well-dressed Iranian Americans, until the two of them are standing facing each other in a secluded corner of the grand ballroom.

"So, who am I being introduced to?" Mona asks, looking around.

"Me," Lucas says, reaching a hand toward her with a cocky smile. "Lucas Sterling. Pleasure to meet you."

Mona chuckles as she grasps his hand. "I know who you are."

"Oh, really?" he asks, eyebrows raised. "Tell me then. Who am I?"

"Let's see," Mona says, tapping her red manicured fingers against her chin in faux reflection. "Lucas Sterling. Only son of President Jordana Sterling. Our modern-day JFK Jr. Beloved by all. Star Harvard lacrosse player." She pauses for a minute, letting her large espresso-brown eyes meet Lucas's more squinty hazel ones before adding, "Also, a player in the more general sense." Lots of girls in Mona's circle have Lucas Sterling stories. None end well.

Lucas laughs, not taking his eyes off hers. "I guess you have me all figured out."

"I'm Mona, by the way," she says. "Now that we're doing introductions."

"Oh, trust me," he says, eyes still locked on hers, smile widening. "I know."

Mona knows she's a household name. Like, duh. She grew up on most people's television screens. Still, she can't help but be a little flattered by Lucas Sterling, America's *first son*, so casually acknowledging he knows who she is. Determined to set herself apart from the throngs of groupies she just saw squealing outside, she does her best to emulate Meesha's notoriously unreadable expression. But she knows her face will give her away, the corners of her mouth already shoving their way upward.

✦ ✦ ✦

Confessional

INT. HARVARD MEN'S LACROSSE LOCKER ROOM—AFTERNOON

LUCAS STERLING, 19, sits on a leather chair in front of his wooden locker. He smirks at the camera quietly for a bit before speaking.

LUCAS

Of course I knew who she was. She's been my celebrity crush since I was ten. I practically jumped on the plane to San Francisco when I heard she'd be at this event.

✦✦✦

Mona's conversation with Lucas is cut short by Roya Daadgar, the event's director of publicity, who politely reminds them the VIP donors at this event paid good money to mingle with each of them during welcome drinks. So, they dutifully go their separate ways—shaking hands, making eye contact, telling stories about their famous families that make you feel like you know them without really revealing anything at all, laughing at jokes that aren't funny—each expertly trained by the world's best PR teams in the art of successfully dazzling virtually any human they come into contact with.

It isn't until they're inside the actual event and Mona is chatting with an elderly Persian lady who knew her paternal grandma that she sees Lucas again. "Your grandmother would have been *so* proud," the lady, Shohreh, is saying as she clasps Mona's hands in hers, her thick Persian accent distorting each word in a way that brings Mona a deep pang of comfort. "You are so funny, just like her. That's why your father loved you so much."

This night is always peppered with little interactions like this, chances to talk to people who weren't just fans of her dad's, but who *knew* her dad and his side of the family. It's one of Mona's favorite things about it. When her dad was alive, Mona would tune out his old stories about growing up between Los Angeles and the Bay Area, writing them off as boring. Now she's desperate for them, for any little tidbit about him she may not have already known. So, when she gets a second to talk to someone like Shohreh, she makes an effort to be extra present, to soak up every little anecdote about her dad like one giant grief-stricken sponge.

But now Shohreh is telling Mona some story about her dad playing pickup basketball with her son growing up, and Mona can't focus. All she can see is Lucas's gaze. He's *staring* at her from across the room. He's in the middle of a conversation with a group of Persian ladies presumably trying to set him up with their daughters but his eyes are staring past them directly at Mona. Like, he's not even making an effort to hide it. It's *blatant.*

Mona must have been staring back because Shohreh pauses her story to look behind her, instantly picking up on what's going on. "Khalee khosh teep hast," she says to Mona. "Oh, I'm sorry. I forgot you don't speak Farsi. He's—"

"Very handsome," Mona finishes the sentence for her with a coy smile. "I still understand a bit."

Shohreh lets out a laugh. "Oh, so you know the important words. Good girl. Just like your grandmother. I love it." Mona smiles, proud. She never knew her grandmother, but based on how her dad talked about her, she was an absolute legend.

Everyone's seated and halfway through their salad shirazi when the president of the charity, Yasaman Darvish, welcomes Mona up to the podium. "Whether you knew him personally or watched him on your television screen growing up, we are all familiar with Ali Mashad," Yasaman says. "America's father, they called him. Here at the Iranian American Mentorship Alliance, we see him as even more than that. He was and continues to be our guardian angel. Throughout his storied life, Ali Mashad still made time to personally mentor hundreds of our students, offering many of them starts to what would become very illustrious careers. He featured these events on his popular show and got dozens of his famous friends involved, giving us an unparalleled amount of global exposure. He donated millions, allowing us to widen our reach beyond our wildest dreams. Tonight, his youngest daughter, Mona Mashad, accepts the Lifetime Achievement Award in his honor."

Mona feels her own eyes watering as she makes her way to the stage, the room full of misty-eyed Iranian Americans fiercely applauding her late father's legacy.

She pauses for a minute when she makes it to the podium, choosing this time to ignore Lucas's eyes once again directly on hers. No time for distractions. *Deep breath*, she reminds herself, desperate to slow her heart rate down. *Deep breath*. She visualizes her dad standing in the back of the room, smiling at her the way only he would. Like he could not believe he had a hand in creating someone so fantastic in every way.

"Hi, everyone," she begins, the words she practiced

hundreds of times seamlessly sliding off her tongue. "Thanks for being here tonight. As you all know, the Iranian American Mentorship Alliance meant a lot to my dad . . ."

By the time she's finished the speech, the once misty-eyed room is now fully sobbing. She did it. She killed this speech. They laughed, they cried, and now she can guarantee they're all going to make some fat donations when auction time rolls around. She takes one last look at the imaginary version of her dad she conjured up in the back of the room. "Good job, azizam," he mouths to her. Mona blinks away a few tears.

"Wonderful job," Majid whispers to Mona as he escorts her off the stage. "Your dad would have been proud."

"Thanks," Mona whispers back, her voice catching. "Actually, before we go back to the table, can I take a minute to myself out on the balcony?"

"Sure," Majid says, changing course to discreetly escort her outside.

<u>Confessional</u>

INT. MARY MASHAD'S LIVING ROOM—AFTERNOON (CONT'D)

MONA

I got through the speech, but it was heavy. I just needed to turn it off for a minute.

Mona won't let herself cry. She can't. Crying will ruin her makeup. So, she'll settle for just being sad for a bit. She stands outside, laughing at the drama of herself wistfully looking out onto the rolling San Francisco hills as she holds back tears in her eyes. For a minute she floats out of her body and watches the moment play as a closing scene on an episode of *Making Mashad*, Eric Clapton's "Tears in Heaven" playing in the background as Mary Mashad's executive producer credit rolls up onto the screen.

She's halfway through this visual when she hears a knock on the sliding door behind her.

"Mind if he joins you?" Majid asks, gesturing to where Lucas is standing off to his right.

"It's a free country," Mona says, a sly smile making its way onto her face.

Before she knows it, Lucas is scooching onto the balcony beside her. "Nice speech," he says. "You're a pro."

"Thanks," Mona says, flashing him a confident smile. "I know."

Lucas laughs. "Humble."

"Very," she says. "Which reminds me. I told you who you are. You didn't tell me who I am."

"Easy," Lucas says. "Mona Mashad. American icon. Insanely talented at the business of being you. Well on your way to billionaire status, purely from being yourself. Wild child. Irreverent. Hilarious. My personal favorite on the show. Always good for a one-liner. A bit of a player yourself."

Mona looks up at him, amused. "You watch the show?"

"Huge fan," Lucas says. "Seen every episode."

"I don't believe you," Mona challenges.

"Fine," Lucas retorts, defiantly crossing his arms over his chest. "Quiz me."

"Okay," Mona says, a delighted smirk on her face. "What did we do for Meesha's Sweet Sixteen?"

"I see what you did there." Lucas snorts. "You thought you were going to get me with a trick question because Meesha didn't show up to her Sweet Sixteen. Your mom rented out SoFi Stadium, threw this massive party, and Meesha never showed. She went to Pete's house and spent the night playing video games with him, which is sort of cute now in retrospect. But the party was still great, especially when you got up on stage and performed 'Work It' with Missy Elliott."

"I won't lie," Mona admits. "I'm impressed."

"Good," Lucas says, beaming. "That was the goal. To impress you."

Mona rolls her eyes, laughing. "Was that the big plan here? Flex some *Making Mashad* trivia and use the same corny lines you probably use on all the models you get with to get me?"

"Depends," Lucas asks, running a hand through his thick chestnut locks. "Is it working?"

Mona pauses just long enough to make him squirm, unwilling to give him the pleasure of an easy answer. "We should get back inside," she finally says, letting her hand just barely graze his chiseled chest as she makes her way past him to open the sliding door.

The rest of the night goes by in a blur of photo ops and emotional conversations with people who knew or knew of her dad. It isn't until the very end of the night, when Majid is escorting her out of the event, that she runs into Lucas again.

"Hey," he says, Secret Service trailing behind him as he files into the service elevator next to Mona.

"Hey," Mona says, suppressing a small smile at the sight of him. "How was the rest of your night?"

"Good," he says. "Spent a solid half an hour talking to the Asemanis about starting a 401(k), so that was thrilling."

Mona laughs. "I can imagine."

They stand quietly for a bit, electricity building in the few inches between them. "Let me take you on a date," Lucas finally says, turning to face her.

Mona looks up at him, a half smile on her face. "No."

Lucas stares back at her, surprised. It wasn't just any no. It was a swift no. A no that could win sprints and races. The fastest no a guy with a dating track record akin to his has likely ever seen. "Why not?"

Mona sighs. "You have a reputation."

Lucas curves the left side of his mouth upward into an annoyingly hot smirk. "So do you."

"Fair," Mona concedes. "But I'm not sure this is a two-wrongs-make-a-right situation."

"What if it was?" Lucas challenges.

"What if I don't want to find out?" Mona retorts, memories of past heartbreaks playing in her head like a pitiful movie montage. "I've done messy before. You've watched the show. You know who my ex is. I'm not looking for more of *that*."

The elevator comes to a halt as it reaches a secluded back section of the lobby and the two wait quietly as their security details file out, creating a human shield to protect them from the dozens of fans milling around, blissfully unaware that two of the biggest megastars on the planet have just descended upon them.

Lucas and Mona take their time walking out, neither of them quite ready to leave the other despite the conversation being over. They've hardly made it out of the elevator when Lucas stops walking entirely.

"Wait," he says, his eyes searching for hers as he fishes something out of his pocket. "Freeze, just like that."

Mona meets his gaze, not exactly hating the way his 6' 3"frame towers over her. "What are you doing?"

Without answering, he pulls a disposable camera out of his pocket and snaps a picture.

"What was that?" Mona asks, laughing as her eyes adjust from the flash. "You moonlighting as a paparazzo?"

Lucas chuckles, stuffing the camera back into his pocket. "What? Can't a guy remember the moment he was turned down by Mona Mashad?"

Mona squints, exploring every nook and cranny of his almost comically perfect face. "You're kinda weird, huh?"

"Oh, I'm weird like you wouldn't *believe*," he says, flashing her a smile. "It's part of my charm. How I, like you said so eloquently, get all the models."

"Right," Mona says, giving him her most dramatic eye roll. "Well, good night, Lucas."

"Good night," Lucas says. "Oh, and, Mona?"

"Yes?"

"I don't care how much time I have to spend to make it happen. I'm gonna take you on that date."

Mona tries to look annoyed but the slight upward tilt in the corners of her mouth gives her away yet again. "We'll see about that."

Chapter 3

The Met Gala is in twelve hours and it's the first year the entire family, along with Josie's best friend turned *Making Mashad* fan favorite, Louise, is invited. Before this year, nobody knew who Josie and Louise were, and Mona was too young to attend. So, in theory, this should be a joyous occasion. Historic, even. But instead of getting their glam in peace as they should be, the family is sitting at the presidential suite of the Carlyle listening to Bunny's newly released diss track, "Desperate 4 Fame."

"It's not that bad," Melody lies, resting a hand on Meesha's increasingly damp shoulder. "Really. Nobody will know it's about you."

This is sort of Melody's role as the eldest sister in this family. Not to *lie*, per se. But to spin. You know, smooth things over. Make it sound like everything's okay, even if it isn't really.

"Maybe it's not about you!" Josie enthusiastically suggests. "I mean, Bunny has definitely dated other people." Mona examines her newfound sister's face, her earnest brown eyes wide with hope. When Melody spins a story, she *knows* she's spinning. But with Josie, it's different. She's genuinely just too green. Naïve to this business and all the dark pitfalls lurking within it.

"Josie, it's definitely about her," Louise says. "She literally closes it out by screaming, 'I hate you, Meesha.'"

Mona is too angry to speak but is suddenly overcome with gratitude that Louise, the only other straight shooter in the room, is here. She's right. This song is *obviously* about Meesha. Someone had to say it. Mona's just grateful it doesn't have to be her for once.

"Maybe she dated another Meesha?" Melody suggests.

Mona rolls her eyes. "Okay, now you're being straight-up delusional, Mel."

"I'm going to be sick," Meesha says, sending Pete chasing closely behind as she books it for the bathroom.

The rest of them—Mona; Josie; Louise; Mary; Melody; Melody's husband, Axle; Josie's boyfriend (and Pete's little brother), Timmy—stand there quietly as the song loops for the second time, its painfully detailed lyrics painting the picture of a "fame-hungry ice queen" who used Bunny to achieve her "vapid dreams" then cheated on her with "some Chad next door."

"Will someone turn it off?!" Mary screams, sending Timmy, who also happens to be a PA on the show, running toward his iPhone, where the song is streaming from.

"This is bad," Timmy whispers, doing a quick scan of the internet once the song cuts out. "Bunny Lee has the most intense fans. They're already obliterating Meesha online."

Mona is fuming. How *dare* that pathetic excuse of a "pop star" Bunny verbally assault her sister in a song like that? Isn't that, like, against the law or something?

Confessional

INT. MARY MASHAD'S LIVING ROOM—AFTERNOON

MONA

Meesha hates being famous! If anyone is *desperate for fame*, it's Bunny Lee. Name-checking Meesha to get more clout. She's a pathetic try-hard loser and, above all else, a liar. There, I said it. Bunny Lee is a *liar*.

[*looks directly into the camera*]

Bunny, if you're watching this, good. It's officially war, you backstabbing, lying, manipulative piece of [BLEEP].

[*PRODUCER gives her a look off camera*]

MONA

What? I promised people this show would be unfiltered!

Mona whips her phone out, instantly logging onto Instagram to pen a scathing rant about Bunny. She's about to hit post when Mary snatches the phone out of her hand.

"Mona, *no*," she says. "We have to think this through."

"Why?!" Mona fires back. "If that psycho Bunny Lee is allowed to say whatever she wants about my sister, why should *I* have to control myself?"

"Patience is a virtue, sweet Mona," Axle says in his annoyingly zen voice. "Why don't you join me for a moment of breathwork? I'll guide us all in a meditation."

"Yes!" Melody squeals as if she's five and he just offered them all candy. "Axy leads the *best* meditations."

Mona is usually good about grinning and bearing Axle's woo-woo vibe. He makes her sister happy. That's all that really matters. But she's in no mood for his New Age hippie nonsense right now.

"MEESHA, OPEN UP," she says, marching past Axle over to the bathroom Meesha and Pete have locked themselves in. "COME ON."

Melody follows behind, gently placing a hand on Mona's forearm. "Maybe she needs some space."

"She doesn't need space," Mona insists. "She needs *me*."

Finally, Pete cracks the door open. "Okay, Mona, she says you can come in."

Mona gives Melody her best I-told-you-so look as she pushes her way past Pete into the bathroom, where Meesha's keeled over the toilet.

Mona says nothing, just quietly hops on top of the bathroom counter as Pete shuffles out. It's not until Pete shuts the door behind him that Meesha turns to Mona. "What am I supposed to do?" she asks, tears making their way down her stoic face for the first time since the song dropped. "I'm being serious. How *in the world* am I supposed to handle this?"

"I'M ON IT, MEESHA JOONAM," Mary yells from the other room. "ON THE PHONE WITH THE PR TEAM NOW."

Meesha groans and falls onto the marble bathroom floor, curling herself into the fetal position. "This is a *nightmare*."

Mona slides off the counter, lying on the floor beside Meesha. "I've got you. You know that, right?"

"Yeah," Meesha says with a small snort. "For better or worse, I know I have you in my corner."

"And who better?" Mona asks, a mischievous eyebrow raised. "Honestly, I *can't wait* to see Bunny and her stupid fans tonight. It will be fun."

"Oh God." Meesha shudders. "Please don't be psycho."

Mona shrugs. "Psycho gets headlines. And, unlike you, maybe I *am* desperate for fame."

Meesha laughs and Mona's filled with a sense of accomplishment. Her work here is done. "Come on," she says, springing up and reaching a hand down toward Meesha. "Let's stop being emo and hang with everyone before Axle insists on cleansing your aura."

When they reemerge from the bathroom, Meesha and Mona find everybody seated in the living room whispering tensely as Mary barks at PR on speakerphone.

"Okay," Meesha declares as she burrows herself into the corner of the gray couch next to Pete, a breathtaking view of Manhattan displayed in the window behind them. "I'm out here on the condition that we *don't talk about it*. Got it?"

Everyone nods in solemn agreement.

"So, Mona," Josie tries. "Have you thought more about

what you want to do now that you're officially done with high school?"

Mona turns her attention to Mary. "I know exactly what I want to do next. My own show. Right, Mom? A chance to tell my own story away from all of you."

"In order to do that, don't you have to get away from us?" Meesha, now resting her head on Pete's lap, asks with a laugh. "What's so different about your life that requires its own spinoff? You're just living in Mom's house hanging out with the rest of us every day."

Mona glares at her sister. "Can you *not*? I was literally just there for you during your mental breakdown."

Mary, still on the phone with PR, sighs as she puts her phone on mute. "Meesha is right," she says. "Mona Joon, in order for your own show, we need a good angle. Give me an angle and I'll give you a show."

"*I* am the angle," Mona insists. "How is that not enough?!"

"Let's talk about something else," Melody tries. "Wait, Mona, I heard you were talking to Lucas Sterling for a bit at the charity thing the other night. Please tell me you at least got his number."

"Mona, *no*," Timmy groans. "That guy seems like such a douche."

"Agreed," Meesha says. "He has an *awful* reputation."

"I've met him a couple times, actually," Pete says. "He's pretty chill. I like him. Plus, doesn't he go to Harvard? I think he's really smart."

"Ah, yes. That's right, Pete Joonam," Mary says, her eyes locked on Mona. "*Harvard*. Very impressive."

Mona focuses her attention on the New York City skyline, willfully avoiding her mom's way-too-intense gaze.

Meesha turns to her mom. "Why are you being weird?"

Confessional

INT. MARY MASHAD'S LIVING ROOM—AFTERNOON

MONA

She was being weird because I got into Harvard. And she simply would not drop it. Even though I *told* her I don't want to go.

PRODUCER

So, why did you apply?

MONA

The world has me written off as some party-obsessed idiot. I wanted to prove to myself that I'm more than that. And I did. Getting in was enough. I don't need to now spend four years away from my *actual* career wasting time reading dusty books in a library just so my mom can tell her friends her daughter goes to Harvard.

PRODUCER

Do your sisters know?

MONA

No. Nobody knows. This was just supposed to be something I did for myself. I didn't even want my mom to know but they sent a letter to the house, and she saw it in my room. . . . So annoying. I mean, who still sends *letters*? What is this, 1998?

Mona checks the time on her phone. *Thank God.*

"As *thrilling* as this conversation about a guy I spent not even fifteen minutes talking to has been," she says, getting up, "I'm doing the 'Get Ready with Me' with *Vogue* and they're going to be in my room in five."

Meesha gets up and trails closely behind her, stopping when they reach the door to Mary's palatial hotel room. "I'm sorry I was snippy."

Mona looks at her sister's giant honey-brown eyes, the same ones that made her Bvlgari campaign so "hauntingly beautiful," as one *Harper's Bazaar* reporter described it. "Honestly? It would be weirder if you weren't."

Meesha laughs. "You'll still have my back tonight?"

"*Obviously.*"

Chapter 4

Meesha is fully shaking as the family's sprinter van pulls up to the Met. And for good reason. Even from inside the van, they can all hear the mass of teen girls scream-singing the words to Bunny's stupid song.

"You'll be okay," Pete reassures Meesha, tightening his muscular basketball-playing arms around her delicate model body. "I've got you."

Confessional

INT. MARY MASHAD'S LIVING ROOM—AFTERNOON (CONT'D)

MONA

I'm fully on board now but, when I first found out Meesha was dating Pete—I'm not gonna lie. It was weird. The Sandersons are like family. Their dad, Scott, was my dad's best friend since college. I mean, the only reason we got this show in the first place is because Scott is the CEO of Yay! Network. Josie dating Timmy was one thing. She'd just entered our family; the first time she met Timmy was on set a few months ago. But Meesha and Pete? They took baths together growing up.

[*gives the camera a wink*]

I guess they're still doing that, amiright?

Mona watches as Pete rubs Meesha's shoulders, her body visibly relaxing a bit at his touch. Something about the moment strikes a chord with her. She takes a deep breath and bites her lower lip to stop her eyes from welling up.

Before he turned out to be a lying, cheating, verbally abusive monster, Mona's ex Max briefly did give her that sense of safety. When they finally ended things, Mona concluded that love must be dead. But now, looking at her sisters all happy in their relationships, she realizes maybe it's just dead to her.

"Meesh, you'll be fine," Mona insists, snapping out of her pity party to focus her attention back on her sister. "I swear I'll punch her if she comes near you."

"We all know she really will," Timmy says matter-of-factly.

Meesha laughs. "Please don't punch her. Ugh, I wish we could just skip the red carpet. That's gonna be the worst of it."

"Why don't you?" Josie naïvely suggests, then adds too eagerly, "Timmy and I will join you! Let's all skip." Josie hates these sorts of things. And the only person who hates them more than she does is Timmy. Mary had to make an ungodly donation to Josie's favorite charity just to get them here.

"The whole point of the Met Gala is the red carpet. And this is a *huge* milestone for our family. The first time we are *all* here," Mary reminds them, before turning to Meesha. "Ghorboonet behram, I know this is hard. But you need to just put a smile on your face and get through it."

Melody pulls an essential oil out of her vegan leather clutch and gently places it in front of Mona's nose. "Here. Sniff this. It's a calming blend of peppermint and eucalyptus scents. All organic. It's coming out in my essential oil line next month. Good, right?"

"Really?" Mona asks, nodding to where Zadie, one of the *Making Mashad* camerawomen, is filming from the front of the van. "We're plugging your brand right now?"

"It *works*," Melody insists. "Right, Meesh?"

Meesha takes a deep breath, then turns back to her older sister. "Didn't work. Sorry."

"Don't be sorry," Melody says, reaching back into her clutch and pulling out a pair of sunglasses. "Just throw these on! They're super tinted. Pretend you can't see anyone."

Meesha accepts the pair of black Celine sunglasses, defeatedly putting them on.

"You ready?" Mona asks as the car comes to a halt at the end of the pink carpet.

Meesha takes a deep breath and reaches her left hand out toward Mona, her right already holding on to Pete's for dear life. "Hold my other hand?"

"Duh," Mona says, gripping her sister's hand as tightly as humanly possible. "I've got you."

As soon as they get out of the car, a mob of Bunny Lee fans are screaming "BOO" in their faces. A few of them even came with TEAM BUNNY signs written in sparkly puff paint.

Confessional

INT. MARY MASHAD'S LIVING ROOM—AFTERNOON (CONT'D)

MONA

I'm sorry. But did they seriously have nothing better to do? Like, honestly. If you are one of those deranged Bunny Lee fans watching this right now, please. Get help.

Mona maintains her tight grip on Meesha's shaky hand, leading her and Pete away from the massive mob of teenagers now loudly bumping Bunny's song. With her free hand she raises her middle finger high in the air, well aware that the stunt might cost her any invites to Met Galas of the future.

"WE HATE YOU," one fan screams right in Meesha's face, nearly leaping over the boundary wall onto the pink carpet. "YOU ONLY CAME OUT FOR THE CLOUT."

Mona hears Meesha's breath catch behind her and knows instantly what's going through her sister's head.

✦

Confessional

EXT. MEESHA MASHAD'S PENTHOUSE BALCONY—AFTERNOON

MEESHA MASHAD, 19, sits curled up on a plush cream lounge chair on the balcony of her West Hollywood penthouse, sweeping views of Los Angeles behind her.

MEESHA

That was the worst possible thing someone could say to me. The minute I fell for Pete, that was my biggest fear. That everything that happened when I was dating Bunny—my coming out on TV, the millions of queer kids it inspired to do the same—would be discounted as some cheap publicity stunt.

✦

Mona looks back at Meesha. They're in public so she looks predictably stoic, but she can read her cues. The shortened breath. The white-knuckle grips on Pete's and Mona's hands. The slight twitch on the upper right corner of her lip. This is about as close to a public Meesha Mashad breakdown as you can get.

In a snap decision, she shakes her hand loose from her sister's grip, turns back toward the Bunny fan who made the comment, and positions her face inches away from theirs.

"Listen, you twerp," she spews. "You have no idea what you're talking about. This is my gentle warning. *Back off.*"

Mona quickly glances at Pete and Meesha. Pete is shaking his head laughing and Meesha is staring down at the carpet completely disassociating. Mona would love to say more, but it looks like saying more might literally kill her sister and the fan is already shaking and mumbling apologies. Her work here is done. She flips off the entire crowd one more time. "THE SAME GOES TO ALL OF YOU!" she yells out.

The paparazzi go wild. She smiles, instantly envisioning the headlines and memes this content is going to generate for years to come.

Confessional

INT. MARY MASHAD'S LIVING ROOM—AFTERNOON (CONT'D)

MONA

This is why I want my own show. I'm good at this, savvy even. I know how to be Mona Mashad. How to play the part. She's wild, she's unpredictable, she's a little bit scary. The girl whose antics you love to hate-read about on the *Daily Mail* the next morning.

Mona makes eyes with Mary, who is just now exiting the sprinter van.

"Stop it," the matriarch mouths at her daughter as she takes her first step onto the carpet. "You're making a scene."

But Mona knows her mom too well to take the warning seriously. She and Mary get each other on an almost telepathic level in these instances. Mary is thinking exactly the same thing Mona is. That moment was PR gold.

It's not until their entire family is posing for a historic picture at the bottom of the Met steps that they see Bunny. She's *the* biggest pop star in the world, with fans so loyal they would literally show up here to protest her ex for breaking her heart. But standing a few feet away from the Mashads and Sandersons, decked out in her gigantic bubblegum-pink gown and matching cape, Bunny somehow looks small. Lonely, even. Mona can hear her dad's voice in her head. "The biggest blessing we have in this life is each other," he would remind them over and over again. "Everyone else in this business is alone. Not us. We have our own *army*." She imagines him watching them posing here, throngs of reporters fighting to document the monumental pop culture moment. To document *his* family. All here together. He would have loved this.

"Bunny!" Melody shouts, a wide smile on her face. "Why don't you join us?"

Mona gives her sister a forceful nudge in the rib.

"What?!" Melody asks through a wide smile. "I feel sort of sorry for her."

"She asked for this," Mona says, making direct eye contact with Bunny as she speaks. "Let her squirm."

"No," Meesha interrupts, locking eyes with her ex. "Melody is right. Bunny, you can join us if you want."

Mona and Mary exchange shocked glances before looking

at Meesha, impressed. It was one thing coming from Melody, who's nice to literally everyone. But coming from Meesha? It was a genius PR move—she just forced Bunny's hand. Bunny can come over and look like the scathing song she wrote really doesn't reflect how she feels at all, or she can choose not to and look like the real villain here. Either way, Meesha comes out on top.

Confessional

EXT. MEESHA MASHAD'S PENTHOUSE BALCONY—AFTERNOON (CONT'D)

MEESHA

[*rolls her eyes*]

I didn't do it for the PR. Bunny and I were together for a long time. I loved her. And, I mean, I may not love her *in that way* anymore. But I still really care about her. I don't want her standing off to the side feeling awkward. That sucks.

You could hear a pin drop as everyone—fans, reporters, celebrities—stared intently to see what Bunny would do.

Finally, she settled on a scowl. "I'm good." With that, the pop star has the absolute *gall* to throw off her cape and reveal the words I HATE YOU, MEESHA spray-painted down the back of her dress.

"Oh," Melody whispers as the crowd bursts out into gasps. "So, that's why she was lurking near us."

Mona lunges forward. "I will rip that dress off your body."

Meesha pulls Mona back, her icy face hardening as she takes in the spectacle her ex just put on. "Don't, Mona," she says, looking Bunny up and down. "She's not worth it."

Mona examines her sister carefully, in search of her trusty tells. But she's breathing steadily. Her grip on Pete's hand is loose. Her lip isn't even slightly twitching. She looks . . . fine?

Confessional

EXT. MEESHA MASHAD'S PENTHOUSE BALCONY—AFTERNOON (CONT'D)

MEESHA

[*shrugs*]

This whole time I thought I was the monster here. But in that moment, I realized it wasn't me. It was *her*. She turned our breakup into one big self-serving publicity stunt. That stupid dress was the best gift she could have given me. I stopped caring.

Once they've finally distanced themselves from Bunny and her ridiculous spectacle, Mona slips away from Meesha and Pete, allowing them to have their first big moment as an official couple without her or the rest of their family cramping their style. Luckily, the optics are very much on their side. Meesha and Pete look unbothered and in love while Bunny, between the throngs of crazed Meesha-hating fans and the dress, looks petty and obsessed. Even without Bunny's antics, Pete and Meesha's spectacularly good looks and generally cool vibe would be enough to make anyone forget about the scandal surrounding their love story. Her sister may have retired from modeling, but she is still so natural in front of a camera. And Pete is no shlub either. A Hollywood nepo baby turned NBA star, he's been blessed with the physique of an NBA legend combined with the ritzy air of a Rockefeller. They look great together.

As Mona makes her way down the carpet solo, it becomes increasingly clear that she has officially absorbed the lion's share of any and all Bunny-related questions. Everywhere she turns, there's another reporter throwing a microphone in her face asking about Bunny's song or the dress. Despite the years of Mary Mashad media training instructing her to do otherwise, Mona gives every single one of the reporters a shady response. "I actually like Bunny's music, honestly. But 'Desperate 4 Fame' is just bad," she tells one *Entertainment Tonight* reporter. "Like beyond being about Meesha, it's not even a good song. Right? You have to agree." That was a lie. The song is unfortunately an absolute banger. But she would sooner die than admit that on the record.

It isn't until she's about to make her way up the famous Met steps that she sees her ex Max and his fiancée, supermodel Chya, posing in front of her. They look annoyingly great together. This year's theme is Guillaume Blanc: A Life in Style, honoring the iconic late designer Guillaume Blanc, and they were the only two granted vintage looks designed by Guillaume himself. Max is in a black velvet tux and Chya is in a white dress with a miles-long train that looks a lot like a wedding dress. At one point, Max pulls her in for a long, passionate kiss and it looks like they could be in front of an altar having just exchanged their vows. The crowd goes wild. Mona wants to vomit.

She turns her attention back toward the hundreds of cameras snapping her photos. She follows each of their instructions as best as she can. "PLACE YOUR HAND ON YOUR HIPS," "BLOW US A KISS," "COME CLOSER," "STEP BACK FARTHER." She's mid flipping her hair when she overhears a reporter ask Max if he's "seen Mona Mashad tonight." And that's when the piece of human garbage responds, "Well, my ex is hard to miss. She's certainly made quite the scene tonight, hasn't she? For a minute there, I thought she was about to throw a punch at poor Bunny Lee." He laughs at his own stupid snarky comment then adds, "You know, honestly? I'll leave it at this. Nothing but love for Mona, but I'm grateful to be with a woman like Chya now."

She balls up the train of her bright blue Valentino gown in the palm of her hand and begins marching the few steps up toward him. How *dare* he? Who does he think he is? Even more infuriatingly, he seems to have absolutely no awareness of his proximity to her. He keeps breezily making his way up toward the stairs, forcing Mona to practically chase him.

She's almost caught up with him when the worst possible thing that could happen happens—the heel of her satin stiletto gets caught on a snag on the carpet and she trips. She *trips*. And the massive crowd of reporters and photographers is too busy trying to get a fun, flirty couple shot of Max grabbing Chya's butt a few steps ahead of her to notice.

As she braces herself for impact, she can already envision the memes and headlines, and this time she's getting significantly less joy than she was with the whole Bunny situation. "Hot Mess Mona Mashad Falls to the Floor on Met Steps Behind Her Ex & His Perfect New Fiancée." It's internet gold.

Then, out of nowhere, just as her head is inches from the pavement, a strong man appears from behind and scoops her into his arms. She looks up, expecting to see Majid.

But it's Lucas Sterling, a crooked smile on his face as he locks his so-absurdly-good-looking-it-should-be-illegal gaze on Mona. "Never a dull moment with you, huh?"

The thing with Lucas is it's not just that he's good-looking. It's his energy. The *way* he looks at you. It's like his gaze is a spotlight and when it's on you, you're the center of not just *his* universe, but *the* universe as a whole. The sun, the moon, the stars. All of it.

Mona wills herself not to blush, desperate to not look all googly-eyed as the throngs of cameras and reporters desert Max and Chya to capture her meet-cute moment with *the* Lucas Sterling. But her stupid mouth gives her away again, those corners curving upward no matter how hard she tries to force them back down.

"I would have been fine," she lies as Lucas gently sets her back down on solid ground.

"Sure," Lucas says with a small laugh, completely unfazed by the hundreds of reporters and fans screaming their names.

"I *would* have!" Mona insists, refusing to be his damsel in distress.

"Okay, fine!" Lucas concedes. "I believe you."

She watches skeptically as he reaches a Tom Ford–clad arm out toward her. "But still. I think you should hold on to me as we make our way in there. You know, for safety."

Mona scoffs. "Are you kidding?" she whispers. "They're all watching us. If we walk in together arm in arm they'll think we're dating."

Lucas shrugs. "So?"

"*So*," she says. "We're not."

"Not yet," Lucas fires back, that cocky grin from the other night back on his face.

Mona rolls her eyes more at herself than Lucas, hating how much his game is working on her. And hating even more how many people are now *watching* his game so effortlessly work on her.

She examines the crowd, her brain tackling a familiar set of PR calculations. On a personal level, she knows what she should do is reject him. He's a scoundrel. Guaranteed to hurt her in one way or another. She should protect herself, give him a curt "thank you" and keep it moving. *But*, if she rejects him now, as everyone watches, after he saved her so dramatically, she would look rude. Ungrateful. Bratty.

That said, in a Hollywood relationship, there are about

thirty-seven steps that come before walking a red carpet together hand in hand. If she grabs on to his arm and walks up those stairs with him, they might as well have just told the crowd they're deeply and madly in love. Which is a huge problem for a multitude of reasons, starting with they're not and ending with, if his unfortunately flawless game *does* work on her and she *does* hook up with him, the whole world will be watching intently when it inevitably blows up in her face.

She needs to find a middle ground. Something that will please the public without being too commital.

"We can walk in together side by side, no touching," she suggests, her tone the same as her mom's when she's in the middle of a high-stakes business negotiation. "Final offer."

"I'll take it," Lucas concedes. He looks Mona up and down, an uncharacteristically shy smile making its way across his face. "You look incredible, by the way."

He is styled in a crisp navy tux and looks pretty incredible himself. But Mona isn't about to go telling him that. Instead, she just settles for a short and sweet "Thanks."

They walk quietly side by side for a minute before Lucas says, "I heard what your ex said to the reporter. That guy is a jerk. You know that, right?"

"Trust me. I'm *well* aware," Mona says, a little surprised by how validating it is to hear someone outside of her family call Max a jerk.

They're about to enter the museum when they spot a group of models fawning over Chya. "You look *so* hot," one gushes. "Seriously. Are you even real?" another coos.

"Girls, *stop* it," Chya faux-modestly responds. "For real. I'm blushing." That's when Max steps in, putting his arm around her. "I am the luckiest guy in the world. The most beautiful girl on Earth, both inside and out, is *my* future wife."

It takes every ounce of self-control Mona has within her to stop herself from rolling her eyes. It's not that she wishes she was with Max or anything. The guy fully gives her the ick at this point. It's not even that she has anything against Chya. She's a literal model. Obviously, she's hot. And, based on the brief interactions Mona has had with her, she's legitimately nice. It's just that Mona and Max were together for years. She was his only other significant long-term relationship. So, it doesn't feel like he's just saying Chya is the most beautiful girl on Earth inside and out. He's also saying Mona *isn't*. If she didn't know him as well as she does, she could reassure herself by saying that's not *really* what he meant. But she does know him well enough. Lucas is spot-on. He's a jerk. A jerk who *would* purposely make a comment like that when Mona is a few feet away just to remind her that he's now with a model who's significantly hotter and an all-around better person than she is. He's purposely trying to get to her. And it still works. That's what makes her livid.

"You know I heard she has a sixth toe?" Lucas whispers to Mona. "And it's super mangled. Bright green fungus growing out of the toenail. Gross. It's why she always wears closed-toed shoes."

It's a weak and blatant attempt at making her feel better but Mona laughs anyway.

Chapter 5

Inside the event, Lucas is seated with the select group of East Coast elite types that get invited every year, while Mona is seated across the room at a table with her family.

Confessional

INT. HARVARD MEN'S LACROSSE LOCKER ROOM—AFTERNOON (CONT'D)

LUCAS

She kept staring at me. It was cute.

INT. MARY MASHAD'S LIVING ROOM—AFTERNOON (CONT'D)

MONA

He said I was *staring* at him? Obsessed with himself much? No. I was not staring at him. He just, like, happened to be seated basically directly in my eyeline. What was I supposed to do? Ask Anna Wintour to re-seat me?

✦✦✦

Mona is trying her best to casually crane her neck without being too noticeable. It's not that she's *staring* at Lucas. She just, like, is curious about what he's up to. She finally makes him out when Melody ducks her head down to wipe some pea soup off Axle's lap. There he is, just chatting with a couple WASP-y-looking guys and a prissy-looking girl who looks like she's never enjoyed the release of a good poop in her life. She can't figure him out. *Why is he being so nice to her?* Obviously, the answer is he wants to hook up with her. Use her and leave her like he does to literally every other girl. But this spark Mona feels doesn't seem like that. Something about the way he treats her feels different.

Oh God. Is she listening to herself? *Something about the way he treats me feels different?* No. This is how guys like him become the way they are. They make every girl feel different. Mona looks at where Ava King, the first Black model to grace the cover of every edition of *Vogue* internationally, is seated a couple tables away from her. Apparently, according to pretty much everyone in Hollywood, Lucas and Ava were talking for weeks when he flew her all the way out to St. Barth's for New Year's. They hooked up the first night, then the next night he completely ditched her for some Brazilian bikini model. Ava probably felt *different* when she was first talking to him, too. But nobody's different to guys like Lucas Sterling.

"Hello! Earth to Mona."

Mona snaps out of her thoughts to see Meesha waving her hand across her face.

"What?" she asks, still distracted by Ava and her golden-brown eyes that look like two bonfires set ablaze against her midnight-colored skin. How could Lucas ditch *her*? She might be the most astoundingly beautiful person Mona has ever seen in real life.

"I was just *thanking* you for what you did out there for me," Meesha says. "I love you."

"Oh yeah. Of course," Mona says, waving her off. "Love you, too."

Mary slides her phone in front of Mona, showing her Page Six's homepage. "You definitely diverted." Mona doesn't want to smile. But she smiles. Right there on the homepage, as the top story, is Lucas holding her in his arms on the Met Gala carpet. LUCAS STERLING SAVES MONA MASHAD FROM NEAR-CATASTROPHIC FALL DOWN THE MET STEPS, the headline reads. Mona quickly pulls up Instagram. Then X. Then TikTok. It's everywhere. Different versions of the same picture littering every corner of the internet. Not a single headline about Bunny.

The memes she was worried about—the ones that would have shown her lying limply on the Met steps behind Max and Chya—have been replaced by ones of Max and Chya looking down at Lucas gallantly holding Mona in his arms alongside the caption "How to Win a Breakup." She was worried about the moment making her a damsel in distress, but it made her a hero to scorned women everywhere.

And, because they didn't walk hand in hand, nobody thinks they're dating. People are just swooning over the *idea* of these two. All she has to do is never be publicly seen with him again and the buzz around them will go as quickly as it came. It wasn't her original plan but, she has to admit, the whole thing worked out pretty spectacularly.

"What is it?" Meesha asks. "Why are you smiling like that?"

Mona wordlessly shows everyone at the table Mary's phone screen.

"Wait, Mona, this is so CUTE," Melody squeals, snatching the phone up. "I'm dying!"

"How did we miss this?" Timmy asks, examining the headline. "You almost fell?"

"Technically, I *did* fall. He just caught me before I hit the ground. You were all inside already," Mona tells Timmy. "It was just a few minutes ago, before we walked in here."

"I saw you two walking in together," Louise says, giving Lucas a once-over from across the room. "He definitely likes you. You're not getting Lucas Sterling's time of day if he has no interest."

Mona feels her hopes rising, then quickly shoves them back down. "He likes anything with a pulse. The moment was PR gold, I'll admit it. But it was really nothing. Everyone was too busy fawning over Chya and Max to even notice I was falling. He's the only person who saw. He *had* to do something. It didn't mean anything."

"Oh, stop with this nonsense," Mary instructs. "Mona, do you know what this could mean for our family? You, dating a *Sterling*? Not just any Sterling, but *the* Sterling? We would get the legitimacy we've always been missing. That all-American gravitas. It's a dream for your brand."

"Can you chill? This is my *life*," Mona shoots back. "Not some strategic business decision."

"Honey, everything in life is a strategic business decision," Mary says, taking her phone back. "Get used to it."

"He has a brutal reputation," Meesha says, her voice in its patent monotone. "Remember what he did to Ava? Oh God, and the story about Annabella Stone."

"What happened with Annabella?" Mona asks, hating how badly she wants to know how Lucas hurt yet another stunning supermodel. "You never told me he dated Annabella."

Before Meesha can respond, Mona's phone lights up with a text from a 212 number. New York. It's gotta be him. She looks past Melody and finds him staring directly at her from his seat across the room.

Part of her wants to play it cool. To throw the phone in her bag and go back to chatting with her family, leave him waiting. But isn't that what she would do if she *did* like him? And isn't she expressly supposed to *not* like him?

So, she opens the message. You going out after this?

Duh. Melody's party at Zero Bond, she quickly writes back. It's not like she's *inviting* him or anything. He's already on the guest list.

Less than a second later, Lucas replies, Huh. I have an early drive back to Boston tomorrow. Was going to skip, but maybe I'll change my plans. . . .

"Why are you staring at your phone like that?" Meesha asks, looking at Mona, then following her eyeline over to where

Lucas is seated. "Oh *God*. Mona, have you been listening at all? Don't."

Mona feels her cheeks brightening. She loves knowing all of Meesha's tells, but she doesn't quite have the same warm sentiment when the tables are turned.

"Why should she not? Which one of us is flawless?" Axle asks, Melody's cheek resting on the shoulder of his dark green velvet tux as her big hazel eyes stare dreamily up at him. "Who are we to judge a man for his past?"

"Especially a man like *Lucas Sterling*," Mary says, red, white, and blue stars already in her eyes.

"It's no big deal," Mona insists, doing her best to drown them all out. "We're just texting about the after-party. It's nothing."

Mona turns her attention back to their short text thread. "Don't do me any favors," she replies before tossing her phone back in her clutch.

She quickly glances back over at him, instantly annoyed by the way her face seems to almost automatically mirror the sideways smile on his as soon as their eyes meet.

Confessional

INT. HARVARD MEN'S LACROSSE LOCKER ROOM—AFTERNOON (CONT'D)

LUCAS

It didn't matter if she told me she was going to a party on Mars. I needed to be where she was.

Chapter 6

After their wedding solidified their spot as everyone's favorite A-list couple of the moment, Melody and Axle were a natural pick to host this year's Met after-party. But really it was Mona who did all the planning behind the scenes. And not begrudgingly, either. She practically begged them for the chance to step in. The past few months she had the time of her life doing everything from selecting the venue to carefully crafting the ultra exclusive guest list. Whether or not she gets the credit for it, this event is her baby.

"Oh God, Mona," Meesha says, making her way over to Mona with drinks. "Look at you. This is pathetic."

"Okay, excuse me. *Rude*," she says, taking a long sip of her espresso martini before asking as casually as she can muster, "What do you mean, anyway?" Mona knows exactly what her sister means, but she hopes by asking she might throw her off a bit.

"You haven't stopped staring at the elevator since we got

here," Meesha says, unfazed by Mona's failed attempt at a Jedi mind trick. "You like him. Even though I *told* you not to like him."

"I *don't* like him," Mona insists, actively resisting the urge to follow up about that Annabella story. "My looking at the elevator has nothing to do with *him*. I made the guest list; I just need to make sure no randoms make their way in."

"Right," Meesha says, a smirk on her face. "Totally."

Mona looks around the expertly decorated room at Zero Bond. She really killed it. This party is insanely A-list. Not even a B-list face in sight. And without phones or fans at the ultra-private members-only club, the guests can actually let their guards down. Make mistakes in peace. That was her goal.

She hears the ding of the elevator and glances slightly over, trying not to be as noticeable as she was evidently being earlier. It's a weird mix. Supermodel Tatiana Marquis, Oscar-winner Antonio Lahoya, rapper Bar None, comedian John Smokes, and tech billionaire Alice Fining. No Lucas.

"Oh, Mona," Melody says, placing a gentle hand on Mona's shoulder as she comes up to join her and Meesha from behind. "I'm sure he's coming. It's still early."

Mona rolls her eyes as dramatically as she can, mortified by how much she needed to hear Melody's words of comfort. "Will you two *stop*? I don't care about him."

Meesha laughs, giving Melody a look. "Oh, yes. Sorry. I forgot this is Mona *not* caring."

Before Mona can get away from her sisters to say hi to Bar None, who happens to live down the street from them in LA, she feels a tap on her shoulder.

"Hi," Lucas says.

Mona stares at him, confused. "How did you get here?"

"A car?" Lucas asks more than answers, equally confused. "How did *you* get here?"

"No," Mona says. "Like, how did you get *in* here? I didn't see you come through the elevator."

"Oh," Lucas says with a shrug. "I took the stairs."

"You took the *stairs*?" Mona asks. "Why?"

"We're in lacrosse season right now," Lucas says. "I thought the extra cardio would be good for me."

"Got it," Mona says, pausing for a second before adding, "I thought you weren't gonna make it with that early drive."

"Well, trust me, I didn't come to *do you any favors*," Lucas says, a crooked smile making its way across his face as he quotes her text. "But I figured I could make it work."

The corners of Mona's mouth briefly curve upward (much to her dismay, it seems he has this effect on her) until she remembers Meesha and Melody are still standing right next to her.

"Oh, um, Lucas, these are my sisters, Melody and Meesha," she says, erasing the sappy smile off her face. "Melody, Meesha, this is Lucas."

"Hey," Lucas says. "Nice to meet you both. I'm honestly a huge *Making Mashad* fan."

Meesha stares at him blankly, completely unimpressed. God, she can be so icy sometimes. She says it's just that she's shy, but Mona has explained to her time and time again that being shy when you're obscenely hot just translates to mean.

Luckily, Melody, the human embodiment of sunshine, quickly counteracts Meesha's chill with a wide smile worthy of the cover of any wellness magazine. "Lucas, it's *great* to meet you. How cute is that picture of you and Mona?!"

Lucas laughs. "Oh no. I haven't been online. Is it everywhere?"

"It's everywhere," Mona confirms.

Lucas gives her that look, the one that makes you feel like the world begins and ends with you. "Can't say I'm mad about that."

Melody clears her throat, reminding them she's there. "So, Lucas, you watch the show?"

"Don't buy it," Meesha says, her eyes narrow with skepticism and her voice so cold it could cause frostbite. "The guy is notoriously full of it."

"Trust me," Mona says, her eyes set on Lucas's. "He watches the show. I tested him and everything."

"I did pass that test with *flying* colors," Lucas brags, his eyes equally fixated on Mona's.

"To be fair," Mona says, "there was only one question. I could test you on more."

"Go for it," Lucas says. "Test me on *anything*. I'll blow you away."

"You'll *blow me away*?" Mona asks, an eyebrow raised. "Big talk."

"What's the matter, Mashad?" Lucas asks, that familiar jolt of electricity building between them as he takes a step closer to Mona. "You don't think I can put my money where my mouth is?"

Mona stares squarely up at him, a smug smile on her face. "I don't."

"I think I'm going to barf," Meesha whispers to Melody, just loudly enough that they can all hear.

"Meesha, can you *not*?" Mona snaps.

"You know," Melody says, yanking Meesha by the arm before she can respond. "We should go check on Josie and Timmy over there. But we'll catch up with you two later."

Mona mouths "Thank you" to Melody, who gives her a wink and a kiss as she pulls Meesha away.

"I'm sorry about Meesha," Mona says sheepishly once her sisters are no longer in earshot. "She's always weird about new people."

"It's okay." Lucas shrugs, his hands stuffed in the pockets of his now disheveled tux. "She's being a protective sister. That's cool."

Mona and Lucas stand there for a second quietly taking each other in as Meesha and Melody walk away.

"There's a vibe here, right?" Lucas asks, breaking the silence. "Between us."

"A *vibe*?" Mona asks, giving it her best attempt at playing dumb. "No. There's no vibe."

Lucas shoots her a sideways smile. "Come on. Admit it. Something about this feels . . . I don't know, special. Different."

Different. There's that word.

The elevator dings behind them and three Victoria's Secret Angels—Janelle Adams, Iman Parik, and Lisabette Rose—walk in, each one looking more stunning than the next.

"Be honest," Mona says as she and Lucas both watch the models file into the party. "How many of them have you gotten with?"

"One," he says.

Mona stares at him, unconvinced.

"Okay, fine," he concedes. "Two. Janelle and Iman."

She's still looking at him, not fully convinced when Lisabette struts over to them.

"Liz, hi," Lucas says. "You know Mona Mashad, right?"

"I don't think we've met," she says to Mona. "Hey."

"Hey," Mona says, looking like a shrimp as the supermodel's six-foot-tall frame towers over her. "Nice to meet you."

Lisabette, or "Liz" as Lucas apparently calls her, ignores her, turning her attention back over to Lucas. "You never called."

"Oh, yeah, I'm sorry about that," Lucas says. "I just got busy with . . . school and stuff."

Lisabette looks around the party, then gives Mona a terrifying once-over before focusing her giant cobalt-blue eyes back in on Lucas. "Right," she says. "It seems like you're really focused on your *studies*."

"All right, maybe I got with all three," Lucas admits to Mona as Lisabette walks away, lowering his voice before adding, "But Liz hardly counts. We went on *one* date. And it was a bad date! Painfully boring."

Mona scoffs. "See?" she asks. "*This* is why there is no vibe. There cannot be a vibe."

"Oh, trust me," Lucas says. "There can still be a vibe. Whether or not we choose to give in to the vibe is a separate matter. But you cannot deny the sheer presence of the vibe."

Just as Mona takes the last sip of her espresso martini, Pete's teammate Robbie Ryder comes over with a fresh one.

"Mona, hey!" he says, boxing Lucas out as he slides into the conversation. "I brought you a drink. I remembered you loved these." It's funny. In almost every other circumstance, Lucas is tall. But Robbie's absurdly tall basketball-player frame somehow manages to make Lucas look short. Small, even.

"Oh, Robbie, hey," Mona says, setting her empty glass down as she accepts the glass that he's holding for her. "Thanks." She takes a sip. "Wow, you even remembered the dash of cinnamon."

"How could I forget?" he asks, before adding, "So, um, anyway, I was thinking, while we're both in New York, maybe we can get together again? Maybe a double date with Pete and Meesha? I know you like to keep things casual, but I thought it might be fun."

"Robbie, I'm going to be real with you," she says. "I don't really want to do that. You said it yourself. I like to keep things casual, and a double date with my sister and her boyfriend doesn't feel casual."

"Oh, um, okay," he says. "I'll see you around then?"

"Yeah," she says. "Definitely."

Robbie sulks away, revealing Lucas still standing there across from Mona.

"And he was . . . ?" Lucas asks, a too-wide grin on his face.

"A friend," Mona says, forcing a nonchalant shrug to really sell the lie.

"Right," Lucas says. "And how about the model over there who hasn't stopped staring at us since I started talking to you?"

Mona turns around to where Jacques, the current face of

Armani, is standing by the bar staring at them. *God*, he's hot.

"Also a friend," she says, a small smile creeping onto her face.

✦ ✦ ✦

Confessional

INT. MARY MASHAD'S LIVING ROOM—AFTERNOON (CONT'D)

MONA

They *are* friends. I mean, I've hooked up with them both. But they're friends.

"I think you're being unfair," Lucas says. "I don't judge you for who you've been with. Why do I have to be punished for *my* history? Honestly, you're slut-shaming me."

Mona laughs. "Why are you here, anyway? Seriously. Don't you have to be up early tomorrow?"

He shrugs. "I wanted to see you. And you won't let me take you on a date, so this was the next-best thing."

"Right," Mona says with a sly smile. "Stalking me."

"I'm not sure it constitutes as stalking when I'm literally on the guest list," he says. "But sure. Whatever you want to call it."

"As the person who made the guest list, I guess I have to take some responsibility there," Mona says. "You're not *fully* a stalker."

Lucas's eyes perk up. "So, are you admitting this was a personal invite?" he asks. "Mona Mashad wanted *me* at her sister's party?"

"Oh, relax," Mona says with a laugh. "I had to include everyone who's anyone and you just so happen to fall under that category. That's all."

Before Lucas gets a chance to respond, Melody comes strolling back with Louise and the rest of Mona's family in tow. "Who wants to do a sibling shot?!" she asks, a bottle of Clase Azul in her hand. "The manager just gave me the bottle as a thank-you for hosting here. Obviously Josie and Timmy are out, but they said they'd do Diet Coke shooters."

"Timmy Sanderson!" Lucas exclaims as Timmy makes his way over with Josie. "The Normal Sanderson. Nice to meet you, man. It's an honor."

Mona looks at Lucas, trying to get a read. He's the son of the president of the United States, and yet he knows deep-cut *Making Mashad* super-fan references like calling Timmy the Normal Sanderson—the moniker the internet gave him because of his desperate attempt to avoid fame despite his family's too-close proximity to it. The guy makes no sense.

"Hey, man," Timmy says, his face adopting a pinkish hue. "Nice to meet you."

"We've heard *great* things," Josie cuts in. "Thank *God* you were there for Mona's big fall. Can you imagine if you weren't there?! Would have been so sad if Mona was just, like, defeated on the floor behind her ex and his fiancée. . . . Oh, um, I'm Josie, by the way."

"Josie's right," Melody agrees. "I want to cry just at the thought of Mona looking all weak and limp behind that jerk. It's heart-wrenching. We're so happy she had you."

Oh *God*. Mona looks over to where Pete is visibly trying to convince Meesha to be nice, and suddenly wishes Josie and Melody could absorb some of her icy coolness. This is so beyond mortifying. How could it be that all three of her sisters could be so embarrassing in such starkly different ways?

"Weren't we going to take shots?" Louise thankfully interrupts. "Let's take shots."

Within seconds, a waiter appears with a tray of the crystal Baccarat shot glasses Mona handpicked for the party. Melody carefully pours the bottle of tequila in each one, making sure to have the bartender fill two with Diet Coke for Josie and Timmy.

They all down their shots, quickly refilling for another round. Then another. Then another. By the fifth round, Lucas has fully won the family over. Even Meesha is laughing as he tells them about the time he ripped his pants trying to do a split at his mom's inaugural dinner.

"All right, fine," Meesha slurs from where she's now seated on Pete's lap, Louise asleep on the couch behind them. "I admit it. You're not that bad."

"Yes!" Lucas cheers in victory. "*Not that bad*. I'll take it."

"I *told* you he was cool," Pete tells Meesha, his arms wrapped tightly around her.

"I knew it," Melody slurs with a sleepy smile. "I knew you were a good egg."

"I should have said this earlier," Josie says, "but I really am a huge fan of your mom. She's, like, the best president we've ever had."

"Listen, Lucas, when you get a moment, I would really like to discuss your mother's policies on organic farming," Axle says out of the blue. "It's high time for a federal mandate."

"Axy, I'm tired," Melody says, stretching her perfectly toned arms out as she lets out a big yawn. "Let's go home."

"We should probably take her home," Josie says, nodding over toward Louise. "I think she had one too many shots tonight."

"I'll help you guys carry her out," Pete offers, grabbing Lou from the couch.

Slowly but surely, her whole family leaves the party. And Mona is drunk so it probably was longer, but it feels like a matter of seconds before she and Lucas are the only two people left at the party.

Mona looks over to where Lucas is sitting on the couch next to her.

"It's probably late," Mona says, unable to check the time without her phone. "We should go home."

"You hungry?" Lucas asks, ignoring everything she just said.

"Honestly, yes," Mona says. "I'm starving."

"Me too," Lucas says. "Let's go grab a slice at Joe's. Have you had Joe's? It's the best."

"Are you *insane*?" Mona asks. "We can't go to some late-night pizza place together. The paparazzi would have a field day. No."

"Fine," Lucas says. "What if you come to my town house?"

Mona opens her mouth, but before she can object, he adds, "*Platonically*. No funny business. We'll take separate cars. I'll get the pizza. You can enter my place on the backside in a Secret Service car. Nobody will know. We can enjoy our pizza in peace."

She thinks about it for a minute, too drunk, tired, and hungry to erase the smile forming on her face. "Fine."

Chapter 7

"Oh my God, *absolutely* no pictures," Mona objects, covering her face with a giant slice of pepperoni as Lucas tries to snap a shot with his disposable camera. "It's four in the morning. I've been up almost twenty-four hours, my eyeliner is smeared, and my mouth is lined with a thick coat of pizza grease. I look repulsive."

"No, you don't," Lucas says, looking her up and down with the cocky grin of a guy who knows his face alone could turn anybody into a pile of human mush. "You look hot."

Mona looks down at the dress the French designer Delphine specifically designed for her to wear to the after-party. It's more like a beautifully and intricately crafted, diamond-encrusted net than a dress, its small openings allowing hundreds of little glimpses at her supple olive skin without really letting you see anything at all. It's not *not* hot.

"Hey," she warns Lucas, lips pursed as she raises one perfectly sculpted eyebrow at him. "You said no funny business."

"That wasn't funny business. That was just fact," he says with an unbothered shrug. "You *do* look hot, just like the sky is blue and two plus two equals four. And the cherry on top is that, whether you admit it or not, I think you know it, which only magnifies the whole effect."

Mona can't remember the last time she let herself really blush, but here she is. Blushing like a twelve-year-old who just got a note from her crush asking her to the school dance. She does her best to distract from the change in skin tone with an eye roll. "You are relentless."

Lucas nods in agreement, cocky grin still on his face. "I really am."

Mona playfully throws the decorative pillow nestled behind her at his face and calls him a cocky prick, but the truth is she likes that he's relentless.

✦ ✦ ✦

Confessional

INT. HARVARD MEN'S LACROSSE LOCKER ROOM—AFTERNOON (CONT'D)

LUCAS

I'm not some creep. If the vibe between us wasn't so blatantly obvious, I would drop it. But it was. So, I couldn't.

INT. MARY MASHAD'S LIVING ROOM—AFTERNOON (CONT'D)

MONA

You try having the most desired boy in America

throwing himself at you and tell me with a straight face you'd actually like him to stop.

Desperate to return her now-rosy skin tone to its natural hue, Mona tries to focus her attention on literally anything else. She takes another bite of her pizza, scanning the cozy den of the Sterling family's West Village town house as she swallows. She likes it here. It feels homey in a way you wouldn't expect from a family as prestigious as Lucas's.

"So, this is where you grew up?" Mona asks.

"Yep," Lucas says, taking a bite of his fresh mozzarella slice. "I was born in the hospital a few blocks away. We had to move into the mayor's mansion for a while when my mom was mayor. And then obviously the White House. But this has always been home."

Part of what makes the room so delightfully cozy is the pictures. On the mantel above the fireplace, there's one of Lucas accepting his high school diploma. And another of him blowing out the candles on his fifth birthday cake, his parents standing on either side of him. Then on the oak side table next to her, there's one of his parents joyfully cutting the cake on their wedding day. If you didn't know any better, you would think this was a normal family.

Mona's eyes zero in on a picture of Lucas's dad propped up on the bookshelf lining the wall across from her. He's asleep on the very same worn pale-yellow couch she's sitting on right now, his glasses halfway down his face as he clutches a copy of *The Catcher in the Rye* against his chest.

Everyone remembers the day Sam Sterling was shot. As the only heir to the famed Sterling family fortune, he was expected by the world to get involved with one of his family's many businesses. Or get super into golf. Or spend his life hanging out on yachts and dating models. Any of the things privileged men do. But, instead, he got into education. A beloved school principal, he was protecting a classroom of kindergarteners when the shooter got to him. Jordana Sterling was just the mayor of New York City then, but after the speech she gave following her husband's death—a young Lucas standing tearfully by her side—everyone knew it would only be a matter of time before she became president.

At this point, Sam Sterling feels less like a person who pooped and ate burgers and probably picked his nose every now and then, and more like some sort of secular all-American version of a saint. People talk about him with such misty-eyed reverence that you almost feel like you need to take your hat off and place a hand on your heart just to mention his name. That's why Mona can't stop staring at the picture. It's just so . . . intimate. Asleep on the couch . . . stubbly chin. He looks so human.

Lucas must notice her staring because, without her asking, he explains, "I took that."

"What?" Mona asks. "The picture?"

"Yeah. Pictures were sort of my dad's and my thing," he says. "He always had a camera on him, I guess you could say I adopted the habit."

"Ah," Mona says, nodding toward where his disposable camera is now placed on the coffee table between them. "So that explains that."

Lucas gives her a shy, almost embarrassed smile. "I've got hundreds of these. If not thousands. I used to try taking pictures on my phone, but that was always a nightmare with tabloids constantly trying to hack me to find dirt on my mom. Eventually, I just deleted all my social accounts, stopped taking pictures on my phone, and went back to taking pictures on disposables like I did growing up."

Mona stares past him to the end table, where there's a framed photo of a young Lucas on his dad's shoulders on the Harvard campus. They're standing by the HARVARD BUSINESS SCHOOL sign, both wearing Harvard T-shirts and baseball caps. It would be massively douchey if it wasn't so cute.

"Can I tell you a secret?" Mona asks, the intimacy of the moment temporarily nudging her guard down.

"Of course," Lucas says.

"I got into Harvard," she admits. "I'm not going or anything. But I got in. My mom is the only person who knows."

Lucas laughs. "*That* was your big secret?"

"Yeah," Mona says, her eyes on the barely perceptible cuticles framing her long glossy red nails. "Everything in my life has been public information. I just wanted to do something purely for me. So, I asked my homeschool teacher to tutor me on the SAT and I studied hard, and I somehow managed a perfect score. Then I put everything I had into an essay. And I got in."

"What was the essay on?" Lucas asks. "I'm intrigued."

"I wrote about a time I failed," Mona says, her voice uncharacteristically small.

"Huh," Lucas says, examining her face quizzically. "I honestly can't really imagine you failing at anything."

They sit quietly for a moment, Mona staring at the old picture of Lucas and his dad at Harvard.

"I didn't speak at my dad's funeral," she eventually blurts out. "That's what I wrote my essay about. I had so much to say. He was my best friend. My favorite human on the face of the Earth. My protector, my . . . just my whole world. And then his funeral came, and it wasn't just me and my family anymore. There were millions of people watching, and everything I had to say just sort of turned into nothing."

"That's not a failure, Mona," Lucas says, scooching closer to gently wrap a Lacrosse-toned arm around her as her eyes adopt a watery sheen.

Mona briefly lets her head sink into his chest, then pulls herself back up and away from him. "Oh God," she says, laughing as she wipes the couple stray tears off her face. "A tearful hug might be worse than funny business."

Lucas chuckles softly, then goes quiet. Mona can tell his wheels are turning but doesn't yet know him well enough to know where they're headed. "So, why won't you go?" he finally asks.

Mona scoffs, the ridiculous question fully catapulting her out of the once-sentimental moment. "I'm already great at what I do. At the business of being Mona Mashad. Getting into Harvard proved what I already knew deep down—that

I'm smart enough to take this all to the next level. I don't need to spend four years in frigid Boston to further prove the point."

"I don't disagree. You're by far the best celebrity in recent American history, no doubt about it," Lucas acknowledges, not a trace of sarcasm in his voice. "But I still think you should at least visit before you go writing Harvard off entirely. What are you doing tomorrow?"

"I'm pretty sure we're currently living in tomorrow," Mona says, flashing her phone in his face to remind him that it's now almost five in the morning. "But ideally nothing. I want to get in my hotel bed, get an IV drip, and watch old reruns of *Housewives*."

That same crooked smile from a few moments ago makes a reappearance on Lucas's face. "Skip that and come to Harvard with me," he says, his optimistic gaze settling on Mona's more skeptical one. "I'll be your tour guide."

"I can't go to Harvard with you," Mona scoffs. "After what happened tonight, I can't go *anywhere* public with you. We're one grainy fan picture away from people expecting us to go ring shopping."

Lucas laughs. "You're probably right. But I swear. This will be low-key. It's not New York or LA, it's Cambridge. People don't expect celeb sightings there."

He reaches behind him and grabs a Harvard baseball cap out of the drawer in the side table, throwing it her way from across the couch.

"Just wear one of these and a big pair of sunglasses while

we're on campus," he says. "Nobody will notice you. And my friends are all chill. None of them will take pictures or care. I promise."

Mona stares down at the Harvard cap, then up at Lucas. The smile is still on his face. His eyes are still set on hers.

"You know what? Why not?" she asks, pulling the cap over her head. "I'm in."

Confessional

INT. MARY MASHAD'S LIVING ROOM—AFTERNOON (CONT'D)

MONA

In retrospect, that was probably not the *best* decision I ever made.

Mona feels her eyes starting to get heavy. "I should probably get back to the Carlyle," she says with a yawn. "I'm exhausted."

"It's already five in the morning and you're coming with me in a few hours anyway," Lucas says. "It doesn't make sense for you to go all the way back uptown. Why don't you just sleep here?"

Mona raises an eyebrow.

"Not like *that*," Lucas says. "Just literally sleep. You can have my bed. It's the most comfortable in the house. I'll take the guest room. And we can stop and grab your clothes or whatever from the hotel tomorrow morning on our way."

"Okay, fine," she says with another loud yawn. "I'm too tired to say no to a comfortable bed."

Mona has to hand it to him; Lucas is a phenomenal host. He gives her a cozy oversized T-shirt and sweatpants to borrow as pajamas, sets her up with a whole host of toiletries President Sterling keeps in their closet for guests, and even remakes his bed for her with fresh sheets.

"Anything else I can get you?" he asks once Mona's comfortably tucked into his four-post bed, crisp white monogrammed duvet pulled up high under her chin. "I left a cold glass of water for you on the nightstand, and there's a TV remote and a bottle of Advil in the drawer if you need it."

"I'm good," Mona says, a small grin on her face as she gives him an appreciative look up and down. He looks almost like a kid on Christmas morning, standing in the doorway in his flannel pajama pants with a big smile and his hair all disheveled. But, of course, he's not a little kid. All Mona needs to do is take one look at his six pack, each ab looking like it was carefully sculpted in some sort of hot-boy lab, to remember that.

"You know," Lucas says, catching her eye, "if you *want* funny business, just say the word."

The truth is the combination of devastatingly cute and impossibly hot is enough to make Mona's heart explode. But she'd sooner die than let him know that.

"Don't flatter yourself," Mona says, her face flushing for the second time this evening as she pulls the duvet farther up.

✦ ✦ ✦

Confessional

INT. MARY MASHAD'S LIVING ROOM—AFTERNOON (CONT'D)

MONA

It didn't matter how obscenely attractive he looked. The last thing I wanted was to be another Lucas Sterling statistic. Another story people whisper about at the next big event while they pretend not to pitifully stare at me. I already have that with Max. I'm not trying to go for a Round Two here.

✦✦✦

Mona scans the nightstand to her right where Lucas has the cold glass of water waiting for her. "Actually," she says, "do you have a phone charger I could borrow?"

"Of course," Lucas says, dashing across the hallway into the study before returning with one. "Sorry, I should have thought of this myself."

He bends down to plug it into the outlet that's conveniently located directly behind Mona's side of the bed, leaving their faces just inches apart from each other. Mona's heart rate picks up speed as Lucas lingers there for just a second longer than he really needs to, their eyes set on each other's, his scent—a mix of musk and leather from his cologne and Arm & Hammer toothpaste from his freshly brushed teeth—filling her nostrils. The AC is blasting, and the room is freezing, but the air between them feels warm. Hot, even.

"We should probably get to bed," Lucas finally says, his face still so close to hers that she can feel the welcome chill of his minty breath as he says it. "Right?"

For a brief moment, Mona hesitates. She thinks about wrapping her arms around his neck and yanking him in here with her. About kissing his perfectly full lips. Running her hands through that famous head of hair of his. It wouldn't be anything she hasn't done with a long list of athletes and models and Hollywood heartthrobs. But the risk here feels higher. Scarier. Like if she lets him get close enough, he might re-shatter parts of her heart she just finished gluing back together.

"Yeah," she finally says, her voice soft as she carefully examines an almost heart-shaped amber speck in his hazel eyes. "We probably should."

Lucas makes his way out of the room slowly, giving her ample time to change her mind. It's torture. And Mona suspects he knows it. Finally, he pauses at the door, one of his chiseled arms nonchalantly touching the ceiling as he stands there watching her watching him

"Good night, Mona."

Mona wants to play it cool, wants to roll her eyes, and say something clever. *Anything* to downplay the sexual tension thickly coating what feels like every square inch of this room. But it's late. And he looks so cute, standing there with that little heart-shaped speck in his eyes. And she's so comfortable in the bed he so carefully made for her. And isn't it enough that she already resisted the urge to yank him in here with her when their faces were almost touching a few seconds ago? So, she just smiles back. "Good night, Lucas."

When he shuts the door behind him, Mona tries closing her eyes, tries sleeping on her side, on her back, on her stomach. But none of it is any use. She's just not as tired as she was twenty minutes ago.

Chapter 8

"See? I told you nobody would notice you," Lucas whispers in her ear as she follows his lead through a brick-lined street slightly off the Harvard campus. "Look at you, Mona Mashad. Just a normal teen."

Mona catches a glance of herself in a nearby window reflection. Between the baseball cap, the massive sunglasses, the N95 mask, and the blond wig that she threw on at the last minute for good measure, she is truly unrecognizable. Yes, if someone flipped the tag on her white tank, they would see it's a limited release Meesha Mashad brand that she was able to snag from her sister pre-market. And her jeans are Khaite, made exclusively for her after she shot a campaign for them. And her sneakers from a Prada x Nike collab set to come out next month. And she's strutting with the confident gait of someone who's walked on more red carpets than sidewalks. But still. At first glance, she thinks she nailed the whole "normal" thing.

The only giveaway would be Majid trailing a few inches

behind her, but mixed in with Lucas's Secret Service team, he sort of just blends in. Lucas seems like the celebrity, and Mona looks like a germophobic, sun-conscious blond friend who's chosen to tag along for his ride today. And boy, is Lucas's ride here something.

"Antonio! Jackie!" Lucas exclaims as they walk into Pinocchio's Pizza & Subs, a hole-in-the-wall spot he has excitedly dragged her to. "How's everybody doing?"

"Lucas!" A woman at the counter, presumably Jackie, comes over and gives him a hug. "I missed you, buddy. You've been gone, what? Almost a week?"

"Not a full week, but it's definitely been a while," he says, turning to Mona. "Jackie, this is my friend Kiki. She's visiting from California." Mona and Lucas spent the whole car ride here from New York brainstorming fake names for Mona before they settled on Kiki.

Confessional

INT. MARY MASHAD'S LIVING ROOM—AFTERNOON (CONT'D)

MONA

I feel like I give Kiki. Don't you think?

"Hey," Mona says, reaching her hand out to shake Jackie's. "Nice to meet you."

"Oh, we don't shake hands around here," Jackie says, waving Mona's hand away. "Give me a hug!"

Mona inhales the mix of coconut shampoo and greasy meat residue wafting off of Jackie's slicked-back bun as the small woman pulls her in for a shockingly tight hug.

"Any friend of Lucas is a friend of ours," she says, releasing Mona and making her way back behind the counter. "What will it be, Lucas? The usual?"

"Already working on it!" the man, who must be Antonio, shouts from the kitchen. "Cheeseburger sub and a small pepperoni Sicilian pizza coming right up."

"You're too good to me, Antonio!" Lucas shouts back. "And make it a double for Kiki here! This is her first time at Pinocchio's."

While they wait, Jackie takes them through pictures of her two-year-old daughter, Evy, who Lucas has apparently babysat for a few times.

"No way," Lucas says after Jackie plays a video of the little girl saying *broccoli*. "I cannot believe she's saying *broccoli*. Does she even eat broccoli? Last time I saw her she wouldn't touch a vegetable."

"She still doesn't," Jackie says with a laugh. "She just saw it on some kids' show and now won't stop saying it. I don't even think she fully knows what it means."

Mona would normally be surprised at the wildly intimate interaction with a pizza shop cashier, but this seems to be par for the course for Lucas around here. They have not crossed paths with a single human Lucas has not waved and said hi to. Not *one*. From the librarian at the Widener Library to the economics professor in Aldrich Hall, and, just before they got here, a shy-looking freshman searching for his classroom, Lucas seemingly has to engage with every single human he sees. "Everyone expects the president's son to be a giant douche," he told Mona after a long exchange with a janitor named Penelope. "It's fun proving them wrong."

"Okay, my friends," says Antonio, interrupting another video of Evy. "Two cheeseburger subs, a large pepperoni Sicilian, and one steak-and-cheese sub with the works since our friend Kiki here has never been."

"Antonio, you are the man," Lucas says, getting up to give him a hug. "Thanks, brother."

"You've got it, buddy."

"This might be the least LA assortment of food I've ever seen," Mona says, feasting her eyes on the gluten-, meat-, and dairy-filled spread as Antonio walks away. "I'm into it."

"Hold on!" Lucas exclaims as Mona takes her now-sweaty N95 mask off, ready to take a bite of the massive sandwich sitting in front of her. "We need to document your first cheeseburger sub."

He pulls out his disposable camera and snaps a shot as Mona bites into the crunchy, flaky slices of bread. "So, what's the verdict?"

"That was incredible," Mona admits, immediately scarfing down another bite. "Oh my God."

"Yeah," Lucas says, grabbing a slice of the pizza. "It's great, right? It's even better drunk when we come here after parties and stuff, but I knew I had to show you Pinocchio's sober first."

On the wall next to them hangs a random assortment of framed pictures. There's an old, framed shot of the Italian soccer team. One of the Harvard women's field hockey team. Another of the kitchen staff posing outside the shop. And then one tiny one in the corner of a cute family laughing at the counter.

"Wait," Mona says, getting up from her seat to get a closer look at the little boy sitting on the counter. "Is that your family?"

Lucas's golden cheeks get a little red. "Yeah," he admits. "I was, like, five."

Mona can't stop staring at the picture. It looks different from any tabloid or official photo of the Sterling family she's ever seen, even different from most of the pictures they have on display at their house. It doesn't feel like a picture where someone told them to smile for the camera. It looks like they just *were* smiling. Like they were truly happy here.

"It's a great picture," she says, sitting back down. "I get why this whole Harvard thing is so special for you."

"Yeah," Lucas says, wiping some pizza grease off his face. "In a weird way, Harvard feels even more like home than New York does. My parents used to have a place here in Cambridge. We would come here for lacrosse games, get a bunch of Pinocchio's for takeout, then go home and watch nineties rom-coms on the couch. It was the best. To this day, I'm a sucker for anything Nora Ephron."

"Wait," Mona says, smiling excitedly as she slams her napkin down. "I thought I dreamed it! You were playing *When Harry Met Sally* in the other room after we went to bed last night, weren't you?! I *knew* I heard Meg Ryan's voice coming through the wall."

"Wow, you're good," he says with a laugh. "Yes. It's my favorite. I always play it when I can't sleep."

"It's my favorite, too," Mona admits. "Honestly, I don't even know why. Of all the rom-coms out there. It's the only one that makes me cry every time."

"It's the ending," Lucas says with confidence. "When he describes her. It's not anything spectacular. But there's something so insanely romantic about how well he knows her."

Mona thinks about it while she chews on her perfectly fluffy Sicilian slice. "You're right," she concedes, her mouth still a little full. "That's the part that always gets me. He sees every piece of her and loves it all. What could be more romantic than that?"

Lucas turns to where Jackie is wiping a table down next to him, "Jackie, what do you think? *When Harry Met Sally* is the most romantic movie of all time, right?"

"Hmm," Jackie says, placing a hand on her hip. "I might be more of a *Sleepless in Seattle* gal."

"No!" Mona and Lucas both exclaim in unison. Mona turns to Jackie and explains, "They don't even meet each other in person until the end of the movie!"

Lucas nods solemnly in agreement. "Kiki is right," he says. "It's over an hour of just waiting for *one* scene at the end."

"That's what does it for me!" Jackie argues. "The buildup to that one *magical* moment."

"Jackie, I love you," Lucas says, "but you're wrong here."

Jackie laughs, walking back behind the counter. "You kids are crazy."

Mona looks around Pinocchio's. It's weird. Lucas is so much a part of her world. Every A-list party, every A-list event. Even if he's not there, he's invited. And that's not even counting all the fancy White House stuff he probably has to attend. The guy sleeps with supermodels and goes to luncheons with foreign monarchs and prime ministers. He was just at the Met Gala with her *last night*. But then he's also a regular at this tiny little sandwich shop that feels like it hasn't been touched or brought properly up to code since 1980.

She narrows her eyes, tilting her head to the side as though he's some sort of optical illusion she's trying to make sense of.

"What?" Lucas asks, cocky grin back on his face as he catches her staring at him. "You more open to funny business in Boston?"

Mona laughs. "Nice try, but—"

Her thought is interrupted by a text from Meesha in the family group text. Oh no is all her sister wrote alongside a viral meme of Mona down on the ground on the Met steps behind Chya and Max.

"I *knew* this was going to happen," Mona mutters, breaking her own cardinal rule and reading through the thousands of comments on the post.

"What happened?" Lucas asks.

Mona flashes him her phone.

He laughs. "Come, on. You have to admit. It's hilarious. Plus, I would take the girl on the floor over the other girl any day."

Mona smiles. She normally hates when guys give compliments like that. Like, "Oh, don't be sad, *I* think you're hot!"

As though their stamp of approval is some sort of prize to be won. Gross. But, for some reason, in this instance, coming from Lucas, it works. The comments still sting, but they sting just a bit less when she can see herself through his eyes.

"I think I have just the thing to take your mind off of this situation," Lucas says, waving her phone away. "Come with me to our date party tonight."

"Is this your way of coercing me into a date?" she asks with a crooked smile. "You really are relentless."

"It was worth a shot," he says with a laugh. "But fine. You can be my platonic date."

"What if people take pictures?" she asks. "It's not like I can go to a kegger in an N95 mask."

"It's a secret society," Lucas says. "You can take all the stuff off. You don't even have to have a fake name or anything. Nobody is allowed to take pictures or mention who they saw there anyway."

Mona picks her phone back up, briefly scrolling down the thousands of comments comparing her to Chya.

"You know what?" she asks, shoving her phone in her pocket. "I'm in."

Chapter 9

"You ready for this?" Lucas asks, pausing in front of a bookshelf in the library.

Mona points to the custom Mugler gown she has on with her diamond-encrusted Versace shoes. "I had this outfit shipped in from New York within the hour," she says. "And, so far, you have taken me to a pregame in your buddy's dorm room and now the library. I am *more* than ready."

Lucas laughs. "All right, all right," he says, slowly pushing the bookshelf. "Mona Mashad, welcome to the Orion Society's annual spring formal."

Mona's jaw drops, as the unassuming bookshelf swings back to reveal a grand oak-paneled ballroom with a massive crystal chandelier hanging from the ceiling. "Whoa," she says, looking around the grand venue. "I have to hand it to you. I did not see this coming."

The room isn't just beautiful. It's lit. The dance floor is filled with hammered kids their age dancing sloppily in their formal attire as the live band plays vintage bangers from the early aughts.

"Sterling!" a tall guy with a buzz cut makes his way over to Lucas, giving him a slap on the back. "Come with me. We're taking shots."

Lucas pauses, reaching a hand toward Mona. "You coming with?"

"Yeah," she says, ignoring his hand and walking toward the bar. "Let's go."

✦ ✦ ✦

Confessional

INT. MARY MASHAD'S LIVING ROOM—AFTERNOON (CONT'D)

MONA

That night got blurry *fast*.

✦ ✦ ✦

"So, let me get this straight," slurs Mona, standing in the center of a circle of Lucas and his friends, now six shots deep. "You guys have these dumb nicknames because you're *all* named John . . . except for Lucas."

"Mona," the douchiest John of the bunch says, his eyes narrow. "I bet a hundred dollars you can't remember all of our nicknames right now."

"No shot she remembers," a short John with orangey-red hair says. "She's a *celebrity*. We're nobody to her."

"I'll do you dorks one better," Mona says, scanning the group. "I'll take two more shots. *Then* name each of you." She swiftly downs the shots, then launches right into it. "Tank, Chef, Goose, Lefty, Jazz, Wiggles, Bobsled, Mack, Flipper, Buck, Brady, Sterling—which, by the way, guys, do better—and . . ." She pauses at the douchey John. "Hmm . . . what was yours again? Oh, yeah. Steve. Because everybody *hates* Steve."

The group of guys erupts into cheers. "Dude, Lucas," Tank, the largest of the Johns exclaims. "I get the hype. This chick is a legend."

"I know," Lucas says, smiling as he glances over at Mona. "Trust me."

"Mona Mashad." Brady, the leader of the pack, steps into the center of the circle. "We normally don't do this. But I think you've earned yourself a nickname. I hereby declare you *Ledge*."

Mona stares at him blankly. "*Ledge?*"

"Yeah, *Ledge*," he says. "Because you're a legend."

Mona laughs as the boys start chanting in the circle around her, "LEDGE! LEDGE! LEDGE!" She loves this. Loves putting on a show. Giving them the full Mona Mashad package.

"All right, Sterling," Mona says, clinking his glass as he takes another shot. "Let's break out of this sausage fest and mingle."

"Your wish is my command, Ledge," he says, downing his shot. "Where do you want to go? We could get food at the buffet. The prime rib is really good. Or hit the photo booth. Or dance *platonically*."

Mona takes a step closer to Lucas, looking into his equally bloodshot eyes. He looks cute in his tux—a different one from the one he was wearing last night. Adorable, even. And she knows she's drunk. But he looked cute even when she was sober. Lucas *is* cute. In fact, he's more than cute. He's objectively hot. Goose said if they didn't nickname him Sterling the runner-up for his nickname was Golden because the proportions of his face so perfectly achieve the golden ratio.

"What if it wasn't platonic?" Mona asks, placing a hand on his rock-hard chest.

Lucas looks down at her hand, a smile making its way across his face. "Mona," he slurs. "You're drunk."

"So?" she asks. "You're drunk, too. We're *both* drunk."

"Yeah, but you made it clear," Lucas says. "You don't want to date me. I have a reputation."

Mona solemnly nods her head. "I did," she says, stepping even closer to him so that her mouth is inches from his before adding, "But, like you said, I have a reputation, too."

"True," Lucas says, sending tingles up her spine as he slides his massive hands around her waist. "But, according to you, mine is worse."

"How about just for tonight, we call it a wash?" Mona asks, wrapping her arms around his neck.

"Deal," Lucas says, pulling her in tight against him. "So, can I kiss you now?"

"Yes."

And then he kisses her. First, it's just a soft peck on her lips. Then another soft peck. Then another, until it feels like the whole party evaporates around them and it's just the two of them standing in the corner of this absurdly gorgeous ballroom making out.

✦✦✦

Confessional

INT. MARY MASHAD'S LIVING ROOM—AFTERNOON (CONT'D)

MONA

We were absolutely hammered. But I have to admit that was a great kiss.

INT. HARVARD MEN'S LACROSSE LOCKER ROOM—AFTERNOON (CONT'D)

LUCAS

Best kiss of my life. Hands down.

✦✦✦

"One second," Mona says, pulling away from him. "I have to go pee."

"Right now?" Lucas asks, pulling her back toward him. "Don't go."

"Ugh, this happens all the time when I'm drunk," she says, scanning the room for a bathroom. "I suddenly have to go pee. And if I don't go ASAP, I'll literally pee myself. Ask Melody. It happened at the VMAs. I legit peed myself sitting next to her last year."

Lucas laughs. "Fine, fine," he says, taking her hand and leading her to the bathroom. "I'll walk you there."

When she finally makes it into the bathroom, she beelines it past a group of girls comforting their crying friend into the only empty stall at the very end of the line.

"Piper, he's an idiot," she hears one of the girls outside her stall say. "A horny idiot."

"Gretchen is right," another one says. "There's no way he *likes* her. She's a Mashad. They're, like, the trashiest family on the planet."

Mona takes a sharp breath in, her heart suddenly feeling like it's going to drop right into the toilet.

"Is it just me or is she kind of fat in person?" the first girl asks. "All her pictures must be *so* photoshopped."

"She *is* kind of fat in person," the sniffly girl agrees with a laugh.

Mona looks down at her body, her bust bursting out of the skintight dress. Her whole life has been spent hearing comments about how *fat* she is, which is especially absurd considering she's a size four. But Melody and Meesha are both tiny. Growing up next to them on TV meant the world has been quite literally measuring the three of them against one another their whole lives. And Mona's measurements always come out bigger. The good news is, by some grace of God—maybe it's her stubborn nature, maybe it was the unwavering adoration of a dad who thought she hung the moon—but Mona doesn't care. She loves her body.

Suddenly, the sniffly girl is sobbing again.

"What you guys have is special," one of her friends tries to reassure her. "You're his girlfriend. No tacky celebrity is going to ruin that."

At this point, Mona goes from upset to nuclear. His girlfriend. He has a girlfriend. He *lied*.

Confessional

INT. HARVARD MEN'S LACROSSE LOCKER ROOM—AFTERNOON (CONT'D)

LUCAS

Yeah. That was my bad. Probably should have dumped Piper before inviting Mona. But *come on*. I asked Piper before I knew I was going to have a shot with Mona [BLEEP]ing Mashad.

Mona grabs her phone out of her Cult Gaia clutch and sends a desperate text to Melody, the only person on Earth who may be able to talk her out of the havoc she knows she's inevitably about to wreak. SOS, need you to calm me down. Might make a scene. Except she's drunk so it comes out more like, sos calm down pls. Mieoa;ight make scne.. Melody immediately responds, What?? What's going on?

"He told me she was just a friend," the crying girl sniffles outside Mona's stall. "And I believed him like an idiot. Then he makes out with her right in front of me. Like I'm nothing to him."

Mona attempts a response to Melody, something like, Lucas sfjiod liar. We madkeo out but Girlfriend outside. Melody quickly writes back, Not fully sure what you're saying. But remember LEAD WITH LOVE. You've been the girlfriend outside. And it doesn't sound like you're in the right headspace to really know exactly what's going on with Lucas. Be calm and be nice.

"Piper, take a breath," one of the friends says. "Why don't you try talking to him?"

"What's there to talk about?!" the girl snaps. "You know he told me he loved me last weekend? And now he shows up here with *her*? That piece of Hollywood *trash*? Why would I trust anything he says ever again? How many times does he have to screw me over for me to actually believe him?"

Mona takes one last look at Melody's text before deciding to ignore it completely. Well, okay, not completely *ignore*. Just put her own spin on it. She bursts out of the stall and marches over to the girls, breaking her way into their circle until she's looking the slim blond girl with puffy eyes up and down.

"You must be Piper," she says, channeling Melody to muster her biggest smile. "Hi. I'm Mona Mashad. The fat, trashy celebrity your boyfriend is apparently cheating on you with."

Mona has to admit. She's impressed. Usually people cower when she comes at them like this. And Piper's crew of minions seem predictably petrified. But not Piper. Piper can hold her ground.

"Hi," Piper says, her voice unimpressed and cold.

Mona pauses for a second, studying every inch of Piper's pale, hollow face. Even in this state, she's pretty. She's got that classic sort of WASP-y, American cool-girl beauty about her. Like the old pictures of Carolyn Bessette-Kennedy. *How perfect.* A Carolyn Bessette-Kennedy lookalike for America's modern-day JFK Jr.

"I'm just here to tell you that, if you want him, he's all yours," Mona finally says. "Enjoy."

Piper looks at her, confused. "What?"

"You heard me," Mona says, making her way past Piper to wash her face. "I want nothing to do with that lying pile of human garbage. If you want him—and honestly, I can't see why you would—you can have him. Really."

Confessional

INT. MARY MASHAD'S LIVING ROOM—AFTERNOON (CONT'D)

MONA

I feel like I handled the rest of the night with class.

INT. HARVARD MEN'S LACROSSE LOCKER ROOM—AFTERNOON (CONT'D)

LUCAS

[*laughs*]

Class? She said she handled it with *class*?

"There you are," Lucas says, pulling Mona in close as she makes her way out of the bathroom. "I missed you."

"Don't touch me," Mona says, shoving him off of her. "I'm leaving."

"What?" Lucas asks, taking a step back. "What's wrong?"

"What's wrong? You have a girlfriend!" Mona screams, the party going quiet around her. "I just met her. Piper. So, what am I? Your mistress? You thought you would just bring me to this party and parade me around with no warning? You twisted sicko."

"Mona, I can explain," Lucas says, his voice quiet. "Please."

"There's nothing to explain," Mona says, staring him dead in the eyes. "You're a liar. I've dated a liar before. I don't need this mess in my life. I'm leaving."

"Where are you going to go?" Lucas asks. "It's two in the morning."

"I chartered a plane," she says, showing him the confirmation on her phone for good measure. "It'll be here in twenty minutes."

"Come on, Mona," he says, pulling her in one more time. "I swear this was all a giant misunderstanding."

Mona spots a can of beer on the table next to her, grabs it, and pours it over his head. The room is now silent except for Goose, who laughs. "*Classic* Ledge."

"Okay," Lucas says, wiping the beer out of his eyes. "Will you chill? That was totally uncalled for."

"I'm sorry, Lucas," Mona says, nodding her head with her brows furrowed in faux understanding. "You're right."

Lucas smiles as she inches closer to him, pulling her in as she gently places her hands on his shoulders. Then she steadies her grip and knees him square in the nuts, leaving the whole party bursting into laughter as Lucas keels over in pain.

Mona smiles proudly. "*That* felt more called for."

And with that, she storms out.

✦ ✦ ✦

Confessional

INT. HARVARD MEN'S LACROSSE LOCKER ROOM—AFTERNOON (CONT'D)

LUCAS

She literally kneed me in the nuts. In the middle of a party. In front of everyone I know.

INT. MARY MASHAD'S LIVING ROOM—AFTERNOON (CONT'D)

MONA

[*smiling proudly*]

It was honestly iconic.

Chapter 10

"Azizam," Mary says, her smile wide as she bursts into Mona's bedroom the next morning. "This is *wonderful*!"

Mona, half-asleep and with a pounding hangover, stares up at her mom confused. "What's wonderful?"

"Oh, you don't know," Mary says, and gleefully offers Mona her phone. "The photograph of you and Lucas. From last night. Mona Joonam, it's everywhere."

Mona's heart rate picks up speed as she grabs her mom's phone out of her hand. *Oh no.* The one grainy fan picture. It happened.

Mary's right. It's everywhere. The same stupid picture of her and Lucas plastered onto the homepage of every gossip site. She can't even scroll through Instagram without seeing it populate her entire feed.

And, of course, it's not a picture of her pouring a beer on him. Or kneeing him in the nuts. It's just the kiss. Someone submitted it to Deuxmoi. Mona remembers what Lucas told her at Pinocchio's. *Nobody is allowed to take pictures or mention who they saw there.* Another lie from the world's biggest liar. God, she really needs to just be done with dating. She clearly has the absolute worst picker in the history of mankind.

Mona buries her head under her plush down pillow as the room starts spinning around her. "This can't be happening," she groans, her voice muffled against her mattress as last night's mascara stains the fitted white Egyptian cotton sheet beneath her. "Mom, I *hate* him. He's a cheater. He lied to me. That's why I came home early last night."

"Well, good luck explaining that to the tabloids. They're already calling you America's first couple," Mary says, opening the curtains to reveal swarms of helicopters hovering above their estate. "Gerald at the front gate said there are thousands of photographers camped outside there as well. Mona, this isn't some model or actor you kissed at Soho House. This is the president's son."

"I'm aware, Mother," Mona says, getting out of bed to shut the curtains again. "But it doesn't matter. Because it's *over*. I'm done with him. And honestly? I'm done with *all* boys. They're awful. Maybe I'll join a convent or something." Mona pauses, an idea taking shape in her mind. "How's *that* for an angle for my show? I join a convent! Like *Sister Act* but my version."

Mary completely ignores hers. "Mona, I'm telling you—not as your mother, but as your manager—dating Lucas Sterling could be huge for your career."

Mona stares at her mother, half hoping she didn't hear her correctly. "You want me to continue dating a total and complete jerk . . . for my career?"

Mary nods calmly as she makes her way toward Mona's bedroom door. "Yes. Now, I have a meeting to get to. But just promise me you'll think about it."

Mona glares at her from across the room. "Absolutely not."

She lies there quietly for a while after Mary shuts the door, staring at the picture she has framed atop the vintage Louis Vuitton trunk she uses as a nightstand to her right. Melody had the picture of her family on vacation in St. Tropez a couple years before her dad died framed in custom silver Tiffany frames and gifted to Mona and Meesha for Father's Day last year. In the picture, the five of them are on the Sandersons' yacht at sunset, Melody and Meesha are each resting a head on Mary's shoulders, and, like always, Mona is in front of her dad, his arms wrapped tightly around her. She wishes she could jump out of her bed and into the image right now, be back on that boat. Back in her dad's arms.

Even when he was dying of cancer, Mona felt like he was her own personal superhero. Like even if she was in trouble on the moon, he would be on the next rocket ship out there to make it better. She misses that feeling of having a parent whose sole interest was *just* being her parent. Mary is her mom *and* her manager. The dynamic is and always will be intrinsically different. She can never *just* be there for her kids. There are too many angles to consider.

She wipes away a couple of mascara-stained tears off her face and grabs her phone from where it's charging by the photo. She skips over the fifty-seven unread texts from Lucas and texts her sisters: SOS: Anyone down to hang?

I have school, Josie writes with a crying face emoji. But I could come over after. I saw the picture of you and Lucas, though—you guys look cute together!

Mona dislikes Josie's text then types back, Not cute. He is the worst. Meesha was right. It pains her to give Meesha the satisfaction, but it's true. She was right.

I was worried about you after your texts last night, Melody writes back with a few heartbreak emojis. What wound up happening? Axle and I have a shoot for Rolling Stone today, but why don't you come over tonight for dinner? You can tell us all about it over some vegan chili.

Mona sighs. She doesn't want vegan chili. And doesn't want to hear whatever woo-woo nonsense Axle is going to offer her tonight. She just wants to hang out with her sisters. Now.

I knew that guy seemed skeevy, Meesha writes. I'm in San Francisco for Pete's game. Let's grab breakfast tomorrow when I'm back.

Seriously?! Mona writes back, fully aware of how dramatic she's being but choosing not to care. NONE of you can hang out with me in my moment of need?

Chill, Meesha responds with an eye-roll emoji.

Just as she goes to reply, another text comes in from Lucas. This time it's: Mona. Please. Just call me. She blocks him, throwing her phone across the room as she resists the urge to cry.

After trying and failing to distract herself with a few episodes of *Real Housewives*, she gets up and cracks her curtains open again. It's only gotten worse since her mom was in here earlier this morning. The helicopters circling above her house have multiplied, and the mass of photographers has gotten so large outside the neighborhood's gates that she can hear them yelling her name from the acres away.

"This is bad," she mutters to herself as she shuts the curtains again. "I have to get out of here."

Chapter 11

As much as Mona loves turning it on—and as *good* as she is at turning it on—sometimes she just needs to turn it off. Like, *really* turn it off. That's why, every once in a while, she has "not famous days." It used to be her thing with her dad. Every few months they would have these days where they'd basically play hooky from being famous. They'd dress as incognito as they possibly could, borrow an inconspicuous car, and drive out the service exit of their neighborhood to Dana Point, where they would have tuna melts and Arnold Palmers at their favorite little beachside diner, Lucky's. Now Mona does it alone.

Getting to Lucky's was a bigger ordeal than usual this time. When her dad developed their ultra-exclusive invite-only gated Beverly Hills neighborhood, Beverly Palms, the whole idea was that it was going to be a place where celebrities and billionaires could truly just *be* in the heart of Los Angeles without any worry of paparazzi invading their privacy. Part of this was giving each home in the neighborhood an underground service exit. For the most part, these exits are used for the many caterers, gardeners, and security personnel regularly popping in and out of their homes to be able to come and go without creating any traffic in the main entrance. But the service entrances also come in handy when residents need a discreet way out of the neighborhood to avoid a media storm, like the one Mona is currently in. The tunnel extends for miles and miles outside their neighborhood, and Ali went to great lengths to make sure it had multiple sneaky exits throughout the city, so that the paparazzi could never quite guess where a celebrity might pop out.

But forty years into the existence of Beverly Palms, the paparazzi has figured out where most of the exits are. Luckily, because the exits are mostly used by staff, the paparazzi don't really bother camping outside of them the way they camp outside the front gate. But, on big news days like this one, there will be at least one paparazzo camped outside each exit point. That's why Mona had to go the extra mile this time. She had Majid dress in a discreet T-shirt and jeans and drive the old Toyota Corolla her dad kept in the garage for occasions like this while she lay down in the back seat, her body covered by a fuzzy blanket.

She could hardly breathe for the almost two-hour drive, having to periodically lift the blanket off her face to get a quick deep breath before throwing it back on, and absolutely caused some permanent damage to her hip with the way the seat belt buckle was digging into it, but it was worth it. They made it to Lucky's without a single paparazzo noticing them.

"How do you want to handle this?" Majid asks as Mona secures her baseball cap over her strawberry-blond-wig-clad hair. "I can wait out here in the car or go inside and sit a table away from you."

"Why don't you come inside?" Mona asks. "You're just in jeans and a T-shirt. Nobody will think anything of it. And you can tip me off if you notice anyone pulling out a phone or whatever to take a picture."

"Of course," he says, nodding loyally. "Let's get inside."

"Hey, Majid?" Mona asks, pausing for a second before opening her car door. "What do you think my dad would have thought? Of this whole situation?"

She and Majid hardly ever do this. Their relationship is strictly professional, and Majid is sometimes annoyingly staunch about never crossing that line. But whether they openly acknowledge it or not, her father's presence is always lingering between them.

✦✦✦

Confessional

INT. MARY MASHAD'S LIVING ROOM—AFTERNOON (CONT'D)

MONA

Majid isn't just some random security guard my parents found. He is a distant cousin of my dad's from Iran. My dad helped him get a visa to come to America after the revolution, and even helped him get into UFC for a while. When he was ready to retire, they hired him to be my security. My dad always said Majid was the only person he would trust with my safety.

✦ ✦ ✦

"Mona Joon, you know it's not my place to say what he would think," Majid says, his eyes glazing over at the mention of him. "But I do know he would be happy you came here. He loved having his special days with you."

Mona nods, resisting tears of her own. "Yeah," she says, her voice cracking. "I just wish he was here with me, you know? He would fix this."

Majid offers her a stiff pat on the back. "He was a great man."

"He was," Mona says with a resolute nod, taking a deep breath before getting up. "Okay, sorry. Enough of this. Let's go inside."

Mona is relieved to see her favorite spot at the counter is available when she enters Lucky's. Better yet, the entire counter is empty. She plops down on the red leather barstool, Majid taking a seat at the booth behind her, and places an order with the waiter for her tuna melt and Arnold Palmer.

In almost every other realm in life, Mona is fast. She talks fast, she eats fast, she walks fast. But at Lucky's she likes to take things slow. When the waiter brings out her tuna melt, she takes each bite slowly. Carefully. Methodically. Chewing sometimes for a full minute before swallowing. Same goes with her Arnold Palmer—she doesn't guzzle it down in one giant gulp like she does pretty much any other beverage that ever comes her way. She takes small sips, swishing each one around her mouth for a long while before finally letting the liquid spill down her throat.

When her dad was around, they would use these little lunch dates as opportunities for Mona to vent. She would unload on him about whatever issue was bothering her at the moment and, like clockwork, he would present her with the perfect solution to her problem. Then crack just the right joke to make her laugh hard enough to evaporate any last shred of upset entirely.

Now that he's gone, she uses her Lucky's lunches as an opportunity to stew in peace. She likes to sit there quietly, replaying every infuriating moment in her head as her blood heats up to a full boil. At home, people are constantly getting in her business. Mary is popping into her room every half hour. Maids are coming and going. PR teams are calling emergency meetings. Media helicopters swarming above them. There's no space to just *stew*. To brood in peace.

Mona is halfway through the tuna melt that she's spent forty-five minutes eating and well into her brooding—memories of the past twenty-four hours successfully bringing her blood to a piping-hot boil—when a waiter interrupts.

The first four times he asks if she'd like a refill on her water, Mona doesn't even hear him. When she's brooding, her thoughts play at the volume of a live death-metal show. It's hard to hear anything else. "Uh, hey," he finally says, tapping his hand down on the counter to get her attention. "You good?" The poor guy didn't know it's dangerous to interrupt Mona mid-brood.

Mona looks up, instantly annoyed by the question. *Of course* she's not good. Before she can think better of it, she goes off. Like, *all* the way off.

"No, Kai," she says, reading the name off the red font on his name tag. "I'm *not* good. Last night, I kissed a guy I thought I liked. A guy who has spent the past few days obsessively trying to get me to like him, even though I *knew* he was a jerk. I really did. I knew! I fully knew I shouldn't have trusted him. And then, what did I do? I trusted him. I trusted the stupid liar, let him kiss me at some dumb party in front of all his dumb friends only to find out he had a girlfriend. A girlfriend who was *there* that night. Who does that? Like, my ex was a jerk, but even *he* wouldn't have done something like that."

"Yikes," Kai says. "That is pretty brutal."

Mona snorts. "That's not even the half of it," she continues. "Then some loser leaked the picture to Deuxmoi. Now the whole world is split between obsessing over my 'relationship' with this guy I kissed once and despising me for being with him, even though—spoiler—I hate his guts! Oh, and don't even get me started on my mom. I told her he was a cheater, and you know what she said? She said she thinks I should date him *anyway*. Because it would be good for my *career*. Who would say something like that to their *daughter*? Normally I would complain about this to my sisters, but they all seem too busy with their own stuff to actually care about the absolute dumpster fire that is my life right now. And so I'm here. Fully unloading to you. A literal stranger."

Confessional

INT. MARY MASHAD'S LIVING ROOM—AFTERNOON (CONT'D)

MONA

Yeah, that was probably a bit of an overshare. Like, I'm pretty sure I broke *several* NDAs over the course of that monologue.

Kai stares at Mona blankly. "Oh, are you, like, famous or something?"

People do this all the time. Pretend like they don't recognize famous people to come off as chill or whatever. It's ridiculous. Mona's face is on every magazine cover and billboard on the planet. Yes, her sunglasses and baseball cap are a decent disguise. But there's no missing her once the connection is drawn. And yet, for some reason, Mona gets the sense Kai *actually* doesn't recognize her. It's sort of . . . refreshing.

"Yeah," she says, looking around before cautiously taking her sunglasses off. "I'm Mona Mashad."

"Like, the reality-TV people?" Kai asks, his eyes still squinted in confusion. "Sorry, I don't really watch much TV."

Mona opens her mouth to say they're so much more than

just "reality-TV people" at this point. That before they got their show, her dad was one of the most prolific real-estate developers in Los Angeles. That her mom was the talent agent who launched the careers of almost every A-list actor in Hollywood. That UC Berkeley teaches an entire course on the empire her family has built since developing their show. That her family has amassed *billions* through their various business ventures. That they have graced the covers of every major magazine in the world.

But she knows saying any of the above makes her sound like an insufferable jerk and, more importantly, she doesn't have the energy for another long monologue, so instead she settles for responding with a simple "Yeah. The reality-TV people."

"Huh," Kai says. "I would have never guessed you were a celebrity."

"What?" Mona asks. "Why not?"

"I don't know," Kai says with a shrug as he wipes the counter in front of her. "I thought famous people's lives were supposed to be fun or whatever. You seem all bugged out and stressed."

"Yeah, well, today is particularly stressful," she says with a sigh. "That's why I'm here."

"You come here and eat tuna melts to deal with being stressed?" Kai asks with a laugh. "Nah, you can do better than this."

"Like what?" Mona asks with an eye roll. "And don't say meditation. I've tried it and I hate it."

"You ever tried surfing?" Kai asks. "It's the only thing that calms me down when I'm feeling stressed."

"I tried surfing once on vacation in Hawaii," Mona says. "My sisters and I took lessons. I *sucked*."

"Why don't you try again?" he asks. "I'll give you free lessons." He smiles for a second before adding, "Not that you need the discount since you're apparently this big celebrity."

Confessional

INT. LUCKY'S KITCHEN—AFTERNOON

KAI, 18, stands in front of the titanium refridgerator, a dish towel slung over his shoulder.

KAI

[*shrugs*]

I don't know. It just seemed like she needed a friend.

Mona looks back at Kai, fully taking him in for the first time as he sheepishly smiles down at her. He's tall. Maybe even taller than Lucas. And jutting out of the short sleeves of his Lucky's T-shirt, she can see his perfectly chiseled arms. His shaggy hair is dark, sun-kissed with a few golden streaks that look nice framing his tan skin. And then there's his eyes. They're brown but not in the same dark, almost black way hers are. They're warm. Kind of like an auburn. Everything about him is sort of like that. Warm. Like a block of ice would instantly melt if she set it in front of him.

She feels herself softening a bit, her eyes still carefully examining every square inch of him. Maybe she doesn't have to be *completely* done with boys. "Free lessons, huh?" she asks, taking a long sip of her Arnold Palmer before delivering her final answer, "I mean, it would just be bad business to say no to an offer that good."

Chapter 12

Confessional

INT. MARY MASHAD'S LIVING ROOM—AFTERNOON (CONT'D)

MONA

For a few hours there, I was actually starting to feel better. Then—and here's where we get into the behind-the-scenes tea you've all been dying for—I got back home to a textbook Mary Mashad ambush.

"You have *got* to be kidding," Mona mutters as she enters her family room to find her mom and President Sterling sitting on the couch across from Lucas.

"Hello, Mona," President Sterling says, standing up from the couch to greet her. "It's wonderful to see you again."

Mona doesn't normally get intimidated, but *God* this woman

is terrifying. Mona takes a deep breath in, willing her hand to stop trembling before responding.

"Hi, President Sterling," she manages to say. "Nice to meet you."

President Sterling gives Lucas a look as she sits back down. "Lucas, don't be rude."

Lucas stays seated, looking up at Mona with his stupid cocky grin. "Hey. You never answered my texts."

"Yeah, I also blocked you," Mona informs him. "I was hoping you would take the hint, but apparently not."

"Well, maybe if you would have just *replied*, I wouldn't have had to make the trip," Lucas responds, infuriatingly cocky smile still plastered across his perfectly symmetrical face. "You really gave me no choice here, Mashad."

If the leader of the free world was not sitting across from him, Mona would lunge over the coffee table and smack him right in the face. How *dare* he show up at her house like this?

"Mom, what is going on?" Mona says, ignoring Lucas entirely. "This whole thing has you written all over it. Just tell me what's happening."

"Mona Joon, have a seat," she says. "President Sterling and I have something we wanted to discuss with you kids."

Mona looks at the empty seat next to Lucas. "I'm fine standing."

Mary gives her a look, but before she can say anything, President Sterling steps in.

"Standing is fine, Mona," she says. "Lucas and I have to be back on our flight soon, so we'll just get right into it. Mary, would you like to kick things off?"

"Sure," Mary says, pulling a file out of the camel Birkin bag sitting to her left and placing it on the white marble coffee table. "Since that picture dropped, something incredible is happening."

Mary opens the file to reveal a series of papers full of graphs and pie charts and draws everyone's attention toward the graph on the first page. "You'll see here, our viewership for this week's episode quadrupled," she says, before flipping to the next visual. "Mona, I'm guessing you missed this when you were off doing God knows what in God knows where today, but your Instagram profile alone got *two hundred million* new followers, officially making you the most followed person in the world."

She flips to the final page, which features what Mona instantly recognizes as the results of a poll conducted by Mary's right hand, the chief brand officer at Mashad Lifestyle Group, Javier. "A market research poll Javier quickly put together said the majority of Americans believed your potential romance with a Sterling gave our family 'gravitas' and 'legitimacy,'" Mary says, pointing to the response to another question at the bottom of the page. "Now this is the key stat here, so look closely. Javier found that eighty percent of Americans who once dubbed watching our show as 'stupid' or 'mindless' now plan on *proudly* tuning in."

Mona would be lying if she said some of those stats didn't at least slightly intrigue her, but she's not about to give her mom that sort of satisfaction right now.

"Are you done?" Mona asks, her arms crossed tightly in front of her chest. "I've had a long day. I need to get to bed.

And, President Sterling, you have a flight to catch, right? You should go ahead. It was great seeing you. I'm sorry my mom dragged you here for this."

Mona can't even imagine what kind of strings her mom had to pull to get the president of the United States to make a spur-of-the-moment trip to their house for one of her marketing presentations. The woman probably has, like, wars and famines to deal with.

"Actually," President Sterling says, as Mona starts making her way out of the living room, "it's not just your family benefiting in this situation."

Ah, so *that's* how Mary got her here. Mona stops in her tracks as President Sterling pulls out a file of her own.

"You'll see here in our graphics, my approval ratings have jumped from a subpar forty percent to a staggering ninety-five percent since this picture went live," she says, looking up from the paperwork to make eye contact with Lucas and Mona. "To be clear, that is the highest approval rating for any president in American history. It seems our association with the Mashads has attracted younger voters who aren't typically very interested in politics. With re-elections around the corner, we cannot afford to be taking numbers like these lightly."

"So, what are you two suggesting here?" Mona asks. "That we keep dating? For your numbers? President Sterling, I'm sorry to have to be the one to tell you this, but your son is a cheater. I'm not interested."

"Oh, please." Lucas speaks for the first time since the presentations started. "I was going to break up with her."

"Said every cheater ever," Mona fires back.

"Enough!" President Sterling cuts in before Lucas has a chance to make his retort. "Mona, you have made your distaste for my son very clear. And, from what I can understand of the situation, I cannot say I blame you. But we are not saying you have to date."

"Yes, we are not forcing anybody into a relationship here," Mary chimes in, casually laughing the idea off as though that isn't exactly what she suggested this morning. "We are simply suggesting that perhaps the two of you just . . . pretend for a bit. For your families."

Mona opens her mouth to speak, but the words don't come out. This is low, even for Mary.

"Not just for your families," President Sterling adds. "For *America*."

Lucas shrugs. "I'm down."

Mona looks at him, equal parts enraged and confused. "WHAT? Have you completely lost your mind? I *hate* you. And, honestly, I kneed you in the nuts in front of all of your friends. You should hate me back. Why in the world would we do this?"

"Were you not listening?" Mary interjects. "For our ratings. For *your* ratings. Mona, you are the most-followed person on Instagram right now. And, Lucas, if you had social media, I'm sure you would be close behind. Do it for your personal brands."

President Sterling adds, "And for *America*."

Lucas rolls his eyes. "I'm not doing it for either of those things," he says, shifting his gaze up toward Mona. "I'm in because I like you."

"Cute," Mona says, her voice flat. "How does your girlfriend feel about that?"

"I dumped her," Lucas says, his eyes still directly on hers. "Right after you left."

"Sure you did," Mona replies, before turning her attention back to Mary. "Mom, I'm serious. I'm not doing this. I'm out." She looks at President Sterling, an unreadable look on her face like she's in the throes of a negotiation with a foreign dictator. "President Sterling, I'd be happy to, like, shoot a commercial or something if you think that would help with your campaign."

Mary takes a deep breath, then hands Mona another sheet of paper from the file. "I did not want to have to do this, but take a look at these stats Scott Sanderson emailed me this morning."

Mona scans the numbers quietly. As of two days ago, only 15 percent of Americans would watch a Mona Mashad solo spinoff show. As of today, 87 percent would tune in.

"Mona, you are always telling me how great you are at playing the *part* of Mona Mashad," Mary says. "Now is your chance. The executives at Yay! think this is all real and they're thrilled about it. Play the part. Give the people what they want . . . and you'll get your show."

Mona stares at her mom, dumbfounded.

Mary flashes her the annoyingly smug smile she reserves only for when she's won a negotiation. "Are you in?"

Mona hesitates.

Confessional

INT. MARY MASHAD'S LIVING ROOM—AFTERNOON (CONT'D)

MONA

It felt like selling my soul to the devil. And, yes, in this case my mother was the devil in question. But my own show? With guaranteed hit-worthy numbers? It's all I've ever wanted.

"Okay, yeah," Mona says, unable to make eye contact with any of them. "Fine. I'm in."

"Great," President Sterling says. "So, it's settled. Now I've got a busy few months ahead campaigning, but I trust Mary's genius PR mind will be able to execute this plan flawlessly."

"Of course," Mary says, pulling NDAs out from a separate file and passing them around the table. "Now, obviously the details of this arrangement are never to leave this room. . . ."

Confessional

INT. VALLEY HIGH SCHOOL SENIOR HALLWAY—AFTERNOON

JOSIE, 18, and LOUISE, 18, stand in front of their lockers.

LOUISE

So, Mary is helping me get started on my modeling career. And we had a meeting set for six thirty to discuss a potential campaign.

JOSIE

I didn't have any plans tonight, so I figured I would just come along for the ride.

LOUISE

Anyway, Josie said we should get there early because Mary is apparently always early for meetings.

JOSIE

She *is* always early for meetings! "If you're on time you're late" is one of her top-five favorite sayings. But obviously this time, we should have probably just showed up right at six thirty.

LOUISE

Yep. Really wish we hadn't heard all of that.

PRODUCER

So how much, exactly, did the two of you hear?

JOSIE & LOUISE

Everything.

Chapter 13

"Are you sure we have the right address?" Majid asks as Alfred, their driver today, pulls the black car in front of an old Santa Ana track house miles away from the beach. "You might want to text your friend."

Mona pulls up her phone and texts Kai, who she now has in her phone as "Hot Surfer." Hey, she writes, snapping a picture to send along with her text. We're here . . . but doesn't really seem like a beach?

Not even ten seconds after her text says it was read, Kai is tapping on her window. Her stomach does the tiniest somersault at the sight of him.

Then she remembers he's a virtual stranger who's somehow convinced her to show up to his home nowhere near the ocean under the guise of "free surfing lessons." Maybe something really is wrong with her picker.

"You coming in or what?" he asks, when she cautiously rolls

her window down just a small crack. "We've got some surfing to learn."

Mona, still not making any moves to get out, looks at him, then back at the almost-dilapidated-looking house behind him. The paint that once presumably used to be white has adopted a brownish hue, the shutterless windows have the sort of hazy fog that comes from never having been washed, and the small front lawn is more a pile of dirt with scattered patches of dying grass.

"This is my security guard," she says, nodding toward Majid. "If this is some sort of creepy plot to rape and murder me, he *will* destroy you."

"Yes." Majid nods matter-of-factly. "I will chop your balls off, then I will kill you."

Kai nods slowly, an unaffected smile sliding across his face. "Got it," he says. "Well, come in and I'll try my best not to murder and rape you."

Mona looks back at Kai, trusting him even though she has absolutely no reason to. Something about him is just so . . . *disarming*. He's got his sort of calm, quiet confidence that leaves Mona feeling stripped of any of her usual defenses. Majid follows Mona's lead as she cautiously takes the first step out of the car, immediately feeling out of place in her thongkini and sarong.

Kai stares at her, and for a second Mona could *swear* she caught him blushing.

✦✦✦

Confessional

INT. LUCKY'S KITCHEN—AFTERNOON (CONT'D)

KAI

[*blushing*]

It was definitely a bold outfit choice. And I mean that in a good way. I learned pretty quickly everything about Mona is sort of like that. *Bold.* And, obviously, she looked great . . . but it wasn't exactly a surfing outfit.

"Next time, just a wetsuit is fine," he finally says with a kind smile, gesturing her to follow as he makes his way toward the front door. "But for now, it doesn't matter. We're not going on the water anyway."

"Are you kidding?" Mona asks, picking up the pace as she tries to keep up with him. "I thought we were going to be, like, relaxed on the ocean."

"Not until you figure out the fundamentals," Kai says, opening the sliding door to his back patio, where he has a surfboard laid out. "You said you sucked when you tried to surf the first time. And that's probably because you hit the water too soon. Let's nail the basics here, then, once you're ready, we'll graduate to the ocean."

Mona stares at the setup, the large surfboard practically taking up the entire back patio.

"I came all the way here," she says with a sigh. "Might as well give it a shot."

"Wait!" an adorable kid shouts as he comes running out to join them. "You guys can't start the lesson without me!"

Mona smiles down at the little boy. He looks like a miniature Kai, but with a pair of blue-rimmed glasses fastened to his head with an elastic band.

"Sorry, bud," Kai says, placing a supportive hand on the child's back. "Mona, this is Rudy. He will be my assistant teacher."

"Rudy Takanasha," Rudy says, reaching a comically professional hand out toward Mona. "Kai's little brother. Big fan."

"Hi, Rudy," Mona says, shaking his hand. "Glad to know *someone* here has heard of me."

"Oh, don't mind him," Rudy says, waving in Kai's direction. "He doesn't know *anything* about pop culture. Unless it's about surfing, he's pretty much completely clueless."

"Whoa," Kai says with a laugh. "*Completely clueless?* That feels harsh!"

Rudy shrugs. "Sorry, man. I've gotta call it like I see it."

Mona smiles, the sitcom-y sweetness of their dynamic tugging at her heartstrings a bit. She's not exactly sure what she was expecting when she agreed to surfing lessons with this hot waiter, but a family-friendly hang with his little brother definitely was not on her bingo card.

Kai laughs and playfully gives Rudy a noogie. "All right, Rudy, what's first up for our lesson here?" he asks. Rudy glances over a paper on the little clipboard he's brought outside with him this morning.

"Hmm," Rudy muses as he looks the paper over. "We've got to figure out which leg is going to be her front leg and which is going to be her back leg."

"How do I do that?" Mona asks.

"The fall-forward test," Kai says, looking down at Mona's gold stilettos. "You, uh, might want to take those off before we do this."

Mona nods, dutifully kicking off her heels.

"Stand with your feet together," Kai says, moving so he's standing directly in front of her. "And just . . . fall forward. Whatever foot you catch yourself with is the foot you'll be forward with when you surf."

"Okay," Mona says. "Here goes nothing."

She falls forward and within an instant, her left foot springs forward.

"Left foot forward!" Kai announces. "Regular."

"Regular?" Mona asks.

"Yeah," Rudy says. "In surfing, we have two groups. *Regular* people go left foot forward. The people who go right foot forward are called goofy. Kai's in the goofy group."

"Wait, what?!" Mona exclaims. "No, let me try again. Goofy sounds like so much more fun. I don't want to be *regular*."

Kai laughs. "It's fine. Not everyone can be as unique and interesting as me," he jokes, the smile lingering on his face as he returns to their lesson. "So, next, we have to clasp this cuff around your back leg—for you, that will be your right. I can help you for the first time." He reaches for the Velcro cuff at the end of the rope and gently clasps it around her right ankle.

Mona laughs, looking down at where he's crouched by her feet. "I could have probably figured this part out myself. How hopeless do you think I am?"

"Well, I made Kai watch the episode of you taking the lesson in Hawaii," Rudy says. "So, pretty hopeless."

Mona's face goes bright red.

✦ ✦ ✦

Confessional

INT. MARY MASHAD'S LIVING ROOM—AFTERNOON (CONT'D)

MONA

There honestly could not be a more mortifying episode for him to have watched. There is an entire minute-long montage featuring scenes of me toppling over. Then the montage ends with a scene of my dad having to save me when I *almost drowned*. And here's the kicker: None of that is even the most embarrassing part. The episode starts with a cold open of me practicing my first kiss on a doll, while Meesha and Melody coach me on my technique. . . . I mean, I was twelve. It is what it is. But *God*. Really brutal episode for me.

✦ ✦ ✦

"You watched that episode?" Mona asks, trying to keep her voice chill. "Like, the whole thing?"

"We were hardly paying attention," Kai reassures her, though the way he's avoiding eye contact makes it clear he's lying. "I just wanted to see your surfing foundation."

"What are you talking about?!" Rudy asks. "We watched the whole thing. Even the scene with you kissing that doll. What was his name? Rupert?"

"Oh my God," Mona says, throwing her head into her hands. "Of all the episodes."

"It wasn't that bad!" Kai says with a laugh. "I mean, the Rupert thing was tough. And you very obviously have no natural athletic ability. But I get why people are so obsessed with your family. Even I have to admit, it was *very* entertaining."

"Yeah," Rudy says with a laugh. "You should have seen him watching that scene where you almost drowned. He kept clutching my hand like he *actually* thought you were going to die. Even though he had just met you!"

Mona grins, oddly touched by Kai's reaction. "So, now that we have established that I'm hopelessly unathletic, what's next?"

"Now," Kai says, "we have to teach you how to lie on the board. The goal is to be somewhere in the middle. It's not a perfect science. But just avoid being too far up toward the tip or too far down toward the bottom of the board, so you don't fall in either direction."

Mona studies the board for a minute, mentally calculating its dimensions before carefully easing down on top of it. "Is this right?" she asks, looking up at Kai and Rudy. She feels ridiculous, like a dead fish flopping far away from the sea.

"Not really," Rudy says, head cocked to the side and arms folded across his chest. "Try scooching a little down."

She scooches, the grain of the surfboard uncomfortably grating against her cleavage and bare stomach. Kai was right. A wetsuit would have been better. She makes a mental note to have her stylist source a cute one when she gets back home.

"This better?" she asks once she's settled a few inches backward.

"Almost," Kai says, bending down toward her. "Do you, um, mind if I guide you with my hands a bit?"

"Oh," Mona says, suddenlly flustered. "Sure . . . I mean, no. I don't mind."

"Okay," Kai says with a laugh, sending a tiny jolt of electricity rushing through Mona's entire body as he gently presses against her shoulders. "Now follow my lead here, just slide a *little* more, until . . . yes! Perfect."

Mona lets her eyes meet his, her expression beaming. "I did it?!"

"You did it!" he confirms. "Now time to do it again. And again."

The rest of the lesson goes by with a lot more of this: Kai insisting Mona has to keep getting off then back on the board in the *perfect* spot in order to fully "nail" the fundamental. For a surfer who seems all chill, Mona is learning Kai has a perfectionist streak that could rival even Mary's. The guy's got layers.

Once the lesson is over, Kai moves the surfboard out of the way.

"Majid, do you want to sit with us?" he asks as he makes his way in toward a closet in their living area.

"I'm fine," Majid says, remaining almost frozen in his position by the sliding door. "Thank you."

"Of course," Kai says, returning shortly thereafter with three foldout chairs and three Juicy Juice apple juice boxes.

Kai carefully folds out each chair, placing them side by side facing the cement wall separating the Takanasha house from their neighbors' place. Once the three of them have taken their seats, he passes out the juice boxes.

Mona stares at her box for a minute, embarrassed to admit she's never had one of these before and isn't 100 percent sure what she's supposed to do with it. It *seems* obvious, but what if she's wrong? She tries to not make a big deal of it, instead pretending like she's fixing her hair while she examines the way Rudy and Kai puncture their boxes.

"I think that lesson went pretty well," Rudy says after a long sip of his juice box. "Nice work, Mona."

"Thanks, Rudy," Mona says, following his lead and poking her straw into the aluminum circle at the top. "But not sure how proud I should be of my ability to lie down at the center of a board."

"You should be *very* proud," Kai says. "Lying down in the right position is half the battle! Well, not half. But a large portion of it."

He reaches across Rudy, who's sitting between them, and clinks his juice box against hers. "Cheers."

"Cheers," she says with a smile.The three of them sip their juices in silence for a while, staring at the unexciting wall in front of them. It's funny. Mary's house comes complete with multiple infinity pools and a fully staffed spa. But Mona feels a type of relaxation sitting here on this dinky patio looking at a decrepit old wall that she hasn't felt in ages. It sort of feels how she used to feel with her dad at Lucky's. Like she doesn't have to be *on*.

"I should probably get going," Mona says, her juice box making loud slurpy noises as she takes the last sip. "I need to be back in Beverly Hills by six."

"Okay," Kai says, getting up out of his seat. "I'll walk you out."

The two quietly walk toward Mona's black car, still parked outside. "That was fun," Mona says, pausing in front of the car. "When's the next lesson?"

"Whenever," Kai says with a shrug. "You're the one with the big fancy Hollywood schedule here. Just text me when you want to come back. Even if I have school or a shift or whatever, I'm sure Rudy would be *thrilled* to give you a solo lesson."

"Oh, I would *love* a solo lesson with Rudy," Mona says. "That kid rules."

"He really does," Kai says, a proud smile forming across his face. "Thanks for being so cool with him."

Mona lets her eyes rest on his. "I think it's sweet you two are so close. I'm a youngest child. I know how good it feels when your older siblings give you the time of day."

Kai grins down at her, his expression somehow simultaneously wildly confident and a bit shy. "I have to say, you're nothing like I expected."

Mona raises an eyebrow. "What did you *expect*?"

"I don't know," Kai says, his grin a smidge more playful now than it was a moment ago. "Spoiled celebrity who can't really hang."

Mona bursts into laughter. "Wow, don't spare my feelings or anything."

Kai's cheeks redden a bit. "Too honest? Sorry. Lying has never really been a strength of mine."

Mona smiles. "No, the honesty is refreshing."

Right then, something passes between them. A moment. It's

clear as day. Mona leans into it, giving Kai his window to make a move.

But he doesn't.

✦✦✦

Confessional

INT. MARY MASHAD'S LIVING ROOM—AFTERNOON (CONT'D)

MONA

I was so confused. Was he friend-zoning me????? Nobody has *ever* friend-zoned me.

INT. LUCKY'S KITCHEN—AFTERNOON (CONT'D)

KAI

Trust me. I *wanted* to make a move. But it had only been a day since she was complaining about all that drama with the other guy. I thought I should give it some time.

✦✦✦

Instead, Kai opens the car door for her. Mona slides into the back seat, pretending to be unfazed by what she's taking as the blatant rejection.

"By the way, what wound up happening with the situation you were telling me about at the diner?" Kai asks before shutting the door behind her. "Everything work out?"

"Oh, not at all," Mona says with a laugh. "It's gotten much, much worse."

Chapter 14

Confessional

INT. MARY MASHAD'S OFFICE—AFTERNOON

MARY MASHAD sits on her plush leather desk chair, the wall behind her covered with *Forbes*, *INC*, and *WSJ Magazine* covers featuring herself.

MARY

If we were going to execute this properly, it was imperative that it didn't *feel* like a publicity stunt. The photo of them kissing was already so big and splashy, we had to move things in a more subtle direction. Slowly tease a few little hints out, giving the fans hope that something real was building between them without really giving them anything concrete. So, for the first outing, we decided they would go to the private Bird Streets Club. They would arrive separately and leave separately. But there's so much paparazzi camped outside of there. As long as they leave around the same time, all the tabloids will be buzzing about it.

✦ ✦ ✦

"I still don't get it," Meesha says, turning toward Mona as their driver, Amelia, approaches the entrance of Bird Streets Club. "I thought you hated him. Didn't you say he has a girlfriend? And didn't he literally kiss you *in front of her*?"

Mona gulps hard, bracing herself for the lie she's about to tell the person who knows her best. She's spent her whole life telling Meesha practically everything. And she knows exactly how Meesha would react to this scheme. She'd be all judgy and holier-than-thou about it, because (contrary to Bunny's stupid song) Meesha is almost annoyingly un-thirsty for fame. She wouldn't get the point. But, under normal circumstances, Mona would tell her nonetheless because that's just what they do. And Meesha would give her grief but ultimately have her back because, again, that's just what they do.

But this isn't just any old NDA she signed. It's an iron-clad NDA from the president of the United States that explicitly bars her from telling anybody, *including* her sisters. So, as near impossible as it is to keep a secret from the one person who knows how to read her facial expressions like they're issues of *Vogue*, Mona has no choice.

"Yeah, well, he dumped her," Mona says, grateful Melody is serving as a human shield sitting between them. "Apparently, it was all a misunderstanding. He wanted to dump her before the party but didn't get a chance to, so now they're actually over." Mona resists the urge to puke at the pathetic words spilling out of her mouth.

"And you believe him?" Meesha asks, the monotone of her voice only making the words cut deeper. "Mona, you're being dumb. The guy is obviously lying to you."

Mona wants to scream, *DO YOU HAVE TO RUB IT IN? I OBVIOUSLY AGREE*, but instead she turns toward Melody, her eyes begging her eldest sister to draw on her unflappable ability to snuff out even the slightest trace of tension.

"Meesha, be nice," Melody pleads, taking Mona's nonverbal cue. "If Mona trusts him, we have to trust her." Mona gives Melody's hand a grateful squeeze as she tries to push down the guilt bubbling up in the pit of her stomach. The thing is Melody isn't just smoothing things over when she says that. She means it. All she's ever wanted since Mona and Max split was for Mona to trust someone again. Watching her hopes get high over *Lucas* of all people kills Mona a little bit.

"Josie and Lou, you two agree," Melody insists, turning toward where they're sitting in the row of seats behind them. "Mona really likes this guy, so we do too. Right?"

"Mm-hmm," Josie and Lou both say in unison, their mouths pressed into equally tight smiles.

Meesha turns to Josie, her eyes narrowing. "You've been acting weird all night," she says. "Do you know something?"

"Me?" Josie asks, a giant bead of sweat dripping down her forehead. "Know something? No! Of course not. It's me, Josie. I'm clueless. I never know anything."

"Don't mind her," Lou says, not at all subtly nudging Josie

in the rib. "She's just all frazzled about finals coming up."

Mona turns her attention over to Josie, carefully examining her face. Their newfound half sister might have just recently joined their family, but it already feels like they've known her forever. And she *does* look incredibly suspicious. Does she know? How could she possibly know?

"Josie, is it what we talked about the other day?" Melody asks. "Because it will be fine. Really, I promise."

"What did you talk about the other day?" Mona asks Josie, her brows scrunched in confusion. "Why is she being all cryptic?" Mona hates to admit it, but she's a little hurt Josie wouldn't come to her with whatever this personal tidbit is.

"TIMMY AND I MIGHT HAVE SEX SOON," Josie finally blurts out loudly.

Confessional

INT. VALLEY HIGH SCHOOL SENIOR HALLWAY– AFTERNOON

JOSIE stands in front of her locker.

PRODUCER

Was that even true?

JOSIE

Yeah, it's what Melody was referring to. I was just so panicked trying to keep Mona's secret. I sort of freaked out and blabbed my own secret instead.

"It's not like we have a date planned out or anything. I just . . . think I'm ready," Josie says as they take their seats around a large table on the roof. "But I'm nervous, you know? How did you all lose it?"

"You know my story," Lou says with a shrug. "Bobby Kim during a party at Jane McFarland's house our sophomore year. The whole experience was average at best."

"Mine was really sweet," Melody says. "I was dating Mauricio the night he won at the Latin Grammys. I was his date and afterward we flew to Brazil to celebrate, and he had this whole beautiful tent set up for us on our private beach."

"I lost mine to Bunny," Meesha says. "That first week we spent together in New York after fashion week. She had this massive suite at Soho House, and we just spent all day in bed together, getting room service and . . . you know. The memory is *obviously* tainted now. But it was a good day."

They all turn their attention to Mona, who launches into her story. "I lost it to Max," she says with an eye roll. "We lost it to each other. It was awful. Neither of us had any idea what we were doing. But I guess the setting was nice. We had this massive suite at the Aman in Venice, and he had set up this cashmere blanket in the center of a bunch of rose petals in front of the fireplace."

"Okay," Josie says. "I have to say. These stories were incredibly unhelpful."

"Josie, you'll be *fine*," Melody reassures. "It's Timmy! You guys love each other. It will be great."

"So, Mona," Meesha says, scanning the rooftop as she takes a sip of her mojito. "Where is he?"

Mona looks around the glitzy crowd of celebrities scattered across the rooftop, hating the way her stomach plummets the moment she sees him. He looks infuriatingly gorgeous with one of his toned arms nonchalantly resting against the wall as he chats up the new face of Calvin Klein, Clare Lane.

"Mona," Meesha says in disgust, her eyes following Mona's. "You have got to be kidding me."

Mona examines the rooftop, hyper-aware of the eyes of everyone at the club fixated on her, waiting for her next move. She knows what they want. They want the classic Mona Mashad special. Slam her napkin down on the table, march right over to them, and pour an espresso martini straight on Lucas's stupid perfect head. Under normal circumstances, she would love to do that. Really, she would. But it's too early into this ruse. She still needs to convince people that she's into this annoyingly gorgeous pile of human garbage.

So, she gets up, composed. Instead of slamming her napkin down, she gently sets it on the table. And, instead of marching over to them, she walks. Casually, leisurely. Making sure everybody sees her *not* caring about her rumored boyfriend chatting up a hot model. Like they were all so ridiculous for even thinking that's what was going on.

"Clare! Hi," she says, ignoring Lucas. "*So* good to see you." She's met Clare a few times through Meesha. Nice girl. Mona's not trying to spark any beef rumors with her.

"Mona." Clare smiles back. "Hey! Oh, wait. The pictures! I'm so sorry. Are you two, like, together-together?"

"No," Mona says, shooting Lucas the quickest death glare she can muster without any of the hundreds of eyeballs on them picking up on it. "We've really just had that one kiss, and you know how these things go. Someone *had* to take a picture."

It takes every ounce of willpower Mona has within her not to rip Lucas's arm out of its socket as he wraps it around her waist. But she knows it's good for this twisted charade, can feel people across the rooftop silently swooning and drafting the tips they'll be sending into Deuxmoi later tonight. "We're just seeing how things go," he says, planting a kiss on Mona's cheek.

"Got it," Clare says, nodding understandingly. "Well, Lucas, it was good meeting you."

"Yeah," he says with a wink. "Really good to meet you."

Clare has made her way back to her table full of her influencer pals when Mona gives the crowd another scan. She wants to lay into Lucas, to rip his head off. To berate him for making her look like a bumbling, pathetic idiot in front of all of these people. But how? All eyes are still on them.

Then it comes to her. She gives Lucas an overt wink, making sure every single glittering face in the crowd of Hollywood hotshots sees as she drags the horny idiot into the bathroom with her. Pictures aren't allowed here, but people will blab. And the tabloids will go nuts for that move tomorrow, fading any mention of Clare into the distance. "Mona Mashad & Lucas Sterling Can't Keep Hands Off Each Other at LA Members Only Club, Sources Say." Mona can see the headline already.

"Well, *this* was unexpected," Lucas says, wrapping his arms around Mona's waist and pulling her in close as she locks the door behind them. She can smell his cologne, the mix of musk and leather. And can see that little heart-shaped speck in his left eye. And part of her—a primal, masochistic part of her—briefly considers tearing his shirt off and letting him pin her against the dark wood door she just carefully secured shut.

Then she comes to her senses. *"Bleh,"* she exclaims, faux puking as she pulls away from him. "I'm not here to hook up with you, you baboon. I'm here to tell you off in private. You *winked* at her. Are you kidding? You were the one who agreed to this whole thing. The least you could do is keep it in your pants for the few hours we're supposed to be here together."

Lucas smiles. "Mona Mashad," he says, his voice adopting an infuriatingly flirty lilt. "If I didn't know any better, I would think you were jealous."

"Oh, get over yourself," Mona scoffs. "Let me be abundantly clear here. I agreed to do this for *me*. For my show. You can do whatever you want when this whole arrangement is over but, for now, I need you to get it together. Everyone was watching us out there. You made me look like an idiot."

"Okay," Lucas agrees. "Then I need you to step it up on your end. You looked like you were going to die the minute I put my arm around you."

"Because I *was*," Mona says. "You are one of the most shamelessly disgusting humans I have ever met. How is it possible you even had a girlfriend in the first place?"

Lucas grabs a disposable out of his pocket and snaps a picture of her standing there with her hands on her hips.

"A picture?" she asks. "Now? Are you good?"

"Yeah," he says, shoving the camera back in his pocket. "You look cute when you're mad."

For a split second, Mona softens. It's something about the flash of the camera. It reminds her of the picture of his dad in the Sterling family living room, of that night in the West Village. But the moment passes as she remembers the night after with Piper. And not even a minute ago, with Clare. How could that guy from that night possibly be the same as *this* horny monster standing in front of her?

"I need a drink," Mona says, turning toward the door as she mutters under her breath, "although no amount of alcohol will ever numb the pain of fake dating a sociopath."

Lucas wraps his arm around her. "Come on, baby," he coos. "Cheer up. It's date night."

Mona resists the urge to vomit all over the marble floor beneath them.

When they approach the bar, the bartender greets Lucas with a too-familiar smile. "Lucas! My man," he says. "What can I get you two?"

"Hey, Greg. Good to see you again, pal," Lucas says. "Mona will have an espresso martini with a dash of cinnamon. I'll take a Blind Pig."

<u>Confessional</u>

INT. VALLEY HIGH SCHOOL SENIOR HALLWAY– AFTERNOON (CONT'D)

JOSIE

It's funny. You would think that, when people are famous, it would be *harder* to order drinks at restaurants and bars because everybody knows how old they are. But, based on my few months in this family, it seems like none of the regular rules apply once a certain number of people know your name.

✦ ✦ ✦

Mona looks over at the bartender, who doesn't have a name tag. Lucas clearly just did his whole *Lucas* shtick with this guy, getting his whole life story at some point. He's so full of garbage, Mona's shocked it doesn't just seep out of his nose and mouth.

"Thanks," she mutters once they get their drinks. "Now let's go hang with my sisters. Heads-up, Meesha despises you."

"I guess that makes two of you," Lucas says, clinking his glass against hers before wrapping an arm around her waist and leading her over to where her sisters are sitting. Mona hates how much she doesn't quite fully hate the feeling of him holding her like that.

They're ten minutes into hanging with her sisters and as expected, Meesha is giving Lucas absolutely nothing to work with.

"Pete's been playing great." Lucas tries for what must be the tenth time to get some conversation going with her. "Think he has a shot at MVP?"

"He *definitely* does," Melody overcompensates, nudging Meesha. "Don't you agree, Meesh?"

"I do," Meesha says, her voice terrifyingly flat. She refuses to make eye contact with him, instead, turning her attention back over to the conversation she was in with Josie and Louise.

"Josie, Louise," Lucas tries. "We hardly got to say hi. Good to see you both."

"Yeah," they both say, their voices slightly too high. "Good to see you, too."

Mona narrows her eyes at them. *Why are they acting so weird?*

"So, uh . . ." Lucas tries again. "How does everyone feel about running it back to the Met after-party? Everybody up for shots? I'm buying."

"I would rather die than take a shot with you," Meesha says, her voice still completely monotone.

Mona's heart softens a bit for her sister. Yes, she's making this entire social exchange painstakingly awkward. But this is her trying to protect Mona, her weird Meesha way of showing love.

Before Lucas can retort, the deejay on the roof changes the music to Bunny's new song. Unfortunately for Meesha, it's gone platinum and is pretty much inescapable at this point. Sure, Bunny's embarrassing antics at the Met helped Meesha let go of some guilt she was harboring about the whole thing. But nothing will quite get anyone fully used to an entire crowd of people singing along as your ex screams "I HATE YOU, MEESHA" out of the speakers.

"Really? They had to play *this*?" Meesha groans, ducking her head down as everyone on the roof starts whispering about and not-so-subtly staring at her.

"Oh," Lucas says, picking up on what's happening. "Is this the song about— "

Before Lucas can finish his thought, Mona has a plan. "WHAT?!" she yells, standing up on her chair. "IT'S ABOUT HER. GET OVER IT!!!!!" The crowd stares back at her, jaws agape, as the deejay stops the song. Mona holds back a satisfied smile, ready to drum up some more headlines and scream at them some more, when Meesha jerks her back down onto her seat.

"Can you *not*?" she asks. "It's already bad enough everyone is staring at me. You screaming at them doesn't exactly make them stare less."

"So, what then?" Mona asks, incredulous. "We're just supposed to let Bunny dominate this narrative? Sit around and say nothing while her song straight-up slanders you?"

"*Yes,*" Meesha insists. "Exactly."

"Meesha might be right," Melody says. "All Bunny and her fans want is a reaction. The best thing we can do is not give it to them."

Lucas laughs. "I thought it was kind of epic."

Meesha and Mona each shoot him death glares for different reasons.

"Mona, I'm glad you said something," Josie says as the song changes. "I think it's the only reason he just switched the song."

"Thanks, Josie," Mona says. "At least *somebody* at this table appreciates me."

"Um, I appreciated you, too," Lucas points out. "Remember?"

"Aww," Melody says. "That's right. He did."

"Come on, babe," Lucas says, pulling her in close. "What's a guy gotta do to get some credit around here?"

"That's right," Mona says through gritted teeth as she forces herself to lean back into him. "Thanks, *babe*."

She pauses for a beat as he gives her a kiss on top of her head. "You know what? I have to go to the bathroom," she announces, suddenly needing to get away as a small bit of heat starts building between them. "I'll be right back."

Before fully walking away, she bends down by where Lucas is still seated, placing a hand on his chest the way she did at the Harvard party before they kissed. Lucas raises his eyebrows, pleasantly surprised as she leans in close.

"Try not to hit on any models while I'm gone," she whispers when her mouth is just inches away from his ear. "Sound good?"

"Yep," Lucas whispers back, nodding toward where her phone is tucked away in her Cult Gaia bag. "And, while I'm busy not hitting on models, how about you stop texting Hot Surfer every time you think nobody's looking?"

Mona's cheeks burn. How did he see that?

Confessional

INT. HARVARD MEN'S LACROSSE LOCKER ROOM—AFTERNOON (CONT'D)

LUCAS

It was obvious! Every time she thought nobody

was looking, she would start smiling at her phone the way people only do when they like someone. So, I glanced at her phone and *boom*. Hot Surfer.

PRODUCER

Were you jealous?

LUCAS

[*pauses*]

A little. See, this whole thing was a chore for her. But for me, I still liked her.

PRODUCER

But you flirted with that model right in front of her.

LUCAS

Yeah . . . not the most mature thing I've ever done, but did you see her reaction? She wasn't just mad I was ruining our little scheme. She cared. It showed me I might still have a shot.

"Not that I owe you an explanation," Mona says with an eye roll, taking a step back from him. "But I was just organizing my next surf lesson." She purposely leaves out the fact that she's praying Kai will finally make a move on this surf lesson. None of Lucas's business.

"Right," Lucas says, with a smirk. "Of course you were."

"I *was*," she reiterates, suddenly too aware of how close their faces still are. "I can't deal with this. I need to go to the bathroom."

She storms away, beelining through the crowd as quickly as she can.

"Wait!" Josie exclaims, running after her. "I have to go, too."

Josie and Mona are quietly washing their hands side by side after using the bathroom when Josie turns to face her.

"I have to tell you something," she says, her face all sweaty again. "I wasn't being weird because of the virginity thing."

"I *knew* something was up," Mona says, relieved Josie's finally trusting her with whatever this is. "What is it?"

"I know," Josie says, her eyes looking down at her sneakers. "Louise and I overheard."

"You overheard what?" Mona asks, heart pounding a bit more than she'd like it to.

"You and Lucas and your mom and President Sterling," Josie admits. "We were early at the house for Mary's meeting with Louise about modeling stuff that night. And we accidentally wound up hearing the whole thing."

Mona slowly nods, processing exactly what Josie is saying. "So, Louise knows, too?"

"Yeah," Josie confirms. "But we haven't told anyone else. It's just us. I wasn't even going to say anything to you, but I don't know. You just seemed so stressed tonight. I thought I should let you know I know. In case you wanted, like, someone to talk about it with."

Mona doesn't say anything, instead just pounces on Josie for a giant hug.

"Thank *God*," she says, resisting the urge to cry actual tears of relief. "Keeping this a secret has been killing me! Josie, I hate him. I don't know how I'm going to keep this up."

"Well, you liked him for real at the beginning, right?" Josie asks. "Maybe just focus on that for the time being."

"I'll try," Mona says. "But everything I learned about him then feels fake. Like, now I know for a *fact* that he really is this slimy cheater. And I just can't unsee it."

"Yeah," Josie says, nodding understandingly. "Well, at least this isn't forever, right? Just do whatever you have to do to get through this whole thing, then you'll have your own show! Focus on that."

"Yes." Mona nods. "You're right. The show. Come on, let's get back out there."

They're two steps out of the bathroom when she spots him in the narrow hallway.

"You have *got* to be kidding me," Mona whispers to Josie. "Let's go back into the bathroom. Quick."

"What?" Josie asks, confused. "Why would we go back into the—"

"Mona," Max says, strolling over to them. "Good to see you."

"Hey, Max," Mona says, resisting the urge to punch the arrogant smile right off his face. "Wish I could say the same."

She looks around, desperate for literally any excuse to leave this conversation without looking like she's desperate to leave this conversation. But there's nothing. They're cornered. There's nobody else in this stupid hallway. Not a singular lifeline in sight.

"How are you holding up?" Max asks. "That was quite the scene you made out there."

"It was not a *scene*," she says. "That jerk shouldn't have played that song while Meesha was here."

"Right," Max says. "Well, the backlash can't be worse than what you got for that fall of yours. Man, those memes were rough. What were they calling you? Messy Mona?" He laughs his infuriatingly smug laugh.

"I actually saw a bunch saying she was relatable and fun," Josie says matter-of-factly. "So, take *that*."

Mona loves Josie to death, but she is the absolute last person you want in your corner at a moment like this. Josie coming for Max is like a puppy coming for a lion.

"And actually, Max," Josie is continuing, "this whole narrative of Mona being a *mess* doesn't even make sense. She's not a mess. The heel of her shoe got caught in the rug. That could happen to anybody!"

"So, Mona," Max says, ignoring Josie entirely. "I saw the picture of you making out with the president's son. And, of course, who could have missed you dragging him into the bathroom just now? Classy."

She hates how he still does this. Says things that make her feel so low that she'd rather nose-dive into the fiery pits of hell than be standing here looking into his soulless gray eyes.

Mona tees up a comeback, a slightly below-the-belt dig about his role in the new Johnny Depp biopic he's currently being critically ridiculed for. She's thinking of quoting one of the particularly harsh reviews Meesha sent her from the *New Yorker* calling his performance and the movie as a whole "an embarrassment to the entire film industry as we know it." But before she has a chance to deliver the zinger, Lucas is standing there with his arm wrapped around her shoulders.

"Hey, hon," he says. "Let's get out of here. This place is boring."

"Great," Mona says, her hatred for Max outweighing her disdain for Lucas as she allows her head to fully relax into her fake boyfriend's chest. "Oh, Max, have you met Lucas?"

"Max Davenport," Max says, reaching a hand toward Lucas. "I attended a few campaign events for your mother."

"Right," Lucas says, maintaining his tight, almost protective, grip around Mona as he shakes his head slowly. "How are you doing, man?"

"I'm fine," Max says, a tight grin on his face. "Just chatting with Mona here. You know she and I—"

"Yeah, she's told me all about that," Lucas says, giving Mona a gentle squeeze. "Well, I guess I just have to say thank you. You two splitting up was the best thing that ever happened to me. Honestly, I just can't believe you let someone this great go."

"Well," Max scoffs. "Just wait and see. Mona is *quite* the personality."

"Right, right, right," Lucas says. "Mona is the personality. And you are what? The emotionally abusive one-hit wonder of an actor who continues to torture her publicly in a pathetically transparent attempt to stay relevant?"

Mona smiles wide as she watches her ex standing there with his mouth hanging open, Lucas's exquisite burn slowly scorching him from head to toe.

She turns her attention to Lucas. "Come on, babe," she says. "Let's go."

✦✦✦

Confessional

INT. MARY MASHAD'S LIVING ROOM—AFTERNOON (CONT'D)

MONA

> Okay, yeah. Fine. That interaction didn't *completely* suck. But I wasn't about to go being besties with Lucas after. The guy was still enemy number two, right after Max.

✦✦✦

"So, where are we going to go next?" Lucas asks, pausing before he and Mona exit the ultra-private club. "You pick."

Mona looks to make sure nobody is within earshot in the coat-check line before responding.

"*We* are not going anywhere next," she whispers once she knows they're in the clear. "Listen, that little interaction was great. I'll give you that. But don't get it twisted. I still hate your guts."

"Boy," Lucas says, his hazel eyes staring down directly at hers as his mouth curves upward, "you really hold on to a grudge, huh?"

"Oh, you haven't seen *anything* yet," she says, snapping into Mary Mashad–mode as she spots her sisters inching closer to them. "Here's the plan: I'll walk out in ten seconds with my sisters, and you follow out ten seconds after us. There are hundreds of paparazzi camped outside. The tabloids will do the rest of the work for us."

For a split second Mona could swear she sees a flicker of disappointment flash across his face, but Lucas quickly reconfigures his mouth into a smile when Melody catches up to them.

"Lucas!" Melody exclaims. "Josie just told us about the moment with Max. I wish I was there to see it! You know, I really try my best to treat everyone the way I'd like to be treated. But I have spent dozens of showers fantasizing about what I would say to that guy if I had the chance to tell him off. Mona, did you just *die*?"

"Honestly, it was pretty great," Mona admits, refusing to look Lucas in the eye as she gives the earnest compliment. "You should have *seen* Max's face. He looked like he was going to poop his pants."

"I still think you're a tool," Meesha tells Lucas as she joins them, Lou and Josie on either side of her. "But I have to respect a Max take-down."

"You should have *seen* it," Josie is excitedly saying. "It was more than cool. It was . . . I don't know, I'm too excited to pick a word. Max looked like he was going to cry!"

"Ugh, I wish we weren't at a private club," Louise groans. "That clip would have gone *so* viral."

"So, Lucas," Melody says, placing a hand on his shoulder. "What do you say we all go to my place for a celebration? Axle just got back from his sound bath and wants to have people over."

Mona locks eyes with Lucas, willing him to remember what they just discussed. *Say no. Say no. Say no.*

"I have an early flight tomorrow morning," Lucas says, pausing for three excruciatingly long seconds before adding,

"But you know what? Who cares? How could I say no to a party with you all?"

✦ ✦ ✦

Confessional

INT. MARY MASHAD'S LIVING ROOM—AFTERNOON (CONT'D)

MONA

That arrogant *prick*.

Chapter 15

The next morning, Mona wakes up to a text from Lucas. Come on. That wasn't so bad, was it? Then another one, Just admit it. You don't fully hate me. She rolls her eyes, wishing she wasn't forced to unblock him.

Okay, yes. The copious number of Melody's Vibe Tea cans they consumed last night might have had her feeling a little looser than she should have. But now she can see things clearly again. The party was *so* bad. Lucas was working overtime, trying his best to charm everyone. Mona even spotted Meesha laughing at his joke at one point. And the worst part was, because everyone was watching them, Mona had to play into it. Every time he pulled her close or rubbed her shoulders or gave her a gentle kiss or whatever, she had to pretend like she was absolutely loving it. After a certain point, even though she would literally never admit this to anyone under any circumstance, a small part of her maybe *was* actually loving it? And that just makes Mona even more furious.

On the one hand, she should be happy. The goal here is to get people to buy it, and if that means letting her guard down for a second and maybe just slightly enjoying the feeling of his slimy, cheater paws on her shoulders, that's a good thing, right? Even Josie—who literally knows this whole thing is fake—called them *cute* at one point. If the people who know her best are buying into their "relationship" this much, the public will eat this up. And if the public eats this up, she gets her show.

But on the other hand, she is still fuming that Lucas might think he's getting away with it. That he spent a night giving her gentle kisses with his stupid perfect lips and making her sisters laugh with his annoyingly witty jokes and sticking it to her ex with his infuriatingly cutting comebacks and all of that is supposed to erase what he did to her not even a week ago. *That* is why she didn't want him to come to Melody's last night. He didn't deserve more chances to charm his way out of the doghouse. But he just *had* to ignore her and come anyway.

Confessional

INT. MARY MASHAD'S LIVING ROOM—AFTERNOON (CONT'D)

MONA

He was being an entitled jerk. I know that's what he did with that girl Piper and with all the other girls he's screwed over. But there was not a shot in hell I was going to let him pull that with me.

✦✦✦

Mona ignores the text, instead jumping over to her group text with her sisters.

Anyone down to get brunch? she asks. I'm so hungover. I need a breakfast burrito.

At school, Lou says, sending a selfie of herself and Josie in class.

I have a doctor's appointment, Melody writes. Then I've got a campaign to shoot for our fall lipstick palette.

I'm at the office prepping for my show, Meesha says. Wanna swing by? I could use a second eye to help me decide on models.

Mona tosses her phone aside and rolls over, examining the bronzer and mascara stains all over her crisp white pillowcases. Did she not take her makeup off last night? Why does she keep forgetting to take her makeup off? She's literally the *face* of makeup remover. She looks out her giant sliding-glass door, their infinity pool glistening pristinely right outside. Maybe she'll lie out by the pool today. Alone. Again. How depressing. Graduating early was fun in theory, but now it's mostly left her lying in bed or by the pool with nothing to do and nobody to hang out with. Okay, fine. Meesha technically just offered her something to do. But, like, the last thing she wants to do right now is go to her retired supermodel of a sister's office to look at a bunch of other hot models when Mona both feels and looks like she was just run over by a semitruck.

Mona is diving down her self-pity rabbit hole, a favorite of hers these days, when Mary bursts through the door with no warning. "It's noon," Mary says, sitting on the foot of her daughter's king-sized bed as she looks her up and down. "It is no longer socially acceptable to be in bed. Come on, get up. We're going to have a meeting with Jorge—Mona, the brand deals have been *flying* in since these Lucas rumors picked up. Since last night alone, you got thirty more offers. And I'm talking big offers. Tiffany's. Versace. *Ralph Lauren!* Everybody wants a piece of you."

Scratch that. *This* is the last thing Mona wants to do on a hungover morning. Sit through a business meeting with her mom and Jorge.

She has to think fast.

"I have plans," Mona lies. "I can't."

"What plans?" Mary asks, an eyebrow raised as she pulls up their shared family Google calendar. "I'm looking at your schedule today. Nothing."

"Yeah," Mona says. "I didn't have anything on the schedule, so I booked a surfing lesson."

"Surfing lesson?" Mary asks. "But you were terrible at surfing."

"Exactly why I need lessons."

Mary stares at her blankly before getting up. "Fine. Suit yourself. But I'm putting a hold on your calendar for tomorrow morning to go through these business prospects."

"Great," Mona says as her mom walks out. "I'll see you then."

She shuffles through her sheets to find her phone. She and Kai technically didn't have anything scheduled for today, but he *did* say she could come over whenever, right?

Hey, she texts him once she finds her phone buried between one of her giant white sham pillows and her custom Hermés orange headboard. You free for a lesson today?

Sure, he quickly writes back. When?

I could be there in two hours, she writes back. That work?

Yep, he says. See you then.

✦✦✦

INT. MARY MASHAD'S LIVING ROOM—AFTERNOON (CONT'D)

MONA

Usually, if I have a crush I like to play it cool. You know, let them come to me and look jaw-droppingly hot when they inevitably do.

[*pauses*]

But there's something about Kai. He's almost intimidatingly genuine. It makes you feel ridiculous putting on any sort of front.

✦✦✦

"Well, this is a shift from yesterday's outfit," Kai says, smiling as he opens the door to greet Mona and Majid. "Still no wet-suit, huh?" Mona looks down at her white tee and baggy gray sweatpants. "I'm not wearing a wetsuit to go flap around on a board on your deck like an idiot," she says with an eye roll. "I'll get one when we go on the water."

"'*When* we go on the water,'" Kai says as she walks in. "I'm loving the confidence."

"Well, duh," Mona says, turning toward where Rudy is waiting for them in the quaint family room. "Rudy, you believe in me. I'm going to be on the water in no time, right?"

"I don't know about *no* time," Rudy says. "It took you a pretty long time to just lie down on the right part of the board."

"Jeez," Mona says, setting her bag down by the door. "Tough crowd."

Kai laughs as he leads them both through the sliding door outside. "So, because, according to your text you're, um"—he pauses for a second glancing down at Rudy before turning his attention back over to Mona—"*not feeling well* today, I was thinking we could take it easy. Rudy? You got the goods?"

"Got it," Rudy says, pulling two blocks of wax out of the pocket of his little khaki shorts and handing them to Kai. "Here you go."

"So, Mona," Kai says. "Waxing a surfboard for me is sort of . . . it's like a spiritual experience. It's meditative."

"Oh God," Mona says. "*Meditative?* You sound like my brother-in-law."

"Well, I don't know who your brother-in-law is," Kai says, "so, I'll go ahead and assume he's a cool guy."

"He's not," Mona says with a smirk. "But please. Continue."

Kai continues by explaining the intricacies of waxing a surfboard. He explains he already *de-waxed* the board, which means nothing to Mona. But says they should sit crisscross applesauce on either side of it, Mona taking care of the left and Kai taking care of the right. Mona missed part of what he said in the middle because she was stuck on how unexpected and cute it was to hear him use a phrase like *crisscross applesauce*, but she got the basic gist: All they have to do is use their little bars of wax to etch a cross-hatch pattern across the board, then go back over and blur it all out in circular motions over and over until it's completely waxy. Seems easy enough.

"Before we get started," Kai says, passing her his phone from where he's now seated across from her. "We have to set the tone. What do you play when you want to feel totally and completely relaxed?"

"Easy," Mona says, queuing her selection up on Kai's phone before passing it back to him. "The Chicks. *Gaslighter* album."

"Country?" Kai asks, an eyebrow raised. "Interesting."

"What?" Mona asks. "Just because I'm a Persian reality star from Beverly Hills I can't like country?"

"Maybe?" Kai says with a laugh. "I don't know, your vibe just isn't super riding horses in the back country."

"Also," Rudy chimes in from where he's seated on a lawn chair next to their board, "country sucks."

"Honestly? There's nothing more calming to me than a scorned singing legend turning her heartbreak into a multi-platinum work of art," Mona says. "Doesn't really matter the genre. Whether it be Beyoncé's *Lemonade*, Fleetwood Mac's *Rumours*, or, obviously, my all-time favorite, the Chicks' *Gaslighter*."

"The fact that a breakup album is what relaxes you most is beyond me," Kai says with an amused chuckle. "But you call the shots around here. *Gaslighter* it is." He presses play and the album starts blaring through the little mini speaker he has set up in the corner of the patio.

"Thank God I've got a playdate in ten minutes," Rudy grumbles, plugging his ears as he goes inside. "Who listens to *country*?"

"Come on, Rudy!" Mona yells after him. "Just give it a shot!"

"Don't mind him," Kai says, laughing as his brother shuts the door behind him. "He can be a real grump."

"My sisters would say the same about me at times," Mona says. "No judgment here."

It turns out Kai was right, waxing the board is pretty meditative. They've been doing it for about fifteen minutes when Mona realizes neither of them has said a word.

"So, what kind of music do you listen to when you do this?" Mona asks, her eyes laser-focused on the board as she rubs in the next few lines.

"It's sort of embarrassing but, if you *must* know," Kai says, his face growing a little pink, "I like to listen to oldies—you know, Sinatra, Ella Fitzgerald, that sort of thing."

"That's not embarrassing," Mona says. "I used to love listening to those sorts of oldies, too."

"Used to?"

"Yeah," Mona says. "They were my dad's favorites. Now they just make me too sad."

"Is your dad . . . ?"

"Dead?" Mona asks with a laugh. "Yeah. You might be the only person on Earth who doesn't know that."

"S-sorry," Kai says, stammering. "I really had no idea. He seemed like a great guy in that episode Rudy and I watched the other day."

"He was," Mona says. "But don't be sorry. Honestly, it's

kind of nice talking to someone who doesn't already know everything about me."

"Good," Kai says. He looks up from the board, offering her a small smile as their eyes meet. "I do get it though."

"Get what?" Mona asks.

"The hype," he says. "Why everyone wants to know everything about you. You're unlike anyone I've ever met."

Coming from anyone else, the line would be corny. Too much. Cheesy. But there's something about the way Kai states compliments. Plainly. Like he's not trying to flatter you, he's just relaying a fact. It sucks any potential trace of corniness or cheese right out of the exchange.

Mona smiles. "Right back at ya."

Confessional

INT. MARY MASHAD'S LIVING ROOM—AFTERNOON (CONT'D)

MONA

I don't know how long we sat out there for after that. I was in, like, a trance or something. We just sat there next to each other in total silence, listening to the Chicks, waxing that board. It was nice.

"We can probably wrap things up," Kai says, noticing the sky darkening above them. "Nice work today. The board looks great."

"Thanks," Mona says, rubbing her hand over the grainy board. "You were right. This was sort of meditative."

"Yeah," Kai says, setting the blocks of wax aside. "I'm sorry I kept you here so long. I lost track of time. I'm sure you've got to get going."

"Honestly, I have nowhere to be," Mona says. "You have plans tonight?"

"No," Kai says with a shrug. "I've got the house to myself tonight and an early shift at the diner tomorrow, so I was just going to smoke a joint and go to bed early."

"How about we smoke that joint together?" Mona asks, any old impulse to play it cool once again escaping her. "I mean, unless you want to be alone. . . ."

"No," Kai says, a shy smile making its way across his face. "I'd love that."

Kai carefully sets the board aside, pulling out two of the same foldout chairs from yesterday. Then he heads to his bedroom and returns with a joint and a lighter.

"So," Mona says once Kai passes her the lit joint. "What *do* you think my vibe is?"

"What?" Kai asks, taking a long drag after Mona passes it back to him. "What are you talking about?"

"Earlier," Mona says, "you said my vibe isn't riding horses in the back country, which, fair. But what *do* you think my vibe is?"

Kai shrugs. "To tell you the truth, I have no idea. It's like I was saying earlier. You're not like anyone I've ever met. And it's not just because you're the only famous person I've ever met. You've just got all these different sides to you that I can't quite piece together."

He pauses, seemingly considering his answer in his head before continuing. "When you walked into the diner, you just kind of seemed like an emo teenager. Then I find out you're some hotshot celebrity. Then you come to my house not once but twice in a row, hanging with my kid brother and smoking joints with me on the porch," he says, glancing back over to where Majid is still standing by the sliding door. "But, also, you travel everywhere with that terrifying guy. So, I don't know. I guess you're just an enigma, Mona Mashad."

Mona gives a small laugh. "I'm not really sure that *I* know what my vibe is anymore," she admits. "I mean, I know what my brand is. You know, who *Mona Mashad* is . . . but being famous for being yourself is weird. There are two versions of me, always have been. The curated version the public gets, and the real version. Lately, I feel like the real version keeps slipping further and further away from me. When my dad was here, it felt like I could always find myself—the full picture—in his eyes. But now he's dead and I'm older and I just don't really know anymore."

Mona looks at Kai nervously, a little taken aback by what she just blurted out. The revelation was one of those dark thoughts she prefers to keep stored away safely in the back of her mind. The kind that creeps up at two in the morning when she can't sleep, only to be shoved far, far away when the sun comes up the next morning. She's not sure how it just found its way out.

Kai shrugs, not an ounce of judgment on his tan face or even a trace of pity in his auburn eyes. "Do any of us really know who we are? I feel like figuring it out is just part of growing up, right?"

"Huh. I never thought about it that way, honestly. I guess you're right," Mona says, comforted by the idea that she might not be as alone as she thought in this. "So, where are your parents?"

"Date night," Kai says, his face adopting a rosy hue as he passes the joint back to her. "They do it once a week. And it's always a different activity."

Mona smiles, her heart warming. "What are they doing tonight?"

"Bowling," Kai says. "Then my dad told me he's surprising my mom with a picnic at the park."

"Just because?" Mona asks, coughing a bit after a too-deep inhale.

"Just because," Kai confirms. "They've been together since high school and, thirty years later, they're still ridiculously in love. I know this is weird to say about your own parents, but it's kind of adorable."

Mona looks over at where Kai is sitting, his eyes focused on the cement wall in front of him and she knows it's probably the joint talking but, for a brief moment, she wonders if he's some sort of angel her dad sent her way when she walked into Lucky's the other day.

"I like this," she tells him. "Hanging on your patio."

"Yeah," Kai agrees. "Me too."

Chapter 16

Confessional

INT. MARY MASHAD'S OFFICE—AFTERNOON (CONT'D)

MARY

The next planned outing was a subtle planting of a seed. Melody and Axle were having us and the Sandersons all over to their house for a family dinner that Sunday evening. Lucas—such a dear, that boy—flew in just for the night to attend. The idea was that superfans would spot him in the background of one of the girls' Instagram stories or in the corner of one of our family pictures. Just another little hint without being too overt.

✦ ✦ ✦

"I don't get it," Mona says as she meets Lucas outside Melody's front door. "Do you not have a life? Aren't you, like, in school?

How do you even have time to be here?"

"Well, hello to you, too," Lucas says with a smile, pulling her in for a hug. "Missed you, babe."

Mona stands frozen in his arms, her eyes zeroing in on a mark on his neck.

"You have *got* to be kidding me," she says, getting closer to the purplish circle. "Are you for real?"

"What?" he asks. "What is it now?"

"What is it *now*?!" Mona asks, stabbing her finger at the dark spot. "You have a massive hickey!"

"It's not a *hickey*," Lucas says, his face reddening. "It's a birthmark."

"You didn't have that 'birthmark' the last four times we hung out," Mona scoffs. "It's a hickey. A hickey you probably got from your girlfriend that you never even dumped. *God*, you are honestly a parody of yourself at this point."

"First of all, I did not get it from Piper," Lucas says. "Because, like I've told you four hundred times now, I dumped her."

"So, to be clear," Mona says, her hands on her hips, "you're admitting it's a hickey."

"Fine," Lucas says. "Yes. I admit it's a hickey. I may or may not have hooked up with someone—not Piper but *someone*—last night. I didn't think she would . . . leave a mark."

"I cannot believe this," Mona says. "You have somehow managed to out-pig yourself."

"All right, can you cool it for a second?" Lucas interjects. "I seriously don't get why this is such a big deal. Are we, like, exclusive or something? You were literally texting that

Hot Surfer guy just the other night."Mona's face reddens at the mention of Kai, who ended their night of smoking joints on the patio with an agonizingly respectful and platonic hug goodbye.

"Not that it's *any* of your business, but nothing has happened between me and him," she hisses at Lucas, briefly grateful being friend-zoned has given her this rare shot at an upper hand. "And the big deal is that, as far as everyone is concerned, we're dating. But now you're strutting around hooking up with randoms and rocking hickeys on your neck, leading everyone to believe that once again I have somehow managed to snag myself a cheating jerk."

"It'll be fine," Lucas says, softening a bit. "I've . . . hooked up with this girl before. She won't tell. People will just assume it's from you. Honestly, it could be great publicity."

He has a point. Mona can see the headline already: "Lucas Sterling Proudly Sports Hickey Amid Mona Mashad Romance." But the headlines would quickly spill into online narratives about the "trashy" Mashad girl corrupting the "sweet, innocent" Sterling boy. And that's assuming this hookup buddy of his *doesn't* blab. Mona gulps hard as she remembers all the brutal memes and headlines that would spring up every time Max cheated on her. They were almost worse than being cheated on.

Before she has a chance to fully explain the magnitude of his little tryst with this flesh-sucking hookup buddy of his, Melody swings the door open. "Well, if it isn't my favorite new couple! What are you two doing just standing out here? Come inside! Axle's got the veggie burgers going on the grill."

Lucas gestures his arms in toward Melody and Axle's wooded entryway. "After you, babe."

"Thanks," Mona responds, her lips pressed into a flat line as she walks past him.

Confessional

INT. MARY MASHAD'S LIVING ROOM—AFTERNOON (CONT'D)

MONA

To say I was fuming would be an understatement. I was livid. How *could* he?

PRODUCER

Was part of you jealous?

MONA

No! Whatever [BLEEP] gave him that hickey could have him as far as I was concerned.

PRODUCER

That sounds kind of jealous.

MONA

I wasn't jealous. I swear. I mean, it was just a bit annoying that he was trying to act like he was all into me and then he randomly went and got a hickey? Yeah. It was irritating . . . but whatever. I couldn't let my family see I was mad. Honestly, I deserve an Oscar for my performance that day.

✦ ✦ ✦

Melody and Axle have set up their plush Japanese-style garden with two tables, one for the "adults" and one for the "kids" with Axle grilling veggie burgers on the barbecue set up on the gravel path between the two.

"Lucas, I don't think you've met anyone here," Mona says, gesturing to the table full of parents. "This is Scott Sanderson, he's Pete and Timmy's dad and the president of Yay!, the network that runs our show. He was also my dad's very best friend growing up."

"Lucas," Scott says, getting up from his seat. "Pleasure to meet you. I got my MBA with your mother back at Harvard. She's a lovely woman."

"Good to meet you, Mr. Sanderson," Lucas says, giving Scott's hand a firm shake. "And yes. My mom actually mentioned that to me once before. She spoke very highly of you."

"That's nice to hear," Scott says. "And please. Call me Scott."

"And this is Scott's wife, Carol," Mona says, gesturing toward the blond woman sitting to his left. "I mean, you probably don't really need much of an introduction to her."

"Carol Sanderson," Lucas says. "Such an honor to meet you. I'm a huge fan."

"Really?" Carol asks with a laugh. "I didn't think anyone your age listened to my music."

"Your *Love Hurts* album is one of my favorites of all time," Lucas says. "I love a good breakup album."

For a second, Mona catches herself wondering if he said that on purpose. Did she mention she loves a good breakup album during an old *Making Mashad* episode or something? But then she shrugs it off. The guy is clearly a manipulative sociopathic liar. There's no point in reading into anything he says.

"A straight man who loves a breakup album," Carol says, nodding toward Mona. "I think you found a keeper here."

"Are you kidding?" Lucas asks. "Your album and the Chicks' *Gaslighter* album. My top two. They get me every time."

"You like the Chicks' *Gaslighter* album?" Mona asks before she can think better of it. "Really?"

"Yeah," Lucas says. "It's one of my favorites. The way Natalie wrote about her divorce. How could someone not love that album?"

"Huh," Mona says, forcing herself not to dig further. "Anyway, moving on, Lucas, this is Matt Lawrence. Josie's adoptive dad."

"Hey, buddy," Matt says, giving Lucas's hand a casual shake. "Nice to meet ya."

"Nice to meet you, too," Lucas says. "Your daughter is great."

"She's really something," Matt says, beaming proudly as he looks over at Josie before turning his attention back to Lucas. "Now, Mary mentioned you go to Harvard. Impressive. How long are you in town for?"

"Just for the night," Lucas says, wrapping an arm around Mona. "Family is so important to this one. I had to make the trip out."

"Isn't he the best?" Mary asks from where she's seated at the end of the table. "Our Mona really found herself a catch."

"Yep," Mona says, her smile tight as she forces her head against his admittedly rock-hard chest. "He is the cutest."

"Awww, you two are adorable," Melody says as she sets a fresh plate of veggie burgers on the kids' table. "And dinner is officially ready for everyone!"

They're halfway through their burgers when Meesha spots it.

"Is that—"

"Wait, Meesha," Mona tries to cut her off. "What wound up happening with the model casting for the big show? I never asked you."

"Don't change the subject," Meesha says, reaching across the table to get a better look at Lucas's neck. "It *is*."

"What?" Pete asks, looking over at Meesha. "What is it?"

"A hickey," Meesha says plainly. "Look at it. It's huge. He has a giant hickey on his neck."

Josie, Pete, Lou, Melody, Axle, and Timmy all crane their heads forward to get a better look.

"Why are we acting as though this is some sort of shameful blemish?" Axle asks. "A hickey is a mark of love. Of passion. It is beautiful. Mona, you created art with your mouth. With your love. With your passion for this man. Be proud."

"*If* she's the one who gave it to him," Meesha says, looking Lucas dead in the eye. "She never said she was the one who gave it to him." Mona loves her sister but, in this moment, she hates her. Hates her and her X-ray vision for the truth.

"Babe," Pete says, nudging Meesha. "Of course she gave it to him."

"Yeah," Josie says, her voice coming out three octaves too high. "It was definitely from Mona."

"Is it just me or does it feel weird that we're debating the details of Lucas's hickey at the dinner table?" Timmy asks. "Maybe we change the subject."

"Thanks, man," Lucas says with a laugh. "Yeah. If you guys don't mind, I'd love a topic shift."

"Why?" Meesha asks, her eyes locked on his. "Why can't you just say who gave you the hickey?"

"Meesha, will you relax?" Mona asks. "It was me! I gave him the hickey!"

Meesha narrows her eyes. "You bit down on your bottom lip. You're lying."

"I'm not *lying*," Mona lies. "I bit my bottom lip because you're berating me in front of our entire family."

"I'm not berating you," Meesha says. "I'm *protecting* you. What are you doing? Why are you letting him treat you like this? It's like ever since Dad died you don't *think*. I mean, do you take anything seriously in life anymore?"

"Meesha," Melody cuts in. "That was too far. Mona's just . . . free-spirited. We love that about her."

Mona looks at her sisters, her eyes watering. "That's really what you think of me, isn't it? That I'm just some brain-dead idiot floating through life with zero self-respect."

On the show Mona knows she's the comic relief. The joke, even when she's not necessarily joking. And somewhere along the lines she suspects she might have become that in her family, too. She knows her sisters love her, there's absolutely no doubt in her mind about that. But she's not sure that they always really see her.

"Of course that's not what we think," Melody says, rushing around the table to engulf Mona in one of her patent hugs. She smothers Mona with kisses, squeezes her tight. "We love you for you. That's all I was trying to say. Every part of you. We love it." Mona's legally an adult now, but when Melody holds her like this, she feels five again. Like a kid who always felt so honored to receive the validation her oldest sister so freely gave her. She says nothing, just lets the scent of Melody's favorite orange-blossom essential oil fill her nostrils as she tightly grips her sister's Pilates-toned arms.

Mona watches as Meesha's outrageously symmetrical face falls at the sight of the hurt Mona knows is currently plastered across her own face. "I was heated and that came out wrong," she insists, pausing to look Lucas up and down before turning her attention back over to Mona. "I'm just worried about you. Something feels off here."

Mona opens her mouth to tell her it's fine, that it happens. Standard sister fight. Sometimes one of them will take it too far and accidentally strike a chord, cut a little too deep. It is what it is, a hazard of being as close as they are. They can just move on. But before she can say any of that, Lucas starts talking.

"Meesha, listen," Lucas says. "I'm sorry I treated your sister so poorly that night. That's on me. Obviously. I messed up. But she's honestly been my dream girl since I was ten. This isn't a random fling to me. I really, genuinely like her a lot. I like how she has no qualms about making a scene in the name of protecting the people she loves, I like how she says exactly what's on her mind no matter who she's talking to, I like how she loves super hard . . . hell, I even like how she *hates* super hard. And all I want to do is spend more time with her so I can figure out all the other things I like about her. I hope one day you can believe me."

The table goes quiet.

✦ ✦ ✦

Confessional

INT. MARY MASHAD'S LIVING ROOM—AFTERNOON (CONT'D)

MONA

[*pauses, then finally speaks, her voice more quiet than usual*]

It was probably a lie. The guy is a master liar.

INT. HARVARD MEN'S LACROSSE LOCKER ROOM—AFTERNOON (CONT'D)

PRODUCER

Mona assumed it was all a lie. What you said that night. Was it?

LUCAS

No. I meant that.

"That was nice of Lucas to say," Pete says, nudging Meesha. "Right, babe? Nice!"

"Yes," Meesha concedes. "Mona, fine. I'll believe you gave him that hickey. Even though you bit your bottom lip, and you only bite your bottom lip when you're lying. And, Lucas, if my sister likes you enough to maul your neck, I guess I'll give you a chance. But you are on *thin ice*. Got it?"

"I think you've made that part clear, Meesh," Timmy says with a chuckle.

"Here's an idea," Pete says. "How about everyone joins Meesha for my game next Wednesday? You can take my courtside tickets. Lucas, I'd love to have you, man. It's the conference finals and these guys are all Lakers fans. I need someone in my corner!"

Mona looks at Lucas, panicked. Courtside at Pete's game was *not* part of Mary's carefully laid-out plan. That would require them going fully public weeks ahead of schedule.

"I don't know," Mona says. "Sitting together *courtside* is a lot. There will be so many paparazzi pictures of us looking all couple-y. Maybe it's too soon. We're . . . kind of enjoying being private for now."

Lucas shrugs. "I'm down. Sounds fun."

Mona resists the urge to punch him in the groin. Why even hope he'll ever do what she wants at this point?

"What do you mean enjoying being private?" Meesha asks. "There's a picture of you sucking his face on every corner of the internet. And now he's walking around with a hickey you so vehemently insist you gave him."

"Meesha's not wrong," Melody says. "Aren't you going to his lacrosse game this weekend, too? How is this different?"

Mona wants to scream that it's different because she did not agree to this as part of Mary's carefully laid-out plan, and thus has not mentally prepared for it. That she doesn't want to have to put herself through two hours sitting next to him as paparazzi snap pictures and fans dissect their every interaction. That she isn't ready for that because she still hates him. But, of course, she can't say any of that. So, she keeps her mouth shut.

"What are you kids talking about?" Mary asks, making her way over to their table. "It's getting boring over there at the adult table, I thought I'd come join you."

"Pete just invited everyone to come to his game," Meesha says. "But Mona and Lucas are being weird."

"Hey," Lucas says. "Let the record show, *I* wasn't being weird. I'm down!"

"I think it's a *fabulous* idea," Mary says, giving Mona a look. "You two should definitely go."

"Well, like I said, I'm in," Lucas says. "Mona, what do you say? You in?"

"Fine," Mona acquiesces, not in the mood to discuss this anymore. "We'll go."

"Great," Mary says, pulling her phone out of the pocket of her black Prada trousers. "Now, kids, squeeze in. Let me get a group picture of you in front of the koi pond."

"I can take one, too," Lucas offers, pulling a disposable camera out of his pocket. "I always have one on hand."

"You know what would be artsy and fun?" Melody suggests.

"What if you took one of our mom taking a picture of us?"

"*Great* idea, Melody Joonam," Mary says. "What do you say, Lucas?"

✦ ✦ ✦

Confessional

INT. MARY MASHAD'S OFFICE—AFTERNOON (CONT'D)

MARY

It worked out better than I could have imagined. I was expecting we would have to strategically crop him out so that there was just enough for fans to see, but the disposable camera did the heavy lifting for us. His face was covered by it. As soon as I put the picture in our group text, Melody posted it to her story, and *boom*. Fans were spotting him all over the internet.

Chapter 17

Confessional

INT. MARY MASHAD'S OFFICE—AFTERNOON (CONT'D)

MARY

A few days after the barbecue Lucas was playing the Ivy League championship game against Yale. It was apparently a big one. So, we decided that Mona would fly out for it. If her last visit to their campus was any indication, we knew photos of her sitting in the bleachers would go viral in no time.

"You didn't have to come to this," Mona says, refusing to make eye contact with Meesha. "Really."

"Yes, I did," Meesha says, following Mona's lead as she locks her eyes on the lacrosse field. "I shouldn't have said what I said the other night. It was out of line. You like this guy. I trust you. I'm *happy* for you."

"You're *clearly* not happy for me," Mona says. "No need to put on this show."

"Mona, the last guy was just the absolute worst," Meesha says. "I'm sorry if I'm a little skeptical of anyone new. Especially when the new person is a cheater."

Mona turns to look at Meesha, an eyebrow raised sky-high. "Excuse me. Are you forgetting the number one song on the *Billboard* charts right now is quite literally about you cheating?"

Meesha stares back at her coolly. "That's different."

It isn't. But everybody has a thing, and Meesha's has always been this. That she's a hypocrite. She doesn't just think she can get away with murder, she also wants to try everyone else for murdering. Mona knows it's not worth her energy to push this subject, especially not for a fake boyfriend she couldn't care less about.

"Whatever," Mona says, turning her attention back toward the field. "Let's talk about something else."

Mona and Meesha sit side by side on the bleachers, pretending not to notice the hundreds of parents and students whispering and taking pictures of them as they watch Lucas play through the dark lenses of their designer sunglasses.

"He's pretty good," Meesha says. "He's scored, like, the last three goals."

"How do you even know that?" Mona asks, suppressing a yawn. "This is so boring."

✦ ✦ ✦

Confessional

INT. MARY MASHAD'S LIVING ROOM—AFTERNOON (CONT'D)

MONA

What?! I agreed I would pretend to like *him*. Not some dumb sport.

✦ ✦ ✦

Mona watches as Lucas twirls the stick thingy in his hand, catches the ball, and effortlessly flings it into the goal. "Harvard goal! Scored by number fourteen, Lucas Sterling!" the commentator announces to the cheering crowd. "That's his forty-third goal of the year, leading the Ivy League for the season."

"So," Meesha presses. "You're telling me you didn't notice that?"

"Isn't that, like, his entire job as a lacrosse player?" Mona asks, lowering her glasses to get a clearer view of the commotion on the field. "To score points?"

Lucas smiles up at the bleachers, prompting every swoony-faced fan in the stands to point their iPhones in Mona's direction as he gives her a wink. The guy has, among pretty much every other form of privilege, *such* hot-boy privilege. If anyone else tried to pull a move like that off, it would be almost painstakingly corny. But when Lucas does it, it's cool. Effortless. Easy.

Mona puts on her best supportive-girlfriend performance—a

smile followed up by a small oh-my-God-stop-I-*hate*-the-attention eye roll, then a kiss blown in Lucas's direction. Lucas pauses for a second, beaming up at her before running back over to his teammates. The crowd all but melts.

"Wow," Meesha says, an amused look on her face as she stares at her sister. "You're really into him, huh? Look at you. You're *blushing*. You never blush."

The comment only makes Mona's cheeks more red. Blushing wasn't part of the performance. That must have come naturally. Call it a chemical reaction to his face. Mona's saying a silent prayer that Lucas can't read her expressions as well as her sister can when she spots a tiny blond girl power walking in their direction.

"Hide me," Mona demands, ducking her head into Meesha's bony shoulder. "It's her."

"Who?" Meesha asks, looking around confused. "What are you talking about?"

"It's *Piper*," Mona whispers. "The girl who is—uh, was—his . . . girlfriend."

The guilt hits Mona like a monsoon. Melody was right in her text. With Max, Mona *was* the Piper. Now, as far as Piper is concerned, Mona is not only dating her Max but throwing it in her face—blushing like an idiot in the crowd after he flashed her a perfect smile.

"If it isn't the Mashad sisters," Piper says, a smile forced onto her face as she stands in front of them. "So nice of you two to make the trip. Must have been hard finding the time between . . . what is it that you people fill your days with? Reality-TV shoots and vapid Hollywood parties?"

Just like that, the guilt evaporates. Mona forgot what a piece of work this girl is.

"I don't think we've met," Meesha says flatly. "Who are you?"

"I'm Piper. Your sister and I met at a party recently," she says, before turning toward Mona. "I just came by to tell you to enjoy your little fling with Lucas. You're the *epitome* of Hollywood trash. A messy, fame-hungry joke. A funny story he'll eventually tell his friends about the reality star who wasn't as hot in person as she was in her overly filtered Instagram pictures. It's only a matter of time before he comes running back to me."

Mona looks around her, taking note of the many eyes glued onto them as she mulls over her next move. She knows what Piper is doing. It's obvious. She wants to get a rise out of Mona. To make her make a scene, like she did at the party. As *if* Mona is about to let her play her like that.

Confessional

INT. MARY MASHAD'S LIVING ROOM—AFTERNOON (CONT'D)

MONA

Piper's plan had one fatal flaw: I only make scenes on *my* terms. Besides, she was so unoriginal. I can't go on Instagram without being assaulted by thousands of different versions of what she said to me, haven't been able to my whole life. Those words are like white noise at this point.

✦✦✦

Mona looks Piper up and down, taking in her predictably chic outfit—a crimson Harvard baseball cap paired with a white tee, white trousers, and a crimson cashmere sweater just casually tied around her waist.

"Thanks for the note, Piper," she finally says, an unnervingly pleasant smile plastered on her face. "Anything else you'd like to attack? Or will that be all?"

"I . . . um. . ." Piper stammers, visibly thrown. "I . . ."

Meesha looks her up and down, her gaze so cold it could freeze the sun. "I think that's your cue to go."

"This is *not* over," Piper says, balling her little hands into fists as she storms toward where her friends are seated in the back row.

It isn't until Piper is no longer in earshot that the sisters let out a small laugh. "At least she has the decency to bully me to my face," Mona points out. "Gotta give her that."

"Fair. The girl definitely has guts," Meesha says, stuffing her mouth with a handful of popcorn. "For a second there I thought I was going to have to fight her."

"*Please,*" Mona says with a laugh. "Like your little birdie hands could fight anyone."

Meesha laughs. "Fair. But maybe I'd have some super strength kick in. Like those moms who lift cars when their babies are in danger."

"Do you think Mom would be able to lift a car if one of our brand deals was in danger?" Mona jokes.

Meesha snorts. "Absolutely."

Mona smiles, taking a handful of popcorn out of Meesha's tub. If they had the type of relationship where they got all sappy, she would tell her that she missed her. That she's so happy for her new fashion line and her relationship, but those things inherently mean she has less time to be attached at the hip to her little sister. And Mona didn't fully realize just how much she'd been missing that attached-at-the-hip feeling until just now.

But they don't have that sort of relationship, so she just takes another handful of Meesha's popcorn and keeps watching her fake boyfriend play this game she doesn't even remotely understand.

"Ooh! Did you see that?!" Meesha exclaims. "Lucas just decked that guy."

"Uh-huh," Mona says, suddenly distracted by a text from Kai, whose name she finally has saved as Kai. The whole Hot Surfer thing was getting embarrassing.

Looks like you have a new number one fan, Kai's text says with a picture of Rudy intently watching an old episode of *Making Mashad* in their living room.

What episode?! Mona immediately texts back, a smile creeping across her face. I have braces so I'm going to guess season five?

I don't know but you're picking an outfit for the Teen Choice Awards, he writes. Pretty thrilling stuff.

Mona is still lost in her phone texting Kai back and forth when Meesha nudges her. "Hellooo," she says. "Are you even paying attention?! Harvard *won*. This is huge! They're the Ivy League champs!"

"Oh, amazing," Mona says, stuffing her phone into her chocolate-brown Bottega Veneta tote. "So, it's over? Let's go."

"What do you mean, 'let's go'?" Meesha asks. "Don't you want to tell your boyfriend congrats on an unbelievable game?"

"Yeah," Mona says, snapping back into fake-girlfriend mode. "Of course. You're the one who dates an athlete. You know this stuff better than I do. Where do we go?"

"I don't know," Meesha says, looking around. "This is different than an NBA game. Let's just . . . follow the parents. They're probably going to see their kids and stuff."

Mona and Meesha follow the large crowd of parents toward an area by the parking lot and wait for the teams to trickle out.

"LEDGE!!!!!!!!!!!!!!!!!!!" Mona hears someone scream from a distance. She searches through the group of Johns from the other night until her eyes settle on her favorite of the bunch, Goose.

"Goose!" she shouts back, embracing him in a hug as he makes his way over to her. "Good to see you."

Meesha stares at the two of them, confused. "What's happening here?"

"Meesha," Mona says, "this is Goose. Well, his real name is John, but there were too many Johns, so he had to become Goose."

"And how did you become . . . Ledge?" Meesha asks.

"Because she's a legend," Lucas says, wrapping his arm around Mona as he strolls into their conversation. "Hey, babe."

Even sweaty, he looks incredible. Like an ad for sweat. It's honestly annoying. She thinks about the last time she saw

Goose, about the Piper of it all. About how that stupid incredible face has let him get away with so much, more than anybody who wasn't Lucas Sterling could ever possibly get away with. The injustice of it all makes her blood boil.

Then she remembers she has a role to play.

"Hey," she says, forcing herself to give him a kiss on his salty cheek. "Good game."

But Lucas isn't paying attention anymore. The arm that was just a moment ago wrapped around Mona is now back by his side and his eyes have shifted their focus onto a guy on the Yale team marching toward them.

"It's the guy he decked," Meesha whispers to Mona. "During the game."

Before she can say any more, the guy is standing in front of them.

"Hey, man," Lucas says, his voice calm as his buddies start standing in a formation behind him. "Good game."

Without responding, the guy shoves him into his friends, sending Secret Service rushing over. Mona's heart rate spikes, her eyes immediately darting to the hundreds of iPhone cameras popping up around them. Habit.

"It's fine," Lucas tells his security detail, standing back up straight. "I can handle this." He returns his attention to the Yale player. "Listen, buddy. I'm sorry you lost. But can you chill? The game is over."

"Well, we wouldn't have *lost* if you didn't play dirty," the guy spits back. "That was a cheap shot you took at me and you know it."

"It was not," Lucas says, his voice calm. "And I suggest you walk away now."

"Oh, spare me the high horse," the guy says. "You were playing dirty the whole game. But I guess that's what I should expect from a Sterling, isn't it?"

"What is that supposed to mean?" Lucas says, taking a step forward.

Mona looks at Lucas, then at the cameras, heart racing. She can read the look on his face, has worn it on her own face a few too many times. That look is a prologue to a story that almost always ends in disaster.

"Mona," Meesha whispers. "*Do* something."

"Lucas," Mona says, tugging on his arm. "What are you doing? The guy is a jerk. He wants a rise out of you. Let's go."

"What it *means*," the guy says, boxing Mona out as he steps even closer toward Lucas, "is that you play dirty just like your mom. Everyone knows she's a liar. Everyone knows the only reason she got to where she got is because your daddy died. And, hell, that pathetic excuse for a wife and mother is so conniving that I wouldn't be surprised if she had something to do with—"

Before he can finish the sentence, Lucas punches him square in the face, knocking him down to the ground.

Mona looks around—hundreds of students and parents are holding up iPhones with their jaws hanging.

✦ ✦ ✦

Confessional

INT. MARY MASHAD'S LIVING ROOM—AFTERNOON (CONT'D)

MONA

I was torn. On the one hand, I would have done the exact same thing. On the other hand, I knew he had just flung open the gates to media hell.

Chapter 18

"Lucas Sterling, nineteen-year-old son of Jordana Sterling, has come under fire for an outburst after a Harvard lacrosse game," CNN anchor Jenna Klein is reporting on TV the next morning. "As you can see, the viral video shows him punching a player on the opposing team square in the face."

Mona glances down at her phone, which is buzzing with a text from Lucas. Sorry if I dragged you into this, it says. I guess I'm the messy one now, huh? Then one from Meesha, Yikes. This is brutal. Poor Lucas.

"Yeah, Jenna, I think we can all agree this was not a good look for the kid *or* for his mother's upcoming re-election campaign," Jenna's co-anchor Mike Abrams is saying, an arrogant smirk on his face. "Approval ratings for President Sterling have dropped twenty points since the video went viral."

Mona hearts Meesha's text, then looks at the long string of never-responded-to texts from Lucas. She replies for the first time since the Met Gala. Watch it. Messy is *my* title.

Mary flips the channel, *Roundtable Roast* now populating the massive TV screen in her office. "Listen, let's just call it what it is," host Amanda Reinhardt is saying. "The kid is entitled! He thinks he can do whatever he wants, punch whoever he wants. And there will be no repercussions. Do we seriously want a woman who instilled those values into her own *son* to continue leading our country?"

"I don't know," co-host Marie Lancic says, shaking her head. "Call me a sucker, but I always had a soft spot for him, especially after everything he went through with his father. My guess? This outburst had something to do with that Mona Mashad."

"That's not a bad point," guest host Penelope Lopez says, nodding aggressively. "She isn't in the video, but Mona *was* at the game and, I mean, if we want to talk about entitled brats. She has to take the cake, no?"

Amanda laughs. "The girl has had more public outbursts than—"

Mona reaches behind her to grab the remote from Mary's meticulously organized desk and turns the TV off.

"Can we be done here?" she asks, swiveling her plush camel leather chair to face Mary. "Why are you making me watch this?"

"Because you need to be *aware*," Mary fires back. "Mona, this isn't just another case of you throwing a tantrum on a red carpet. This is the president of the United States' son *punching* another kid in the face, while you were there! Thank God you were somehow out of frame in that video. It's our only saving grace."

"Excuse me," Mona says. "Are you seriously blaming *me*? Lucas punched the kid!"

"Mona, how many times do I have to drill this into your head?" Mary asks. "Always think ten steps ahead. You look at those idiots pointing their cameras in his direction, and you have to see the headlines. You have to see what they're going to say. You have to see how it's going to reflect back onto *you*."

"Mom, I am *constantly* thinking about the headlines," Mona fires back. "Literally constantly. They haunt me. You cannot blame me for this. I mean, if anything, *you* are the one who wanted me to enter this train wreck of a fake relationship in the first place."

"This is a disaster," Mary says, letting out an exasperated sigh. "I have a Zoom booked with Jordana this afternoon during your surfing lesson. You and I are going to have to circle back this evening. I hope she doesn't want to call the whole thing off. Honestly, I have to touch base with Jorge on how the numbers are looking on our end. *We* might want to be the ones to call it off, depending on how Lucas is polling."

"Oh no," Mona deadpans. "That would be terrible."

"Everything okay with you?" Kai asks as he adjusts Mona's stance atop the surfboard. "You've been a little quiet."

"I'm fine," Mona says, a now-familiar small rush coursing through her body as she lets Kai guide her legs a bit closer together. "Just had a rough morning."

"Wanna talk about it?" he asks, his expression once again

managing to do two contradictory things at once. This time, he's completely earnest and still a little aloof. Like he's here if she wants to talk about what's bugging her, but he doesn't *need* to know what's going on either. Mona shrugs. "Not really." This is her time with Kai. The last thing she wants to be talking about is *Lucas*. Besides, venting to your real-life crush about the PR fiasco your fake boyfriend has found himself in is not exactly a fast track out of the friend zone.

"Fine by me," Kai says before reaching out to gently tap her left leg. "Watch your front leg there, it's going just a bit too far forward."

Mona quietly adjusts the leg, relieved to be here with Kai at the one place on Earth that doesn't seem to be buzzing about her and her scandalous fake boyfriend.

Kai takes a step back, examining her form. "Honestly, Mona? I think you've got it. You free tomorrow afternoon? I have to work in the morning, but I think you're ready for some real water if you want to meet me at the beach later."

"The ocean?!" Mona asks, suddenly understanding how that NFL guy Melody used to date must have felt when his team made it to the Super Bowl. "Are you kidding?!"

She grabs his chiseled shoulders and starts jumping up and down, any trace of residual Lucas-related upset evaporating as Kai returns her excitement. "Not kidding!" he confirms with a small chuckle, his warm gaze fixed on her. "You earned it."

Mona smiles up at him, sure something is finally gonna happen as he inches his head down closer to hers, but then—

"Kai!" Kai's mom, a tall woman in scrubs interrupts as

she walks out onto the patio. "Oh. I didn't realize you had company."

Kai and Mona both instinctively step a respectable six inches away from each other.

"Sorry, sweetie," his mom continues. "I was just going to ask if you could help us unload the groceries."

"I told you!" a man's voice, presumably his dad's, booms from the kitchen. "I've got it!"

Kai's mom rolls her eyes, but a small smile gives her away. "Your father *insists* on doing it for me, even though we know he shouldn't be lifting heavy groceries with his bad back."

His dad—a tall guy whose face looks like someone slapped one of those aging filters on Kai's—makes his way out onto the patio, his strong arm wrapping around his wife's slender shoulders like a scarf custom made for them. "Unloading the groceries for you gives me *joy*," he tells her. "Didn't one of those podcasts you made me listen to say that's the greatest thing you can do for your wellness? Live a joyful life? Let me have this!"

Kai's mom looks up at her husband, beaming. She's got to be at least in her fifties, her full head of black hair heavily salted with strands of grays and gentle lines creasing the corners of her eyes and mouth. But looking at him with that goofy smile on her face, she looks like a teenager.

"You guys," Rudy says, trailing behind them. "This is *Mona*. The one I was telling you about. Kai's famous friend."

"Where are our manners?" Mrs. Takanasha asks, shifting her attention onto Mona. "I'm Kai's mom. It's a pleasure to meet you."

"Same here," Kai's dad agrees, glancing over at Rudy. "I've never met a *famous* person before."

Mona laughs. "Hi, Mr. and Mrs. Takanasha. It's nice to meet you both."

"Don't mind them, Mona," Rudy says. "They're even more hopeless with pop culture than Kai, if you can believe it."

"How much longer will you two be out here for?" Mrs. Takanasha asks as she pulls her long salt-and-pepper hair into a loose bun. "Mona, we're having the Takanasha house special for dinner tonight if you'd like to join us."

"I think we're just about done here," Kai says. "What do you say, Mona? You up for a little Takanasha house special?"

"Well, I have no idea what that is," Mona says. "But I'm too intrigued to say no."

It takes about ten minutes for Mr. and Mrs. Takanasha to get the meal together and onto the small black circular Ikea dinner table. This would simply never happen at Mona's house. Not just because they don't eat frozen food and they have a staff of chefs and six dining areas to choose from. But because everything in the world of Mary Mashad is a giant *to-do*. A simple family dinner is never just a simple family dinner, it's an elaborate event that takes weeks of intricate planning and coordination with everybody's g-cals. Mona can hear her dad's voice in her head. "It doesn't have to be this *complicated*," he would groan when Mary would spend weeks coordinating chefs and floral arrangements for a casual weeknight dinner with just the five of them.

Mona looks around her, the Takanasha family all seated

together laughing and chatting as the scent of pepperoni fills their small track home. No floral arrangement. No chef. No g-cal invite. Just a family having a casual spur-of-the-moment dinner at home. Maybe this is what her dad meant.

"Mom," Rudy says shaking his head in dismay as Mrs. Takanasha plops the piping-hot box of pizza onto the table. "This is so embarrassing. You can't give *Mona Mashad* DiGiorno pizza with some cheap dressing on the side. She eats at Nobu!"

"Of course I can," Mrs. Takanasha says with a laugh as she takes her seat between Mona and Mr. Takanasha. "I'm doing it right now, aren't I?"

"Now the key here, Mona," Mr. Takanasha adds, his free hand demonstrating while the other settles down on his wife's scrubs-clad thigh. "Is you take a slice of the pizza, then you mix the Hidden Valley Ranch with the Newman's Own Caesar as your dipping sauce."

Rudy, Kai, and Mrs. Takanasha watch intently as Mona carefully squeezes the two dressings onto her plate, dips her pizza into the mixture, and takes a bite.

"You know what?" Mona says, covering her still-full mouth. "That's not half bad."

"See? *Everybody* likes the Takanasha house special," Mrs. Takanasha tells a relieved Rudy before shifting her attention back to the whole group. "So, how was everyone's days? Did you see that crazy video of the president's son?"

Mona sets her slice back on the plate, opting for a sip of her water as a sudden wave of nausea washes over her.

✦ ✦ ✦

Confessional

INT. MARY MASHAD'S LIVING ROOM—AFTERNOON (CONT'D)

MONA

Listen, I'm not dumb. I knew that I was going to Santa Ana, not Mars. And Rudy might be the most pop-culture-savvy person since Perez Hilton in his heyday. But for a brief minute there it felt like their house was my little safe haven away from all of the never-ending headlines.

✦ ✦ ✦

"I didn't see the video firsthand," Kai says. "But everyone was talking about it at the diner today. Didn't he punch a guy or something?"

"You have to see the clip," Mrs. Takanasha says. "It is reprehensible."

Mr. Takanasha vehemently nods in agreement. "Out of nowhere, this spoiled brat just punches an innocent kid in the face."

"Well, I don't think it was totally out of nowhere," Mona says before she can think better of it. "I . . . heard the kid he punched actually was pretty rude."

"No," Mrs. Takanasha says, shaking her head. "I saw the video multiple times. It was *completely* out of nowhere."

"Oh, this is painful," Rudy says. "Do you three seriously not know Mona is his girlfriend?"

Mona's face goes bright red as Kai and his parents stare at her in shock. Kai, in particular, doesn't just look shocked. He looks hurt. And the expression kills Mona a little bit.

"I'm not his *girlfriend*," Mona insists, more to Kai than the rest of the table. "We kissed once. It was nothing."

"Weren't you at the game when he threw the punch?" Rudy asks. "That's what all the tabloids are saying. And it's why you know what the guy said, huh?"

"Well, yeah. And the guy *was* totally out of line. Trust me. But my being there didn't really mean anything. My sister Meesha was there, too," Mona says, desperate to change the subject. "Kai, could you pass me the Caesar?"

"Is this the guy you were venting to me about the day we met?" Kai asks as he passes her the Caesar. "The cheating jerk who your mom wants you to date?"

Mona briefly considers lying. Admitting to Kai that she's still hanging out with Lucas after everything she told him earlier is . . . well, embarrassing.

But then she looks at Kai's expression. It's trusting, like he will accept whatever it is she tells him as fact. You'd think that might make it easier to lie. But it does the opposite.

"Yeah," Mona admits, unable to fully look Kai in the eye as she says it. "Him."

"But you're not dating him?" Kai asks. "Even though you were at his game yesterday?"

"And you just defended him now?" Rudy adds.

"Boys," Mrs. Takanasha says. "Enough. This is Mona's private business. Let's stop with the third degree here."

"No, it's fine," Mona reassures them, her eyes now focusing on Kai's. "I'm not dating Lucas. Really."

Confessional

INT. LUCKY'S KITCHEN—AFTERNOON (CONT'D)

PRODUCER

Did you believe her?

KAI

I mean, she looked me in the eye and said she's not dating him. So, yeah. I believed her.

PRODUCER

Do you think part of you wanted to believe her? Because you were starting to have feelings?

KAI

[*smiles shyly*]

Probably.

Chapter 19

"Mona," Mary says, knocking on her door the next morning. "Meet me in my office in fifteen minutes."

"Do I have to?" Mona asks from where she's lying in bed. "I have my first surfing lesson on the water today! I still need to pick out a wetsuit."

"Well, if you would have bothered to come home in time for our meeting after I spoke with Jordana last night, you wouldn't have to," Mary says, letting herself in and taking a seat on the foot of Mona's bed. "But you were too busy doing God knows what, so here we are."

"I told you I had surfing lessons," Mona says. "I even put it on the calendar."

"Yes," Mary concedes. "But where were you last *night*? Your surfing lesson was in the afternoon."

"I had dinner with a friend," Mona says. "After my lesson."

"What friend?" Mary asks. "I know all of your friends."

Mona rolls her eyes. "You don't know *all* of my friends."

"Something is going on here," Mary says, an eyebrow raised. "And it better not be anything to interfere with your relationship with Lucas—"

"My *fake* relationship with Lucas," Mona corrects. "Now can you please let me get ready so I can meet you in fifteen minutes?"

Mary gets up, smoothing out a small crinkle from her black St. Laurent blazer. "You know if you're any good at this surfing thing, we should consider a brand deal," she suggests. "Maybe a line of Mona Mashad surfboards. At the very least a collaboration with Billabong."

Mona laughs. "You are relentless."

She immediately regrets the word choice; hates the version of Lucas it reminds her of.

Fifteen minutes later, Mona shuffles into her mom's office on the ground floor of the house.

"So, what's up?" she asks as she sinks into her go-to plush camel leather seat across from Mary's. "You talk to President Sterling? We calling this whole scam off?"

"Quite the contrary. President Sterling and I are both *thrilled*," Mary says, mirroring her computer screen full of graphs onto the TV. "Every young person in the world is infatuated with you and Lucas right now. And, while parents are critical of Lucas, they're finding President Sterling's experience as a single mother dealing with a rebellious teen to be incredibly relatable. Our viewership has never been higher, and her approval ratings are shockingly through the roof."

"So, is Lucas not in trouble with her?" Mona says. "For the punch? I heard he got suspended for the season."

"She's less than pleased with Lucas, of course," Mary says. "But she feels the suspension is punishment enough. And the appearance at the Lakers game couldn't come at a better time. It will distract from all the negative attention he's been getting and put the spotlight back on something happy."

Mona stares back at Mary blankly.

"Your *relationship*."

"Right," Mona says, a flurry of future headlines suddenly popping into her head. "You don't think it's a bad look, though? That he got in trouble and now he's sitting courtside at a Lakers game? It doesn't exactly come off like he's listening and learning."

"Trust me, Mona Joonam," Mary says resolutely. "We've thought this through. The game is a good idea. You look like the supportive girlfriend; he looks like a sweet kid in love."

"Whatever you say," Mona says, getting up from her seat. "Now, if you'll excuse me, I have a wetsuit to pick out."

"Well, well, well," Kai says, grinning from ear to ear as Mona walks over to where he's standing on the beach. "Look who got herself a wetsuit."

"You like it?" Mona asks, doing a twirl to show off the custom colorful Pucci wetsuit her stylist was able to snag on the condition that Mona would post a few selfies in it later. Before Kai can answer, she pauses, suddenly noticing Kai's and Rudy's black wetsuits with royal-blue accents. "Wait. Are you two matching?"

"Yeah," Kai says, his face reddening as he shyly brushes a hand through his shaggy golden-brown hair. "Santa got them for us this Christmas."

"This is the cutest thing I've ever seen," Mona all but squeals. "You guys look adorable."

"Thanks," Rudy says. "Did you notice the blue accents? The elves purposely made them to match the frames on my glasses. See?"

"Oh, yeah," Mona says. "You look *amazing*."

"All right, enough of the fashion talk, you two," Kai says with a small grin, before turning toward Mona. "Let's get you on the water."

Mona scans the quiet beach, trained to spot any potentially embarrassing pictures before they're taken and spread across the internet. "Oh God," she says, looking around nervously. "I can already see the paparazzi shots of me toppling over spread across Page Six."

"Nah," Kai says. "I chose this beach on purpose. Not many people know about it. Mostly just locals. I highly doubt paparazzi will find you here."

She's sure he's wrong, but she nods anyway, her smile tight. Even if there's no paparazzi, it's only a matter of time before someone gets a picture with an iPhone. This is how her life is and always has been. She simply can't do anything embarrassing in public and expect there *not* to be pictures. She looks down at her wetsuit and lets out a sigh. If she's going to be caught on camera toppling into the water like an idiot, at least she's going to look good doing it.

Kai and Rudy enter the water first, and Mona watches intently as they move through the same steps they've walked her through over and over again on their little patio.

"Okay!" Kai yells from the water. "Mona, you're up!"

Mona places the board on the water, then stares at it, carefully taking in the same dimensions she's taken in so many times at this point. She looks around one more time, making sure she can't spot any paparazzi or nosy civilians with iPhones. *Nope.* The beach is almost shockingly empty.

She closes her eyes and plops onto the board, relying on muscle memory more than anything else.

"Oh my God!" she exclaims. "I did it! I didn't tip backward or forward! I'm balanced!"

"No offense, Mona," Rudy says from where he's floating atop his board beside her. "But there's a lot more to do after this. I wouldn't get too excited."

"What? No!" Kai says, giving Rudy a playful noogie. "She mastered the first step. This is huge."

Rudy looks away from them as he spots a group of boys his age walking over toward the shoreline. "Those kids are in my class! I should probably say hi," he says, turning to Mona. "You gonna be okay here without me?"

"I think I'll manage," she says with a smile. "But don't go too far. I want to make sure I have backup if your brother gets too strict."

"Promise I won't!" Rudy shouts, his glasses covered in salt water as he paddles away.

"I think he might be the cutest kid I've ever met," Mona tells

Kai once it's just the two of them on the water. "I can't handle him."

"I know," Kai says, watching as he runs toward the group of boys. "He's pretty great. I do worry about that group of kids, though."

Mona narrows her eyes as she looks over at the group of little boys snickering as Rudy runs up toward them waving excitedly. "Yeah. They look like little jerks. Should we go over there?"

"No," Kai says. "Let's just hang back. We don't want to embarrass him. He'll call over if he needs us."

"Fine," Mona says, stills watching Rudy out of the corner of her eye. "So, what do we do next?"

Kai is helping her get into her stance on top of the board when they hear Rudy cry out. "HEY!" he shouts, his voice choking up as he holds back tears. "You guys, that wasn't very funny. Where are my glasses? They're my only pair. I can't see."

Confessional

INT. MARY MASHAD'S LIVING ROOM—AFTERNOON (CONT'D)

MONA

If Piper wanted to get under my skin the other day, she should have tried to pull something like *this*. Come for someone I cared about. When that happens, I sort of see red.

INT. LUCKY'S KITCHEN—AFTERNOON (CONT'D)

KAI

[*laughs, a lovey look in his eyes*]

She was *fierce*. Like a superhero out of one of Rudy's comic books. There was no stopping her.

Before Kai can stop her, Mona is paddling back to shore.

"All right, you little twerps," she says, her perfectly manicured fingers clutching Rudy's little shoulders tightly as she stands behind him. "Which one of you did it?"

They all sit there, staring at her, their eyes wide.

"Are you . . . ?" one of them asks, unable to finish the question.

"I think my older brother has a poster of you in his room," another says.

"She's my older brother's lock screen," another chimes in.

"I think my older sister got a selfie with her at an airport once," another says.

"Yes, it's *me*," Mona confirms. "Now quit staring and tell me which one of you has my friend's glasses."

"We don't have them," one of them quietly says.

"Well, he doesn't have glasses on right now, does he?" Mona asks. "So, clearly something happened to them. Who wants to fess up?"

"We threw them," one of the boys quietly mumbles, nodding toward a cliff to the left. "That way."

Before Mona gets a chance to march over there and grab

them herself, Kai comes over with the glasses. "Found them," he says, wiping the sandy frames off with his sleeve before gently placing them back on Rudy's head.

"Now listen here," Mona says, inching closer to the boys as she nods over toward where Majid is standing by the entryway to the beach. "You see that giant guy over there?"

They all look over as Majid gives them a wave.

"That's Majid," she says. "Majid knows Rudy is my very best friend. And, you see, it's Majid's job in life to protect me and my best friends. So, the next time you go messing with my best friend, I need you to know that I *will* find out about it. Even if he doesn't tell me, just know. I have my ways. I will find out about it. And that means Majid will find out about it. And together, the two of us will destroy each and every one of you."

The group of boys sits there silently staring up at Mona, their mouths hanging wide open.

"I'm, uh, I'm sorry, Rudy," the boy who threw the glasses mumbles. "I won't be mean to you ever again."

"None of us will," the boy whose brother has a poster of Mona chimes in. "We promise. You can even sit with us at lunch. Right, guys?"

They all nod enthusiastically.

"Can we just go home?" Rudy says, looking at Kai. "I'm kind of over the beach."

"Of course, buddy," Kai says, taking his hand. "Let's go."

The three of them walk toward the parking lot, Majid trailing behind as the group of boys stare at them in a collective state of shock.

"Hey, Rudy," Mona says before he gets into Kai's beat-up station wagon. "I hope you know you are the coolest kid I've ever met. Those other boys have nothing on you."

"They're the popular kids in my class, though," Rudy says, his eyes low.

"Listen," Mona says, crouching down so she can look him in the eyes. "I'm pretty popular in the world, wouldn't you say?"

"I mean, you *are* the most followed person on Instagram," Rudy says. "So, I guess that literally makes you the most popular person in the world."

"Right," Mona says. "So, trust me here. You are *way* cooler than any of them."

Mona smiles as she sees the corners of Rudy's little mouth start to curve upward. "You really think so?"

"I *know* so," she promises. "And you'll tell me if they give you any more trouble, right?"

"Yeah," Rudy says. "I will."

"Pinkie promise?" Mona asks, reaching a pinkie out toward Rudy.

"Pinkie promise," he confirms, clasping her pinkie in his.

"All right, little man," Kai says, opening the car door. "Let's get you home. I'm thinking ice-cream sundaes and *maybe* a round of *Mario Kart*."

"Yes!" Rudy exclaims, hopping onto his booster seat. "Let's do it."

Kai helps Rudy with his buckle, turning his attention toward Mona once he shuts the door behind him.

"Listen, I'm sorry your first day on the water was a bust,"

Kai says, flashing her a small smile as he looks her up and down. "I know you got a wetsuit and everything."

Mona tries to ignore the way his gaze seems to set loose an army of butterflies in her belly. "There will be other surfing days," she reassures him. "If anything, *I'm* sorry if I took it too far with those kids. I know I can get . . . carried away. I just get so protective sometimes, I almost black out."

"Don't be sorry. Rudy will probably ride the high of you calling him your best friend for the rest of his life," Kai says, pausing for a few seconds then adding, "Hey, listen. What are you up to Thursday night?"

"Uh, Thursday night?" Mona asks, pulling out her phone to check her calendar. "Nothing. You want to do another lesson? At night? You better not be demoting me to patio duty again."

"No," Kai says with a laugh. "You're not being demoted to patio duty. I don't have plans Thursday either. My parents and Rudy will all be gone. I was thinking maybe you could come over for dinner or something."

Mona looks up at him tentatively, a small smile making its way across her face. "So, like, a date?"

Her heart starts pounding, one second feeling like one year as she waits for him to respond.

Then he smiles back, his warm eyes set on her and her only. "Like a date."

Chapter 20

Confessional

EXT. AXLE & MELODY'S GARDEN

MELODY MASHAD, 22, is dressed in a flowy floral sundress, her bare feet digging into the grass beneath her as she sips on a mug of green tea.

MELODY

Lucas may not be related to us, but he was dating my little sister. And I take my job as the oldest sibling seriously. I knew he was going through it after the whole punch thing, so I told Mona she and Lucas should join me and Axle for lunch at Nobu the day of the Lakers game. Maybe we could cheer him up a bit, remind him he has us in his corner. The poor guy doesn't have any siblings of his own for that sort of thing, you know?

"I didn't know you knew how to drive," Lucas says from the passenger seat as Mona pulls her matte-black G-Wagon into the Nobu parking lot, Majid and the Secret Service trailing behind them.

"I think that's the first I've heard out of you this whole car ride," Mona says as she pulls into a parking spot. "Not that I'm complaining or anything."

"I've got a lot on my mind," Lucas says, looking nervously out the window at all the paparazzi camped outside. "This is going to be rough, isn't it?"

"Depends on your definition of rough," Mona says, grabbing a baseball cap and a pair of sunglasses from the back seat and tossing them over to him. "But, yeah. You'll probably want these."

Lucas secures the old cream-colored Polo baseball cap over his thick chestnut-brown locks and shields his eyes with the tinted lenses of the Oliver Peoples sunglasses. He pulls down the visor and looks at himself in the mirror, then takes another glance outside.

"All right," he says after a deep breath in. "I guess we have no choice, right? Gotta get out there."

"What do you mean we have no choice?" Mona asks. "What are we, prisoners of war? We have a choice. I'll text Melody right now and tell her you're not down for lunch if you can't handle it."

"I can *handle* it," Lucas says, an edge to his usually unwaveringly friendly voice. "It's fine."

"Jeez," Mona says. "Sensitive much?"

Lucas sighs. "Let's just get this over with."

The minute Mona and Lucas exit her car, it's absolute pandemonium. They're swarmed by photographers and fans alike. So much so that Majid and a few of the Secret Service men have to run to the front to make way for Mona and Lucas to be able to safely enter the restaurant without getting trampled by the massive mob.

The crowd of people is so large Mona and Lucas can't even tell who's yelling what as they follow their security detail toward the front entrance, their heads down.

"MONA! LUCAS!"

"JUST ONE SHOT OF THE TWO OF YOU TOGETHER!"

"GIVE HER A KISS!"

"YOU'RE COUPLE GOALS!"

✦✦✦

Confessional

INT. MARY MASHAD'S LIVING ROOM—AFTERNOON (CONT'D)

MONA

It was like . . . I don't even know what to compare it to. Picture the biggest pop culture moment in your head and multiply it by a thousand. It was total and complete mayhem.

✦✦✦

Of course, not everyone in the crowd is a fan. Since the clip went viral, the kid Lucas punched—apparently a guy named

Teddy—gave a tearful sit-down interview claiming Lucas attacked him "out of the blue." The whole thing was pathetic and, as far as Mona was concerned, so *blatantly* phony. But some idiots bought the bogus performance. So, the crowd is also peppered with people yelling variations of "LUCAS STERLING YOU ARE A DISGRACE" and "JUSTICE FOR TEDDY." The Secret Service even has to forcibly remove one woman after she tries to spit in Lucas's face.

Mona hears Lucas's breath catch behind her as one person yells, "PRIVILEGED JERK. THEY SHOULD HAVE EXPELLED YOU." She stops in her tracks, scanning the crowd until she meets the eyes of the middle-aged woman who must have just hurled the insult.

"YOU HEARD ME! THEY SHOULD HAVE EXPELLED YOU," the woman repeats, her eyes cold as she stares down Lucas. "YOU ARE A DISGRACE TO YOUR MOTHER AND TO THIS COUNTRY."

A woman standing next to her chimes in, "YOUR FATHER WOULD HAVE BEEN ASHAMED."

"Do you two seriously have nothing better to do than attack a teenage boy?" Mona asks the women, instantly sending the crowd into an even larger frenzy.

"Come on," she whispers to Lucas, taking his trembling hand in hers. "Let's get inside."

Confessional

INT. MARY MASHAD'S LIVING ROOM—AFTERNOON (CONT'D)

PRODUCER

That moment went *so* viral. Not just you telling those women off. But the handhold. Did you know that would happen?

MONA

I mean, in retrospect, yeah. *Obviously* that was going to be major. But I wasn't really thinking about that at that moment.

PRODUCER

So, what were you thinking about then?

MONA

As much as I still hated him, I honestly just felt bad for the guy. Like, he's a teenager with an impulse-control issue. Not a disgrace to our *nation*. People are so dramatic.

"Mona! Lucas! Over here!" Melody shouts, waving excitedly as the hostess escorts them out to the beachfront patio.

Just the sight of Melody instantly regulates Mona's nervous system, and Mona quietly hopes she'll be able to work some of her magic on Lucas. There's a reason America loves Melody so much. The woman is like Xanax in human form.

"Hey, Melody," Lucas says, his voice still not quite back to its normal cheery pitch. "Good to see you."

"You poor thing," Melody says, bringing him in for a tight hug. "This is just *awful*. I heard them screaming out there. I'm so sorry. We should have chosen somewhere more low-key."

Mona watches as, like clockwork, Melody's kindness starts slowly melting away a bit of Lucas's discomfort. Then Axle gets involved. Unfortunately, these days you can't get Melody's kindness without a dose of Axle's weirdness.

"Give me your hands," Axle demands of Lucas before he sits down. "Both of them."

"Uh, okay," Lucas says, cautiously placing his hands on top of Axle's. "Here you go. . . ."

"Lucas," Axle says, staring directly into Lucas's eyes. "This is a test. Of your strength. Of your character. Allow this hardship to build you up. And resist the urge to let it tear you down."

"Thanks, man," Lucas says, blinking away what Mona can't believe are tears. "I actually really needed to hear that."

Confessional

INT. MARY MASHAD'S LIVING ROOM—AFTERNOON (CONT'D)

MONA

Axle was making him emotional. If that's not rock bottom, I don't know what is.

"Nah, ah, ah," Axle says, pulling Lucas's hands back in as he tries to remove them from his grip. "Allow me to give you some strength. From my spirit into your soul."

Axle closes his eyes and tightens his grip around a confused

Lucas's hands. "Great, beautiful universe," Axle says, his eyes shut tight. "I ask that you allow me to transfer my strength into the core of this young man."

Suddenly, without any warning, he releases Lucas's hands, sending them flinging back toward his sides. "It is done," he says. "Go forth."

"Oh," Lucas says, staring down at his hands as he takes a seat next to Mona. "Uh, thanks. I feel better already."

"So," Melody says. "Let's talk about something else."

"That sounds great," Lucas says with a smile. "You guys excited for the game tonight?"

Before any of them can respond, they're interrupted by a small group of protestors standing beneath them on the beach. Mona squints her eyes and makes out the two middle-age women from earlier leading the charge, this time with megaphones in hand. "LUCAS STERLING MUST PAY! LUCAS STERLING MUST PAY! LUCAS STERLING MUST PAY!"

Mona looks over at Lucas, noticing his breath getting increasingly shallow as he tightly clutches his menu.

"I'm over this," she says, grabbing Lucas's hand. "Come on. We're leaving."

"What?" Melody asks. "No! I'll just ask them to move us to a private room."

"No," Mona says, her decision already made. "This is insane. We're leaving. I'll see you both tonight."

"Where are we going?" Lucas asks as he follows her out the restaurant toward the parking lot. "I feel bad ditching your sister."

"She'll be fine," Mona says. "Just get in the car."

Chapter 21

Confessional

INT. MARY MASHAD'S LIVING ROOM—AFTERNOON (CONT'D)

MONA

Getting out of there without being followed was a nightmare. I had to drive with the security trailing behind me to my mom's place in Malibu. There we had to quickly swap into the back of one of the SUVs with extra-tinted windows and have one of the drivers take my car back to Beverly Hills to throw the paparazzi off.

"So, *this* is where you put all this effort into taking me?" Lucas asks as the car pulls into the gravel parking lot at Lucky's. "Some random diner?"

"This diner is where I go when I just absolutely cannot deal," Mona says, checking her reflection in the mirror as she secures her black Favorite Daughter cap and slips a pair of oversized black Loewe sunglasses on. "And it seems like you absolutely cannot deal right now."

She reaches into the back seat to grab a UCLA cap and a pair of Ray-Bans. "Here. You're going to want a new disguise," she says. "The pictures of us from earlier are everywhere already." She hands him her phone, knowing he doesn't have any social media feeds of his own to look through.

"They're calling us couple goals," Lucas says, his signature smirk making an appearance for the first time all day as he scrolls through her feed full of pictures of them walking hand in hand through the crowd outside Nobu.

"I know," Mona says, taking the phone back. "My mom has sent me, like, four hundred texts. She's pumped. The brand offers are pouring in."

Lucas stares at her, smiling.

"What?" she asks, knowing exactly what but refusing to admit it.

"You know what."

She doubles down. "I don't know what."

"Fine. If you won't say it, I will. We look *good* together," he says. "Admit it. America is into it because it *works*."

"America is into it because I'm Mona Mashad and you're Lucas Sterling," she insists, adding an eye roll for good measure. "Two wild-child nepo babies. America's two first families merging. It's a great story. Even if it's a lie."

"Come on," Lucas insists. "Just admit it's not a total lie. We wouldn't be here right now if you didn't *slightly* care about me."

"I'm being nice to you right now because I *pity* you. Don't get it twisted," she says, nodding toward the UCLA cap and Ray-Bans. "Now put those on so we can enjoy our tuna melts without a mob of crazed fans attacking us. And maybe take Pete's Lakers sweatshirt in the back there. Everyone knows what we were wearing."

Mona already changed out of the colorful Prada floral silk printed mini dress at her mom's place and into a pair of baggy low-rise Levi's jeans and a cropped white tee for this very reason.

"Fine," Lucas says, throwing the sweatshirt on. "But before we go in, one selfie."

He pulls the disposable out of his pocket, taking a picture of them both.

"Really?" Mona asks. "You want to remember *this* day?"

Lucas puts the new cap, sweatshirt, and sunglasses on, pausing for a minute to smile at Mona before opening the car door. "I want to remember *every* day."

It's only when they've actually entered Lucky's and are waiting by the white plastic host stand that Mona realizes this maybe wasn't her best idea ever.

"Mona?" Kai asks when he sees her and Lucas standing there, both with sunglasses and baseball caps. "What are you doing here? Did we have a surfing lesson scheduled for later?"

Mona's not sure why. It's not like she's doing anything

wrong. She just brought a friend to the diner! But the confused expression on his face breaks her heart the tiniest bit.

"Hey," Mona says to Kai, her voice low. "No surfing lesson. Just . . . needed somewhere safe to duck out to."

She offers him a soft smile and, to her relief, he returns the expression. "Got it. Let me get you two—"

Before he can finish his sentence, Kai's coworker, a redhead named Jade based on her name tag, looks over at Mona, then back at Kai.

"Wait," she says, between smacks of gum. "You're not . . . ?"

"Alyssa Miller," Kai quickly says. "She graduated a few grades above us at Santa Ana. I'm giving her surfing lessons to make some extra cash."

"Huh," Jade says, looking her up and down. "For a second I thought you were Mona Mashad."

"Right," Kai says with a laugh. "Like Mona Mashad would be coming to Lucky's at three thirty on a Wednesday."

Mona shoots Kai an appreciative look.

"True. I just saw she and the new guy were at Nobu anyway," Jade says, looking over at where Lucas is standing with his extremely oversized Lakers sweatshirt and women's sunglasses. "And no offense, but he was dressed *way* better than that."

"Here," Kai says. "Let me get you two seated."

They follow as Kai walks them over to the last two seats at the counter.

"This work?" he asks quietly, setting a couple menus down on the table. "I remembered this is where you sat last time."

"Yeah," Mona says, blushing. "Thanks. This is perfect."

"AHEM," Lucas says, obnoxiously clearing his throat as they take their seats.

"Oh," Mona says with an eye roll. "Kai, sorry, this is— "

"Jack," Lucas says, reaching a hand toward Kai. "Jack Ryan."

Confessional

INT. LUCKY'S KITCHEN—AFTERNOON (CONT'D)

KAI

I know I don't really know anything about pop culture. But that was obviously him. The other guy.

PRODUCER

How did it feel seeing them together?

KAI

[*sighs*]

Not great. I mean, she told me they weren't dating and I still believed her. But there was . . . I don't know . . . *something* there between them. It was clear.

Mona winces, incapable of looking at Kai's face as he raises a skeptical eyebrow at Lucas. "Like . . . the TV character?"

"Yeah," Lucas says. "Funny coincidence."

"Got it," Kai says, his voice flat. "Well, I'll leave you two to it. Just let me know when you're ready to order."

"Thank you!" Mona exclaims, her voice coming out too pitchy and too loud.

"So, that's Hot Surfer, huh?" Lucas asks, a coy smile. "Okay, I'll hand it to you. The guy *is* pretty hot. . . . I mean, not as hot as me. Obviously. But hot. Lives up to his name."

"Will you be quiet?!" Mona asks, her face reddening. "And what was that about Jack Ryan? He obviously knows who I am. And his stupid coworker *just* said we were together. It was a pathetically obvious lie."

"Yeah, and the stupid coworker was still standing a few feet away. I didn't want to risk any slip-ups," Lucas says, a playful smile making its way across his face before he adds, "I think he likes you."

Mona rolls her eyes. "Honestly, you bring him up so much I'm starting to think *you* like *him*."

Lucas is about to respond when his face falls at the sight of a new text on his phone.

"What?" Mona asks. "What happened? Why aren't you being annoying anymore?"

"It's my coach," Lucas says with a sigh. "He's been fighting to appeal my suspension and just got denied. The school thinks it's a bad look to cut me slack right now."

"I'm sorry," Mona says. "If it's any consolation, I would have punched that guy, too."

"The difference is you punching that guy would have maybe been a headline on Page Six," Lucas says. "Not some national emergency that's being discussed on every news station globally. You know there were people protesting outside the White House this morning? All because I lost my cool in one stupid moment."

"People are nuts," Mona says. "So, you messed up. You're a *person*. Not some robot."

"Yeah, but that's the thing," Lucas says. "I can't be human. My mom has drilled that into my head. I have to be a Sterling, not a human. I don't have the privilege of impulsive moments like that."

Mona scavenges every corner of her brain for something to make him feel better, until she finds something. It's not ideal, but it's worth a shot. "You know, it literally kills me to cite one of Jorge's polls, but when my mom showed me the most recent numbers this morning, it turns out most young people actually like you *more* after that impulsive moment. You're the hot, lovable bad boy."

"So, you think I'm hot?" Lucas asks, a sideways smile making its way across his face.

"I didn't say *I* think you're hot. I just said *they* think you're hot. The people," Mona says, a sly smile flashing on her face as she looks him up and down. "Unfortunately for you, the whole perfectly symmetrical face, megawatt smile, Ken-doll-abs thing doesn't do it for me."

The truth is it very much does. It's actually just the lying, cheating jerk thing that doesn't do it for her. But there's no need to get into all of that right now.

"So, uh," Kai says, interrupting as he walks over to them. "Sorry to bug, but the kitchen is gonna close soon. You guys want anything?"

Lucas looks over at Mona. "I'll follow your lead, babe."

"Ew. Don't call me that," Mona says, turning to Kai. "Sorry about him. Yeah. We'll order. A tuna melt, a patty melt, and two Arnold Palmers please."

"You've got it," Kai says, writing it all down. "Anything else?"

"No," Mona says. "We're good. Thanks, Kai."

They stare at each other for a few seconds of awkward silence before Mona can't take it anymore. "So, what's Rudy up to?" she asks, turning to Lucas. "Luc—uh, Jack—Rudy is Kai's younger brother, and he is *so* cute."

"How old is he?" Lucas asks. "I always wished I had a younger sibling . . . or any siblings, really."

Kai looks a little taken aback by the earnest comment. "He's nine," Kai says. "Uh, anyway, I'll go put that order in."

"*Babe?*" Mona asks as soon as Kai isn't in earshot anymore. "What was that? We're not pretending in front of anyone right now."

Lucas just stares back at her, an amused look on his face.

"*What?*" she demands.

He takes a long sip of his water, seemingly enjoying how the wait makes her squirm. "He doesn't just like you," Lucas finally says. "You like him."

Mona flashes him a sly smile. "So what if I do? You jealous or something?"

Lucas smiles back, his eyes squarely on hers. "Do you *want* me to be jealous?"

"Whatever," Mona says, taking a sip of her water to make sure he can't see the corners of her mouth curving upward.

"Let's change the subject. You ready for the game tonight?"

Lucas shrugs. "Why wouldn't I be?"

Mona scoffs. "Um, I don't know, because it's our first official outing as a couple and you're, like, having a mental breakdown today? Not exactly the ideal circumstance going into two hours straight of professional cameras pointed in our faces, fan pictures, jumbotron footage, media box commentary, and endless tabloid dissection the next day. . . . I mean, don't get me wrong. *I* will be fine. I'm a pro. But are you up for pretending at that level?"

Lucas flashes her an unbothered smile. "I don't have to pretend. And honestly? I don't think you do either. We've got a vibe, Mashad. Whether you choose to admit it or not."

"A tuna melt and a patty melt," Kai interrupts just as Mona's face goes pink, sliding their orders onto the counter. "And two Arnold Palmers."

"*Yum,*" Mona says, grateful for the distraction. "Thanks. Hey, by the way, are we still on for your place tomorrow night?"

Kai's face lights up. "Yeah," he says. "How does seven sound?"

Mona's mouth spreads into a wide smile. "Sounds great. Need me to bring anything?"

"Nah," Kai says. "I've got it covered."

"Hmm," Lucas muses as Kai walks away. "A seven o'clock hang tomorrow night at his house? Forgive me, I'm not much of a surfer, but I don't believe people take nighttime surfing lessons at their instructors' houses."

"*Fine,*" Mona concedes. "If you must know, Kai asked me on a date. And I said yes. Not that it's any of your business."

"I mean, it *sort of* is my business," Lucas says as he takes a bite of his fries. "You're literally going on a date with this guy after you chewed my head off for hooking up with someone."

"Oh, *please*," Mona says. "Spare me. I chewed your head off for getting a *hickey*. Hickeys are public. Nothing about what I'm doing with Kai is public. We're going on a date at his house. Nobody will ever know."

Lucas smiles, that amused look back on his face. "*I* know."

"For someone who's not my boyfriend," Mona says, pausing to take a bite before continuing, "you sure do seem jealous."

"No, actually," Lucas says, his voice so chill it could pass for Meesha's. "I've thought about it. And I'm not."

Mona scoffs. "Oh, really? Tell me more about how not jealous you are."

Lucas shrugs. "I mean, I'll admit. Seeing you blatantly like someone else right in front of me isn't exactly *paradise*. But I realized I have nothing to worry about. You and I are clearly endgame. If you want to hook up with a hot surfer and I want to hook up with a couple girls at school before our happily ever after, that's perfectly fine with me."

"Oh, trust me. You've made it perfectly clear that you're more than fine with hooking up with 'a couple girls at school,'" Mona says with a chuckle. "But Kai and I are not just hooking up. We actualy like each other. We're going on a *date*. It's different."

"Sure, whatever," Lucas says, that infuriatingly confident

smirk on his face. "Do what you need to do. When all is said and done, it's gonna be you and me, babe. I know it in my bones."

Mona rolls her eyes. "Can you read that text from your coach again or something?" she asks, reaching over to grab the patty melt from his plate. "I miss sad, mopey Lucas."

Chapter 22

Confessional

INT. MARY MASHAD'S OFFICE—AFTERNOON (CONT'D)

MARY

Forget Mona and Lucas. That was a big night for our entire family. Me, Melody, Axle, Josie, Mona, Meesha, Matt, *and* Louise, Timmy, Carol, and Scott Sanderson. Then, of course, Lucas. Not to mention, Ali was such a huge Lakers fan. After he died, they vowed to keep a courtside seat open at every game in his honor. They seated all of us in a row next to Ali's honorary seat. The images weren't just front-page news. They were museum-worthy.

"You okay?" Josie whispers to Mona as they sit courtside. "I know this is a lot."

Mona looks out at the thousands of faces staring at her and Lucas from the stands. It's not like she's much of a basketball person anyway. But she hasn't processed a single second of this game. All she can see is all the people seeing *her*. All the photographers crouched down on their knees getting good shots—not of the players—but of *her* every interaction with Lucas. Usually, this sort of attention would fuel her, each click of the camera encouraging her to give them an increasingly worthwhile show. But tonight, something feels . . . different. Off.

"Be careful," Mona says, covering her mouth as she whispers back to Josie. "Sometimes they have lip readers to try to figure out what we're really talking about."

"What?" Josie whispers back, this time covering her mouth tightly. "That is crazy! Shouldn't there be, like, a law against that or something?"

"SANDERSON!" the commentator exclaims before Mona can respond. "Spinning it up and in. Incredible shot, just before halftime."

"As you can see here, this is a very special night for the Los Angeles native," the TV commentator chimes in from behind them as the camera pans over the Sandersons. "His entire family has come out to support him this evening."

Carol and Scott wave excitedly as Mary nudges for Timmy and Josie to follow suit.

The camera starts zooming in on the Mashads as the other TV commentator adds, "It's a sentimental night here at the Staples Center as the Mashad women have also shown up to support the star athlete, sitting right next to the seat perennially left empty in honor of the late Ali Mashad."

"For those of you who don't know," the first TV commentator adds as the camera starts zooming in on the Mashads. "Because of the tight friendship between their parents, Pete Sanderson grew up incredibly close with the Mashad family. He's now dating Meesha Mashad and, actually, Josie Lawrence—love child of Ali Mashad—is now dating Pete's little brother, Timmy Sanderson."

Mona looks over as Josie's face turns bright red, Timmy wrapping a reassuring arm around her shoulders. Josie *hates* when they refer to her as Ali Mashad's "love child." And Mona can't blame her. She's a living, breathing person. Not the result of some scandal.

"But, of course," the other commentator adds, "there's only one couple everyone is talking about tonight. Mona Mashad and President Jordana Sterling's only child, Lucas Sterling."

The crowd goes wild as the camera zooms in on Mona and Lucas, flashing their image up on the jumbotron.

Lucas grins widely as he puts his hand on her knee. "Will you loosen up?" he manages to say without moving a singular muscle on his face.

Mona tries her best to force a smile but falls short. She looks up at the thousands of fans cheering, some even crying, screaming about how much they love them. Then looks over at the empty seat in honor of her dad. Suddenly, the room is spinning. At first it's slow. Like, it's just wobbling a bit. Then it's fully circling around her, a blur of adoring fan faces and tributes to her late father swirling around her like some sort of sentimental cyclone.

"I need a minute," she whispers back to Lucas, getting up and rushing into the hallway.

"Mona!" Mary exclaims from her seat as she speeds past her. "What are you doing? Boro besheen. Hanooz daran feelmet ro meegeerand." *Sit down. They're still filming you.*

Confessional

INT. MARY MASHAD'S LIVING ROOM—AFTERNOON (CONT'D)

MONA

My mom does that sometimes. When everybody is staring, and she has to say something. She'll just say it in Farsi. People still wind up translating. But it at least buys us some time before the world figures out whatever she was saying.

"I have to go to the bathroom," Mona snaps back at her mom, careful to make sure the cameras see her excuse. "Chill."

Mona can't even make it all the way through the hallway into the bathroom. Her breath gets increasingly shallow until she finally looks around to make sure nobody is watching, slides against the wall and has a seat right there on the hallway floor.

She has no idea how long she's been sitting there when Lucas comes over, taking a seat next to her. "Hey," he says. "I thought you were going to the bathroom."

"So did I," Mona says, her voice small. "I couldn't make it."

"You ever had one of these before?" Lucas asks.

Mona stares at him confused. "One of what?"

"A panic attack," Lucas says, gently placing a hand on her knee. "I think you might have just had a panic attack."

"Oh," Mona says, nodding slowly, her breath now nearing its normal rhythm again. "That makes sense. No. I've never had one. I thought I had one once after Max and I broke up. But that was nothing compared to this. For a second there I thought I was gonna die."

"I know the feeling," Lucas says. "I get them from time to time. They're awful."

They sit there quietly for a little while, Mona still trying to get her breath back to a state of total normalcy.

"It was just a lot," she finally says. "When Pete invited us, I knew the whole *you* aspect would be a lot. But I forgot about that seat for my dad. And then I kept staring at the seat. Then up at the fans. Then back at the seat."

Mona pauses when she feels her breath catching again.

"He really loved me," she eventually continues, her voice now cracking. "I mean, obviously he was my dad. He had to love me. But he *really* loved me. He would always say I was a star. I had all this personality. That I was going to take the world by storm."

"He was right," Lucas says, his voice soft. "Mona, you are so influential that the president of the United States is asking you to fake-date her son to win an election. You are the biggest star in the *world*."

"But that's not what he meant," she says through sniffles. "I mean, listen, I always put on a show. Play it up a little for the cameras. But I feel like I've crossed some sort of point of no return. That girl they're all cheering for out there? She's not *me*. The real me, the version that he loved so much, would never lie to anyone, let alone the entire world. She'd never agree to parade around some fake relationship to juice her numbers. I just wonder . . . like, if he was still here, how disappointed would he be?"

The last part barely makes it out of Mona's mouth before her sniffles turn into sobs. Lucas says nothing, just quietly rubs her back until her tear ducts go dry. "Listen," he finally says. "If you want to call this whole thing off, I'll respect that."

"Really?" Mona asks, making a feeble attempt at a laugh as she looks up at him. "I thought you were *loving* this whole setup."

"Honestly? The truth is, even when you hate me, I kind of love spending time with you," Lucas admits. "But seeing you like this . . . nothing is worth this. I don't want to torture you."

Mona thinks about it for a minute, her gaze hyper-focused on that little heart-shaped amber speck in his left eye. For weeks, this has been all she wanted from him. An out. And here he is giving it to her. So, why does the thought of finally deleting this lying, cheating, entitled nuisance of a guy from her life feel like . . . this? Like there's suddenly 10 percent less oxygen in the room?

"No," Mona eventually answers, letting out a long exhale. "My own show is all I've ever wanted. For better or worse, this is the only way to get it." That's part of the truth, the unspoken part being she's suddenly realizing she might not quite hate having this lying, cheating, entitled nuisance of a guy in her life as much as she thought she did.

Lucas plays it cool, just barely suppressing one of his megawatt smiles. "All right," he says, offering her an arm as they both get up. "Then let's do this."

Mona pauses in front of him, suppressing a smile of her own as she clutches onto his arm. "Then let's do this."

"Are you okay?" Meesha asks Mona as she and Lucas walk onto the court arm in arm. "Pete made, like, six shots you two missed."

"We're *fine*," Mona says, settling back into her seat next to Josie's. "I just had to go to the bathroom."

"So did I," Lucas says. "There were super long lines."

Timmy looks at them, confused. "I was just in the bathroom. There were no lines."

"Oh God," Meesha says, covering her mouth. "Did you guys just hook up? Ew!"

"Why ew?" Melody asks. "That's fun! *Hot.*"

Josie and Lou both shoot Mona confused looks.

"We didn't hook up," she says, laughing. "We just had to go to the bathroom at the same time. Really."

"Hey," Lucas says, pointing up at the jumbotron. "It's us."

Lucas wraps his arm around Mona, and she settles her head against his shoulder, smiling as she gives the cheering crowd a relaxed wave. Just before the camera moves away from them, Lucas bends down and plants one sweet kiss on top of her head.

✦ ✦ ✦

Confessional

INT. VALLEY HIGH SCHOOL SENIOR HALLWAY– AFTERNOON (CONT'D)

LOUISE

I was so confused.

JOSIE

Same. I don't know what happened when they left but they came back looking . . . I don't even know what the word is here.

LOUISE

In love. The word is *in love*.

JOSIE

Technically that's two words. But yeah. Lou's right.

Chapter 23

Mona doesn't know what's been up with her the past couple days. First, her weird panic attack at the basketball game yesterday. Now, she's standing outside Kai's front door feeling like her stomach just hopped on a Tilt-A-Whirl. Her phone buzzes with a text from Lucas, You ready for your big date?? Mona rolls her eyes, letting out a small laugh. He really is relentless in every sense of the word. NONE OF YOUR BUSINESS, she types back before stuffing her phone in her Loewe tote. She looks down at the colorful knit Missoni maxi dress she has on, a smidge embarrassed by how many outfit attempts it took to land on this look. *Is* she ready for her big date?

The truth is she's been bugging out all day. She begged Majid to wait in the car instead of coming in with her like he normally would. And now she's been standing outside Kai's front door, incapable of knocking, for almost five minutes. "This is ridiculous," she mutters to herself. It's not like she hasn't been on dates before. She's casually dated half of Hollywood. Why is she being so weird about this particular date? She squares her shoulders, lets out a giant exhale like she's about to walk onto the stage at an award show, and gives the pale blue front door a knock.

"Hey," Kai says, opening the door in jeans and a plaid flannel button-down.

So far she's only ever seen Kai in his Lucky's uniform, sweats, or his wetsuit. Jeans and a plaid flannel button-down are probably formal attire as far as he's concerned. And the effort instantly melts Mona's heart.

But something feels off. It's his energy. A little more chilly. Guarded. "Hey," she says, forcing a smile. "I, uh . . . brought a gift." She digs her hand into her tote and fishes out a bottle of Newman's Own Caesar dressing.

Kai accepts the bottle coolly, a tight smile on his face. "Thanks," he says, heading inside. "That'll actually go great with what I had planned for us tonight."

Mona follows along, her nerves building, as he leads her into the kitchen. There, she sees he has two flattened chunks of pizza dough laid out on the table alongside bowls of red sauce, shredded mozzarella, pepperoni, sausage crumbles, peppers, onions, and mushrooms waiting for her.

The sight instantly makes Mona smile. Again, the effort tugs at her heart. Maybe the weird energy is just standard first-date nerves.

"I was thinking we'd do a make-your-own-pizza night," Kai says, gesturing toward the table. "I have everything laid out here. And the oven is already preheated. All we have to do is top our pies and pop them in."

"Fun!" she exclaims, plopping down on one of the seats. "I've never made pizza before. Honestly, I've never made *anything* before. I don't think I'd even know how to fry an egg."

"Really?" Kai deadpans. "I'm shocked."

"Hey," Mona says. "Watch it with the sarcasm. I bet I would be a *great* chef if I gave it a whirl. I just haven't gotten around to it."

"Well, this will be a good start," Kai says, looking her up and down. "You want an apron? Your outfit looks kind of . . . fancy."

Mona opens her mouth to tell him that, of the thirty-six outfits she tried on, this was actually her dressy casual option. But then she shuts it. Probs better to play it at least somewhat cool. "No," she says with a shrug. "I'm fine."

"Suit yourself," Kai says, sitting across from her. "So, what are you thinking for your toppings?"

"I'm thinking everything," Mona says as she smears a large dollop of sauce onto her hunk of dough. "I've always been a more-is-more kind of girl."

Kai chuckles as he carefully spreads a small bit of sauce onto his crust. "I'm the opposite," he says. "All about the minimalism. I'm thinking just cheese."

"Just *cheese*?" Mona asks, appalled. "Come on. How could anyone be so boring?"

"I don't see it as *boring*," Kai says. "I see it as pure! Simple. There's something beautiful about that to me."

Mona looks up at him, enjoying the way his dimples crinkle around his mouth when he smiles. And suddenly she's not thinking about why she was so nervous or whether or not his energy seems off. She's just here, enjoying her time with him. For the next half hour while they craft their pizza pies, they just talk. Like, it sounds so unbelievably corny to say they get *lost in conversation*. But that's sort of exactly what happens. Mona conveniently leaves out what she's currently doing to get it, but she tells him about her plans for her own show. How she's finally going to have the chance to tell her story her way. Kai tells her his plans to go to community college nearby. He got into San Jose State and briefly considered going there, but he figured community college made more sense money-wise. Plus, he'd miss his family too much up there in Northern California. They talk about Rudy, who's at his best friend Julia's house tonight. Then they talk about Kai's parents, who are out at a karaoke bar for their date night this week, which somehow leads them to talking about how Mona would just about die if her mom ever dated again. Even though she knows a boyfriend might be the only thing to get her mom to be a little less obsessed with work and thus a little less obsessed with *her*.

It feels like they just sat down when Kai tells her he's done with his pie. "So, how's yours coming along?" he asks. "I think I'm all set."

"I think I have a sort of lasagna situation going," Mona says, adding another layer of cheese on top of the mushrooms. "I might be a while."

Kai laughs. "That's fine," he says. "I've got nowhere to be. I can wait." And for a while they sit there quietly as he watches Mona build upon her increasingly high mountain of toppings.

"Okay," Mona eventually says, dumping the entire bowl of sliced peppers on top of her pie as the final touch. "And *fin*."

"Huh?" Kai asks.

"And *fin*," Mona repeats. "Like, it's done."

"Oh," Kai says with a laugh. "All right, cool. Let's pop them in the oven."

Kai takes both pizzas and carefully places them in the hot oven.

"These should be done in, like, twenty," he says. "Want to go hang on the patio while we wait?"

"Sure," Mona says, following him out the sliding door. Once they make it outside, she sees he already has two folding lounge chairs set up for them, this time with a small plastic table in between. On the table is a mason jar with a single yellow daisy in the center.

"Whoa," Mona says, taking a seat in the foldout chair. "Did you set this up yourself?"

"It was nothing," Kai says with a shrug, flipping a switch so that the string of Christmas lights lining the cement wall turns on. "Here. So we don't have to eat in the dark."

Mona smiles at the twinkling string of colorful lights. She knows he's lying. This isn't the *only* way for them to not eat in the dark. She's been on this patio after dark before. There's plenty of light that comes in from the living room.

"Kai," Mona says, taking a seat on the folding chair. "This is amazing. I love it."

Kai takes a long look at her, and Mona notices something shifts. Like she's watching in real time as his heart balloons, then deflates. The weird energy is back.

He sighs, taking the seat across from her. "Okay, I didn't want to do this. But I have to ask you something or it's going to keep bugging me."

Mona's heart speeds up a bit. "What's up?"

"Did you lie to me? When you said you weren't dating the president's son?" he blurts out. "The guy you brought into the diner. That was him, right?"

Mona gulps. "Yeah, that was him but— "

"No," Kai stops her. "Don't do that. Don't give me a 'yes, but.' Just give me a straight answer. Please. What's going on, Mona?"

Kai's phone starts blaring one of the signature elevator-jazz tunes that seem to come with every iPhone. "Pizza's ready," he says, getting out of his seat. "Be right back."

Mona sits outside, chewing the inside of her cheek as she decides whether she's really about to break an NDA with the leader of the free world for this hot, painstakingly sweet boy and the patio he carefully decorated for her.

"I know you don't want a complicated answer," Mona says when he comes back with the pizzas. "But the fact of the matter is the answer *is* complicated. So, do you want it or not?"

Confessional

INT. MARY MASHAD'S LIVING ROOM—AFTERNOON (CONT'D)

MONA

I told him everything. About coming home from the diner the day that I met him. The ambush from my mom and President Sterling. The numbers. The offer for my own show. All the planned appearances. Everything.

PRODUCER

Weren't you worried? That he was going to tell?

MONA

No. Kai is just . . . implicitly trustworthy.

"So, you have to spend all of your time pretending to date this guy who humiliated you?" Kai asks. "That's brutal."

Mona shrugs. "It's not that bad. He's grown on me recently, to be honest. We've kind of become friends at this point."

"Isn't that sort of his thing?" Kai says, carefully cutting his pie into little slices.

"What do you mean?" Mona asks.

"That's how he gets away with everything, isn't it?" Kai asks. "I mean, you know the guy better than I do, but from the outside it seems like he makes these massive errors in judgment, then sort of charms his way out of them."

Mona pauses for a second, a little taken aback by how right Kai is. Lucas *does* that. She's always known he does that. It's how saps like Piper wind up in never-ending loops with him.

You give him an inch; he swipes your whole heart. It's why she vowed to completely cut him off the first time he lied to her. And yet, here she is, falling for the very routine she's so carefully been avoiding. Yesterday's slip-up can't happen again. It *won't* happen again.

"That was a dumb thing to say," Kai says, interrupting her thoughts. "Sorry. I spoke out of turn. I hardly know this guy. Who am I to judge? Let's just . . . talk about something else."

Mona smiles at Kai, more than happy to stop thinking about Lucas as her eyes settle on the bright yellow daisy sitting in the mason jar between them. "Why a daisy?" she asks.

"The reason is kind of dorky," Kai says, his face turning red. "Promise not to make fun of me?"

"Promise," Mona says, taking a forkful of her lasagna-style pizza.

"Okay," Kai says. "Well, I saw that daisy and it sort of reminded me of you. The color is just so . . . bright. Bold. It sort of commands your attention. But in the best way. Like, you can't miss it. And once you spot it, you can't help but instantly feel a bit happier than you were before you did."

Mona's whole life has been narrated by other people's definitions of her. The good, the bad. She's heard all of it. And, after a while, she sort of just became desensitized to it. What's one more opinion of you when you've heard millions?

But Kai's opinion somehow manages to matter. Maybe it's what she's learned is his no-nonsense way of presenting compliments like they're objective truths. Maybe it's just that she's come to not just like him, but respect him. And so she cares what he thinks of her. Whatever it is, his words manage to break into a part of her heart she was sure was impenetrable. Mona smiles, her gaze now on his. "That's really nice," she says quietly.

"I meant it," Kai says, sending shock waves vibrating

through Mona's whole body as he leans in closer. "Mona, do you mind if I— "

"Please," she answers before he can finish the question.

Then he leans across the small table and kisses her on the lips. It's a gentle kiss. A peck, really. And yet, Mona feels dizzy. Giddy. Like cartoon hearts might start shooting up out of her head.

"Hey, Kai?" she asks once they're both back in their seats, quietly eating their pizzas.

"Yeah?"

"I'm really glad you asked me out."

Kai smiles sheepishly. "Me too."

Chapter 24

Confessional

INT. MARY MASHAD'S OFFICE—AFTERNOON (CONT'D)

MARY

This was it. The biggest appearance on their schedule. Meesha's New York fashion show, debuting her new couture collection. It was going to be a who's who of the fashion and entertainment industries with a red carpet leading into the event at the Highline Hotel. We decided this is where Mona and Lucas would make their red-carpet debut. It felt fitting a few days after the courtside pictures went so viral.

"Knock, knock," Lucas says, letting himself into Mona's suite at the Crosby Street Hotel. "You almost ready?"

"Wow," Mona's hair stylist Jamie whispers as she secures a final bobby pin into Mona's updo. "He's even hotter in person."

Mona watches wordlessly as Lucas casually plops himself down on the colorful striped couch across from hers. Unfortunately, Jamie is right. He looks absurdly hot in the bleach-white tee he's paired with the black Ralph Lauren suit she knows the brand personally sent him. But Mona can't let that distract her. The goal of tonight is to make him re-dead to her. It's her only choice. Look what happened after she was nice to him for *one* day! Now he's just casually letting himself into her hotel room unannounced and telling her how good she looks, like they're some sort of married couple. This is exactly how guys like Lucas suck you in. How they slowly build your trust brick by brick, just so they can eventually run a bulldozer through it.

Well, not on Mona's watch.

"What are you doing here?" Mona asks Lucas, chilling her voice to the most freezing temperature she can muster. "I thought we were meeting in the car right before the event."

"Yeah, but I got ready early, so I figured I'd just head over to the hotel now," Lucas says. "Then I ran into your mom in the lobby and she gave me a key."

Mona flattens her mouth into a straight line. "Okay, well, I think we should just stick to the original plan. I don't know what you're going to do just hanging in my room for the next hour."

Lucas stares at her quizzically. "Are you not ready?"

Mona's makeup artist Joaquin laughs loudly. "Oh, honey,"

Joaquin says. "*No*. I haven't even started contouring her."

"Well, I don't mind waiting," Lucas says with a shrug. "I've got nothing else going on. I'll just hang here and do some homework on my phone or something until you're ready."

"Or maybe we should just stick to the plan," Mona says again, this time making sure her eyes are set directly on his. "And meet later."

Lucas looks at her, confused. "Um, all right," he says. "I guess I'll just see you in an hour then."

"Good," Mona says, careful to erase any semblance of disappointment from her expression as she watches him walk away. "See you then."

"Girl, that was *cold*," Joaquin says once Lucas is out of the room.

"Yeah," Jamie agrees. "What was that about? You two in a fight or something?"

"No," Mona lies. "No, we're fine . . . I just needed some me time before the big debut."

When Mona eventually makes her way through the mob of fans and paparazzi shouting her name outside the hotel, the black car is already parked outside waiting with Lucas inside of it. The small glimpse of him sitting in there once Majid opens the car door sends the already crazed fans into a full frenzy. They're screaming, chanting for them to kiss.

Mona looks out at them, seamlessly snapping into Mona Mashad mode. "Will you guys have some *chill*?" she jokes with a sly smile and a wink. Lucas plays along, rushing out of the Escalade to help Mona into the car, his chin gently grazing the top of her head as he wraps both of his perfectly sculpted arms around her waist. It feels good, him holding her like this. And that infuriates her. How is it possible that someone so emotionally dangerous can make her feel *this* physically safe? What is wrong with her wiring?

"Oh my *God*," Mona hears a tween girl gush behind her. "He is such a gentleman." An older woman, likely her mom, agrees. "Now *that* is the kind of man you marry."

Mona does her best not to snort. If only they knew.

Lucas flashes her an easy smile once the door shuts behind them, pulling a disposable out of his pocket. "Mind if I take one? BTS of our first official *red carpet*. Exciting stuff."

"Sure, whatever," Mona says, barely making eye contact with him—let alone his camera.

Lucas snaps the shot, then puts the camera back in his pocket, he and Mona each staring out their respective windows as an increasingly uncomfortable silence builds between them.

"Are we good?" Lucas finally asks, turning to face Meesha. "Because it feels like we're not."

"I don't see why we would be *good*," Mona says, her eyes still staring out the window as they pass a Calvin Klein ad featuring Meesha in a pair of baggy jeans and a bra. "You're still a lying, cheating jerk."

"*This?*" Lucas asks. "We're still on *this*? Are you going to rake me over the coals until the end of time because I messed up *once*? I had a girlfriend when my celebrity crush since I was ten years old waltzed into my life. Even when I brought you to that event, I didn't think I actually had a *shot*. Then I did. And I took it, even though I still hadn't dumped Piper. That's on me—"

"Yes," she says before he can continue. "That *is* on you. Once a cheater, always a cheater."

"I just don't get what's happening right now," Lucas says, rubbing his temples. "I thought we were past this. After the Lakers game, I thought we were finally in a good place."

"Yeah, you thought you suckered me into your little web again," Mona says, making eye contact with him for the first time as the car pulls up in front of the red carpet. "And I almost fell for it. But no. This—what we have going on here—is strictly a business arrangement."

Lucas stares at her, his normally warm hazel eyes frozen. "Fine by me."

They sit there silently for a few more beats, the weight of everything they just said hanging heavily in the air between them until the driver swings open the car door revealing a swarm of fans so large it makes the mob outside of Nobu look like an intimate gathering.

✦ ✦ ✦

Confessional

INT. MARY MASHAD'S OFFICE—AFTERNOON (CONT'D)

MARY

I got a final head count after the event. Ten thousand people were crowded outside to see them get out of that van. *Ten thousand* people.

✦✦✦

"MONA! LUCAS! MONA! LUCAS!" The crowd is cheering their names so loudly that Mona can hardly hear herself think. Like clockwork, she flashes them a wide smile and gives them a confident wave. Lucas dutifully wraps his arms around her, the same way he did earlier outside the Crosby Street Hotel. But his touch feels different now. Colder. More distant. *Good*, Mona tells herself. Cold and distant is *good* when it comes to Lucas Sterling.

She's repeating that last sentence in her head like some sort of mantra Axle would force upon her at a meditation retreat when Meesha comes rushing over on the red carpet, Pete by her side. "I'm so glad you're here," Meesha says, clutching tightly onto Mona's forearm. "Anna Wintour just showed up. I might puke."

"You'll be fine. Just look how hot my dress is," Mona says, sending the crowd into hysterics as she does a twirl in her sheer black gown. She turns to face Meesha. "You *made* this."

Mona looks at Lucas, half expecting him to make some sort of comment about how fantastic she looks. But he doesn't. "Hey, dude," he says to Pete, his eyes not even remotely on Mona's. "Great game the other night."

If that's how he wants to play it, *fine*. She can ignore like the best of them. Mona looks around the carpet, turning to face Meesha. "Where's Mom?"

"She's backstage with Josie trying to pump Louise up before her big modeling gig," Meesha says. "Lou's nervous, but I think she'll be fine. She was crushing it at rehearsal."

Mona is about to ask if she has time to pop backstage to wish Lou luck when the crowd erupts into squeals as Axle and Melody step out of their sprinter van.

"Hi!" Melody exclaims, ignoring the crowd as she rushes toward her sisters. "Meesh! I can't believe it's here! The big show!"

"Don't remind me," Meesha says, nervously biting her lower lip. "I'm so nervous."

"Well, being nervous just means you care," Melody says. "And that's okay."

"Meesha," Axle says when he catches up to the group. "The dress you have created for my Melody is exquisite. It is divine. It is the most magnificent piece of art I have ever laid my eyes upon."

"Axy," Melody says, smiling. "I'm blushing."

They all look at Melody's backless satin emerald-green gown, the fabric hitting her toned body in exactly the right places.

✦ ✦ ✦

Confessional

INT. MARY MASHAD'S LIVING ROOM—AFTERNOON (CONT'D)

MONA

I mean, she looked great. Meesha killed it with the design. But *magnificent piece of art*? That was a bit much.

✦ ✦ ✦

"A PICTURE OF ALL THE MASHAD SISTERS!" one of the photographers calls out. "SISTERS! GET TOGETHER!"

The guys step back as the three sisters scrunch in close, each settling into their signature poses—Melody, a giant, radiant smile; Meesha, a chic scowl; and Mona, a sexy smize—as the photographers snap the thousands of photos that will be plastered all over the internet in a matter of seconds.

"NOW WITH THE GUYS!" another photographer calls out. "GUYS, GET IN THERE!"

The guys shuffle in, each wrapping their arms around their respective dates.

"It was your date, wasn't it?" Lucas whispers in Mona's ears as he wraps his arms around her. "I can't believe I'm just realizing now. You went on a date with that guy last night. And now you hate me again. It was the date. That's why you're turning on me. Because you went on your date and now you feel guilty getting along with me."

"I have nothing to feel guilty about," Mona hisses back.

"LUCAS AND MONA, OVER HERE!" another photographer calls out. "WE NEED MORE OF THE TWO OF YOU!"

Mona and Lucas break away from the group, Mona's smoldering smize turning more into a Meesha-style scowl as Lucas holds her close. "Sure, you do," he whispers. "Because getting along with me makes this real."

She turns around, the crowd going wild as she wraps her arms around his neck and whispers into his ear. "Have you ever for a second considered the fact that my negative feelings toward you might just simply be because you're a gigantic douche?"

"Honestly?" Lucas asks, sending the crowd into hysterics again as he twirls Mona around. He pauses for a minute, smiling widely at the cameras before whispering in her ear. "No."

"YES!" one of the photographers shouts out. "THIS IS GREAT! HUG AGAIN AND WHISPER IN EACH OTHER'S EARS!"

Lucas embraces Mona tightly. "It's wild what a high horse you sit on," he whispers. "You ripped me a new one for just hooking up with another girl during this . . . arrangement. Now you're going on a date with another dude pretending like you're this absolute saint. And I'm somehow still the one in the wrong. Even as you toy with that poor guy's heart like it's a new car your mom got you for your birthday."

"I'm not *toying* with Kai," Mona whispers. "What I have with him is real. Unlike *this*."

She turns around, sending the crowd into an absolute uproar as she smiles widely, her head resting against Lucas's chest.

"COME ON, YOU TWO LOVEBIRDS," Melody calls out from the end of the carpet. "THE SHOW IS ABOUT TO START."

✦ ✦ ✦

Confessional

INT. MARY MASHAD'S LIVING ROOM—AFTERNOON (CONT'D)

MONA

The show was . . . I mean, you've all seen the reviews by now. It was iconic. It's a weird feeling realizing your sister might be a legit creative genius, you know? Every single look was unlike anything I had ever seen before. Not to mention the fact that Lou absolutely killed it for her runway debut. I swear I even saw Anna Wintour's jaw drop at one point.

PRODUCER

That clip of you at the end of the show went *so* viral.

MONA

[*laughs*]

Yeah, I was fully unwell. Screaming and sobbing so loudly that I lost my voice. I couldn't help myself. I was so proud.

PRODUCER

How did you all celebrate after?

MONA

We had an *epic* party at Casa Cipriani.

PRODUCER

Did Lucas come?

MONA

[*pauses*]

No.

INT. HARVARD MEN'S LACROSSE LOCKER ROOM—AFTERNOON (CONT'D)

PRODUCER

Why didn't you go?

LUCAS

I don't know. It was a long night, and we had an early morning the next day. I wasn't really in a party mood.

Chapter 25

Confessional

INT. MARY MASHAD'S LIVING ROOM—AFTERNOON (CONT'D)

MONA

The Ralph Lauren thing just happened sort of by accident. Lucas was wearing that Polo baseball cap I gave him before we got out of the car in Nobu, remember? Well, the pictures went so viral that Ralph Lauren sold out of the caps in every color. So, Ralph got in touch with my mom and President Sterling about Lucas and I being the faces of this new campaign he wanted to do releasing a limited edition capsule of his classic American flag sweater.

PRODUCER

And the campaign was shot in the Hamptons?

MONA

Yeah. The day after Meesha's show. The vibe was tense, to say the least.

"Remind me again why we had to drive together," Lucas says, his eyes hyper-fixated on the road ahead as Mona drives her old Range Rover down Montauk Highway toward the Sterling family's East Hampton estate. "Honestly, you're probably still drunk. This whole thing is a horrible idea."

Mona nods toward the people snapping pictures of them on the side of the road. "*That* is why we're driving together," Mona tells him. "And Majid made me take eight Breathalyzer tests before I got in the car. I'm *more* than fine to drive."

They sit there for a few quiet beats before Mona can't help herself. "Why didn't you come last night anyway?" She keeps her eyes on the road ahead, hoping it makes the question come off as casual. Nonchalant. Like it hasn't mildly plagued her for the last twelve hours.

Confessional

INT. MARY MASHAD'S LIVING ROOM—AFTERNOON (CONT'D)

MONA

I get it. I told him to back off. But, like, isn't not backing off his whole *thing*? What if his not showing up was, like, a cry for help or something! I was just doing my due diligence.

"Huh," Lucas says, his hand on his razor-sharp chin as he feigns pensiveness. "I'm no expert here, but that sounds like a *personal* question. And, according to you, this is a business arrangement. Correct?"

Mona rolls her eyes, refusing to dignify his snark with a response. So, they drive a few more miles in silence until Mona has to pull the car over on the side of the road, the four security cars tailing them obediently following suit.

"No," Lucas says. "You cannot be puking again. You realize people can see you."

"Who cares?" Mona says, rushing out of the car to puke on a patch of hydrangeas outside the Bridgehampton Citarella. "It's *relatable*."

Two girls walk out of the grocery store and hand her a seltzer. "Not to be creepy but we're *huge* fans," one of the girls, a tall blond, says to Mona. "You seemed like you were going through it, so we got you this."

The other girl, a shorter brunette, points to her own seltzer bottle. "We're also struggling today."

Mona wipes the last bit of puke off her face and flashes the girls a smile, accepting the bottle of seltzer. "I feel *seen*. Thank you."

"Duh," the brunette says, lowering her voice to a whisper

to add, "Wait, be real with us. Is that Lucas Sterling in your passenger seat?"

Mona looks over to where Lucas is staring out at them from the car, visibly confused. "Yep," she says. "That's him."

"I *cannot*," the blond says. "You are living the dream."

Mona laughs. "Something like that."

"You're not actually going to drink that are you?" Lucas asks when Mona gets back in the car. "It could be poisoned. Or roofied or something. Those girls were strangers."

"I would drink straight anthrax if it would make me feel better right now," Mona says, taking a large sip out of her plastic bottle of lemon Hal's. "But thanks for the concern."

They drive the next fifteen minutes in total silence until Mona pulls the car into the long driveway leading up to the famed Sterling family estate.

"So, are we going to talk about last night?" Lucas asks once Mona puts the car in park. "At all?"

"I don't see what there is to talk about," Mona says, focusing her attention on the small brown shingled guest house behind him to avoid having to look at Lucas directly. "I think we both made our stances pretty clear."

"Fine," Lucas says, unbuckling his seat belt. "I'll see you inside."

"Fine," Mona says, downing the last sip of her seltzer, then flashing him a smile. "See? Still not dead."

Lucas shakes his head, opens the car door, and walks over to where the Ralph Lauren team is waiting to greet them alongside Mary and President Sterling at the front door.

Mona sits in the car a few beats longer, not yet ready to get out.

✦✦✦

Confessional

INT. MARY MASHAD'S LIVING ROOM—AFTERNOON (CONT'D)

MONA

I had no idea President Sterling was going to be there. And let me tell you: Doing a photoshoot hungover with your fake boyfriend who you hate is already a nightmare. Add polite small talk with the president of the United States into the mix and it's literal hell.

✦✦✦

Mona exhales into her hands, checking her breath for signs of the many tequila-flavored puke sessions she had on the car ride over. "*Ew*," she mumbles, sifting through the dashboard for a mint. "This is bad."

Just as she's considering swallowing a rogue dusty Tic Tac she found under a pile of takeout napkins, Mary opens the car door. "For the love of God. Do not eat that disgusting old Tic Tac," she says, pulling a pack of Listerine breath strips and eye drops out of the mint-green alligator Birkin she reserves for the Hamptons. "Here. Have these."

"Thanks," Mona says, popping a strip into her mouth.

"Melody said you had to take me home last night. Are you mad?"

"Yes," she says matter-of-factly. "I was worried about you."

Mona has to squint to make it out, but she notices Mary's eyes watering just a small bit. Ali was all emotion all the time, but Mary's always dispersed her small snippets of emotion like this. In brief, blink-and-you'll-miss-it glimmers. It doesn't take a psychology major to tell you why. Mary grew up in one of Iran's wealthiest families, her loving parents regularly sending her to Europe and America to attend fancy boarding schools and summer camps. Then the revolution happened. Mary was in Paris at a summer camp when she got the call. Not only had they seized all of her family's considerable assets, but they had murdered her parents. She showed up at her aunt and cousin's apartment in Los Angeles an orphan without a penny to her name. And as much as she loved him and as wonderful as he was as a father, Mona has to acknowledge the fact that Ali *did* eventually cheat on Mary and conceive Josie with that very cousin, the only family Mary had left after her aunt died. Then, of course, that cousin tragically died in a car crash while she and Mary were still not on speaking terms. And the kicker? Ali died shortly thereafter, leaving Mary with three kids and a media empire to maneuver on her own. The woman's life hasn't exactly been a walk in the park. She had to harden any of her soft edges to survive.

So, if she pays enough attention to catch it, in a moment like right now, for example, Mary will say something casual like this, just six words: *Yes, I was worried about you.* Her voice will be flat, casual, totally collected. But her eyes will tell the real story. In there, Mona can see the pain flicker through. And it's just *so much* pain. It's every heartbreak she's ever had, plus the one Mona just nearly put her through. All in one look.

Mona's eyes hang low. "I'm sorry."

"No time for apologies," Mary says, the glimmer of sadness gone so quickly Mona wonders if she imagined it. "Mona, the *president* is here to greet you personally. Your hangover does not take precedence in this situation. Come on."

"Fine," Mona groans, unbuckling her seat belt. "I'll suck it up."

"And by the way," Mary whispers as they march toward the Sterling family front door, "whatever is going on between you and Lucas, *squash it*. These people are shooting a campaign based on your *love*. Your *love* is what's going to sell sweaters."

"Don't you think the fact that I don't *love* him might be an issue?" Mona whispers back.

"Oh, please," Mary says, laughing. "You spent the entire car ride home last night yammering on about him."

"What?" Mona asks, her face crimson. "What was I—"

"Mona!" President Sterling exclaims, swinging the door open before Mona has a chance to finish the question. "How are you, sweetheart?"

"President Sterling," Mona says, trying her best to ignore the wave of nausea and flash her a large grin. "I'm doing . . . well. Thanks so much for coming out today. I heard you missed a speech in Michigan to be here!"

"I was thinking about you two shooting this campaign here

and I just thought, 'You know what? Michigan can wait,'" she says with a smile. "Come on, let me give you a tour of the house while the Ralph Lauren team sets up out on the beach."

The giant shingle house with its white trim and rosebushes lining the sides is stunning. And the interior even more so. It's got the same homey feel that the Sterling family town house in the West Village had, but this time with a coastal Nancy Meyers–esque twist. Lucas and President Sterling take Mary and Mona through the house room by room, stopping to share little anecdotes, highlight sweet old family photos, tell them about any old memories. It's not until they're all huddled up in Lucas's favorite room, the darkroom he and his dad used to use as part of their photography studio, that they get the text that Quincy, the creative director from Ralph Lauren, is ready for them out on the beach.

"Now, Lukey," President Sterling says, slapping on a megawatt smile so bright it could only compete with that of her son's, "remember what we talked about when you're out there."

Lucas rolls his eyes. "Got it."

Mona and Lucas make their way through the expertly decorated house, past the large pool area, toward the beach, where the photographers are waiting.

"So I take it your mom just gave you the same speech mine did?" Mona says, before they set foot on the sand. "Look in love?"

"Yep," Lucas says. "Not sure how we're supposed to do that given the current circumstances. But I guess we can try."

Mona sighs. "Worth a shot."

"Hi," Quincy says as they approach him and the camera

crew. "Quincy Adams. Creative director for this shoot. It's an honor to meet you both."

"Thanks," Mona says, shaking Quincy's hand. "Honor to meet you, too."

"Same here," Lucas says. "This is actually, uh, my first *fashion* photoshoot. So, go easy on me, okay?"

Quincy gives a reassuring laugh. "I have a feeling you're going to be a natural. I've got hair, makeup, and costume set up in your pool house. Why don't you two get ready and meet me back out here in an hour?"

When they both step out, Mona is wearing her cream American-flag sweater half tucked into a pair of boyfriend jeans. She's got on makeup and her hair is very much done, but it all looks minimal. To the naked eye, it would look like she rolled out of bed like this (and not with vomit crusted on the side of her lip).

For his part, Lucas is wearing a men's version of the same sweater in navy over a chambray button-down shirt and a pair of khakis. His chestnut locks have been gelled just enough to look strategically messy.

Confessional

INT. MARY MASHAD'S LIVING ROOM—AFTERNOON (CONT'D)

MONA

[*sighs*]

Yeah, fine. What do you want me to say? He looked great.

✦✦✦

"You two look *perfect*," Quincy exclaims as Mona and Lucas, both barefoot, step back onto the beach. "Now, here's what I'm thinking. You roll up your jeans, put your feet in the ocean and just talk. I'll stand back here and get the shot from afar."

"Sounds good," Mona says, making her way toward the shore.

"Yep," Lucas says, following suit.

The two are standing at the shore, awkwardly staring at each other. "So, what do you want to talk about?" Lucas asks. "Since you apparently think we have nothing left to discuss."

Mona rolls her eyes. "We *don't*," she says. "And by the way, I'm not toying with Kai. You said I was toying with him last night. That's not true."

"COULD YOU TWO GET A LITTLE CLOSER?" Quincy shouts from where he's standing with the photographer about twenty feet away from them. "THESE ARE LOOKING A LITTLE . . . TENSE."

They inch closer to each other. "Okay," Lucas says with a shrug. "I believe you. You happy?"

"I mean, it would make me happy if you actually *meant* it," Mona says. "You clearly don't."

"Why do you care what I think anyway?" Lucas asks. "I'm just a lying, cheating jerk, right?"

Before Mona can respond, Quincy is marching over to them. "Okay, so this body language isn't really translating great on camera," he says. "Lucas, how about you come behind Mona and just hold her while the two of you stare into the ocean?"

"Sure," Lucas says, halfheartedly wrapping his arms around Mona's waist. "This work?"

"Hmmm," Quincy says, staring at them intently. "Not quite. Mona, why don't you rest your head on Lucas's chest? And, Lucas, you rest your chin on her head."

Quincy circles around them, considering their pose from every angle. "Okay," he says. "Better. Let's give a few a try this way. And remember. Just . . . relax. The way you were in those photos outside Nobu. Or at the Lakers game. Those were great shots."

"For your information," Mona whispers, "I *don't* care what you think. You were just being annoying, and I wanted to set the record straight."

"Great," Lucas whispers back. "Consider the record straightened."

"You have a weird thing with Kai," Mona says. "You said you're not jealous. But you're *clearly* jealous of him."

"I'm honestly really not," Lucas says. "I know it's not what you want to hear right now. But I stand by what I said at the diner. As irritated by you as I am in this current moment, I still think you and I are endgame. So, please go ahead and have your fun with Kai or whoever else it is in the meantime."

Mona turns around, fully aware that she's breaking Quincy's instructions. "You see? *That* is what I'm talking about," she says. "*You and I are endgame*. Stop feeding me with stupid lines. I'm not some dumb groupie you met at a party."

"You're right!" Lucas exclaims, exasperated. "How are you

not getting it? You're *not*. That's what I'm literally trying to tell you here."

"Okay," Quincy says, rushing over. "How about we just take a break for a minute? A little breather. Sometimes it takes a bit to get into the groove for these things."

"Fine by me," Lucas says, storming up toward the pool.

"Same here," Mona says, sitting on the shore.

Confessional

INT. MARY MASHAD'S LIVING ROOM—AFTERNOON (CONT'D)

MONA

I love the ocean. We scattered my dad's ashes in the ocean out in Malibu and, no matter where I am in the world, I like to think he's close by when I'm near an ocean . . . maybe that's why I was excited to learn surfing.

[*pauses*]

Before the haters come for me, I know Malibu is on the Pacific Ocean and East Hampton is on the Atlantic Ocean. I'm just saying every ocean makes me think of him.

Mona has been sitting there silently staring out at the ocean for nearly a half hour when Lucas comes back with Quincy.

"I had a new idea," Quincy announces. "I saw Lucas

tinkering with his little disposable camera up there. So, I suggested he try taking a few snaps of you to include in the campaign. It could be fun."

"With a disposable camera?" Mona asks, an eyebrow skeptically raised. "Not sure that's going to translate well on a billboard."

"I agree," Lucas says, pulling something out of his pocket. "That's why I brought this. My dad's old film camera."

"Let's just give it a try," Quincy says, walking back toward the crew. "I'll leave you two alone."

"So, what do you want me to do?" Mona asks, turning toward Lucas as he crouches down next to her. "Do I look at you or the ocean?"

"Listen," Lucas says, setting the camera down. "If we're going to get one decent shot, we need to clear the air here."

"I have nothing to say," Mona says, turning her attention back toward the ocean.

Lucas sighs. "Fine, then I'll go. That night at Harvard haunts me. Even when I'm thinking about other things, I'm thinking about it. It's constantly playing on a loop in the back of my mind like some sort of sadistic new soundtrack to my life. The night I got you and lost you all in the span of ten minutes. The world's worst magic trick. I blew it. I know I blew it. And if you think you hate me for it, trust me, I hate myself a hundred times more."

He pauses for a beat, letting a loud wave crash onto the shore in front of them before continuing. "If what I did means you can only stomach me in your life as a business acquaintance until I can earn your trust back, I understand. That surfer guy is probably more deserving of you anyway. He didn't lie to you. I did. I get that. But I won't apologize for saying things like we're endgame. Trust me, I've got plenty of lines. That's not one of them."

Mona lets her eyes meet his. He looks at her in a way she's never been looked at before, like she's a work of art on display for a limited time only. Like she's going to evaporate any minute and so he must memorize every detail of her face—of her entire existence—before she does.

She stares back at him stunned, blinking quickly as an unexpected wave of tears pushes up against the backs of her eyes. "Now," she says, her voice barely audible. "Take the picture."

Lucas doesn't respond, just holds her gaze for a couple brief seconds. Then he grabs his camera from the sand and snaps a picture.

Chapter 26

"It's just stunning," President Sterling says, more to herself than anyone around her. "It's so . . ."

"Intimate," Mary finishes the sentence for her. "It's incredibly intimate."

"Yes," Leslie Smart, editor in chief of *Elle*, agrees. "It looks less like an advertisement and more like art."

"She's fully dressed, more so than many other photo shoots she's done," their family friend and French designer Delphine says. "But she somehow still looks naked. Like she has stripped all of her defenses away."

"That's what love does, doesn't it?" British fashion critic Jones McLaren chimes in. "It strips you of all your guards and just leaves you there, raw in front of the person you care for."

"It's not *just* love though, is it?" John Allen, fashion editor at the *New York Times* says. "There's a pain in her eyes. A heartbreak. A hesitation."

"But is all of that not part of what it is to experience love?" Leslie says. "This photo is love . . . and everything that comes with it—the fear, the vulnerability, the intimacy. All wrapped up into one breathtaking image."

Mona stands a few feet behind them, considering the picture for herself. The raw emotion in the photo is palpable. There are no tears in Mona's eyes, but it's like you can just *feel* them trying to make their way out. And the inscription, *Mona Mashad: As Shot by Lucas Sterling*, scribbled across the bottom tells the viewer everything they need to know. It's iconic. And, of course, Mona knew it would be.

Even before Lucas developed the pictures and Quincy was so happy he declared they had to unveil the campaign at this last-minute party at Mulford Farm tonight, Mona knew. A lifetime spent as Mary Mashad's daughter trains you to have a sixth sense for these things. You're never fully in the moment. Never just feeling a feeling. In fact, even now, Mona couldn't tell you *what* she was feeling in that moment. It was a mix of a million different things she can't quite yet put words to.

But what she *could* do is what she's always done. Float up and out of her body and consider the real-life moment from above, flashing forward to the fan reactions, the headlines, and the brand partnerships that could stem from it.

<u>Confessional</u>

INT. MARY MASHAD'S LIVING ROOM—AFTERNOON (CONT'D)

PRODUCER

How did you and Lucas leave things off after the shoot?

MONA

We didn't, really. What he said was so heavy. I just . . . didn't have the words to say anything back. We wrapped up, I went home with my mom to get ready. And then I saw him again at the party.

"You know what we really captured, right?" Lucas asks, walking over to her from where he was standing across the sprawling garden.

Mona rolls her eyes. "You better not say *love*."

"It's the vibe that you insist we don't have," Lucas says. "At its core, there it is. The vibe. People can *feel* it. That's what makes the picture so good."

Mona chuckles, her gaze shifting back toward the picture. "I still don't think I can trust you," she says, her voice so soft it's barely audible. She's spent all afternoon thinking of how to respond to everything he said to her before snapping that picture. This was the best she could do.

"I get that," Lucas acknowledges with a solemn nod, before adding with his cocky grin, "and I'm still going to try to change your mind."

"You really are relentless," Mona says with a laugh, her

eyes still stuck on the photo and the crowd of people ogling it. Usually it's cut-and-dried for Mona. There's Mona, the person. And there's Mona Mashad, the megastar. It's easy to separate one from the other. But every once in a while, there are moments, like this picture, that blur those lines.

Confessional

INT. MARY MASHAD'S LIVING ROOM—AFTERNOON (CONT'D)

MONA

Not to get all meta and philosophical here but it's just like . . . What happens when something starts as a vulnerable moment but then you commodify it? Which version of yourself is left then? You know what I mean?

She cocks her head to the side. "Did you ever watch the show *Hannah Montana* growing up?" she asks Lucas, her eyes still on the picture.

"No," he says. "The old Disney show, right?"

"Yeah," Mona says. "She lives a double life, half pop star, half normal teen. Do you ever feel that way? Like there are two versions of your life?"

"Sometimes," Lucas admits. "Yeah."

"Same." She opens her mouth to offer further explanation,

then shuts it. Outside of her sisters, Lucas might be the only other person who actually gets what she means here. "How do we know which version is the real us?"

"I don't know," Lucas says with a shrug. "I sort of think it's all just us, right? I mean, we don't have to be just one thing."

Before she can respond, Mona hears a glass clink. She looks up, spotting Quincy standing in front of the giant ad with a champagne glass in hand.

"This was *not* on the itinerary," Mary whispers as she marches over to Mona. "I hate when people go off book."

"Don't I know you do," Mona whispers back.

"Excuse me, everyone," Quincy says. "I just wanted to thank you all for coming here tonight. Mona, Lucas, if you could join me up here, I would love to say a few words about this shoot."

Mona takes a sharp inhale, cognizant of the hundreds of high-profile eyes glued on them. She looks at the picture, the one they're all so entranced by, and her heart picks up speed. It's not just her standard Mona Mashad show this crowd is expecting from her. It's *that*. She has to live up to *that*. And she's not sure if she quite has *that* in her right now.

"You coming, babe?" Lucas asks, his hand reached out toward hers.

Mona didn't realize she was frozen.

"What are you doing?" Mary whispers. "Follow him."

"Coming, babe," Mona coos, snapping herself out of it. No time for overthinking.

She dutifully lets his giant hand engulf her tiny one, smiling for the crowd as she follows Lucas up to where Quincy is standing. "I have done many high-profile shoots over the course of my over thirty-year-long career," Quincy says. "Those of you who know me know that I don't often say much at these sorts of events. But I simply had to take a moment to say this was one of the most beautiful moments of my career. Watching the way this young man really *sees* this young woman. Watching the way she allows herself to just be seen by him . . ."

Mona resists the urge to roll her eyes as Quincy tears up. "It was just incredibly beautiful," he concludes, his voice cracking. "So, thank you both for allowing me—and now the world—to bear witness to what you share."

"You know," Lucas says, looking at Mona as he speaks into Quincy's mic. "I told Mona from the moment I met her that there's something special here. A certain vibe we share. I'm glad we have that on film." Lucas flashes Mona one of his annoyingly cocky smiles as the crowd bursts into variations of *aww* and, before she can quite figure out how to best react for the crowd's sake, she finds herself laughing, giving him one of her patent eye rolls. It's just her natural, knee-jerk reaction. Not really a show. But it also sort of works. She looks like the adoring, bashful girlfriend. The crowd eats it up.

"Now, I know Ralph has a fabulous dinner laid out for us inside the barn," Quincy says, taking the microphone back from Lucas once the crowd finally stops their applause. "What do you say we all head inside for a feast?"

The crowd cheers, all heading into the barn like an obedient herd of incredibly well-dressed sheep.

"You coming?" Lucas asks, reaching a hand toward Mona.

"I think I'm going to go to the bathroom," she says. "I had to miss Josie's high school graduation to be here, I want to call her to say congratulations."

"Mona, stop beating yourself up about that," Mary says. "Josie told us she did not want any of us there. Too much attention."

Mary's right. Josie made it abundantly clear she didn't want to make a big deal of her graduation. But Mona wanted to show up anyway, maybe in some sort of disguise.

Confessional

INT. MARY MASHAD'S LIVING ROOM—AFTERNOON (CONT'D)

MONA

When Josie entered our family, everyone expected us to be mad or, like, mean to her. Especially me. But honestly? I was excited. It was like we got a bonus piece of our dad back. Now I can't really even imagine what life was like before she was one of us.

"I have to pee anyway," Mona tells Mary. "I'll just try her while I'm in line."

Mona walks over to the fancy trailer full of bathrooms

they have parked outside and dutifully takes her place at the end of the line, pulling out her phone to FaceTime Josie while she waits. She tries twice before she gets a text, I'm still here at the ceremony! Love you! Mona quickly writes back: I wish I was there!!!!! She catches up on her thread with her sisters, which has upward of a hundred unread texts. Mona's hardly been on her phone all day. After dozens of texts about Josie's graduation, it seems as though the conversation in her group text with her sisters has shifted toward the photo shoot. Are you kidding me with this picture?????????????????????????? Melody wrote in the group text along with a picture of the ad Mary had presumably sent them earlier. MONA, IT'S INCREDIBLE. Meesha chimed in, Wow. This is going to be huge. I've never seen you look like that on camera. For her part, Josie emphasized Meesha's and Melody's texts, then separately sent Mona a group text with Lou on the side, Okay, we're confused. Is this still fake? Mona quickly writes back, YES! Enjoy your graduation. Love you both.

She's still sifting through her texts when she's interrupted by the girl in front of her in line, "AHEM." Mona looks up to see Piper, dressed in a camel-colored turtleneck with a tan belt and a pair of white linen shorts. "I have to tell you something," she says, hands on her hips.

"Honestly, Piper?" Mona says, suppressing a yawn. "It's been a tough couple days for me. Can we not do this right now?"

Piper ignores her, instead looking around them to make sure

the people ahead of them in line are too lost in their own conversations to hear before continuing. "Listen, Lucas is probably the most infuriating person I could have chosen to fall in love with . . ."

It takes all the might Mona has in her not to hit her with an *Amen*.

"But I've known him practically my whole life," Piper continues. "I know when he's lying and when he's not. I thought what he was doing with you was some dumb fad. It's why I weaseled my way into this event tonight, to get him back. But I saw the way he looked at you. He's never looked at me that way. . . . He's never looked at *anyone* that way. Whatever it is he feels for you—and let me be clear here, I don't get it—it's real."

Mona cocks her head to the side, trying to fully process what Piper just said. "Why are you telling me this?"

"Because you win," Piper says, her glassy eyes giving away her cool voice. "I'm not going to stand in the way of something real. . . . I can't do that to him."

Mona nods, standing quietly for a beat before speaking again. "My ex was also infuriating," she admits.

"Yeah," Piper says. "I think I've read about him."

"Right," Mona says. "Well, I just wanted to say, when I was still in love with him, I would have *never* done what you just did. You're a good person."

Piper smiles. "Thanks."

✦ ✦ ✦

Confessional

INT. MARY MASHAD'S LIVING ROOM—AFTERNOON (CONT'D)

PRODUCER

Did you believe her?

MONA

I mean, I believed that she was telling me *her* truth. And I respected her for doing it. I meant what I said. I would have never had the guts to do what she did when I was still obsessing over Max.

[*pause*]

But we have to consider the narrator here. This is a girl who he's successfully manipulated a million times over. Her buying what he was selling wasn't exactly a golden seal of approval.

Chapter 27

Confessional

INT. MARY MASHAD'S LIVING ROOM—AFTERNOON (CONT'D)

PRODUCER

So, the date with Kai. How did it end?

MONA

We made plans for my next surf lesson for the day I got back from the Hamptons, then he gave me a kiss on the cheek good night, and I went home. It was all pretty G-rated, honestly.

✦ ✦ ✦

"You ready to give the ocean another shot?" Kai asks, grinning widely as Mona makes her way over to where he and Rudy are posted up on the shore in their matching wetsuits.

Mona smiles, instantly happy to see him. "Depends," she

says, turning to Rudy. "Those buttheads aren't going to be giving us any more trouble today, are they?"

"*Please,*" Rudy says. "Ever since they realized you and I are friends, each of their moms has called my mom asking for a playdate."

Mona shakes her head. "Social climbers are the *worst.*"

"Agreed," Rudy says. "It's, like, I've *always* been cool. Now that I'm best friends with a celebrity you're suddenly getting it? That's a you problem, buddy."

Kai laughs. "Yeah, joke is on them," he says, his attention shifting to where Mona is fumbling with the Velcro cuff around her right ankle. "You need help there?"

Mona covers her mouth as she lets out a small yawn. "No, I'm good," she says, finally securing the cuff. "Just tired."

When she agreed to meet Kai for this lesson, she didn't exactly take into account the fact that she would be both physically and mentally exhausted. And surfing lessons—while incredibly fun when they're with your practically perfect crush/instructor and his little brother who is slowly but surely becoming one of your favorite people on the planet—are still a lot of work. What Mona really needed today was to be horizontal. Not to be fighting for her life in the ocean. But she can hear Mary's voice in her head. *Mashads* never *cancel their engagements. It doesn't matter if you're on your deathbed, you show up.* It's the one rule Mary and Ali actually agreed upon. Even when he was on his *literal* deathbed, Ali would tune in for Zoom interviews and film scenes for the show.

So, anyway, this is all to say, canceling today was not an option as far as Mona was concerned.

"You sure you're up for a lesson today?" Kai asks, his eyes squinted with concern. "I know you just got back from that photoshoot thing."

Rudy nods enthusiastically. "Yeah," he says. "On the drive here, like, four of the billboards we drove past were being replaced with that picture Lucas took of you."

Mona inches closer toward Kai's ear, her heart racing a bit. "You didn't tell him . . ."

"No," Kai whispers back. "I figured that was a secret."

Mona flashes him an appreciative smile before turning back toward Rudy. "Okay," she says, clapping her hands together. "Rudy, you're usually on top of this stuff. Where do we begin today?"

"Well," Rudy says. "First things first, let's see if you can get situated on your board without any instruction."

Mona lets out another small yawn, then places her board on the ocean. "Please. Give me a *challenge*."

Kai and Rudy stand behind her, both examining her technique with their arms crossed on their chests as Mona takes a leap and goes for a confident plop on her board.

Confessional

INT. MARY MASHAD'S LIVING ROOM—AFTERNOON (CONT'D)

MONA

I wiped out, hard. It was brutal. I went too far forward and nose-dived right into the sand beneath me. Then the board flipped over behind me, and I was all tangled up with it because of the stupid cord thingy. It was a nightmare.

✦ ✦ ✦

"Your first real wipeout!" Kai exclaims, reaching his hand up for a high five as Mona comes up for air. "Congrats."

Mona spits out a mouth full of sand, leaving Kai's hand dangling. "*Ew,*" she says. "I hated that."

"Yeah, wiping out isn't the most fun. Why don't we take a little break before getting back out there?" Kai asks, turning toward Rudy. "Hey, dude, you know where my keys are, right? Can you go grab those sandwiches we packed?"

"You've got it," Rudy says, dutifully grabbing Kai's keys from the quilted blanket they have laid out on the sand and heading toward the parking lot. "Be right back!"

"Come on," Kai says, gesturing toward Mona once it's just the two of them. "Let's chill for a bit."

Mona follows Kai back to shore and watches carefully as he unzips the top part of his wetsuit, revealing his almost cartoonishly chiseled six-pack of abs. She knows he's no longer Hot Surfer in her phone, and she's glad he's not. Kai's kind, trustworthy, and walks around with this sort of quiet confidence that instantly puts anyone at ease. . . . He's so much *more* than just some hot surfer. But he does also happen to be painfully, almost comically good-looking. Mona lets her eyes settle in on a sand dune in the distance to avoid completely staring as he pulls a neatly folded beach towel off the blanket for her.

"Want a towel?" he asks, nodding toward Mona.

"Oh, uh, sure," Mona says, slowly unzipping the bright orange zipper on her sleek navy wetsuit to reveal the skimpy Versace string bikini she has on underneath. Now it's Kai's turn to pretend not to stare. Mona tries to suppress a smile as she watches him gulp hard.

It takes her an annoyingly long time to actually get the stupid wetsuit off, but once she does, she lets her eyes meet Kai's. "Can I have that towel?" she asks, a small smile on her face as she watches him stand there almost frozen at the sight of her in this bikini.

"Oh, of course," he says, snapping back to life. "You want me to—" He takes a step closer to her, towel in hand.

"Sure," Mona answers before he can finish the question.

Kai delicately wraps the big fuzzy towel around her body, letting his muscular arms linger around her for just barely a moment longer than absolutely necessary. It's brief. And even if there was someone on this empty beach who was able to snag a picture, it would register as nothing. Just a friend quickly helping another friend out. But between the two of them, the moment feels special in the way that every small point of physical contact feels special when you have a new crush on someone.

"So," Kai says, taking a seat on the blanket. "Is everything okay? Whenever I'm wiping out like that it's usually because something deeper is bothering me."

Mona looks at him apologetically. "I feel like I'm always dumping my drama on you."

Kai shrugs, a small, kind smile on his face. "I don't mind."

"Okay" she says with a sigh. "Well, this past weekend was

confusing. Things between Lucas and I are just . . . tough. And weirdly intense. But then not at all. And the whole thing is just draining."

"I mean, I've never been in one myself," Kai says, "but being in a fake relationship does sound like it would be taxing."

"It *is*," she says, her eyes shifting downward. "And, um, also this time of year is just always tough for me. It's kind of this weird thing my family does. Next week, on June tenth, we all get together to remember my dad."

"That's not weird," Kai says. "Was it his birthday? Or the day he . . . ?"

"Died?" Mona asks. "No, it's neither of those. That's what's sort of weird about it. If he was a normal person, if we were a normal family, I'm sure we'd be able to do this on those days. And I mean, we do. But he was just so famous. It feels like we wind up mourning him alongside the rest of the world on those days. It's not really about *our* grief when we have to go speak at the Ali Mashad Memorial Parade or host the *Ali Mashad Memorial Special* on TV. You know?"

"I can't say I know firsthand," Kai says. "But that makes sense."

"Yeah, so, a couple years after he died, we decided we would pick a day to mourn him that could be just us," she says. "June tenth is the day we settled on. He always said that was the most perfect day of the year. I honestly love the ritual, but I always get a little . . . weird leading up to it. Now, combined with the whole fake-relationship situation, I guess I'm feeling extra weird."

"BACK WITH THE SANDWICHES!" Rudy shouts from

across the beach, proudly holding up three brown paper bags as he runs over toward them.

"THANKS, BUDDY," Kai yells back, then turns back to Mona. "I have an idea."

"Let's hear it," she says, intrigued.

"I think we should do something fun," he says. "You free Friday? One of my friends is throwing a party. Why don't you come? Hang out with normal people at a normal party and just . . . let loose for a bit."

"You think everyone would be cool?" she asks. "No pictures or anything?"

"I've known most of these people since I was in diapers," Kai reassures her. "They're all cool."

Mona thinks about it for a minute. "You know what? Sure. I'm in. I'm doing an appearance with Lucas on *Late Night with Amira Norris* on Friday promoting the ad campaign, but that shoots earlier at, like, five. I'll come right after."

"No rush," Kai says. "Party shouldn't start until nine or ten anyway."

"Perfect," Mona says with a smile. "A *real* party with a *real* boy I *really* like. I can't wait."

Kai smiles back, practically beaming. "I never expected you to be such a cheeseball."

Chapter 28

"Do you both think this is fine?" Mona asks, pointing toward her sequined nude Ralph Lauren maxi dress. "To wear to a normal high school party?"

Josie and Lou look up at the outfit from where they're seated across from Mona on the couch in the dressing room at the *Late Night with Amira Norris* studio.

"It's *perfect* for a late-night-show appearance," Lou says enthusiastically. "But I don't know if it's right for a normal high school party."

"Yeah, I mean, throughout my entire high school career I only attended one party," Josie says. "So, I'm by no means an authority here. But do you have anything more . . . casual you could change into?"

Mona sifts through the rack of clothes her stylist Allison left for her to pick from. "Okay, so maybe I keep this dress on for the appearance, then I change into this?" She pulls out a long-sleeved turquoise catsuit.

"Not quite," Lou says, getting up to sift through the rack herself. "How about something more casual? Like, maybe these jeans and . . . this red top?"

"I'm into it," Mona says, nodding in agreement. "With some gold jewelry? Gold hoops, a gold watch. Simple."

"Yes," Lou says. "Perfect."

"And you two will come with me, right?" Mona begs more than asks. "Please."

Josie bites her lip nervously. "I don't know, Mona," she says. "Are you sure you want us coming with you? Like I said, I've only been to *one* party. I'm not sure I'll be much help."

Lou sits back down on the couch, giving Josie a playful nudge on the shoulder. "Come on, Mona *needs* us," she says. "We'll be there."

Mona lets out a sigh of relief. "Thank *God*," she says, double-checking her freshly applied glam in the mirror. "You two are the only people I know with even a slight connection to normalcy. I need you with me."

Louise narrows her eyes. "You like this guy, don't you?" she says. "That's why you're so nervous. You're into him."

Mona takes a seat in the swiveling vanity chair and spins until she's facing Josie and Lou. "Circle of trust?" she asks. "Whatever I say here doesn't leave this room."

"Of course," Josie says. "What's going on?"

"I went on a date with him the other night," she says. "Before I went to New York. And I think I really like him."

"Mona," Josie says, her voice panicked. "But what about Lucas?"

"What *about* Lucas?" Mona asks. "You two know that's all a sham."

"You say that," Josie says. "But then every time you're with him . . . there's something there. You have to admit it."

"Even if it's *not* a sham," Lou adds. "The whole world is now fully obsessed with the two of you together. What happens if someone sees you with Kai? The backlash would be awful."

"Nobody will see anything," Mona says. "My world with Kai is completely separate from all of this. We just, like, hang at his house."

"And at a public beach," Josie says. "Where anyone could take your picture."

"Not to mention the party we're about to go to," Lou adds. "With a bunch of random strangers from his school."

"It's a *local-only* beach. There's never anyone there," Mona says. "And he said he's known the people at the party since he was a baby. They're all cool."

"Does Lucas know about him?" Louise asks.

"I don't see how that's relevant, considering we are not even dating at all," Mona says, avoiding eye contact with Josie and Louise before fully answering. "But yes. If you must know, he does know about Kai. And it's annoying. He accused me of *toying* with him the other night."

"Which him?" Josie asks. "Lucas or Kai?"

"To be fair, you're sort of toying with both," Lou notes. "Right?"

"I am *not*," Mona insists. "I like Kai! Only Kai! And I've been clear about that to Lucas."

"Maybe in your *words*," Josie says. "But you have a certain . . ."

"Vibe," Lou finishes the sentence for her. "When you're with him. There's a vibe. Everyone can feel it. I know you feel it."

"Can everybody stop saying that?" Mona asks with a sigh. "There's no vibe."

"There's definitely a vibe," Josie says. "He really likes you. It's obvious. I sort of feel sorry for him."

"If you both remember correctly, the guy cheated on his girlfriend with me," Mona says. "Then showed up to a family barbecue at Melody's house with a *hickey* from another girl shortly after launching this fake relationship. He's not exactly crying himself to sleep every night."

"Fair," Lou says, nodding toward the hallway just outside the dressing room door. "Is he here now?"

"Yeah. He's got his own dressing room down the hall," Mona says, hesitating before adding, "You know something weird? The *producer* had to tell me that. He didn't tell me himself. Usually, he's blowing up my phone, but I haven't heard from him once since I got back from New York."

"Maybe he's giving you some space," Josie says. "That's good, right? Since you like Kai?"

"Yeah," Mona responds a smidge too quickly. "It's *great*. All I've wanted from him."

Josie and Lou stare at her unconvinced.

"What?" Mona asks. "It *is*. . . . Let's talk about something else. Wait! Josie, whatever happened with you and Timmy finally doing it?"

Josie turns bright red.

"Oh my *God*," Mona says. "You did it!"

Lou looks over at Josie, a silent exchange happening between them before she speaks. "Not exactly."

"I thought I was ready, then the time came and I just . . . wasn't," Josie explains, her head down. "I mean, I just had my first kiss a few months ago, you know? It felt like a lot!"

Mona nods. "I get that. So, how did Timmy react? Are you two—"

Before Mona can finish her question, there's a knock on the door. "Ms. Mashad," the producer Beatrice says, from the other side of the door. "You're up."

Mona sighs. "Just when the conversation was getting interesting," she mutters, turning her attention back over to Josie. "I am getting *every* detail after my appearance, okay?"

"Fine," Josie groans. "But really. There's nothing scandalous to tell. It weirdly still wound up being this perfect, romantic night."

"Excuse me?" Mona asks as she makes her way out the door. "*Perfect, romantic night*? We are absolutely circling back."

Once in the fluorescently lit hallway, Mona follows Beatrice over to the area just off the stage where Lucas is already waiting. "Now, Mona, you've been on this show so many times before," Beatrice whispers. "You're good here, right?"

"Yep," Mona says. "Thanks, Beatrice."

"Of course," she says, turning her attention toward Lucas. "And I hate to be such a fangirl here but that picture you took . . . it's *magnificent.*"

"Thanks," Lucas says, flashing her his perfect smile. "I appreciate it."

"Really," Beatrice says, her attention back on Mona. "Both of you. What you created is history. We never get to see celebrities like that. So just . . . unguarded. And, Lucas, you were behind the camera, but I feel like we still somehow get so much of you, too. It's like we can *feel* you in the picture."

Mona lets out an uncomfortable laugh. "You're being too nice to us."

"Okay, okay," Beatrice says, taking a step away from them. "That's a wrap on my fangirling."

"Hey," Lucas says to Mona once they have some privacy. "You look nice."

"Thanks," Mona says, her eyes looking past him to where Amira is doing her monologue on stage. "Haven't heard from you in a bit."

"Yeah," Lucas says, his voice low. "I'm taking the hint, I guess. Giving you a little less of me. I'll see you at these events, but no more texts in between. No unplanned drop-ins or hanging around later than I need to. Just Mary's set schedule."

"Wow," Mona says, an eyebrow raised. "Dreams really do come true, I guess."

"Yep," Lucas agrees, his eyes now also focused on Amira. "Lucky you."

"I have to say," Mona says, "as truly elated as I am to hear this update, I didn't think you would give up this easily."

Lucas laughs. "Who said I was giving up? Just tweaking my approach."

"Without further ado, folks," Amira says to the crowd before Mona is able to respond to Lucas, "our first guests for the night: Mona Mashad and Lucas Sterling!!!"

Beatrice rushes back over to them, giving them both a nudge forward. "And *go*," she whispers.

The crowd erupts into cheers as Mona follows Lucas's lead onto the stage. Not just cheers. Roars. They are screaming so loudly that Mona can feel the stage vibrate beneath her nude mules.

"*Wow,*" Amira says as Mona and Lucas take their seats in the two cream boucle chairs next to her oak-wood desk. "I have been hosting this show for what? Ten years now? And I have to say I have *never* heard a crowd erupt the way this one just did. You two sure seem to have a hold on your fans."

Mona and Lucas each let out their version of a shy laugh.

"So, tell us," Amira says. "Now that we know the two of you are together, nothing has ever made more sense. But how did this *happen*? Was it the moment at the Met? We're all dying to know here."

Lucas looks at Mona, a playful smirk on his face. "You want to tell the story, babe?"

Mona looks over at the cheering crowd.

Confessional

INT. MARY MASHAD'S LIVING ROOM—AFTERNOON (CONT'D)

MONA

He thought he was messing with *me* by being so over-the-top cute and couple-y. Two can play that game.

✦✦✦

"Sure, *babe*," Mona says, flashing Lucas a wide smile. "Okay, so, it was actually *before* the Met."

She pauses, giving the crowd a moment to let out their audible gasp.

"We were at this fundraiser in San Francisco for the Iranian American Mentorship Alliance," she continues, grateful for the opportunity to quickly plug her dad's favorite charity. "And I was in the middle of a *perfectly* pleasant conversation with my parents' friends."

"Please!" Lucas cuts in. "You were bored out of your mind."

"Okay, fine," Mona admits, looking directly into the camera. "I was bored out of my mind."

The crowd and Amira erupt into laughter. Mona's been on this show enough times to know Amira has two laughs. Her real one, and her fake one. *This* is her real one.

Mona continues, energized by the feedback. "So anyway, I'm in the middle of this conversation when, out of the blue, Lucas interrupts, telling me he needs to introduce me to someone. Now mind you, I've never met this boy in my *life*."

"Which is *why* it made total sense that the person I needed to introduce you to was me," Lucas adds, cocky grin on full display as he turns to wink at the crowd. "Smooth, right?"

The crowd bursts into a resounding "*Awwwwwww.*"

Mona gives them a playful eye roll. "I mean, is it *aww* or is low-key egomaniacal?" she asks them with a laugh.

Like clockwork, the resounding "*Awwwwwww*" shifts into more fits of laughter.

✦✦✦

Confessional

INT. MARY MASHAD'S LIVING ROOM—AFTERNOON (CONT'D)

MONA

I had them eating out of the palm of my hand . . . God, I love that feeling.

✦✦✦

"Well, *egomaniacal* or not, it worked," Lucas continues, tenderly wrapping an arm around Mona's shoulders. "We wound up talking the rest of the night."

Mona watches how the audience softens at Lucas's gesture, each person in the crowd saying a silent prayer that maybe one day they'll find their own Lucas Sterling to wrap his big muscular arms around them like that. So, she does what she does best: stokes the fire.

"Now, here's the biggest plot twist," she adds to the audience, her hand now strategically clasping the one Lucas has casually draped over her shoulder. "It turns out Lucas Sterling is a closet *Making Mashad* mega fan."

"Um, excuse you," Lucas says. "There's nothing closeted about my fandom. I'm loud and proud about it!"

"Actually," Amira says, "we heard about this fandom of yours. And we decided to put together a little *Making Mashad* quiz for you, Lucas. Mona, you okay with administrating?"

Mona smiles at the cheering crowd. "Oh, I would love nothing more."

Confessional

INT. HARVARD MEN'S LACROSSE LOCKER ROOM—AFTERNOON (CONT'D)

LUCAS

[*grinning proudly*]

I absolutely smashed that quiz. And Mona made this huge scene about trying to stump me. She tore up the rest of the flash cards with the preplanned questions and said she was going off-script. And I *still* [BLEEP]ing crushed.

INT. MARY MASHAD'S LIVING ROOM—AFTERNOON (CONT'D)

MONA

[*sighs, defeatedly*]

Yeah. He killed it.

Lucas is bowing proudly as the crowd gives him uproarious applause, Mona standing back playfully rolling her eyes with her hands on her hips.

"Well, that was an absolute blast," Amira says as they sit back down, wiping tears of laughter off her face. "And before we get into this gorgeous Ralph Lauren campaign you two shot, I do have one more small request."

"Let's hear it, Amira," Lucas says. "I'm up for whatever."

"Same," Mona quickly adds. "Duh."

"Well," Amira says, flashing the picture of them from Harvard up on the screen behind her. "*This* is the first and only picture we have of the two of you kissing! What do you say you do the crowd the honor of another smooch?"

Lucas looks over as Mona's heart starts pounding hard against her chest.

"I don't know," Lucas says. "Mona isn't much of a PDA person. That picture was sort of a . . . fluke."

"Come on!" people start cheering from the audience. "Just do it!!!! Kiss!!!!!!!!!!!!!"

It's not long until all of them are chanting in unison, "KISS! KISS! KISS! KISS!"

Mona gulps, looking at Lucas, then at the camera, then at the audience.

"We really don't have to do this," Lucus whispers to her, covering his mic with his hand. "Seriously."

Mona gently covers her own. "No," Mona whispers back. "It's just a stupid kiss. Whatever. Let's do it."

"The lady has agreed," Lucas announces to the cheering crowd.

"Yay!" Amira exclaims, clapping her hands excitedly. "Let's get the kiss cam going!"

Mona and Lucas stand in front of each other, the crowd waiting in silent anticipation as the camera zooms in on them.

"Last chance to back out," he whispers to her, their faces now so close she can feel the minty chill of his breath. "You sure?"

Mona lets her eyes meet his. "I'm *sure*."

"Okay, then," Lucas says, sending far more fireworks than Mona would care to admit exploding down her spine when he takes her face in his hands. The kiss starts gentle, Lucas's hands cradling Mona's face as she wraps her arms around his neck, their lips just softly grazing each other's. But then something shifts. Her body relaxes into his as the kiss grows deeper, Lucas's arms sliding down Mona's back, pulling her in more and more tightly until their lips are fully locked. The crowd goes wild as Mona and Lucas continue kissing long after the director yells cut.

Confessional

INT. HARVARD MEN'S LACROSSE LOCKER ROOM—AFTERNOON (CONT'D)

LUCAS

It was like all of the tension building between us over the last few weeks was released in that one kiss. We just kept going and going. Honestly, I don't think we even *heard* the director yell cut.

INT. MARY MASHAD'S LIVING ROOM—AFTERNOON (CONT'D)

MONA

[*blushing*]

It was whatever. The crowd wanted a kiss. So, I gave them a [BLEEP]ing great kiss.

[*pause*]

You have to understand this is my *job*. I was doing my job.

✦ ✦ ✦

"Admit it," Lucas says as they walk offstage, the crowd still in hysterics. "That was an epic kiss."

Mona shrugs, her face still flushed from it. "It was fine."

"Oh, *give me a break*," Lucas says with a laugh. "You were into it! Just admit it!"

Before Mona can respond, the next guest—a hot guy with shoulder-length blond hair and piercing blue eyes—interrupts.

"You guys really crushed out there. Tough act to follow," he says, reaching a hand forward to shake theirs. "Liam Schroeder."

"Right!" Lucas exclaims, giving Liam's hand an enthusiastic shake. "Liam Schroeder! How's it going, man? You're starting that new show, right? About the surfers?"

"Yeah," Liam says, tucking a strand of his hair behind his ear. "It's gonna be sick, man. We're trying to find ten surfers and make them *huge*, give them each a full season documentary-style just following their lives."

"You know," Lucas says, nudging Mona, "Mona here is an amateur surfer."

"Really?" Liam asks, a surprised grin on his face. "You got any interest in coming on the show? I can't even imagine the sort of viewership a Mashad guest spot would bring us."

"Amateur surfer is *generous*," Mona says, shooting Lucas a death glare for putting her on the spot like this. "But actually . . . if you're still casting, I know someone who might be perfect."

"Cool," Liam says, handing her his card. "I'm going to be out on Surfrider beach in a couple days. Why don't you bring your friend?"

"Definitely," Mona says, slipping the card into her nude clutch.

"ALL RIGHT, Y'ALL," they hear Amira yell from the stage. "LET'S GIVE IT UP FOR PRO SURFER LIAM SCHROEDER."

"Wish me luck," Liam says, flashing Mona and Lucas a nervous smile before running onstage.

Mona takes the card out of her clutch again, carefully examining it before shooting Kai a quick text. I have a MAJOR surprise for you.

"Ooooh," Lucas whispers to Mona, glancing down at her phone. "Is Hot Surfer about to become Famous Surfer?"

"Aren't you supposed to be not talking to me?" Mona says, shooting him another death glare.

"You're right," Lucas says, giving her an unbothered smile as he walks toward his dressing room. "See ya."

Chapter 29

"Okay," Mona says, taking a deep breath as the black SUV pulls up in front of a track house a few blocks away from Kai's. "You two are *sure* this outfit is fine?"

"Yes," Louise says with confidence. "You look great."

"Like, I'll fit in?" Mona asks. "I don't want to embarrass Kai."

Josie laughs. "Mona, you are showing up to a suburban high school party in full glam," she says. "You are not going to *fit in*. But you're definitely not going to embarrass Kai, either."

"Agreed," Lou says. "You just look abnormally hot. Nobody is ever mad that their date is the abnormally hot one."

Mona turns toward Majid, who's sitting in the far back seat with Josie's security guard, Blake. "You guys are fine with hanging back here, right?" she asks, her eyes pleading. "Walking into a party with a security detail doesn't exactly scream normal."

"Blake will be in here keeping an eye on the exterior, but,

Mona, I have to come in," Majid insists. "I'll be out of your way, but your mother told me it's of utmost importance to make sure nobody sneaks photos of the three of you out here tonight."

"You told her we're coming here tonight?" Mona asks. "I purposely left it off the family calendar! Come on, Majid. Work with me here!"

"Sorry, Mona Joon," Majid says with a deep exhale. "This is for your safety and privacy."

"Fine," Mona acquiesces. "It is what it is. I'll just be the freak with a bodyguard."

"All right," Lou says, opening the door. "We going in or are we going to sit here all night?"

Mona takes a deep breath, using her iPhone camera to check her makeup. "Okay, fine," she says, pleasantly surprised by what she sees. "Let's go in."

"Hey," Kai says, a wide smile on his face as he opens the door to greet them. "You came."

"Duh," Mona says, trying not to blush. "I said I would be here."

"Well, I'm glad you made it," Kai says. "You look great."

"Thanks," she says, turning toward Josie, Lou, and Majid. "This is my sister Josie. And our friend Lou. And you obviously know Majid."

"Nice to see you, Majid," Kai says, turning his attention toward Josie and Lou. "And Josie and Lou, it's nice to meet you both. Come on, follow me. The party is in the garage."

They all follow Kai through a shag-carpet-lined hallway, until he opens the door to the party.

Confessional

INT. VALLEY HIGH SCHOOL SENIOR HALLWAY—AFTERNOON

LOUISE

[*laughing*]

The music didn't stop, but, I mean, it might as well have.

JOSIE

Yeah. Mona walked in and the whole room froze.

LOUISE

It was like God entered the building.

JOSIE

Yep. I don't think I've ever had a real-life reason to use this word, but they were *awestruck*.

PRODUCER

You two are pretty famous yourselves at this point. You don't think you had anything to do with the shock?

LOUISE

[*pauses*]

I think us *with* Mona helped build the picture. But you have to understand Mona stopped in the hallway to fix her makeup in a mirror. So, we entered the room first. It went Kai, then me and Josie, *then* Mona . . . then Majid, but at that point the crowd was already done for.

JOSIE

[*nodding*]

Yeah. We literally watched the room freeze in real time.

EXT. JUNO FRAZIER'S DRIVEWAY—NIGHT

Two of Kai's classmates—BRIANNA GARCIA, 18, and NIA BAKER, 18—stand outside the party.

BRIANNA

I mean, can you blame us?

NIA

Kai gave us a heads-up to be cool and, like, not take pictures or whatever.

BRIANNA

But *nothing* can prepare you for what it's like when she walks in a room.

NIA

Not just *any* room, either. Juno's garage! We are at parties in Juno's garage almost every weekend. It's, like, musty and gross and one time we saw a mouse running by. It's not exactly where you expect Mona Mashad to casually stroll in.

BRIANNA

And she was with Josie Lawrence and Louise Adams. I thought I was dreaming.

NIA

Same. It didn't feel like real life.

✦✦✦

It's funny. Mona strikes awe in crowds of people all the time. And, usually, she lives for it. Thrives under the circumstances, really. But something about *this* particular situation makes her uncharacteristically . . . nervous.

Mona stares back at the room full of regular-looking faces, eyes all glued to hers. "Hey," she says, offering them a patent Mona Mashad wave. "I'm Mona. Who wants to party?" From the outside, she sounds confident. Bold. Classic Mona Mashad. But, if Meesha were here, she would know to look more closely. As she stands there, every eye in the crowd still super-glued to her, Mona quickly bites the inside of her cheek and runs a hand through her luscious jet-black locks. A one-two punch of her nervous tics.

✦✦✦

Confessional

INT. MARY MASHAD'S LIVING ROOM—AFTERNOON (CONT'D)

MONA

Listen, I'm not one of those insufferable celebrities who complains about being a celebrity. I get it. My life rules. But I will say, growing up famous does leave you with a few blind spots when it comes to the "normal" teenage experience.

[*pauses*]

Let me put it like this. You know how if you grow up normally, the thought of going to a Hollywood party is exciting but intimidating? That's how I feel about going to a regular high school garage party. I've only seen them on TV.

They're all silent for a few more excruciating seconds until Mona speaks again, this time nodding toward Majid. "This is Majid. I promise he won't hurt anyone." She purses her freshly glossed lips. Another tic.

"Unless you try to hurt these three," Majid adds in. "Or take pictures. We clear here?"

The room full of stunned teenagers nods in silent agreement, their hands clutching their red Solo cups tightly. Finally, Louise marches over toward a cooler in the corner of the room, grabs a beer and yells, "Woo! Anyone down for a shotgun?"

Mona flashes her an appreciative smile as everyone excitedly starts shuffling toward the Styrofoam cooler full of beers.

"Sorry about that," Kai whispers as they follow the crowd. "I thought everyone would be more chill than *that*."

"It's fine," Mona says, attempting her most casual shrug. "I'm on TV. A little weirdness comes with the gig."

"You want one, Josie?" Kai asks, noticing Josie standing off to the side with a bottle of water. "We've got plenty."

"Oh, I'm good," Josie says. "Not a big drinker."

"Yeah," Mona tells him. "Josie doesn't drink. But she did get wasted at my eighteenth birthday party. You should have been there. It was nothing short of iconic."

"Not being there will be one of my biggest regrets until the day I die," Lou says, shaking her head sadly. "A once-in-a-lifetime chance to see my best friend drunk and I missed it."

"Ugh, it was *awful*," Josie says, burying her head in her hands. "I fell off the stage during a dance routine our sisters had come up with for Mona, and I gave her ex a wet willy."

"I told you," Mona says, grabbing a Bud Light from the cooler. "Iconic."

"Nia!" Kai calls out. "You have to meet Josie. She doesn't drink, either."

"Hey," Nia says, walking over with a bottle of water of her own. "Not to be weird but I'm a big fan. I know only the first couple episodes of your season have aired. But I'm *hooked*."

Josie gives her an awkward smile. "Thanks."

"And you and Timmy are so cute together!" Nia practically squeals. "Do you think he's, like, the one?"

"Nia," Kai interrupts with a laugh. "Chill, dude."

"Sorry," Nia says, hands in the air. "Kai, you brought three A-list celebrities to our garage party, and I'm not even allowed to take a picture. At least let me have my fangirl moment."

Josie laughs. "It's okay," she says. "I'm just happy to hear you're liking the show. I spent half the time filming that first episode completely silent because I was so terrified."

"Yeah, but that's what makes you so *relatable*," Nia says. "Like, I would be the exact same."

"Okay," Lou says, turning toward Mona, Kai, and the rest of

Kai's friends standing around the cooler, beers in hand. "Who's ready?"

"Let's do it," Mona says, turning toward Kai. "You got a key?"

"Yep," Kai says, handing her what must be the key to his house. "Go for it."

In a line, Mona, Kai, Louise, and the rest of the party each slit a hole into their beer cans, open the tabs, and start chugging. "Done!" Mona exclaims, wiping the remaining foam off her face as she throws the empty can on the ground and crushes it under her black stiletto.

"Wow," Kai says, finishing his own can a few seconds later. "I have to say I'm impressed. I didn't think there was much shotgunning going on at the fancy Hollywood parties you're usually attending."

"I kind of had a thing with a guy in the British royal family last year," Mona says. "They were weirdly into shotgunning."

Kai laughs. "You might be the least relatable person on Earth."

Mona shrugs, looking up at him. He looks dressed up again, this time in a white T-shirt, dark-wash jeans, and an open gray shacket. "You look nice tonight."

"You don't look so bad yourself," Kai says, a bashful smile on his face. "I can't believe you actually came."

"I told you I would," Mona says. "And you were right. This is exactly what I needed. Uncomplicated fun."

"Good," Kai says. "By the way, are you going to give me any more details on this surprise you have for me?"

"Nope," Mona says. "But you are going to *die*."

"Whoa," Kai says. "Really not worried about overselling here, are we?"

"Not even slightly," Mona says. "This is a great surprise."

"Mona!" Louise calls from the beer pong table set up in the center of the room. "Come on, let's play a round."

A guy standing by Lou with curly hair and dimples smiles mischievously over at Mona and Kai. "Kai, what do you say we take these two down?"

"Let's do it," Kai says with a smile. "Mona, this is my friend Joey, by the way."

"Hey, Joey," Mona says, walking over to stand next to Louise on the far end of the plastic foldout table. "Looking forward to beating you."

"Wait," Lou whispers to Mona once they're standing side by side. "Have you ever played beer pong before?"

"*Yes,*" Mona whispers back with an exasperated sigh. "Why do you all assume I've never partied before?"

"Trust me," Lou says with a laugh. "Nobody on Earth thinks you've never partied before. I just, like, wasn't sure if there's beer pong at the *types* of parties you go to."

Mona rolls her eyes, grabbing a ball, and immediately sinks it into one of the red Solo cups on Kai and Joey's side. "Trust me," she says. "I've played beer pong."

Lou and Mona continue crushing Joey and Kai for three straight rounds until Kai gives up. "I quit," he says with a laugh. "You two are too good. I'm not going to be able to walk by the end of the night if we keep playing you."

"Come on, man," Joey insists. "I think we could have had them the next round."

"Nah," Kai says, walking toward the door. "I've gotta go to the bathroom, anyway. I'll see you guys in a bit."

Mona turns to Lou. "Should we find another duo to challenge?"

Lou scans the garage, her eyes settling on where they left Josie with Kai's friend Nia a while back. "Maybe later," Lou says. "But let's check in with Jos."

"Mona!" Josie exclaims, flashing her a nervous smile. "Nia is a huge fan and just got an alert about your episode of *Late Night*. It just went live and is making *lots* of waves."

"Wow," Mona says, her heart rate accelerating. "That was fast. Have you . . . watched it?"

"No, I haven't watched the whole thing," Nia says. "But the clip of you and Lucas kissing is, like, everywhere online already. You two are *so* hot together."

Another girl with a light smattering of acne and flat-ironed dirty-blond hair standing with Josie and Nia chimes in, showing them the screen of her phone. "Look at my Insta feed right now," she says. "It's all you two. You *have* to tell us what he's like in person."

"This is Brianna," Josie tells Mona. "Nia's best friend."

"Oh," Brianna says, laughing. "My bad. Honestly, I feel like I know you already. It's so weird having to introduce myself."

"So, come on, give us the scoop on Lucas," Nia insists. "Is he *really* a bad boy?"

"After everything he went through with his dad," Brianna

says, dramatically clutching her heart. "Who can blame him for being a little troubled?"

"All I know is he's *hot*. Way hotter than your ex," Nia says. "I mean, at least he looks that way in pictures. Is he that hot in person?"

"*Nia,*" Brianna says, nudging her friend. "Don't be weird. That's her boyfriend."

Mona freezes for a second, racking her brain for how to respond when Louise catches her gaze and jumps in. "He *is* pretty hot in person," Louise tells the girls. "I can confirm that much."

"What's everyone talking about?" Kai asks, making his way back over to the group from the bathroom. "Who's pretty hot?"

"Mona's boyfriend," Nia says. "Lucas Sterling."

Brianna rolls her eyes. "Kai probably doesn't even know. He is hopeless with pop culture."

"I know who Lucas Sterling is," Kai says, flashing Mona an apologetic look before turning his attention back to Nia and Brianna. "Now, can you two leave Mona alone?"

"Kai, come on," Nia says, pressing play on the video of Mona and Lucas making out. "Tell me this is not the hottest kiss you've ever seen."

"Oh," Mona interjects, nonchalantly waving her hand across Nia's phone. "We really don't have to watch it." If Meesha was here, she would know to check the inside of Mona's cheek, which, at this point, has been chewed raw.

"No," Nia insists. "Kai, she's just being modest. You're

friends with one half of the hottest couple on the planet. You have to see this."

"I can't believe you're here," Brianna says to Mona, her eyes glued to Nia's phone screen. "If I had a kiss like that, I would be in bed for three straight days just recovering."

"Yep. That is one hot kiss," Kai says, turning toward Mona. "I, uh, have to go to the bathroom real quick. I'll be back."

"But you were just in the bathroom," Mona says, her voice soft. "Is everything okay?"

"Yeah," Kai says, flashing her a forced smile as he runs his hand through his hair. "I'll be back. Have fun."

"You know," Brianna says, "I read somewhere once that boys have smaller bladders than girls."

"Huh," Josie says. "Really? That's wild. I wonder why."

"I'll be right back," Mona says, handing Louise her red Solo cup full of beer. "Hold this for me?"

Mona marches up toward the door leading into the house, stopping where Majid is posted in front of it.

"Did you see where Kai went?" she asks. "I know he's not in the bathroom *again*."

"Blake is monitoring the activity on the front yard," Majid says. "He told me he saw him step out a moment ago."

"Thanks," Mona says, rushing past Majid.

Mona frantically walks through the shag-carpeted hallway, passing the few couples making out against the butter-yellow walls, then through the family room, where another couple is doing much more than making out on an old brown polyester futon until she's outside facing Kai on the front lawn.

"You said you had to go to the bathroom," Mona says once they're standing inches apart.

"Yeah," Kai says, refusing to make eye contact. "I lied. Sorry. Just needed some air."

"Got it," Mona says. "Listen, I'm sorry you had to see that dumb video."

They stand there quietly for a few moments, both staring out at the suburban street until Kai speaks again, this time his voice hoarse. "Mona, what is happening here? Between us?"

Mona looks up to see his amber eyes staring down directly at hers. "I like you. I thought that was obvious," she says. "We went on a date. I'm *here*."

"Yes," Kai says, his eyes glassy. "But you're here after you were *there*. Kissing *him* on national TV."

"Kai," Mona says, her voice low. "I told you. That's all *fake*. It's like acting. I'm playing a part."

"That kiss seemed pretty real," Kai says, his eyes still focused on hers.

Mona steps an inch closer to him, so that their bodies are just barely touching. "No," she whispers, wrapping her arms around his neck and pulling him in toward her. "*This* is real."

"What if people see us?" Kai whispers, pausing just as their lips are inches from meeting.

Mona nods toward where she knows Blake is camped outside in her black car. "Let him deal with that."

Kai looks at her for a minute, his mouth spreading into an agonizingly adorable smile. "Okay, then," he says, gently brushing a rough hand across her soft cheek before he pulls her in close. Mona lets out a long, luxurious exhale as her lips finally meet his, her hands running through the shaggy golden-brown hair that caught her attention that first day she met him at the diner.

Kai kisses like he behaves in the world. Thoughtfully. Honestly. Sturdily. It's a kiss you can list as your emergency contact. A kiss you can cash checks and swear your life on. A kiss that makes you feel safe, calm, restored. While kissing Lucas felt like spending a rowdy night drunkenly dancing on tables in Mykonos, kissing Kai feels like a tranquil day at the spa.

"You live close by, right?" Mona asks Kai, briefly coming up for air. "Just a few blocks away?"

"Yeah," Kai says, his arms still wrapped tightly around her. "Like, a five-minute walk."

"Cool," Mona says, smiling up at him. "Mind if I spend the night?"

Confessional

INT. LUCKY'S KITCHEN—AFTERNOON (CONT'D)

KAI

[*smiling*]

Of *course* I didn't mind.

Chapter 30

The next morning, Mona wakes up with her head nuzzled against Kai's chest.

"Hi," she says, smiling up at him.

"Hi," he says, rubbing his hand up and down her back. "How you doing?"

"I'm doing pretty great," she says. "And you?"

"I'm pretty great myself," he says, smiling widely. "Actually, I was thinking . . . My parents are out this morning to watch Rudy's chess tournament. What do you say I make us some breakfast?"

"That sounds amazing," Mona says, reaching for her phone where it's sitting on Kai's nightstand. "But it's already ten. I have to get going for that thing I was telling you about for my dad. There's no shot my mom doesn't already have a car waiting outside for me."

Mona and Kai both peep through the plastic blinds on his window facing the street. *Yep*. Majid waves at them from the passenger seat of a black Cadillac SUV parked right outside.

"The woman should honestly work for the CIA," Mona says. "The way she has her tabs on everything and everyone at all times."

"Have you heard from Josie and Lou?" Kai asks. "I hope they weren't too mad we ditched them."

"No, they thrived," Mona says, sifting through her many unread texts from Mary. "Lou hooked up with your friend Joey, and Josie and Nia are thinking about going to a poetry slam together in a couple weeks."

Kai laughs. "Good. I'm glad they had fun."

"Same," Mona says, looking apologetically at Kai as she sets her phone aside. "If this wasn't the *one* day I get to mourn my dad without the rest of the world breathing down my neck, I'd stay."

"No, you should definitely go," Kai says, giving her a reassuring smile from bed. "We'll hang out later."

"Yeah," Mona says, sliding her jeans and shirt back on. "I have your big surprise tomorrow!"

"Oh *right*," Kai says. "The big mysterious surprise. You're still not going to give me any intel here? Nothing?"

"Nope!" Mona says, grabbing her black Loewe Squeeze chain leather bag and heading out the door. "I'll pick you up here tomorrow around noon!"

"Mona Mashad," Lucas says, shaking his head in mock disapproval as Mona steps out of her SUV onto Mary's cobblestoned front driveway. "Is that the same outfit I saw you leaving the studio in last night?"

"Stalker much?" Mona asks, rolling her eyes. "Why are you here anyway? I thought you were only doing *official* planned appearances with me from now on."

"I am," Lucas says. "This was on the schedule."

"What?" Mona asks, pulling up her phone. "No, it wasn't. This isn't a day for the public. It's just me and my family."

"Your mom invited me," Lucas says, showing her his phone. "Look. Here it is."

Mona pushes past him, storming into Mary's house, weaving through the acres of space until she finds her mom seated with her sisters by the infinity pool.

"Melody Joonam you're *right*," Mary is saying with a laugh. "He did always hate bananas. And, you know, the doctor was always saying he was low on potassium. God, I tried *everything*—"

"Can I talk to you for a minute in private?" Mona interrupts, aggressively tapping her mom on the shoulder. "Now."

Meesha looks at her from the other end of the table, an eyebrow skeptically raised. "What do you have to say in front of Mom that you can't say in front of us?"

"Mona Joonam, you are late," Mary says, looking at the time on her vintage gold Piaget watch. "Whatever it is you want to discuss, it will have to wait until tonight."

"I'm on time. And I *really* insist we go somewhere and talk right now," Mona tries again, her blood scalding.

"Lucas!" Melody exclaims as Lucas finally catches up with

Mona in the backyard. "Hi! I didn't know you were coming."

"Lucas Joonam," Mary says, getting up to give him a hug. "I'm so glad you came."

"Hi, everyone," Lucas says, giving the whole family a polite wave. "Thanks for including me on everything today. I know it can't be easy."

"Here," Meesha says, pulling up the seat next to her. "Have a seat. Your girlfriend is throwing a tantrum for God knows why."

"Mom," Mona begs. "Please. A word."

"Fine," Mary says with a sigh, tossing her hands in the air as she walks away from the table. "Let's talk."

"Why would you invite him?" Mona asks, once she and Mary are standing inside the pool house. "Today of all days?"

"Isn't it obvious?" Mary retorts. "All we have to do is post one picture with him in the background. Once the world knows he was here supporting you today, it will fully seal the legitimacy of this whole thing."

"Is nothing sacred to you?" Mona says, her voice shaking. "This day is supposed to be about *Dad*. Not about selling the world on some stupid fake relationship you know he wouldn't have agreed with."

"Where is this coming from?" Mary asks, her voice low. "Is this about the *surfer* I hear you spent the night with? Because I hope to God you're being careful, Mona. Do not ruin this."

"This isn't about Kai," Mona says, now sobbing. "Do you even miss him?"

"Miss who?" Mary asks. "What are you talking about?"

"DAD!" Mona screams. "Dad! I'm obviously talking about Dad because this day is supposed to be about Dad. Do you even miss him at all?"

"You're being ridiculous," Mary says, her eyes also gaining moisture. "Of course I miss him. That man was the love of my life."

"I don't believe you," Mona says, her sobs intensifying. "Do you know how hard it is for me? Every single morning, I wake up hoping it was a nightmare. Then I remember he's really gone, and I have to spend the rest of my waking hours actively resisting the urge to walk around in public sobbing like this. I miss him so much it feels like I swallowed a ball of fire and it's scorching me from the inside out. This is the *one* day I get to express that pain without owing anything to the rest of the world. And you took that away from me. If you truly missed him, you would have understood that."

"Mona Joonam," Mary says, rubbing a hand on her shoulder. "Ghorboonet behram man. I miss him, too. Really. I do. But this isn't that big of a deal! We will still have our day honoring him. Lucas is just here, too, for optics."

"You really don't get it, do you?" Mona asks, snot dripping down her nose into her mouth. "I don't need a manager right now. I need a *mom*."

"Mona. Azizam—" Mary starts.

"No," Mona says, walking back outside. "Please. You're just going to make it worse."

Mona marches over to the table where her sisters are still seated, snot and tears still streaming down her face as she grabs her bag from where she left it on her chair.

"What happened?" Melody asks, jumping out of her seat to give Mona a hug. "I know. Today is hard."

"I just need to go," Mona says once Melody lets go of her. "Sorry. You guys will probably have a better day without me anyway."

"What?" Meesha asks. "You're *bailing*? On today?"

"I'm not bailing," Mona says, her voice hoarse. "I just can't be here."

With that, she storms away from them all.

"Mona!" Melody calls after her. "Just tell us what happened! I'll talk to Mom for you!"

"I'll get her," Lucas tells the table, scooching out of his seat. "Sorry for, um, this whole thing."

Confessional

INT. HARVARD MEN'S LACROSSE LOCKER ROOM—AFTERNOON (CONT'D)

LUCAS

Mary's house is massive, and Mona is shockingly fast. It took forever to find her. But I finally did in one of the garages. She was lying across the back seat of an old Bentley, sobbing alone.

"Hey," Lucas says, knocking on the half-cracked window of Mona's car. "Can I come in?"

"No," Mona says, sniffling. "You are the *last* person who can come in here."

"Okay," Lucas says. "Then I'll stay out here."

"Suit yourself," Mona says, rolling her window back up.

The car was Mona's dad's. Technically, according to his will, it's Mona's now. But as far as she's concerned, it's still his. It will always be his. She remembers the day he bought it. Mona was in first grade when he pulled up in the brand-new silver GTC with its top down to pick her up from school. Mary had a thing about convertibles. She hated them. Said they were unsafe. But, somehow, he had convinced her not only to let him get one, but to let him drive one of her precious babies in one. It was nothing short of a miracle. But, of course, this part didn't surprise Mona. She expected miracles from her dad, which is probably what made the whole him dying thing hit extra hard.

Anyway. Back to that day in first grade. It was the first time Mona rode in the front seat, and, even though she was big for her age, it was probably highly illegal. But Ali didn't care. He just wanted to make this ordinary Wednesday afternoon extraordinary for his little girl. She remembers gleefully slipping into the passenger seat next to him and him telling her she could pick *any* radio station she wanted. She flipped through the stations as he drove out of her school parking lot, listening carefully to a sampling from each until finally settling on one that was playing LMFAO's "Party Rock Anthem." She and Ali looked at each other at the same time while stopped at a red light and said the same thing, "I love this song." Then, "Jinx!" Ali blasted the song as loudly as the speakers would let him and the two of them scream-sang the song as they cruised down Mulholland, Mona's little jet-black pigtails flying wildly in the air. She remembers looking over at him and thinking she won the cool-dad lottery. Maybe it's because he died just before she got to that age where your parents inherently start becoming uncool, but Mona never really stopped feeling that way.

Nowadays she reserves this car for emergencies, coming here only when she's missing him so much that she can hardly breathe. Today is one of those days. She wants to be in here for as long as she humanly can be. She cries in here for a *long* time. She cries and cries and she even falls asleep for a bit. Then she wakes up and cries some more.

✦✦✦

Confessional

INT. MARY MASHAD'S LIVING ROOM—AFTERNOON (CONT'D)

MONA

[*voice uncharacteristically soft*]

Lucas just stayed outside the whole time.

✦✦✦

Mona peeks out the car window after what must be her seventh session of crying and sees Lucas sitting exactly where she saw him last. He's not even on his phone or anything. He's just sitting there, his head resting against the car door.

"Don't you have anywhere to be?" she asks, rolling the window back down as she notices the sun start to set through the glass garage door. "It's been hours."

"I've got nowhere to be," Lucas says. "And you've already called me a stalker, so not much to lose in terms of dignity with you."

"Fair," Mona says, still sniffling. "Well, I'm not ready to leave the car."

"That's fine," Lucas says. "Are you ready to talk?"

"There's no point," Mona says. "You wouldn't get it."

Lucas laughs. "*I* wouldn't get it?" he asks. "Are you kidding? I might actually be one of the few people on this planet who really, really, intensely gets it."

Mona considers this for a few moments. "Fine," she says, unlocking the door. "You can come in."

Mona sits up, scooching down to the left passenger seat so that Lucas can take the right one.

"Melody always says my mom does the things she does as a coping mechanism," Mona shares once Lucas is sitting in the car next to her. "That we need to cut her some slack. But using *him*? Using *this* day?" She thought she was done but, like clockwork, the tears are back.

"Do you know when my mom announced her presidential bid?" Lucas asks. "The day after my dad's funeral. His body was barely cold, and we were off on the campaign trail."

"That's a total Mary Mashad move," Mona says, nodding. "She was always a workaholic, but when he died, it reached another level. She became all manager, no mom just when I needed a mom most." Mona's cries turn into sobs and eventually her head is resting on Lucas's shoulder, covering the sleeve of his crisp olive-green T-shirt in snot and tears.

"You're lucky you have your siblings," Lucas says, his arm gently wrapped around her. "Sometimes I feel like I'm the only one remembering my dad."

Mona's heart breaks for him. Losing her dad was hell. Losing him without her sisters would have been unbearable. "Tell me about him," she says, her eyes looking up at that heart-shaped amber speck in his.

"Well," Lucas begins, thinking. "He would make fun of you in a way that never felt mean. He somehow always smelled like Christmas trees. He was the smartest guy in every room but never felt a need to prove it. He would say 'I love you' so many times a day, I'd just tune it out half the time. But now I'd give an arm just to hear him say it one more time."

Mona clasps his hand in hers the way she did at *Late Night with Amira Norris*, except this time it's not to please any crowd. It's because she wants to. "Sounds like he was a great guy."

"He was," Lucas says, letting his fingers intertwine in hers. "And I know your dad was, too."

Mona nods, her eyes welling up again. "I think I'm going to sleep here tonight."

"Okay," Lucas says, not a trace of judgment in his voice. "Want me to get you anything before I go? A pillow?"

Mona looks up at him, her eyes wide and wet. "Stay with me." The words surprise her as they escape her mouth, but all this emotion has her brain on a delay tonight.

"Are you sure?" Lucas asks. "You want me . . . ?"

"Yes," Mona answers swiftly. "Please."

"Sure," Lucas says. "I'll stay."

Lucas softly strokes Mona's hair as she lays her head on his lap, now covering his jeans with their own fresh coating of tears and snot.

"Sorry." Mona sniffles. "I'm really ruining all your clothes tonight, huh?"

"It's fine," Lucas says, his grin kind. "I can always get new ones."

Mona looks up at him, her eyes watery. "You have no reason to be nice to me."

Lucas chuckles. "Right back at ya," he says. "But I want to be here. Really."

She lies there quietly for a few more minutes, her gaze fixated on the tan leather passenger seat in front of her until she speaks again. "All in all, you're a pretty great guy, too."

Lucas swallows hard. "Thank you."

They look at each other, both their eyes moist and then Mona sits up, softly giving him a kiss on the lips.

Confessional

INT. MARY MASHAD'S LIVING ROOM—AFTERNOON (CONT'D)

MONA

I know. I know. I know. I made a giant [BLEEP]ing mess of it. But . . . I wasn't thinking that night. I was just doing what felt right in the moment.

✦✦✦

"Good night, Lucas," she says, lying back down on his lap.

"Good night, Mona," Lucas says, leaning down to give her a kiss on the forehead.

Mona closes her eyes and within seconds she falls asleep.

✦✦✦

Confessional

INT. HARVARD MEN'S LACROSSE LOCKER ROOM—AFTERNOON (CONT'D)

PRODUCER

Did you get any sleep?

LUCAS

No. God no. It was so uncomfortable. My head was pressed against a window and my lap was soaking wet . . . but I was happy. It felt like we finally made it out on the other side.

Chapter 31

Confessional

INT. MARY MASHAD'S LIVING ROOM—AFTERNOON (CONT'D)

MONA

Lucas left early the next morning to go to some campaign thing with his mom. And I had to go take Kai for his big surprise.

PRODUCER

Were you nervous to see Kai? After what happened with Lucas?

MONA

Honestly? I couldn't even go there in my head. I mean, I knew I eventually *had* to go there. But I decided for one day I just wouldn't think about it. I mean, it's not like Lucas and I had sex. It was one quick peck. And Kai and I weren't in, like, a relationship. We hooked up once! Nothing *that* scandalous happened when you really think about it.

PRODUCER

Right.

MONA

Okay, no need to take that tone. The truth is I was confused. I had no idea how I felt about who. Or what to do about any of it. So, I just decided I wouldn't deal until later. That day was supposed to be about Kai anyway.

"You're not going to kill me, are you?" Kai asks, adjusting the blindfold Mona put around his head. "I saw a movie once where rich people had this ceremony where they each befriend a normal person, then sacrifice them at a ceremony in the woods."

"No," Mona says with a laugh as she parks her car in the lot. "I'm not sacrificing you in a creepy rich-person ceremony. Promise."

"Plus," Majid chimes in from the back seat, "if it's any comfort, I couldn't let her do that under my supervision."

"I guess that is a bit of a comfort," Kai says as the car comes to a halt. "Is this it? Can I take my blindfold off now?"

"No!" Mona exclaims. "Where's the fun in that? Just wait for me. I'll guide you."

"Well," Kai says as Mona opens his door, "you made me

bring my wetsuit. And I can smell the salt air. So, I'm going to assume we're at the beach. It took a little over an hour to get here so I'll guess Surfrider?"

"Creepy that you were able to calculate that. But *where* we are isn't the surprise," Mona says, scanning the parking lot to make sure she doesn't spot any photographers before taking his hand. "Come on."

Kai laughs. "If where we are isn't the surprise, then why do I have to keep this on?!"

"Honestly," Mona says, "that's not a bad point. Fine. Take it off."

Kai slips off the mask and looks out at the ocean ahead. "Surfrider! I knew it."

"Yes," Mona says, grabbing his surfboard from the back. "And Rudy already gave me this, so we're all set."

"So, is this the surprise?" Kai asks. "You're just watching me surf?"

Mona rolls her eyes, scanning the lot once more for photographers before grabbing his hand again and dragging him out of the lot onto the beach. "Will you just trust me on this?"

When they finally hit the sand, Liam is already waiting by the shore to greet them.

"Mona!" he exclaims. "You showed up."

"Yes!" Mona says. "Liam, this is my friend Kai."

"Liam Schroeder," Kai says, his eyes wide. "I'm a huge fan, man."

Mona looks at Kai, an eyebrow raised. "So *him* you know?" She turns to Liam. "The guy knows nothing about pop culture;

this is the first I've ever seen him recognize anyone. You should be honored."

"Liam is a legendary surfer," Kai excitedly tells her. "One of the best to ever do it. Epic surprise, Mona."

Liam chuckles. "Pleased to meet you, Kai. Mona tells me you're not a bad surfer yourself."

"I try," Kai says with a shrug. "She honestly hasn't seen me do much surfing. I've just been giving her lessons."

"She mentioned something to that effect," Liam says. "I said she would be a great guest spot on the show."

"Show?" Kai asks.

"Yes!" Mona jumps in. "So, meeting Liam wasn't the surprise. The *show* is. Liam is making this show about amateur surfers. About their lives. So, it wouldn't just be you on the show. It could be your whole family. Oh my God. Can you imagine how much America would love Rudy?"

"Wait," Kai says, his mood shifting. "Can you backtrack for a second here? You want me to go on this show?"

"Well," Liam says, "I'm going to need to see you out on the water for a bit right now just to make sure you don't totally suck or anything. But that's really just a formality. Mona was pretty enthusiastic about you and, if a Mashad doesn't know who has the chops to make it on reality TV, who does? As far as I'm concerned, unless you go out there and drown, it's pretty much a done deal."

"Ah!" Mona squeals, giving Kai a tight squeeze. "Did you hear that?! A done deal! You're going to be a *star*!"

"Um . . ." Kai says, looking at them both. "Liam, it was

nice meeting you. But I think there's been a miscommunication here. I need to go."

Liam shrugs at a stunned Mona as Kai starts speed-walking back toward the parking lot. "Surfers have this chill rep," Liam says. "But we're like artists. We're temperamental, man."

"Excuse me," Mona tells him, her eyes laser-focused on Kai. "I'll be right back."

Mona rushes up the sand toward Kai. "Kai!" she shouts behind him. "Will you slow down? Where are you even going? I drove you here."

"I can take the bus back," Kai says, still marching forward.

"Will you just stop for a second?" Mona insists, out of breath. "Kai, *what* is going on?"

Kai stops in his tracks, turning to face her. "Fine," he says, his expression so hard you could build a house on it. "You want to know what's going on? That was messed up. You ambushed me."

Mona looks up at him, perplexed. "Yes, I 'ambushed' you by presenting you with an opportunity to become rich and famous by *surfing*. How is that not a dream scenario?"

Kai runs a frustrated hand through the same head of golden-brown hair Mona was blissfully running her hands through just a couple nights ago. "Mona, I like my life the way it is," he says, his eyes on the ocean behind her. "I don't want to be famous. I don't want to be rich. I don't want to be *you*."

Mona's breath catches as his eyes meet hers. "What's that supposed to mean?"

"Nothing," Kai says, walking away. "Sorry. That came out wrong. I'm too heated to be doing this right now. I should go."

"No," Mona says, grabbing him by the arm to stop him from leaving. "Tell me."

"Fine," Kai relents. "Your life works for you. But the fake relationships and the tabloids and the watching over your shoulder for photographers before you do anything . . . all for what? For more money? To be *more* famous? I don't want that. Not even on a smaller scale."

"So, you think my life is frivolous," Mona says, her voice deliberately steady. She expects digs like this from trolls online. But Kai? He *knows* her. Or at least she thought he did.

"Can we talk about how *you* feel about *my* life?" Kai asks, his feet kicking into the sand. "Because clearly you think it's too small. A cute little charity case for you to invest in."

"You know that's not true," Mona says, anger replacing her hurt.

"What was this then? It was basically a make-a-wish for your poor friend," Kai says. "*Let me surprise you with a chance to be like me!*"

"I'm gonna go," Mona says, storming toward her car. "Enjoy the bus."

Confessional

INT. MARY MASHAD'S LIVING ROOM—AFTERNOON (CONT'D)

MONA

There was no point just standing there going back and forth anymore. We were never going to see eye to eye.

Chapter 32

Confessional

INT. MARY MASHAD'S LIVING ROOM—AFTERNOON (CONT'D)

MONA

That night, we were doing a sister night at Meesha's place. But I just couldn't stop thinking about my fight with Kai. I mean, he was being a jerk, right? I was doing something *nice* for him.

PRODUCER

Did you tell your sisters about it?

MONA

Meesha and Melody barely knew who he was. And Josie could hardly discuss anything having to do with Kai or Lucas without basically having a stroke. It wasn't worth it.

"Mona, are you good?" Meesha asks, taking a big bite of her salad. "You've hardly said anything all night."

"What?" Mona asks, staring past Meesha at the view of the Los Angeles skyline behind her. "Yeah. I'm fine."

"Is it Mom?" Melody asks. "What happened between you two yesterday?"

"It's not about Mom," Mona says, pushing the few pieces of lettuce around on her plate. "We got into a blowout, but you know how it is. I'll see her tonight; we'll ice each other out for a few days and then we'll pretend it never happened."

"It doesn't *have* to be that way," Josie suggests. "You know, she seemed really sad yesterday. After you left. Maybe it's worth actually resolving things with her."

"Trust me," Mona says. "It's not. And I'm fine. Seriously. Can we go back to talking about literally anything else?"

"Whatever you say," Meesha says. "Josie, keep going. What happened next? After you went to Timmy's?"

"I feel bad Mona has to hear this twice," Josie says, helping herself to more of the salad sitting at the center of the table. "But I don't know what came over me. I went there fully thinking I was ready, then we got to his house, and he had this whole cute setup with candles and roses and I just . . . choked. I started getting all weird and sweaty and blabbering on and on and finally I just told him I wasn't ready."

"She said it was still a 'perfect romantic night,' though," Mona chimes in, perking up a bit.

"Yeah," Josie says, her face reddening. "It honestly made me love him more than I already did. He was so sweet and understanding. We just cuddled and watched our favorite movie, *Island Rock*."

"Is it weird that makes me want to cry?" Melody asks, smiling as she wipes a tear. "I mean, that whole story is just so *pure*."

"Yes," Meesha tells Melody. "Very weird it makes you want to cry. But I do agree it's pure. I'm happy for you, Josie."

"Sorry," Melody says, pulling her phone out of her bag as it makes a dinging noise. "I know we said no phones, but let me just quickly check this. It might be Axy. He's in Tulum right now and hardly has any service."

Mona rolls her eyes and does her best Melody impression. "*God forbid I let Axy go an extra hour without getting in touch!*"

Meesha cracks up. "*There*'s our Mona."

Melody looks up from her phone, her expression suddenly scrunched with concern.

"Mel, I was just kidding," Mona says. "I'm sorry. I wasn't trying to be a jerk. Take the call or respond to his text or whatever. Really. It's totally fine." Hurting Melody feels like punching a baby deer square in the face. It's the worst.

"Yeah, Mel, come on," Meesha says. "It was just a joke. I mean, you have to admit. Mona does a killer you impersonation."

Melody just stares back at them frozen, her eyes wide.

"Melody?" Josie asks, reaching next to her to grab her hand. "What's wrong?"

"It wasn't a text from Axle," Melody finally says, passing her phone to Mona. "You're going to want to see this."

Mona grabs the phone out of her sister's hand, looking at the piping-hot new TMZ article: "Mona Mashad Galavants with

Mystery Man Days After Kissing Boyfriend, Lucas Sterling, on National TV." She clicks into the article and there they are. Dozens of photos someone took from the shrubs of Mona excitedly pulling Kai out toward the beach from the parking lot this morning. They look happy. They look in love. She looks like a cheater.

Her heart stops.

Confessional

INT. MARY MASHAD'S LIVING ROOM—AFTERNOON (CONT'D)

MONA

I mean, it was a disaster. A [BLEEP]ing disaster. It looked like I cheated on the president's son. I knew what was coming. I knew I was done for.

"Mona," Meesha says, scrolling through the pictures on her own phone. "What is going on? Who is this guy?"

"Well, the guy is clearly just her surfing instructor," Melody says, her patent optimism kicking in. "You were obviously just excited for your lesson, right?"

Mona looks down, avoiding her sister's hopeful gaze.

"Oh gosh, Mona," Josie says, throwing her head into her hands. "This is bad."

Mona gulps hard. "I know. And the worst part is nothing even *happened* with Kai today."

"Huh," Melody says, nodding slowly. "So, things *have* happened?"

"Yes," Meesha says matter-of-factly, a tinge of hurt in her eyes as she squares them on Mona's. "Clearly she cheated on Lucas with this Kai guy."

"I didn't *cheat* on—" Mona begins, shutting her mouth when Mary comes storming out of the elevator opening into Meesha's penthouse.

"Hi, Mom," Meesha says. "So glad you're putting that spare key to use."

"You've really done it this time," Mary says, ignoring Meesha as she marches straight up to Mona. "I warned you. Did I not? Yesterday. Before you spewed all of that vitriol on me, I *warned* you. I told you to be careful with this surfer boy. And what did you do? You chose to go gleefully skipping to the beach with him? Were you even using half of your brain?"

"*Mom* knew?" Meesha asks. "You didn't tell us about your affair, but *Mom* knew?"

"I'm telling you," Mona says, turning to Meesha. "It was not an *affair*. Besides, you're one to talk. I don't remember you looping us all in on your little affair with Pete."

"Yeah, but I didn't tell *Mom*," Meesha says. "Why on Earth would you tell *Mom*?"

"Meesha, enough. Air your grievances with your sister later. We have damage control to get to," Mary says. "Mona, of all the antics you pulled, this has to take the cake. As far as the public is concerned, you cheated on the *president's son*. Every major hard news station is going to pick this up. People who don't even follow pop culture are going to know about this.

They are going to hate you. Hate us. How could you let this happen?"

Mona's eyes well up at the thought of Lucas seeing the pictures. The timing could not possibly be worse. She doesn't know what last night was, but she knows it was . . . a step. This is going to hurt him. Really hurt him. Maybe more than he hurt her that night in Harvard.

And Kai! As if he wasn't already livid enough with her. Now every tabloid on the planet is going to be hounding him. Mary's right. *How* could she let this happen?

"I swear I checked," Mona tells Mary, picking her phone up and immediately setting it back down upon seeing the growing mountain of notifications. "I scanned the parking lot twice to make sure nobody was taking pictures."

"Did it not occur to you that people might *hide*? Mona Joonam, you are young. But you have been in this industry for too long to be this naïve," Mary says, turning toward Meesha. "At least take a page out of your sister's book here and have an affair in private."

"Will everyone stop using the word *affair*? It was not an *affair*," Mona says, turning to Mary. "You know that."

"As far as the public is concerned, you just had an affair," Mary says. "And the worst part is the story is not in our hands. We're playing defense here."

"What do you mean 'as far as the public is concerned'?" Meesha asks. "Mona, why does Mom know more about your love life than we do right now? What's going on?"

✦ ✦ ✦

Confessional

INT. MARY MASHAD'S LIVING ROOM—AFTERNOON (CONT'D)

MONA

[*takes a deep breath*]

I had no choice. I had to tell them everything. I took it from the top. Every behind-the-scenes detail from the day President Sterling and Mom ambushed me to that moment.

"No," Melody says. "This can't be true. We spent so much time with you and Lucas. You two seemed so . . . good together."

"To be fair," Josie interjects, "she's pretty cute with Kai, too."

Their words slice through Mona like a freshly sharpened knife because it's all true. It was weird and messy and confusing, but somewhere along the line Mona started falling for both Lucas and Kai. Now she's somehow managed to lose them both in one fell swoop. A Messy Mona record.

"You *gaslit* me," Meesha says, her voice terrifyingly steady as her eyes lock in on Mona's. "All this time. I knew. I *knew* something was off! And you made me feel like I was being some sort of evil psychotic monster."

"Bold request here, but could you maybe not make this about you right now?" Mona snaps. "You don't think it hurt when I found out you had spent *months* lying to me about Pete? But it didn't matter. I knew you were hurting, so I had your back anyway. I *still* have your back."

"That was *different*," Meesha says, her voice freezing. "That wasn't some dumb publicity stunt I baked up with Mom. It was my *real* life. I was in love. It was complicated."

Mona scoffs. "Right. It's always different when it's you. Did you ever think *this* is why I didn't tell you? Because I wanted to spare myself the holier-than-thou shtick?"

Meesha sets her napkin on the table and gets up. "I'm going to Pete's."

"Do you not get what's happening here?" Mona asks, her eyes watering. "The world is about to hate me. I need you."

Melody gets up, grabbing Meesha's hand. "We're at your house. Just stay. Please."

"I need some space," Meesha says, shaking Melody loose as she strides toward the elevator. "I'll see you later."

Melody, Mona, Mary, and Josie watch as the elevator door shuts, sending Meesha straight down to the private garage. Mary stands by the table for a moment longer before quietly taking Meesha's seat at the table.

Mary lets out a dramatic sigh as she scrolls through her phone. "Jordana is not responding to any of my emails. Maybe I should give her a call. What time is it in Washington right now?"

"I think President Sterling might be in Nevada," Josie says. "I'm looking online now, and it seems like that's where she was earlier today at least. She was there for a rally. Lucas too."

Mona looks down at her phone, knowing she has to reach out to them. To say *something*. But what? She starts with Kai, sending him a quick You OK? text. She watches and watches and it never says delivered. He blocked her.

"Give me a minute," Mona says, getting up to walk into Meesha's bedroom and dial Lucas.

She takes a seat on the comically large custom bed Meesha had made to fit Pete's large basketball-player body and steadies her eyes on a family photo Meesha has sitting on her burlwood nightstand. It's the same photo Mona has by her bed. The one Melody gave them both for Father's Day. Her dad wouldn't be pleased with her right now. She turns her attention toward her phone, no longer able to meet his gaze.

The first call goes straight to voicemail. So, she tries again. And again. And again. It's not until the twelfth call that she musters up the courage to leave him a message.

Confessional

INT. MARY MASHAD'S LIVING ROOM—AFTERNOON (CONT'D)

MONA

The funny thing is I think if that voicemail was leaked to the press or something, people wouldn't even believe it was me. It was all Mona, just scared, sad, tiny little Mona. Every confident, sparkly trace of Mona Mashad stripped away.

"Hi," Mona says in the voicemail, her voice instantly cracking. "It's, um, me. Mona. I know you're busy with your mom right now, but I was just wondering if maybe you could call me? Whenever you get a chance. Please. I'm sorry."

"I think President Sterling should be back in Washington later tonight," Josie is telling Mary when Mona unsteadily takes a seat back at the table. "A few outlets shared pictures of her and Lucas boarding their plane. They're probably in transit."

"Yeah," Mona says, her voice quiet. "I just tried him a bunch of times. All straight to voicemail. Hopefully that's why."

"Poor Lucas," Melody mumbles, her eyes back on her phone. "These pictures are probably crushing him."

"And *Kai*," Josie says. "It's only a matter of time before the world finds out who he is. And I know firsthand what a nightmare that can be."

"Is that really helpful right now?" Mona asks, rolling her watery eyes. "Obviously I know this is terrible for everybody involved. I messed up. Royally. I think we can all be clear on that."

"Oh, Mona," Mary says, shaking her head in defeat. "How on Earth am I going to bail you out this time?"

Chapter 33

Confessional

INT. MARY MASHAD'S LIVING ROOM—AFTERNOON (CONT'D)

MONA

I hardly slept that night. I mean, how could I sleep? I was just up all night glued to my phone, watching as more and more people all over the internet called me different variations of the word [BLEEP].

Meanwhile, Lucas is coming off great. The poor sweet playboy who got cheated on the one time he gave love a real shot. Mona's the devil. The vixen from the trashy reality-TV family. And he's the sweet angel. It's a great story.

Mona looks down at her string of unanswered texts to him

and resists the urge to cry as she considers the possibility that she might never hear from him again. And it would be completely her fault. Last night, when she told Mary on their car ride home that she was scared Lucas might never speak to her again, Mary scoffed. "That would just be absurd," she said, her eyes on her phone when they probably should have been on the road. "As if he's some sort of saint himself."

"I think what I did might have cut deeper," Mona said, "than what he did to me." The confession wasn't exactly the typical kind of conversation she and Mary have. They're not really the touchy-feely, gab-about-boys kind of mother-daughter duo. But Mona was feeling low and desperate. The words needed to break out of her.

"You know," Mary said, setting her phone down, "you sure seem to care about the feelings of someone you told me just a week ago that you definitely don't love."

The response annoyed Mona, so they spent the rest of the car ride in silence.

She lets out a long sigh, her eyes still glued to her pitiful thread with the boy she may or may not love. A therapist would tell her to get outside. To touch grass. But she can't. The FAA had to declare an air traffic warning for the cluster of helicopters above their house this morning. And, according to the last text she got from Mary twenty minutes ago, there were 1,200 reporters camped outside. Even leaving her room to move around the house is difficult with the dozens of staff milling around whispering about her.

So, she's trapped in her room with her thoughts and her

phone. She exits out of her one-sided conversation with Lucas and heads back to Instagram, expecting to sift through the barrage of horrific posts and comments hating on her, but, instead, she sees millions of people have tagged her in a post the Comments by Celebs account shared a few minutes ago. It's a comment from Meesha that seems to currently be going viral.

Apparently, it all took place in the comments section of the original TMZ post reporting the scandal. Some troll commented, *What did he expect? That girl is a mess.* Compared to a lot of what Mona has spent the past twelve hours reading, the comment is not even that harsh. But it apparently set Meesha off. Her sister replied to *fortheloveofgod9484933499 why don't you get a life? Or I don't know maybe a hobby other than berating my 18-year-old little sister on social media? You have no idea what really happened. Nobody does.* Mona smiles, quickly texting her sister, Thanks. Meesha immediately responds, Still not talking to you.

✦ ✦ ✦

Confessional

EXT. MEESHA MASHAD'S PENTHOUSE BALCONY—AFTERNOON (CONT'D)

MEESHA

What? I was still pissed at her. But she's my sister. Nobody can call her a mess but me.

✦ ✦ ✦

"Bad news," Mary says, bursting through Mona's door. "I just got a tip that someone identified Kai. I've tried everything to stop tabloids from releasing his information, but a few won't budge. I think we need to send security to his house."

Mona pulls her somehow still crisp white covers over her head. "No," she says. "This is the *last* thing Kai wants."

"Luckily, he is very good-looking," Mary points out. "That helps. People like a good-looking underdog. It's a fact. You know, if he's willing to work with me, I really think we could—"

"He's not," Mona interjects. "Trust me."

"So, what then?" Mary asks. "The boy wants to just work in a diner the rest of his life?"

"Apparently, yes," Mona says. "He doesn't care about money or fame. He's not . . . like us."

Mary snorts. "You really know how to pick them, don't you? Anyway, we need to get him security, preferably before this all blows up. The *last* thing we want is him getting hurt and us being blamed for it. You have his address, correct?"

"Yeah," Mona says. "I'm going to go there myself today. I'll tell him about the security."

Mary looks up from her phone, her nostrils flared the way they only do when she's truly furious. "For the love of God, Mona. Please tell me you are joking. By the time you get there, his information will have been leaked. Everyone will see you. Do you have any idea how that will look? You showing up to your *lover*'s house? Before you're even seen with Lucas?"

"I know how brutal it's going to be," Mona says, willing her voice to remain calm. "But I *owe* this to Kai. I just flipped the guy's life upside down. He deserves an in-person apology."

Mary sighs. "You know what? I don't have the energy for this today. Fine," she says, giving Mona a once-over. "But if you insist on making this abysmal decision, skip the glam. You look haggard. People will feel sorry for you."

Mona takes a look at her reflection, her hair in a greasy top knot and circles so dark that they're almost black rimming each of her eyes. They aren't showing yet, but if she traces her finger across her chin, she can feel a collection of stress zits about to form. Mary's not wrong. She definitely looks like she's been going through it.

"Thanks for the compliment," Mona deadpans, swapping her Meesha Mashad–brand sweats for a ribbed gray tank and a pair of boyfriend jeans. "But really. You're overreacting. I'm leaving right now. There will hardly be anyone there by the time I arrive."

Confessional

INT. MARY MASHAD'S LIVING ROOM—AFTERNOON (CONT'D)

MONA

Turns out, she was not overreacting. It was an absolute nightmare out there.

Between the many cars that followed Mona here and the mob of reporters already camped outside on Kai's street, Mona is absolutely swarmed the moment she steps out of her car outside the Takanasha house. In fact, "outside the Takanasha house" is not even accurate. There was such a massive crowd of fans and reporters that Mona's driver had to park a full block away. Majid and the backup security detail Mary sent with him had to spend a full thirty minutes before Mona got out of the car clearing the path for her to safely approach the house.

"Just keep your head down and make it to the front door," Majid instructs as she walks. "No eye contact. No comments."

Mona tries her best to follow his instructions, ignoring the many slurs and insulting questions being thrown her way until she hears one fan in the crowd say to another, "I mean, it's honestly kind of sad. She blew up a shot with *Lucas Sterling* for this? For a guy who clearly used her to be famous?"

"Mona," Majid whispers, clocking the same conversation. "We are almost at his front door. Just let it go."

But she can't. "Excuse me," Mona says, cutting into the crowd until she's facing the two girls. "I couldn't help but overhear."

"Oh my God," one of them, a mousy brunette with pale blue eyes, says. "It's you."

"Mona, hi," the other one, a much taller girl with jet-black hair and a faint unibrow says. "We're, uh, we're huge fans."

"Yeah, I heard your conversation," Mona says, hyperaware of the thousands of cameras now on her. "Clearly you're huge fans. Thanks so much for looking out. I just wanted to say you're wrong."

"We're what?" the black-haired girl asks. "What are you talking about?"

"You're wrong. About Kai," Mona says, now turning her attention toward the crowd at large. "He does not *want* this. Actually, believe it or not, most people don't. If anything, in my experience, my fame seems to be less something people use me for and more a contagious disease I have that people try to avoid like it's the bubonic plague."

"Oh," the mousy brunette says. "Well, thanks for clearing that up."

"Sure thing," Mona says, turning her attention back toward the crowd. "And, now that I have, why don't you all lay off him? This story isn't about him. Nothing happened that day. Just drop it."

Confessional

INT. MARY MASHAD'S LIVING ROOM—AFTERNOON (CONT'D)

MONA

I mean, they obviously didn't listen. If anything, my little monologue just sparked more questions. But . . . I tried.

By the time Mona reaches Kai's front door, she doesn't even have to ring the doorbell.

"Mona," he says, opening the door just the tiniest crack. "What are you doing here?"

"You blocked me. This was my only way of getting in touch

with you," she says, pausing to gesture toward the increasingly rowdy crowd watching them like hawks. "Are you seriously not going to let me come inside?"

Kai sighs. "Fine." He quickly opens the door, ushering her in, the security team following behind her.

"Where are your parents and Rudy?" she asks, looking around the empty house.

"They're hiding out at my aunt's house for a few hours," he says. "They needed a break from all this craziness."

"You didn't want to go with them?"

"If I went with them, this stupid crowd would have just followed."

"Right," Mona says, nodding slowly. "Well, my mom got you security. They're here with me. A whole team. Enough for you, your parents, and Rudy. We're obviously paying for it. It's, um . . . the least we could do."

"I don't want your mom's charity," Kai snaps. "I'll be fine."

"No, you *won't* be," Mona says. "Why are you being so stubborn? You said it yourself. Your parents and Rudy are currently *hiding* because it's too crazy."

"Okay," Kai relents. "I'll take the security. Can you leave now?"

"Well, that was rude," Mona says, a hand on her hip. "Don't you want to hear me out? I had a whole apology speech ready for you."

"Mona, I honestly don't want to hear what you have to say," he says, resting his head in his hands as he slinks down onto the small pleather couch in the living room. "I should have never gotten involved with you. On some level, I knew that the whole time. But I asked you out anyway. And that's on me."

His words stab Mona like a dagger. "So sorry our time together was such a colossal regret of yours."

"Before I met you, my life was easy," Kai says, his voice measured. "No drama. No stress. No *scandals*. And definitely no mobs of people parked outside my front door. All I want is to go back to that. Please."

"Fine, then," Mona says, trying her best to blink away a sudden wave of tears. "I'll go."

Halfway through the dead-silent car ride back to Beverly Hills, Mona's phone lights up. It's Lucas. Her heart beats so fast it could win an Olympic sprint.

"Hi!" she answers, wiping away a stray tear. "I wasn't expecting you to call."

"Well," he says. "Here I am."

"Listen," she says. "I just wanted to say I'm sorry. After all the hell I gave you, it was me who blew it all up in the end. Classic."

There's silence on the other line, but, if she listens really hard, Mona can faintly hear him breathing. "You still there?" she asks.

"I'm here," he says. "Can I just ask one thing?"

"Of course," Mona says. "Anything."

"Those pictures," he says. "Were they before or after . . . that night? I know the tabloids are saying after, but sometimes they're wrong."

Mona wipes away a fresh set of tears. "They were, um . . . yeah. The tabloids were right. They were after."

It's like she can hear his gut being punched. "Okay," he eventually says. "I think I should go."

"Lucas," she says, her voice cracking. "Wait. I'm sorry."

"Don't be," he says. "Taste of my own medicine, right?" He makes a half-hearted attempt at a laugh that crushes the few remaining pieces of her already shattered heart and hangs up the phone.

Chapter 34

"Get up," Mary demands. "Get showered. We're going to Maryland."

Mona cracks her eyes open to find her mom standing over her bed, arms crossed expectantly. "What time is it?" she asks, still groggy. "Why are we going to *Maryland*?"

"It's six in the morning and we're going to Camp David," Mary says casually, as if Camp David is just somewhere they vacation from time to time. "Jordana has called an emergency meeting to discuss the situation."

"I thought Lucas's numbers were through the roof right now," Mona says, her brain trying desperately to catch up. "What's there to discuss?"

"I have no idea what *she* has in mind, but I know exactly what I'd like to discuss with her," Mary huffs. "I don't care who she is. If that woman wants me to lie down, roll over, and let them carry on with my daughter being the villain while her scoundrel of a son gets to be America's sweetheart, I will fight her to the death."

"So . . . we're going to Camp David," Mona says, still processing. "For you to fight with the leader of the free world in person."

"Potentially. Yes," Mary says nonchalantly. "Now, get up. We need to be on our plane within the hour. All you have to do is shower. I already had your bags packed and arranged glam for the plane to take care of *this*." She gestures to Mona's chocolate-and-tear-stained face.

"Do you, um, think Lucas will be there?" Mona says, unable to look her mom in the eye as she asks the embarrassing question.

"I know he will. And it will be great press. Hopefully ramp up some reconciliation rumors," Mary says, walking out. "Now, get a move on. I'll see you outside in twenty minutes."

Mona sighs, sending a mountain of chocolate crumbs flying around her room as she drags herself out from under her plush white duvet.

All her life, Mona has been notoriously difficult. It's what makes her such fantastic television. She's always ready, willing, and able to put up a fight. Especially with her mom. So, under normal circumstances, if her mom just waltzed into her room willy-nilly and told her to *get a move on* for some godforsaken trip to Camp David with the boy whose heart she heard break in real time on the phone last night and his MOM of all people, Mona would have refused. She would have dug her heels in, thrown a fit, chained herself to the bed. Done whatever it took to get out of it or, at the very least, put up a good fight before her hand was eventually forced.

But today, that version of herself feels distant. If her conversation with Kai pushed her to the edge, her call with Lucas shoved her off of it. And that's not even considering the internet of it all. Mona had to delete social media and put her phone on Do Not Disturb to give herself a break from the overwhelming onslaught of hate being hurled her way. But Mona has been in this business too long for a "break" like that to ever truly be a break. She doesn't have to log onto social media to know what's being said, to be able to distinctly imagine the memes, the TikToks, the comments. All she has to do is close her eyes and it's all right there.

Melody wound up coming over, holding Mona for hours as she cried and housed Milk Duds. Then Melody eventually left, and Mona cried some more. Housed more Milk Duds. By the time Mary waltzed into her room, she had only been asleep for half an hour.

This is all to say, at this point, Mona has no fight left in her. Every last bit of that patented Mona Mashad fire has been extinguished.

✦ ✦ ✦

Confessional

INT. MARY MASHAD'S LIVING ROOM—AFTERNOON (CONT'D)

MONA

I wasn't just brokenhearted. I was *broken.*

✦ ✦ ✦

The minute Mona sets foot on the tarmac at Camp David, President Sterling rushes over to embrace her in a hug.

"Mona," President Sterling coos, gently rubbing her back. "Honey, how are you holding up?"

Mona gives her a surprised smile. "Oh, I'm fine," she lies. "It's no big deal."

"It *is* a big deal," President Sterling says, gesturing for Mona and Mary to follow as she makes her way into a cute cabin labeled ASPEN LODGE. "Listen, I don't care how much good press my son is getting. I am first and foremost a feminist president, and I will absolutely not stand for a young woman being slut-shamed the way you are right now."

Mona and Mary exchange confused glances as they nod along.

"So, is Lucas here?" Mona asks, willing her voice to stay casual.

"Yes, sweetie," President Sterling says. "He's around here somewhere in one of the cabins. I was thinking you could take some time to rest, then we'll all meet at six to discuss strategy."

"That sounds lovely," Mary says before Mona has a chance to respond. "Thank you for organizing this, Jordana. Really."

"Of course," President Sterling replies. "We got our kids into this mess. Now it's time to fish them out of it."

"I could not agree more," Mary says, beaming. "I'll see you at six then with a few ideas for how to smooth this whole thing over."

"Wonderful," President Sterling says. "My team will prep a few ideas as well."

Confessional

INT. MARY MASHAD'S LIVING ROOM—AFTERNOON (CONT'D)

MONA

The minute we dispersed, my mom went into business mode. She had Jorge on speaker phone, and they were going on and on with different ideas about how to handle the situation. . . . I hung around there for a little but I just needed a break. So, I dipped out for a bit.

PRODUCER

Dipped out for a bit to see Lucas?

MONA

[*pauses*]

What do you want from me? Fine. Yes. I dipped out for a bit to see Lucas.

Mona goes back to her room and is reading over the list of activities President Sterling's assistant provided her with. *Hiking*? Pass. *Mountain biking*? Hard pass. *Skeet shooting*? Extra-hard pass. She looks out the window of her wood-paneled bedroom. It's one of those weird East Coast summer days where it's scorching hot and pouring rain. The last thing she wants is to do anything outside.

She flips the list over to find a map of the compound alongside a list of indoor activities. *Hickory Lodge* immediately stands out. It's got a bowling alley, a movie theater, and a bar. Her kind of lodge.

Mona throws on a Burberry raincoat her mom packed in her suitcase and follows her increasingly wet paper map outside the Aspen Lodge through the trees over to the wood-paneled gray-green building she recognizes as the Hickory Lodge. Even with the raincoat, she's sopping wet by the time she arrives.

"Hello?" she asks once she enters the old wooded building. "Anyone here?"

She laughs at herself, embarrassed she even asked. This building is huge. Even if someone *was* here, there's no way they would hear her pathetic little call-out. Mona makes herself at home, opening the many doors until she finds a bathroom where she can towel off, her once perfectly styled hair now damp and wavy and the makeup that was previously disguising her dark circles and stress-induced zits now completely washed away. She spends a few minutes trying to fix the situation, toying with the idea of controlling her hair with a French braid or reviving her skin with a splash of cold water. But she eventually gives up. It is what it is. For better or worse, this is what she looks like today.

She continues her expedition through the Hickory Lodge,

making her way past the bowling alley, the bar, and the billiard room, until she hears a noise coming out of what must be the movie theater. Mona walks closer toward the sound until it evolves from a muffled noise to what she can distinctly tell is Meg Ryan's voice. *When Harry Met Sally*.

She pauses by the door, taking a deep breath before letting herself in.

"Mind if I join you?" Mona asks, her voice adopting an uncharacteristically timid tone once she spots Lucas sitting on an old upholstered floral couch, closest to the screen.

"It's a free country," Lucas says with a shrug, his eyes still glued to the screen.

"Cool," Mona says, cautiously sitting on the opposite end of his couch.

Mona stares at him for a few seconds, silently willing him to say something. *Anything*. But he doesn't. Instead, he just keeps eating his popcorn, his eyes hyper-focused on Harry and Sally on the screen.

"It was pouring outside," she blurts out. "That's, um, why I look like this. . . ."

Lucas nods. "I'm, uh, trying to watch the movie."

"Right," Mona says, mimicking his nod. "Of course. Let's just watch the movie."

Mona dutifully shuts her mouth, watching in painful silence as Harry and Sally spend an hour and a half figuring out what the audience knows all along: that they're meant for each other. The movie is loud, but the silence exchanged between Mona and Lucas feels louder. It's not just the silence, either. It's the space. The five empty feet between them on this massive couch. All of these voids, these abysses between them. They're in the same room, watching the same movie. But they might as well be on different planets.

"Lucas," Mona finally says, once the credits start rolling. "Can we talk?"

"There's nothing to talk about," Lucas says, checking his phone. "It's almost six. We should head back to Aspen for the meeting."

Mona checks the time on her phone. It's 4:30. "We have a full hour and a half before the meeting," Mona says, her eyes watery. "Come on. Just talk to me. Please."

For the first time since she entered the theater, Lucas looks at her. Not just looks at her. *Sees* her.

Confessional

INT. HARVARD MEN'S LACROSSE LOCKER ROOM—AFTERNOON (CONT'D)

LUCAS

It was sad. I mean, I've seen her upset before. I've seen her down. But this was different. She looked . . . fragile. Broken.

"Okay," Lucas says with a sigh, his eyes locked on Mona's. "Let's talk."

"I'm sorry," Mona says, bursting into tears. "You were

nothing but nice to me the whole time. And I couldn't let that one night go. I raked you over the coals. Then I finally let you in. *I* initiated that kiss. I know I did. Going off with Kai the next day was messed up, even if those pictures didn't happen. It was messed up. I just . . . I didn't know what to make of everything yet. I needed a minute. It all felt so complicated. And now the pictures obviously just made it all *more* complicated. I hurt you both and set my own reputation on fire in the meantime."

"Mona," Lucas says. "You don't have to apologize. Really. Honestly? I hate how mopey I'm being. I hate how hurt I am by this situation. It's embarrassing. And trust me, the hypocrisy of my being this way is not lost on me."

"You're not a hypocrite," Mona says, wiping a few of her remaining tears away. "What I did was different."

"We had one peck the night before," Lucas says. "You didn't owe me anything."

"It wasn't just any kiss, though," Mona says, now avoiding his eyes. "That kiss . . . that *night*. It was different. I know that."

"Yeah," Lucas says, his voice just barely audible. "It did feel different."

"So, will you accept my apology?" Mona asks, her eyes back on Lucas's hazel ones. "Please?"

"Sure," Lucas says. "I accept. As long as you know you didn't have to apologize in the first place."

"I wanted to," Mona says, her heart rate lowering to a normal speed for the first time in days.

"And, Mona?" Lucas adds. "You know you don't deserve the way they're talking about you, right?"

"Do I not?" Mona asks. "As far as the public is concerned, I cheated on *you*. The president's son. America's most troubled sweetheart."

"But that's not what actually happened," Lucas reminds her. "It's like you said. *Hannah Montana*, right? There are two versions of our lives. The one the public gets is a half-truth, it's not reality."

"It's not," Mona agrees. "But sometimes it's the only one that matters. . . . You have Harvard. You have lacrosse. You have all these other things. My reputation to the public is *everything*. It's my livelihood. There's no show without it. There's no *me* without it."

"Hey," Lucas says. "What's going on here? What happened to the Mona at the Met Gala? Who doesn't mind being the villain?"

"This feels different," Mona says. "This isn't just classic Messy Mona leaning into the character to give people a good show. This is me being a *bad* person when I thought nobody was watching. People saw my true colors and they *hate* me . . . and I'm not sure I blame them for it."

Lucas looks at her for a minute, and Mona notices something different in his eyes. It's not pity. And it's not sympathy. It's sadness. Empathy. Like, she can see that he's palpably feeling her hurt. He scooches over, closing the giant gap of space between them.

"We'll figure this out," he says, leaning over to give her a reassuring squeeze on her thigh. "I promise."

Mona's lips curve into a small smile. "Thank you."

Lucas pulls a disposable out of his pocket, snapping a picture. "Your first smile since we started talking."

"After careful consideration with my team, I'm going to give a speech defending Mona," President Sterling announces once they're all seated in the cozy den of Aspen Lodge. "I will say that the Sterling family stands firmly by Mona Mashad's side and against slut-shaming of any kind."

Confessional

INT. MARY MASHAD'S LIVING ROOM—AFTERNOON (CONT'D)

MONA

Having the president of the United States essentially put out an anti-bullying PSA in my defense? No. Absolutely not. I could not imagine anything more mortifying.

Mona gulps hard, giving Lucas a panicked look from across the table.

"I have an idea," Lucas says, slapping his hands on his lap excitedly. "What if Mona and I address the rumors head-on? We'll hang out with Kai at a party, take a selfie of the three of us with some sort of nod to the fact that none of us are bothered by this supposed scandal, have Mona post it on her Instagram, and let that be the end of it?"

"That's not a bad idea," Mary says, nodding. "It definitely won't be the *end* of it. It will generate more intrigue and conversation, which could be a good thing for Mona's spinoff show."

"But it would definitely take some of the heat off of Mona," Lucas says. "And Kai."

"It does require you to continue the fake relationship, though," President Sterling says. "This whole thing has already been so hard on you both. Are you sure you can handle that?"

Mona looks over at Lucas, not wanting her eyes to look as hopeful as she knows they do in this moment.

"Yeah," Lucas says after a pause. "It'll be fine. We'll just do this, have a couple more appearances, then tell the tabloids we naturally fizzled out."

"Yes," Mary agrees. "A good fizzle out is always a good option. We'll say your schedules weren't aligning. The long distance was too hard."

"So, Mona, what do you think?" Lucas asks. "You in? One last hurrah to end this drama, then we wind this whole sham of a relationship down once and for all?"

For months, all Mona wanted was to be done with this whole stupid fake mess. To be having *this* exact conversation. And now it's finally here. The end. She looks over at Lucas, at the little heart-shaped amber speck she's gotten so used to focusing her attention on. And then she imagines never seeing it again. Scrolling through Instagram and stumbling upon images of him with his arms around some other, nicer, more deserving girl all over Deuxmoi. Him telling *her* she's "endgame," them eventually saying "I do," standing barefoot on the same sandy beach they shot their Ralph Lauren campaign on. The thought makes her feel sick. Dizzy. Overwhelmingly, devastatingly, heart-wrenchingly sad.

The Mona Mashad people watched grow up on their television screens would have said something. The other one, the one who existed behind the scenes, probably would have said something, too. Neither of them would have let him slip away so seamlessly. Not without a fight. But neither of those Monas are in the building right now. Whoever's left sitting here is a shell. A shadow of them both.

"Um, sure," she says, a tight smile on her face. "I guess I just have to ask Kai, but—"

"Nonsense," Mary interjects. "We will make *sure* Kai is on board."

Chapter 35

"So this is where he lives?" Mary says, looking out the window of the SUV at Kai's small front lawn. "Interesting."

Mona rolls her eyes. "Can you not be such a snob?"

Mary ignores her. "Remember the plan. If you can't close, I'll come get the job done."

"Will you stop talking like a mob boss?" Mona asks. "I'm just asking the guy to take a picture with me. It's not that big of a deal."

"You and I both know it's a huge deal," Mary retorts. "Not just for you but for him, too."

"Fine, it's a big deal," Mona admits. "But trust me. If he says no to me, he's *definitely* not saying yes to you."

Mary laughs in the smug way you can only pull off when you're truly great at what you do, and you know it. "You seriously underestimate me," she says, before checking the time on her gold Cartier watch. "Okay, it's almost noon. His security said he has a shift in an hour. If you want to see him, you need to stop wasting your time going back and forth with me and get in there."

Mona takes a sharp inhale, fidgeting with the gold bangles she paired with her bright aquamarine Dannijo slip dress as she looks out at the few reporters still camped outside of Kai's house. "Okay, fine. I'm doing it."

She opens the car door, raising a middle finger up high as the dozens of photographers jump out of their cars to snap photos of her.

"Mona!" Rudy exclaims, opening the door before Mona even knocks. "Hi!"

Mona's heart swells at the sight of the little boy, who's dressed in khaki cargo shorts and a baby-blue T-shirt that matches almost exactly the color of his glasses. She's been so focused on the Kai of it all that she didn't take a second to realize how much she missed his little brother.

"Rudy!" she says, crouching down to engulf him in a big hug. "How are you, buddy?"

"Well, I've been dealing with that grump," Rudy says, gesturing to where a shirtless Kai is waxing his surfboard outside on the patio. "So, not great."

And just like that, Mona's heart deflates again. What was she thinking? It's not just Kai she hurt. It's all of them. His whole family. Maybe Lucas was right that night at Meesha's show. Maybe she *was* just toying with Kai, haphazardly tossing the guy's entire life into a blender without so much as a second thought.

"I'm sorry," she says as she steps inside the sparsely

decorated living room, Rudy shutting the door behind her. "I came here to apologize to Kai the other day. But I really owed one to you also. And your parents."

"Do *not* apologize to me, sister," Rudy says. "I'm the most popular kid in my class! You know, a few kids didn't believe that the beach incident when you stuck up for me really happened. But, after these pictures came out, now *everybody* believes you and I are best friends."

"Well, we are," Mona says with a shrug. "Duh."

Rudy smiles. "Hey, Mona?" he says. "Even if things don't work out with you and my brother, can we still be friends?"

Mona smiles down at Rudy, his brown eyes brimming with hope behind his little glasses. "Of freaking *course*."

"Cool," Rudy says, a relieved smile on his face. "Thanks."

"Thank *you*," Mona says. "I'm honored to be your pal."

Rudy smiles quietly as the two of them settle their eyes on where Kai is still waxing his board, his back facing them.

"So, what do you think?" Mona asks. "Any chance he's going to forgive me?"

"I'm here this time," Rudy reassures. "And I've got your back."

"Thanks, dude," Mona says, gesturing for him to follow her. "Come on. Let's go give it a shot."

Mona's inches from the glass sliding door when she freezes, her hand unwilling to just pull the door open. *It's just Kai*, she reminds herself. But, of course, it's not just Kai. This is a different Kai. A new, broken version, only in existence because she destroyed the original model. The guilt sizzles something deep inside of her.

Rudy eventually slides the glass door open for her, and they're both immediately hit with the sound of Frank Sinatra's "My Way" blasting on Kai's little portable speaker. Kai's calming music.

"Um, hi," Mona says, tentatively tapping an index finger on his bare shoulder. "Got a second?" Her voice comes out like that of a shy tween giving a presentation in science class.

"Oh," Kai says, turning around to face Mona and Rudy. "Mona. Hey. My music was so loud, I didn't even know you were here. Sorry. I would have come in."

"Don't worry about it," Rudy breezily says. "Mona and I had some catching up to do."

"We *did*," Mona says with a smile. "And, um, Kai, I wanted to apologize. Not just for the pictures. But for that whole day. You have to understand, being famous is literally the only thing I know. I couldn't see where you were coming from. But now I do and I'm genuinely so sorry."

"It's okay," Kai says, slipping the bar of wax into the pocket of his gray sweatpants. "Honestly, I was pretty harsh on you, too. I know you didn't mean any harm. I just sort of freaked out."

Rudy shakes his head in disapproval. "And this guy is no peach when he's freaked out."

"You've got me there," Kai admits with a chuckle before settling his kind gaze on Mona. "How are you, though? The media has been pretty hard on you. I've been seeing the headlines."

"*You* have been keeping up with the headlines?" Mona asks with a laugh. "Man, fame really does change people."

Kai mirrors her laugh. "I guess I had a vested interest."

"I'll be fine," Mona says, taking a nervous pause before continuing. "Actually . . . I swear you can say no, and I will never bring this up again. But, um, we sort of have a plan. To smooth this whole disaster over for all of us."

Mona takes another beat, her heart now pounding.

Confessional

INT. MARY MASHAD'S LIVING ROOM—AFTERNOON (CONT'D)

MONA

I was terrified that asking the favor would sort of undo the apology, you know? Like it would seem like the only reason I showed up would be to get him to do this for me.

"Okay, here it goes," she eventually says, her voice a tad shaky. "My family hosts this annual Fourth of July party at our house in Malibu. We were thinking maybe you could come. Lucas will be there, the three of us can take a picture and I'll post it with a funny caption to show the world we're all cool, that you're just a friend and there's no drama to see here."

Mona watches intently as Kai stares at her, his razor-sharp jaw clenched tightly.

"It was stupid," Mona quickly says. "Forget I said anything. You've already—"

"No. Don't forget it," Rudy interrupts, turning to Kai. "She's our *friend*. Don't you want to help her?"

"Seriously," Mona says, her stomach in knots. "I knew it was a bad idea to—"

"I'll do it," Kai says. "I'll be there."

"What?" Mona asks, relief washing over her like a warm bath. "Really?"

"Yeah," Kai says with a smile. "Really."

<u>Confessional</u>

INT. LUCKY'S KITCHEN—AFTERNOON (CONT'D)

KAI

[*shrugs*]

Rudy was right. She's our friend.

Chapter 36

"Hey," Meesha says, gently knocking on the door of the glam room in Mary's Malibu mansion before letting herself in. "Mind if I join you?"

"So, we're talking again?" Mona asks, raising the one eyebrow not currently being filled in by her makeup artist Jacques.

"Yes," Meesha says, sinking into the camel leather swivel chair next to Mona's. "I even brought you a peace offering." She reaches into her navy suede Khaite Lotus tote and pulls out an Erewhon smoothie.

Mona examines the light-green concoction, instantly recognizing it as the Melody Mashad Rejuvenation Smoothie. "Thanks," Mona says, taking a sip. "I know she's our sister and we're biased. But it really is an insanely good smoothie."

"I know," Meesha agrees, taking a sip of her own matching drink. "So, no more secrets?"

"No more secrets," Mona promises, offering Meesha her pinkie for good measure.

Confessional

INT. MARY MASHAD'S LIVING ROOM—AFTERNOON (CONT'D)

MONA

That's how Meesha and I make up. We keep it brief. To the point. No tears, no hugs. Honestly, it's for the best. Making up with Melody is the *worst*. She wants to talk everything to death. One time she even made me go to couple's therapy with her after a fight. Then, as if that wasn't enough, we had to go to a Reiki healer afterward to cleanse out "the bad energy living between us." Season nine, episode eight. The whole thing's on camera. *Brutal* day.

The two sisters sit there quietly for a few minutes, looking around at the hundreds of framed magazine covers with their faces splashed across them lining the well-lit room.

"So, Mom told me the plan for today," Meesha eventually says, her eyes staring at the ocean view visible through the one large window to the left of Mona. "It was Lucas's idea?"

"Yeah," Mona says, careful not to move her head as Jacques

applies her eyeshadow. "He's been super supportive ever since Camp David."

"Well, he has no reason to not be," Meesha says. "It's not like you actually cheated on him."

"I guess not," Mona says. "But I don't know. It was complicated."

Meesha sighs. "It's always complicated with us, isn't it?"

Confessional

EXT. MARY MASHAD'S MALIBU MANSION—AFTERNOON

Kai and Rudy stand outside the massive dark-wood front door of Mary Mashad's sprawling Mediterranean-style clifftop Malibu mansion.

RUDY

Okay, I've seen the aerial shots on TV. But this house is even bigger in person.

KAI

[*chuckles*]

Come on, dude. You promised if I brought you, you'd keep the fanboying to a minimum.

RUDY

I'm only human! Do you think it's bigger than my school? It's definitely bigger than my school.

KAI

[*looks up at the house*]

Yeah. It's probably bigger than your school.

PRODUCER

So, Kai, how are you feeling? About being here today?

KAI

Um, I guess I'm a bit nervous. I've never been to anything like this before.

"Thanks again for doing this," Mona tells Lucas as they stand by the huge rectangular pool, the ocean crashing beneath them. "I know you probably had, like, a million Hamptons parties this weekend."

"I did," Lucas says, his cocky smirk flashing across his face. "But it's no big deal. The hottest Hollywood event of the summer isn't the *worst* second choice."

Mona looks around the star-studded bash, wondering how many collective billions the guest list has in terms of social media followings.

"Wait," Lucas says, pulling a disposable out of his navy shorts. "Keep staring out at the crowd like that."

"Really?" Mona asks as Lucas snaps the picture. "What do you want a picture of me right now for?"

"This whole thing . . . whatever it is we had," Lucas says, shoving the camera in his pocket. "It's coming to a close. Gotta preserve all the Mona Mashad memories I can before it's fully over."

"So, this is really it, huh?" Mona says, her chest constricting. "No more stalking?"

"*Aww,*" Lucas says with a laugh. "Don't look so sad! We can still be friends. You were right. We were never going to work as more anyway. It was my bad for pushing it."

"Yeah," Mona says, forcing a smile on her face. "I guess I was right."

"Look who just got here," Lucas says, nodding toward the house behind her. "You ready to go viral?"

Mona looks over, spotting Kai and Rudy walking out of the living room into the pool area, where the party is in full swing around her.

"Rudy! Kai!" Mona exclaims, waving a little too excitedly as she rushes toward them. "I'm so glad you came."

"Hey, man," Lucas says to Kai, coming up from behind Mona. "I'm—"

"Not Jack Ryan," Kai says with a crooked smile.

Lucas lets out an awkward laugh, his cheeks growing pink. "Yeah. Not Jack Ryan."

"I told you that was a weird move," Mona says with a playful eye roll. "Who even still watches that show, anyway?"

"If you're going to go with a John Krasinski character, at least go Jim Halpert. He's timeless," Rudy suggests. "I'm Rudy, by the way."

Rudy offers a hand toward Lucas, who accepts the gesture, giving his little hand a firm shake.

"Nice to meet you, Rudy," he says. "I'm Lucas. And if I'm making fake names up in the future, I promise to take your advice."

"Sounds good," Rudy says. "So, this is pretty awkward, isn't it? The three of you hanging out?"

"There's nothing awkward about this," Kai lies to Rudy. "It's fine. This is fine."

"Yeah," Lucas says with a shrug. "So, uh, Kai, you a big sports guy?"

"I surf," Kai says. "But I've never really been big into recreational sports. You're into lax, right?"

"Yep," Lucas says. "I was playing at Harvard this year, until . . ."

"Oh, yeah," Kai says. "The punch. Sorry for bringing that up."

"No big deal," Lucas says. "It happened. It is what it is."

Mona and Rudy watch, both cringing as Lucas and Kai's pitiful attempt at small talk comes to an anticlimactic close.

Mona lets out a deep exhale. "Let's just get this picture over with, okay?"

"Not so fast," Mary says, rushing over. "Kai, hello. I'm Mary Mashad. Mona's mother."

"Hi, Mrs. Mashad," Kai says. "Nice to meet you."

"You can call her Mary Joon," Rudy says. "She never goes by Mrs. Mashad."

"This little boy knows what he's talking about," Mary says with a pleased smile. "You must be Rudy. Mona has told me a lot about you. Kai, yes. Please. Call me Mary Joon."

Mary takes a step back, pulling her large black Prada sunglasses on top of her head to carefully examine the three of them.

"Okay," she says. "Mona, you go on the left. Then Lucas. Then Kai. Lucas, maybe give her a kiss on the cheek while you wrap an arm around Kai? That will establish all the relationships without spelling it out for everyone."

"No," Mona interjects. "It shouldn't feel staged."

Mona grabs her iPhone out of her vintage Gucci bucket bag, reaches her hand out as far as she can, and focuses the camera on herself and the two boys.

"What do you want us to do?" Kai asks from behind her.

"Whatever you want," Mona says. "Don't overthink it."

Kai eases his mouth into a closed-mouth smile, placing his hands in his pockets as Lucas flashes one of his signature Lucas Sterling smiles, putting a hand on Mona's shoulder. And *boom*. She snaps the shot.

"Not bad," Mary says, stepping forward to get a closer look at Mona's phone.

"Let me see," Lucas says, scooching in close. "Yeah. I have to agree. Not bad, Mashad."

"Okay," she says. "For the caption I'm going with, 'We're FINE.'"

"That's it?" Mary asks. "Don't you want to give them a little more? It leaves a lot of questions unanswered."

"Yes," Mona says. "Questions I can answer on my show. But for now, it at least shows there's no big drama happening and lets Kai off the hook a bit."

Mary considers Mona's point for a moment, a hand on her waist. "Okay," she finally says, a proud smile on her face. "You're right. It's a very good caption."

"Great," Mona says, throwing her phone back in her bag after pressing post. "Done."

The phone has barely plopped down onto the bottom of her bag before Melody is strutting over, her flowy red maxi dress cascading behind her. "Lucas!" she exclaims. "I'm so happy to see you."

"Hey, Melody," Lucas says, giving her a hug when she finally reaches them. "It's good to see you, too."

"Listen, I know this was all *fake*," Melody says with a whisper. "But, for what it's worth, I was always rooting for the two of you. You seemed so good together."

"Melody," Mona groans. "Can you have some chill?"

"What?" Melody asks. "You'll never say it. So, let me say it. You two were cute together."

Lucas gives her an awkward laugh. "You know, for a minute there, I thought so, too. But I think we're better off as friends. . . . So, where's Axle today?"

"He's around here somewhere," Melody says, scanning the crowd. "Last I saw he was teaching Josie and Timmy how to properly execute a juice cleanse."

Confessional

INT. MARY MASHAD'S LIVING ROOM—AFTERNOON (CONT'D)

MONA

I was standing there listening to Melody tell Lucas all about Axle's juicing preferences when I noticed Kai had slipped away.

✦✦✦

"Excuse me," Mona says to Melody and Lucas. "I'll be right back."

She sifts her way through the crowd until she reaches Kai where he's seated alone at the bottom of the ceramic-tiled steps leading down from the clifftop house toward the ocean.

"Hey," Mona says, giving his shoulder a light tap. "Mind if I join you?"

Kai says nothing, just scoots over to make space for her to sit down next to him.

"Where's Rudy?" Mona asks once she's seated, her shoulders lightly grazing against his biceps.

"He introduced himself to Louise, who introduced him to some of her model friends and now he's doing magic tricks for them," Kai says. "I just needed a break."

"Yeah," Mona says. "It's a lot up there."

Kai nods, his face turned wholly toward the ocean in front of them. "Whatever we had," he says, "the romantic stuff, that's over, isn't it?"

Mona picks up a small twig she finds in the sand and fiddles with it a bit before answering the question. "Yeah," she says, her eyes refusing to look up from the tiny piece of wood. "I think it is."

Kai nods slowly. "I figured. But I guess I just wanted to . . . say it out loud."

"I wanted it to work," Mona says, gesturing up toward the party raging above them. "But *this*? This is my life. I need to be with someone who can handle that."

"I wish I could," Kai says, his usually steady voice hoarse. "Trust me. You're worth handling that for. But I just . . . It's not . . ."

"It's not you," Mona says. "That's okay."

"I know I said I regretted it that day when I was upset," Kai adds. "But I hope you know I didn't mean that."

Mona hadn't realized how much she needed to hear him say that. "Thanks."

"It's just weird, you know?" Kai says, looking up at the party. "You got to know all of me. And I only got to know this one small part of you."

"It was a real part," Mona says, her voice soft. "But yeah . . . it was just a part."

They sit there quietly, both staring out at the ocean. "I'll still give you surf lessons," Kai offers. "You know, if you want them."

Mona smiles. "I do."

"Good," Kai says. "I mean, Rudy will be thrilled."

"Hey, speak for yourself," Mona says. "Rudy and I already agreed to stay friends no matter what you and I decide."

Kai laughs. "Of course you two did."

They both turn their attention back up to the party, where Rudy is now doing magic tricks for Louise, Josie, Melody, Timmy, and Lucas.

"Can I say something?" Kai asks. "As a friend?"

"Shoot."

"Why not him?" Kai asks, nodding toward Lucas. "I know things were messy for the two of you in the beginning there.

But that feels so long ago now. And, well, he's here. He clearly cares about you."

Mona gives him a small smile, her eyes misty. "You're here, too."

"Yeah," Kai says, his eyes adopting a similar sheen. "That's how I know he must care."

Mona stares up at the party, watching Lucas fake shock at one of Rudy's tricks.

"I don't know," she says with a sigh. "I think that ship might have sailed."

Kai says nothing for a while, giving Mona's mind space to wander. "We should probably save them," he eventually says. "Rudy is cute. But he's a god-awful magician."

Chapter 37

"Mona Joonam, wake up," Mary says, bursting into Mona's room in the Malibu house. "You have to see this."

"What now?" Mona groans as her mom pulls the cream linen curtains open, revealing the sun rising over the ocean.

"*Good* news, for once," Mary says, showing Mona her phone. "The response to the photo has been phenomenal. *Vogue* called. They want an exclusive interview with you on the cover. ASAP. They're bumping Gigi Hadid for you! Plus, you have three late-show offers for tonight alone. Everybody wants to know the story behind the story. You were right. Fantastic promo for your show."

Mona sits up, the tequila shots she took with Meesha and Pete at the end of the night tempering her excitement as they pound heavily against her skull. "Whoa, okay," she says. "So, which do we start with?"

"Actually," Mary says, taking a seat beside Mona on her bed,

"I told them all to hold off. Today you and I are going to do something different. Not work. It's a surprise."

Mona stares at her mom blankly. "Are you dying?"

Mary laughs, getting up from where she had made herself comfortable at the edge of Mona's oak four-post dark-wood bed. "No. Now, come on. Get dressed. I'll meet you in the car in half an hour."

Confessional

INT. MARY MASHAD'S LIVING ROOM—AFTERNOON (CONT'D)

MONA

I mean, she *said* she wasn't dying. But it was the only logical explanation. My mom and I hadn't just hung out for the purpose of just hanging out without any cameras or my sisters there since . . . I don't know. I honestly can't even remember.

A couple hours later, Mona is quietly following her mom into UCLA's Boelter Hall, panting as they make their way up five flights of stairs. "We couldn't take the elevator?" she asks, last night's tequila shots threatening to make their way back up. "I'm dying here."

"I didn't exercise this morning," Mary says, surpassing Majid and her own bodyguard, Yousef, as she seamlessly ascends upward. "This will have to do."

"Right," Mona says, catching her breath as they finally stop at the fifth floor. "Are you going to explain what we're doing here?"

"Yes," Mary says, guiding Mona through a set of glass doors into a market full of junk food called SEAS Café. "We're coming here."

Mona looks at her, confused. "We came all the way to UCLA to get Cheetos and Twix?"

"It's not *just* Cheetos and Twix," Mary says, grabbing a pack of Oreos as she makes her way toward the cash register. "They also have the cheapest coffee in Los Angeles. Well, they used to at least. We'll see."

Mona and Mary make their way up to where a young girl about Mona's age is working the register. "I'll have a high-tech coffee, please," Mary says. "And she'll have one as well."

"Yeah," Mona says. "That would be great, thanks."

"Oh!" Mary exclaims. "And, Mona, go back there and grab us a couple packs of Cup Noodles."

"Excuse me?" Mona asks, both eyebrows raised. "How do you even know what that is?"

Mary rolls her eyes. "Just *do* it."

Mona walks over, grabbing two containers of Cup Noodles and placing them at the register where her mom is currently checking out.

"I'm sorry," the cashier says. "I hate to do this . . . but are you—"

"Yes," Mary says, flashing the girl a gracious smile. "Mary Mashad. Class of 1987. And this is my daughter Mona."

"Wow," the girl gushes, her blue eyes gleaming. "I'm Allison. I'm a sophomore here. *Huge* fan."

"Thanks," Mona says with a smile. "Nice to meet you."

"Do you mind if we take a selfie?" Allison asks. "Sorry. Not to be super cheesy. My friends are just not going to believe me when I tell them."

"We don't mind," Mary says, pulling Mona in tight as Allison takes a selfie. "Just please don't let people know until after we've left. We don't want to cause a scene."

"Sure," Allison says, setting her phone back in the pocket of her jeans and going back to ringing them up. "Definitely. That will be five dollars."

"*Five dollars*," Mary says, swiping her Amex black card. "Can you believe that? Two cups of ramen, a pack of Oreos, and two coffees for five dollars. Now *that* is a deal."

Mona stares at her mom, perplexed as she uses the hot water dispenser to prepare their cups of ramen and makes her way over to a table for two. "Are you going to join me or what?" she asks, gesturing toward the empty seat across from her.

"Oh," Mona says, not realizing she hadn't moved. "Yeah, yeah. I'm coming."

"My *God*," Mary says, slurping up a spoonful of her ramen. "This is delicious. Do you know how long it's been since I've had this? At least thirty years. Have you ever even had it?"

"No," Mona says, slurping up her own mouthful. "But you're right. It's good."

"If Melody was here, she would tell us all about the toxins in here that will probably kill us," Mary says with a laugh. "But, you know, sometimes it's worth it."

Mary looks around the empty café, the only other table with patrons occupied by Majid and Yousef. Mona expects her to say something, to explain why in the world they're at UCLA outside of the normal school year having black coffee and ramen for breakfast if she's *not* dying, but she says nothing. So, the two just sit there for a while, looking out at the palm trees through the window next to them.

Mona finally cracks. "Mom, why are we here?"

"Everybody thinks your dad and I met when he asked me out on that bench," Mary says, her focus still on the palm trees outside. "But that's just when I first agreed to go on a date with him."

For a second Mona wishes the cameras were with them because her jaw drops in a way jaws seldom genuinely do. The moment would have made for great TV. Mary makes no mention of it, but Mona knows the same thought just crossed her mind as well. Thoughts like these are instinctual for them at this point. Second nature. Totally unavoidable.

Confessional

INT. MARY MASHAD'S LIVING ROOM—AFTERNOON (CONT'D)

MONA

The jaw drop didn't just come out of nowhere.

That bench is a big deal. Not just to our family, but to the world. On my parents' twentieth wedding anniversary, my dad got my mom a plaque on the bench that literally marks it as the spot where he first asked her out. It was on the most-watched episode of the show to date. And to this day people, like, travel to LA just to take pictures in front of it.

✦ ✦ ✦

"We met at a frat party," Mary reveals. "Very undignified, I know."

Mona snorts. "I cannot imagine you at a frat party."

"My roommate dragged me there," Mary says, turning so she's fully facing Mona again. "Your father was at the center of the party doing a keg stand when I walked in, and he just froze. His friends were holding him up and he just stopped chugging. His shirt was halfway down his chest, beer was pouring down his face, and his mouth was hanging wide open. That was my very first image of him. He looked absurd."

Mona laughs, the image crystallizing in her mind.

"Once he got it together, he flipped back over and made it his mission to talk to me," Mary continues. "Even after looking like such a buffoon, he pursued me with such confidence. That man really could have broken through a brick wall with his charm alone."

✦ ✦ ✦

Confessional

INT. MARY MASHAD'S OFFICE—AFTERNOON (CONT'D)

MARY

When I say he was confident, you have to understand the context. Ali and I were freshmen in 1983. The crisis when the Iranian kids held the United States embassy hostage had just happened and American people still carried a strong hatred for anyone Persian. The hatred ran so deep that it didn't really feel safe to go to parties that weren't predominantly Persian. It's why I started going by Mary. *Marjan* felt a little too overtly Persian. A little unsafe. But not Ali. He would go wherever he wanted whenever he wanted, and he would be exactly who he was no matter where he was. Anyone can be confident when life is easy. Ali was confident even when it wasn't.

✦ ✦ ✦

Mary pauses for a second, the faraway look in her hazel eyes indicating she just hopped aboard some sort of mental time machine. "Anyway, here we were," she goes on. "The only two Persian kids at this quintessentially American frat party. One of us, against all odds, the star of the party, the other desperate to leave. But we started speaking Farsi and chatting about home until eventually I was able to get the image of him on that *disgusting* keg out of my head, and I let him walk me back to my dorm."

"Ooooh," Mona says. "*Scandalous.*"

"It was!" Mary says. "I let him walk me back and we even had a little kiss outside my door. But that was *it*. He kept begging to take me on a date and I told him he wasn't my type. I wanted someone more serious."

"Of course, you did," Mona says with an eye roll.

"I didn't really see him again until the first day of the next semester when it turned out he was in one of my business classes," she says. "He was an engineering major, but his dad was making him minor in business, so we had a bit of overlap in our classes."

Mary looks out the window, a dreamy smile making its way across her face. "He saw me first. And it was one of those big lectures with, let's say, a hundred kids. But he managed to make his way to the seat next to mine. That's when I realized he wasn't just a dumb frat boy. He was *smart*. Very smart. I really couldn't figure out this one concept we were being tested on and he offered to tutor me. We met here, and it became our spot. We would spend hours guzzling ramen and drinking coffee while we studied together."

"And he never asked you out?" Mona asks. "On any of those study dates?"

Mary snorts. "Oh, he *always* asked me out. But then one day, I was sitting on that bench, and he came up to me so casually and said, 'Next Friday. It's happening. Our date.' And I don't know. Something came over me. I said yes. The best decision I've ever made in my life."

Mona looks down at her now-empty Cup Noodles. "Mom, why are you—"

"Of course I miss him," Mary answers before Mona can finish the question, her eyes wet. "Every second of every minute of every hour of every day. I miss him. He knew me like nobody else did. He *saw* me in a way that I still have trouble seeing myself. Sometimes I feel like the best parts of me existed through a lens only he had access to."

"I know that," Mona says, her eyes now also puddling with tears. "I know I made it seem like I don't. But I do. I just . . . wish you said it more."

"I can't say it, because if I do, I fall apart," Mary says, her voice cracking. "And I can't fall apart. For *you*. For your sisters."

"Mom," Mona says, reaching her hand across the table. "You can fall apart."

"No." Mary shakes her head emphatically. "I can't. I want you all to grieve recklessly, loudly, wildly. And know that I'll be here, strong. Steady. Here to catch you like an unwavering net. When my parents were killed when I was fifteen, that's all I wanted. I loved my Khaleh Farrah, her taking me in meant the world to me. But I couldn't act out, drive her crazy the way I could my own mother. There was always this awareness that she was affording me this kindness. That she didn't *have* to do this for me and so, in turn, I should be making life easier for her."

"I'm sure you didn't *have* to do that," Mona says, her voice quiet. "You went through something awful. It would have been fine if you just let it all out."

"Maybe," Mary says. "But logical or not, that's how I felt

at the time. And I don't want that for you girls. You deserve to crumble. You had the best father in the world, and he was taken away from you too soon. I tried to give you everything, protect you from all of the horrors I had to face growing up. But I couldn't protect you from that. And I'm sorry."

Mona watches as tears stream down her historically stoic mother's porcelain face. "Mom," Mona, now also crying, says. "You lost him, too. It wasn't fair to *any* of us."

Mary nods solemnly, her focus now back on the palm trees outside the window. "He was so good at this," she says, her voice quiet. "At being a parent. At making you feel loved exactly the way that you needed to. I was always missing the mark. I'm *still* missing the mark."

"You are both great parents," Mona reassures her through tears. "In your own ways."

"The business," Mary says, looking at Mona. "Being your manager. Especially as you get older, I push it because it's what keeps us connected. It's my way of staying involved in your life. Of continuing to give you everything I wanted you to have and more."

Mona looks at her mom, whose large brown eyes are mirrors of her own. "I'm sorry I'm so hard on you," she says. "Deep down, I know all of this. I know how much you love us. But sometimes, when I'm frustrated with everything else in the world, it's just easier to take it out on you."

Mary smiles at her, tears still wetting her face. "Good. I'm your mom. That's the way it should be."

Mona scooches her chair over next to Mary's and rests her

head on her mom's shoulder. "I'm glad we did this."

"Me too, azizam," Mary says, squeezing her tightly against her chest.

They sit there for a while, both sipping on the remainder of their coffees. "And, Mona Joon," Mary says, "if you want to be done with this Lucas thing, let's be done. I'll have Jorge start sending quotes to *Us Weekly* and *People* saying things have run their course between you two. Fans will wonder about the Kai element, but maybe that's not so bad. Maybe that will allow you to just be with him if that's what you really want. The public historically is forgiving of affairs if you stay with the person who you had an affair with."

Mona takes a long sip of her now-cold coffee. "Kai and I are done."

"Oh," Mary says. "Okay, well, then those rumors will take care of themselves."

Mona looks up at her mom. "When you decided to say yes to Dad that day, on the bench, how did you know it was time?"

"Hmmm," Mary says, dipping an Oreo into her coffee and taking a bite. "I guess I knew that on some level, it was destiny. He and I. As much as I wanted to deny it, there was just something there."

Mona doesn't respond. Instead, takes two Oreos out of the sleeve, stacking them on top of each other, and takes a quiet bite.

"Why?" Mary asks. "What's on your mind?"

"This is my first time saying this out loud," Mona says, her voice at a whisper even though nobody but her mom is within earshot. "But I might have feelings for Lucas. Real ones."

"Then what are we sitting around here for?" Mary asks. "*Do* something about it."

"I don't know," Mona says. "It might be too late."

"Mona Joonam," Mary says, wrapping her always-soft hands around Mona's face and turning her head toward hers. "In life, I look back on so many of my decisions and think about what I could have done differently. Giving in to how I felt about your father is the one decision I have *never* regretted. Not even when we were at our worst. If you think there's a chance you and Lucas have even a fraction of what we had, please, as your mother, I'm begging you: Don't let it slip away."

"Okay," Mona says. "I think I might have an idea."

Chapter 38

"Are you ready?" Mary asks as their SUV pulls up to Van Nuys Airport. "I checked with Jordana. The plane is scheduled to leave in twenty minutes."

Mona takes a deep breath, watching as Lucas slips out of his own SUV and starts walking toward the private Sterling-family plane parked in front of them outside on the massive lot. His headphones are on, and his head is ducked, the look of a guy not at all expecting a grand romantic gesture.

"I feel like a stalker," Mona tells Mary, twiddling her thumbs nervously. "What if he's creeped out?"

"Then he's creeped out," Mary says with a shrug. "Do you think your father cared how *anybody* reacted to him? Channel him."

"You're right," Mona says, straightening her spine. "But . . . stopping him at the airport? Is this too cheesy?"

"It is incredibly cheesy," Mary says. "But cheesy works when it's coming from the right person."

"And Lucas does love rom-coms," Mona says. "That's the whole point of this, right?"

"Right," Mary says. "Now get out there. He's about to make his way into the plane."

"Okay," Mona says, pausing before she rushes out. "Mom?"

"Yes?" Mary asks.

"I love you."

"I love you too, ghorboonet beram."

Mona takes a step out of the car, speed-walking toward the stairs leading up to the Sterling-family private jet. By the time she's at the bottom of the steps, Lucas is at the top, lowering his headphones so he can ask the flight attendant how her sick mother is doing in the hospital.

Confessional

INT. MARY MASHAD'S LIVING ROOM—AFTERNOON (CONT'D)

MONA

The timing couldn't have been worse. The woman was, like, tearing up telling Lucas about how her mother was on dialysis. I had to just awkwardly stand there waiting for them to stop hugging.

"Lucas!" Mona shouts as soon as Lucas and the middle-aged woman separate from their hug.

"Mona?" Lucas asks, squinting down at her. "What are you doing here?"

He looks over at the flight attendant standing next to him, then back down at Mona. "Oh, sorry. That was rude. Veronica, this is Mona," he says. "Mona, this is Veronica. She's been a flight attendant for our family's plane for years."

"Hi, Veronica," Mona says. "Nice to meet you. And, um, I'm sorry. I saw you crying."

"Oh, don't worry about it, sweetie. *Life*, you know?" Veronica says, slapping her hands energetically on her thighs like a little reboot. "So, tell me. Will you be joining us this flight?"

"No, I'm not joining you," Mona says, turning her attention back toward Lucas. "Um, can you come down here for a second? There's something I need to tell you."

"Sure," Lucas says, making his way back down the steps until he's facing her. "What's up? Is everything okay?"

Before she can answer, he takes a disposable out of his pocket and snaps a picture of her. "Sorry," he says, stuffing the camera back into the pocket of his Harvard Lacrosse sweatpants. "Probably not the right time. Habit."

She looks into his hazel eyes, that little heart-shaped speck glimmering under the sheen of the bright Los Angeles sun.

"Okay, I'm just going to let this rip," she says. "And if you hate what I'm about to say we can just pretend it never happened. Deal?"

"Deal," Lucas says with a chuckle. "Mona, what's going on?"

"I love that little heart-shaped speck in your eye," she blurts out. "I don't even know if you know it's there. It's in your left eye and I love staring at it. I love the way you always have that camera with you. The way you can't let a single moment go by without capturing it, like every human experience is a piece of art worthy of savoring forever. I love how you can't meet someone without learning their name. And actually *remembering* it. I love how you stop and take your headphones off to check in with Veronica. I love that you even remember whether or not Veronica's parents are in the hospital. And how Jackie's daughter says *broccoli*, even though she hates vegetables. . . ."

Before she can continue, the corner of Lucas's mouth curves upward. "Mona Mashad, are you *When Harry Met Sally*–ing me?"

"Trying to," Mona says, shifting her gaze toward the pavement for the next part. "Lucas, I know the timing might be off and I might have missed my window. But I . . . don't want to be just friends."

She moves her focus back up toward him, so their eyes are locked. "You were right! I tried to deny it. But you were right. There's a vibe between us. It's undeniable. We might . . . actually be endgame. And I want to give it a shot. For real."

Lucas stares at her for a minute, nodding his head quietly. "I . . . should go. My flight is about to take off and I can't be late for this campaign event with my mom."

"Oh," Mona says, blinking frantically so that the tears can't escape her eyeballs. "Got it."

She turns around, trying her best not to fall to the floor in mortified hysterics as she speed-walks back toward the SUV where Mary is still sitting waiting for her.

"Oh no," Mary says once she's in the car. "Didn't go so well?"

"Went *terribly*," Mona says. "He just stood there."

"Well, at least you tried," Mary says. "Now you don't have to wonder."

Mona nods, wanting that to be enough to make her feel better, but it's not. This did *nothing* to make her stop wondering. If anything, she has more questions than ever. At what point did she lose him completely? Was it the pictures with Kai? Or was it now? When she showed up offering something real? Sure, he was down to flirt and joke around, but maybe the real thing is too scary. Another guy who just loves the chase. If her heart didn't feel like someone just took a sledgehammer to it, she'd laugh at the cliché.

"Can we just go?" she asks Mary, tears welling in her eyes.

"You *might* want to check your phone first," Mary says, nodding toward where Lucas is standing at the base of the stairs pointing toward his phone.

Confessional

INT. MARY MASHAD'S LIVING ROOM—AFTERNOON (CONT'D)

MONA

And that's when I got the notification on my phone. Well, actually, it was two notifications. First, it was "Lucas Sterling followed you." Then it was "Lucas Sterling tagged you in a post."

INT. HARVARD MEN'S LACROSSE LOCKER ROOM—AFTERNOON (CONT'D)

LUCAS

I wanted her to know I was in. *All* in. So, I quickly made a profile and posted all of our pictures in a little slide-show thingy.

PRODUCER

Carousel. They're called carousels.

LUCAS

Right. Whatever. I'm new to social media. But I posted all of them. That first night at the Fairmont. My house after the Met Gala. Before that awful party at Harvard. Even the one from Camp David. Everything I had developed.

INT. MARY MASHAD'S LIVING ROOM—AFTERNOON (CONT'D)

MONA

And he captioned it, *Endgame*.

Mona bursts the car door open, rolling her still-wet eyes at where Lucas is standing there outside the plane, a cocky smile on his face.

"You *jerk*," she says, marching back over to him. "You had me stewing there for a second."

Lucas wraps his arms around her, pulling her close to him. "Are we really doing this?"

"Yes," Mona says, leaning in so their lips are just barely touching. "We're really doing this."

Mona's heart picks up speed as Lucas lets his lips wrap around hers, and, even though they've technically kissed three times before, this kiss feels entirely different.

Confessional

INT. MARY MASHAD'S LIVING ROOM—AFTERNOON (CONT'D)

MONA

The first time we were wasted. The second time we hated each other. The third time was just a peck. But that fourth time . . . I don't even know how to describe it. It was unlike any other kiss I've ever had.

INT. HARVARD MEN'S LACROSSE LOCKER ROOM—AFTERNOON (CONT'D)

LUCAS

Standing outside having this one long, perfect kiss with my dream girl. Knowing she finally felt for me the way I have for her since day one. That might be the closest to pure, unadulterated joy I've ever felt.

Confessional

EXT. STERLING FAMILY COMPOUND—AFTERNOON

MONA and LUCAS sit next to each other outside on the beach where they shot their now famous Ralph Lauren campaign.

MONA

So, there you have it.

LUCAS

Our whole story.

MONA

Completely unfiltered.

Acknowledgments

The acknowledgments are always my favorite part of a book. And I wrote a very long name-droppy one at the end of *Finding Famous*, so I will try my best to be more brief here.

For my husband, Brian, this book is dedicated to you because it's a love story, and how could I properly write a love story if I hadn't lived one out in my own life? Also, you truly read so many drafts of this book. It would not be what it is without your input. I'm sorry some of the sports references are definitely still wrong.

For my parents, my aunties, my uncles, my grandparents, my sister, my nephew, and my cousins—the village who raised (and was raised alongside) me. You taught me what family and unconditional love are all about, and you made me want to infuse those themes into my books. Thank you from the deepest part of my heart.

For my in-laws, thank you for the endless love and support

for me and my work. I got very lucky to stumble into such a wonderful bonus family.

For my best friends—so much of everything I write is inspired by the relationships I have with all of you. It's amazing what having a few friends who love you for you can do for your confidence. I hope every girl reading my books has at least one friend like each of you. (Special shout-out to Annie, without whom Kai would not have been a surfer.)

For my writer friends. When I first came to New York to intern at *Cosmo* over a decade ago, I was terrified. I flew in with my mom and nephew and they stayed a few days to help get me settled. I remember being too nervous to eat at breakfast with them that first morning before work. My nephew asked what I was so scared of and I told him I was worried people would be mean to me. I had no journalism experience and I was sure I was about to walk into some sort of *The Devil Wears Prada*–esque hellscape. But I wound up having the best summer and making friends I've kept to this day. In the years that have followed, my experience working in media and writing professionally has continued to be filled with some of the best, kindest people I know. From my writers group to the friends and mentors I've made at *Elite Daily*, *Cosmo*, Girls Write Now and beyond, I'm so grateful that my career has gifted me with each of you. Writing can be a really lonely endeavor. Having you all to bounce ideas off of, vent to, and just generally commiserate with helps so much.

For my agent Amy, I feel so grateful to have worked with you for as long as I have had the chance to. My career in this industry has been entirely defined by your efforts to transform my dreams into realities. That is not lost upon me. Thank you.

For every person who had a hand in bringing this book to life. Rebecca, you gave me the chance to create not one but *two* books in the Mashad universe. Thank you for loving these characters as much as I do and thank you for all of the time, effort, and care you invested in them. Cassandra and Jocelyn, thank you both for taking this book on and giving me the thoughtful notes that really helped add another layer of emotional depth to Mona's story. Zareen and Bahar, thank you for incorporating the design elements that turned this book into something my fourteen-year-old self would have sprinted toward at my local bookstore. To everyone else at Hyperion who played even the smallest role in this process, thank you, thank you, thank you.

For my publicist, Brittani. Thank you for the endless support and the commitment to getting the word out there. Putting a book out into the world is terrifying and having you there as a support is an immeasurable comfort.

For my elementary school teacher, Phyllis, thank you for making me believe I could write. And for the bookstore I grew up going to as a kid with my dad, Book Passage, thank you for giving me all the books I needed to spark my love of reading.

For the many pop culture influences who inspired this story, from the Kardashians to *Laguna Beach* (Mona definitely has a touch of *Laguna*-era Kristin to her, no?) to the late JFK Jr. and Carolyn Bessette-Kennedy, to Paris Hilton, Lindsay Lohan, Britney Spears, and the other early-aughts party girls who defined the culture of my teen years. And, on that note, to the pop culture podcasts I listen to religiously: *Shameless* (special shout-out to the *Scandal!* series!!!!), *Comments by Celebs*, and *The Toast*, you all feel like my virtual friends I gab about this stuff with every morning. And, Meggy, there's nothing more fun to me than listening to one of these then debriefing with you. Thank you for that.

As always, for my holy trinity of YA and middle grade authors: Meg Cabot, Lisi Harrison, and Cecily von Ziegesar. You three made me believe writing novels was the coolest job in the world. Thank you for igniting a dream.